# BLACK HEARTS

# WHITE BONES

by

## William Charles Furney

*I don't make excuses for them, they don't deserve any. But, in a world that only leaves room for heroes and demons, so much of this story has been left untold.*

...Alysia Bennett

# THE CAROLINA COLONIES

BATH

CEDAR ISLAND

OCRACOKE INLET

BRUNSWICK TOWN

CHARLES TOWN

# TABLE OF CONTENTS

# PROLOGUE

## April 1721
## Spanish Town, Jamaica

A SOOTHING NIGHT BREEZE from the coast drifted through the barred window and across the dank, putrid cell to kiss the perspiration collecting on Mary Read's forehead. She had lain motionless on her cot so long that the straw in her mattress were as needles, piercing the rags she wore, sinking ever deeper and deeper into her back. Her bloated bladder screamed for release, compounding the misery, but she gritted her teeth and held her water. If she made her move too soon, the birds would soon be picking her bones as her body rotted in the gibbet on Deadman's Cay.

Adding to her torment was the small, smooth stone nestled in the pit of her arm – the arm on the open side of the cot that the good doctor would use to check for a pulse. The plum-sized rock felt as though it had grown to the size of an orange, but the numbness of her limb meant it was serving its purpose well.

Turning her head just enough to steal a look across the dark cell, the woman who had once wrought death and despair throughout the Caribbean was not surprised to see that the Hollow had returned once more. Its undulate form waxed and waned in the gloom, never defining itself and discernible only by its varying shades of gray.

She loathed the apparition. Not because it haunted her, and not because it made her remember the death, deceit, and betrayal that had taken place in this cell. She hated it because it taunted her sanity. Escape from jail would not only free her from the hell that was Spanish Town and her looming execution, it would also free her from the fear that she was losing her mind. Or so she hoped.

Being careful to keep pressure on the stone so it would stay in place, Mary Read extended her throbbing arm beside the cot and placed her numb hand into a bucket of water. Grasping a soaked rag, she squeezed the water out and applied the damp cloth to her forehead. Half a day had passed since her fever had broken and the warm ruddiness of life was returning to her skin – an unacceptable condition for a supposed dead person.

As she dropped the cloth back into the bucket she heard the familiar jingling of the watchman's keys and the soft shuffling of leather soles on stone that preceded him and his betters – the jail's life-weary keeper and Spanish Town's esteemed Dr. Nathan Riley. A week earlier the venerated jug of rotting haggis had facilitated Anne's release from prison and that of the baby's. And though the lust to wreak vengeance upon the doctor's sorry personage ran hot, she knew that was a ledger that would have to be balanced another day.

Again, the vision of her body, stuffed in the gibbet just as they had done with Calico Jack, flashed through her mind, a rotting, stinking mass of flesh left as a warning to anyone who believed that he – or she – would find profit doing the work of pirates.

*Now, before they come too close.*

Relaxing her bladder, foul liquid waste flowed through the fabric of her ragged clothes and the straw mattress to puddle on the floor beneath her cot. The odor mingled with the stench escaping from the open sewage bucket sitting in the corner. Use of a privy was a luxury not afforded to prisoners of the Crown in Spanish Town.

Squeezing her arm tighter against the stone, she dismissed any thoughts of shame.

*Soiling myself is a damn small price to pay for freedom...and life.*

Closing her eyes and parting her lips just wide enough to breathe, she prepared herself. The footsteps stopped at the door to her cell and the clinking of the watchman's keys announced that the three men were about to enter.

"Hold the lantern this way more, damn you," Major Anders, the jail keeper, said.

Thorne, the plump, sweaty watchman bit his tongue and did as he was told. He hated the jail keeper but knew better than to challenge him.

Mary Read listened with dread as the bolt disengaged from its seat with a metallic clank, followed by the protesting screech of iron hinges as the door was pulled open. Their shoes made shuffling noises on the cobblestone floor as they approached her cot. With each step, her heart beat harder until she feared its thumping would give her away. In a flash of panic she considered using the stone as a weapon and try to fight her way out, but reason clawed its way back into her consciousness, forcing her to dismiss the idea. She was far too weak. Instead, she drew in a final deep breath, stilled the motion of her chest – and became as the dead she knew too well.

"Is this where she was when you left her?" Major Anders asked the night watch.

"Well...of course it is, gov'nor," the watch said. "I told you, she's dead. Dead as dead. Dead as ol' King William. Dead as–"

"Shut up, fool!" Anders said, already having lost his patience with the man.

Though well past his prime, the jail keeper was still an imposing figure. A former army officer, he had been awarded the jailer's post when the wounds he suffered in battle no longer allowed him to maintain a commission.

The adrenaline flowing through Mary Read's veins heightened her senses as the men spoke. Even a room filled with the rank odor of human waste could not mask the smell of the jailer's breath, an odor so foul it might have been mistaken for a rancid hog carcass.

"Give me the lantern," Dr. Riley said, growing annoyed with both men.

He was not happy to have been wakened from his slumber for the purpose of declaring the death of a pirate. On the other hand, he was glad to at last be done with the circus that had been Calico Jack Rackham and his so-called lady pirates. The seagulls had long since feasted on Rackham's flesh and Anne Bonny was now gone too. With Mary Read dead, he knew that the people of Spanish Town would have to look elsewhere to satisfy their prurient curiosities.

Taking the lantern from the night watchman, he held it over Mary Read's head to better see her face. Her skin was white and clammy, as it should be when devoid of blood. Her dark, sable hair was matted and tossed wild about her face, creating a stark contrast against her pale skin. She looked dead, to be sure, but his professional training demanded a more thorough examination.

Grasping her wrist with his free hand, he sought and found the sweet spot where life should pulse. Nothing. He released her arm, letting it drop back onto the cot, and held the lantern higher to take one last look at the infamous piratress.

Anyone who saw her now would find it hard to believe that the woman was only twenty-nine. She had lived hard and notorious, and had known adventures most men only dreamed of. Though the years of fighting, murdering and stealing had taken their toll, the sharp features of her face held steadfast against time and toil's assault on her beauty.

A small glint of light reflecting off Mary's forehead caught the doctor's attention. It was the sort of refraction caused by the air's dampness collecting on her skin...or perspiration. Shifting closer for a better look, he heard a slight splash as he put his foot down. He pulled the lantern back to see what he had stepped in, though sure he already knew.

"Damn it!" he said, stepping back from the cot. "My shoes...ruined. I've seen enough."

The doctor spun on his heels and left the cell, forcing the other two men to scramble after him lest they be left in the dark. He had examined enough corpses to know that they always emptied their bladders – if not their bowels – when they passed. It was the nature of things, and all the evidence he needed to know that the piratress' soul had gone to a higher place to answer for her crimes.

Mary Read listened to the scuffling – and occasional squish – of the men's shoes as they left the cell. When sure it was safe, the not-so-dead reiver drew in a deep breath. The first part of her plan had succeeded, but she was not free yet. The second part might not go as well.

After exiting the jailhouse, Dr. Riley disappeared into the dark streets of Spanish Town to return home, leaving Major Anders to deal with Mary Read's body as he saw fit.

"I want you to bury the woman right now, tonight," Anders said to the night watch. "We don't need gawkers and token hunters gettin' in the way. It was bad enough after we hanged Jack Rackham. The poor bastard had nary a stitch left on him 'cause of the human buzzards rippin' off pieces of his clothes before they got him into the gibbet. Go get Mabó and the wagon and bury her before word gets out. It'll be dawn soon enough, so you better make quick about it."

Mabó was an oddity in Spanish Town, neither slave nor Englishman. He was born from the blood of both African Maroons – slaves left behind by the Spanish – and the last of the Tainos – the native Indians who had escaped European death and disease by seeking refuge in the mountains. Because he was of several races, Mabó belonged to none. Jamaica's English conquerors allowed him to move through the former Spanish settlements with little bother, though they never treated him as an equal. He made his way through life hunting, fishing and doing odd jobs for the English.

Thorne hated Mabó almost as much as he hated his job as night watchman, almost as much as he hated the major. Other than slaves, the dark-skinned Indian was the one person in town afforded less respect than he was. The bloated watchman never passed up an opportunity to denigrate his charge, his one opportunity to feel superior to someone. Anyone.

"Wake up, Own!" the watchman ordered, kicking Mabó in his ribs. "Own" was Thorne's mispronunciation of "Ao'n," the Taino word for "little dog."

The half-breed, who had been sleeping in the straw of an open stall as was his habit when he stayed in town, sprang to his feet and squared his body to attack. Though only a little more than five feet tall, he was stocky and muscular. Tattoos on his face and half-naked body added a ferocity that unnerved men of far greater mettle than Thorne.

Scared that he had pushed the Indian too far this time, the night watch stepped back and gripped the hilt of the knife sheathed on his belt. They glared at each other for a few moments until Mabó, realizing that his life was not threatened, relaxed. The watchman eased his grip but kept his hand on the knife's handle.

"Hitch the red nag to the wagon, and hurry," Thorne said, using the flame from his lantern to light a couple of the stable lamps. "We have to bury Rackham's wench before the dawn."

With the hierarchy of their relationship reestablished, the watchman felt his confidence returning. As long as Mabó was around, there would always be a "little dog" even lower in the pecking order for him to kick.

After loading Mary Read's body onto the wagon, Thorne snapped the reins and guided the old horse through Spanish Town's dark, stagnant streets. By the time they reached the paupers' cemetery on the outskirts of town the first tinge of orange was beginning to peek above the horizon. It would be morning soon. They had to hurry.

"This is it," the watchman said as he brought the wagon to a halt. "Remove the boards covering the grave down this row, then come back and help me get 'No Beard the Pirate' started on her final voyage."

Thorne laughed at his bad joke as Mabó disappeared between the markers in search of the grave. How Bonny and Read – two mere women – had gained such notoriety was something he had never understood. He began to imagine himself as one of Captain Jonathan Barnet's men, leaping from the *Snow-Tyger* onto the deck of Rackham's sloop, *William*, with a cutlass in one hand and a dirk in the other. Forcing the two women to submit in short order, he must decide whether to let them live to meet the hangman – or take their lives right then and there with their precious Calico Jack looking on.

Thorne let the fantasy play through his mind several times, each new variation becoming more bloody and sadistic than the previous. He was so absorbed in his daydream that he neither heard Mary Read rise to her feet nor felt the wagon shift as she crouched behind him. The crude knife she clutched was fashioned out of a brick shard taken from the prison's wall, cord from the cot's roping, and a splinter of wood for the handle. In one swift motion, she pulled the watchman's head back with her free hand to expose his throat, then slashed across it with the knife. His soft flesh yielded with ease, but the brittle blade snapped before its work was halfway done.

Thorne bolted upright, clutching his throat, then turned to see who had attacked him. He tried to call out to Mabó but only wet, gurgling sounds burbled from his mouth. Realizing that he was about to die, Thorne grabbed the dagger from his belt and made a desperate leap toward Mary Read. She tried to sidestep his lunge, but sickness and months of confinement had dulled her reflexes. The fat watchman made several wild slashes until the knife raked down across the left side of her face. The blade sliced through skin from her forehead to her jawbone, its tip tearing through the soft jelly of her eye. Despite the excruciating pain, she swallowed back a scream and placed a hand over the mutilated orb. Warm blood flowed between her fingers as freely as the rage surging through her veins.

For the first time in her life, a man had dealt the raven-haired hellion a serious injury. She had broken up many fights as a tavern keeper, fought in the army as a man, and as a pirate had boarded ships more times than she could recount. Through all of that, no man had ever managed to do her any worse than a bruised lip or a black eye.

Finding new strength in her fury, she jammed the broken blade of her knife and half of its handle into the watchman's throat. Thorne dropped his dagger and grabbed at the protruding shank with both hands, gagging out guttural noises meant to be curses.

As he slumped to his knees, Mary Read shoved him off the wagon with her foot and picked up his dagger. Slipping onto the seat, she grabbed the reins and gave them a snap. It wasn't far to Port Royal where she would be able to sneak onto an outbound ship. Any ship to anywhere. Freedom was so close now she could taste it.

Before the mare had gone three steps, the tattooed native jumped from the darkness to snatch its bridle, bringing the big nag to a halt. Mary Read locked eyes with the half-breed, each wondering what the other's next move would be.

"Help bury," Mabó said, pointing to the night watchman.

His thick accent made the words almost impossible to understand, but Mary knew what he meant. She had no choice but to go along. Fighting the guard had drained all her strength. The native she faced was a young, strong warrior. Even the knife would not give her enough advantage.

Stepping down from the wagon, they each grabbed one of Thorne's legs and dragged him to the open grave meant for her. They rolled the fat guard into the hole and began shoveling the sandy soil on top of him as fast as they could. Mary watched the native from the corner of her eye as they worked. If he let down his guard even for a moment, she was ready to hit him over the head with her shovel. But the native was far too savvy for that, and the opportunity never came.

"Go," he said when they were done. Then, pointing to the coast, "I return wagon. Eng-lish man drink. Miss much work. Me tell others...we bury woman. Go now."

She hesitated for a moment, not sure whether to trust him, then realized she had no choice. After all, if he was going to kill her, he would have already done so.

"Thorne not man." The native smiled. "Thorne is Own."

Mary did not understand the joke, but she understood his intent. The native was not helping her, he was rewarding her. Without another thought, she turned and began walking toward the coast. She had to get off the open road as soon as possible. She still knew people in Port Royal who owed her a favor. All she needed was a good meal and a set of seaman's clothes and she would be able to disappear in plain sight. She had spent most of her life pretending to be a man. The transformation would be easy. And the best part – everyone would believe that she was dead and buried. No one would be looking for her.

*Your day will come, Anne Bonny,* she vowed as she walked toward town. *You left me to hang like Jack and the others, while you were spirited away in the middle of the night with the boy...to freedom. I will find you and when I do, I will show you despair you have never known.*

As she crested a small rise marking the halfway point between Spanish Town and Port Royal, she stopped. She might regret looking back, but she had to look. She had to know.

With her remaining eye she peered back down the narrow road that had brought her through a grove of avocado trees. Though partially hidden by the dark shadows beneath the boughs, she saw it. There – watching from the trees as unformed and wavering as it had been in the prison – was the Hollow.

# PART ONE

## CHAPTER ONE

### April 1729
### Town of Bath, North Carolina

PEG BRENNAN SAT IN THE OPEN DOORWAY of the grain barn's loft with her back against its sturdy jam, her legs stretched out along the threshold. Shimmering in the sunlight, her long, crimson hair cascaded around her shoulders and over the front of her worn gown. She refused to wear her hair up under a mobcap as did most of the women in Bath. She had been able to reassume most of the cultural norms of her gentility, but displaying her magnificent red locks in full glory was her one remaining act of rebellion.

Blossoming wildflowers and early magnolia blooms along the woodland riverfront were both fragrant and pleasing to the eye. Not yet heavy with the humidity that would come with the thick of summer, spring in Bath was much like the ones she had known in Charles Town. It was a pleasant memory in a rare moment of idleness, and she was making the most of it by doing nothing at all.

From her second-story perspective she could see Bath Creek and the Pamlico River beyond, their flows coming together before continuing to the vast open waters of the Pamlico Sound. Between her and the creek a pandemonium of Carolina parrots was attacking a cocklebur bush with ravenous abandon. Oblivious to everything around them, the colorful birds tore open the burrs and devoured the sweet meat inside, a bounty of spring. If the townsmen saw them they would rush out with their fowling guns and slaughter them for their stunning feathers. But the screeching birds were safe for now. Most of the men who would have hunted them were in the woods working a tar kiln or collecting sap from the pines they had boxed during colder days. Later, she would visit the cocklebur bush to collect any feathers the parrots may have shed. There were many ways she could craft the plumage to earn a farthing or two – a modest booty for a poor woman.

The back quarter of the loft was her home, such as it was. She had cordoned off a corner by bundling armfuls of loose straw together with twine, standing each bundle on its end, and then tying each bundle to the next to make a wall. It wasn't much, but it was private and it was dry, and for that she was thankful. She was a mother without a husband and had to provide. The space was hers as long as she managed the gristmill, as was any meal she might be able to scrape from the grindstones at the end of the day. It was a fair trade.

Below her, about fifty feet in front of the barn's main door, her son coaxed an ox around the gristmill's bed stone. Tye was only eight, but more mature than most adults and far more intelligent. To the casual eye, he looked the same as any other boy his age, but the mothers of other children his age knew different. Tye was so far ahead of their offspring, it made them seem slow in comparison. Their whispers were often laced with warnings that Peg should be regarded with suspicion, because a boy that smart couldn't be natural.

In truth, few people in the community had come to accept them during the seven years they had lived in Bath. The townspeople had always had more questions than she had answers – wanting to know where they were from, what had happened to her husband, where was the rest of her family, why had she settled here? The information she volunteered had always been vague, leading to yet more questions. But it had to be that way. Far better to have them distrust her for what she did not say than to shun her for being caught in a lie – or for giving an honest answer.

The satisfying sound of the grindstone crushing the final bushels of last year's corn conspired with the warm spring sun to laden her eyelids. She was falling asleep, but for once she didn't care. It felt good to steal again, even if the prize was only a few idle moments.

Succumbing to the serenity, her musings became a blend of fleeting memories and meandering daydreams. She both loved and hated this place. Bath was an odd mix of crude dwellings made of wood, stone, and brick. Precisely fixed upon a series of uniform lots, they represented the unfulfilled promise of refinement and sophistication made by its founders – though the residents did try.

Bath was the name its founder John Lawson had given the town more than twenty years earlier. Some said he had named it after the City of Bath in England. Others said he had dubbed it Bath in tribute to Lord Proprietor John Granville, the Earl of Bath. The only person who knew for sure was John Lawson, though he could no longer be consulted. Lawson was long dead, murdered by the Tuscarora eighteen years back.

Exactly when Carolina had become separate colonies of North and South was also a matter of debate. During the past forty years, the two regions had been governed both as one province and as two. Sometimes there had been no governor at all. There were times when the Eight Lord Proprietors had appointed one governor to rule over the entire area. Other times they named separate governors to preside over each region separately. And then there were times when the people elected their own governor. The prevailing rumor these days was that the Proprietors would soon return their claim on the land to King Charles, a move that would make the two Carolinas royal colonies. But England was an ocean away and news traveled slowly.

The settlers here had been left to govern themselves more often than not, and they preferred it that way. People in the other colonies called the area "Rogues' Harbor" for a reason, and not just because it was an official haven for debtors. The northern part of Carolina had settled differently than other English colonies. Massachusetts, Pennsylvania, New York and the others had expanded from coastal footholds to establish new cities farther inland. The region now known as North Carolina was populated by people who had migrated up the coast from its sister colony, South Carolina, and down the coast from Virginia to carve out homesteads in the vast pine forests between Charles Town and Jamestown.

Most of the villages in North Carolina were typical frontier towns, centers of commerce for farmers and trappers. Bath was the exception. Its population numbered fewer than a hundred in the town proper, though several hundred more lived in the surrounding area. The majority of them worked to produce naval stores for the shipyard and visiting merchant vessels. The town itself was an odd mixture of French Huguenots from Virginia, German Palatines, English Barbadians who had migrated up from Charles Town, and a spattering of former merchant ship captains, privateers, and pardoned pirates from many ports. Though its population was small, the people of Bath believed that their town would one day become the colony's cosmopolitan center by virtue of its growing importance as a port of entry, shipyard, and trade center of furs and naval stores.

"MOTHER!" Tye shouted from below.

Peg opened her eyes, vaguely aware that her son must have called several times before rousing her.

Tye stood a few feet below the loft door looking up at her. His friend, the skinny, carrot-topped William Gibbs from town stood beside him. Peg wondered how long she had been asleep.

"Mother," Tye said, combing his dark curly hair back with his fingers. His voice was calm and measured, the way it was about everything. "Will says the men at the kiln are sword fighting...with rapiers. If we go now, we might be able to see some of it before they're finished."

"Wait!" Peg said. The sounds of metal clanging on metal and blades slicing air rustled in the background of her memories. "Fighting? To the death? What? Why?"

"No. It's an exhibition."

"Oh," Peg said, beginning to understand.

"It... it's...Cap-tain...Rad-er," Will said, struggling to get the words out. "He... He..."

"He showed up at the kiln about a half-hour ago," Tye finished for his friend. "He said he'd give a shilling to anybody who could best him. There weren't any takers, so he said he would give instructions to anybody who wanted to learn."

"I see. All right then...go on. Have fun."

"What about you?" Tye asked, though it sounded more like a request. "You should come too."

Peg started to say no, but the ring of striking blades called to her again. It was a sweet sound that made her blood run hot – a siren song she could not resist.

"Yes," she heard herself say. "You two go ahead, I'll be along in a minute."

Tye looked at her for a moment, trying to decide if her promise was sincere. It would not be the first time his mother had given the answer he wanted to hear but not deliver.

"I mean it," she said with a snip. She didn't blame him for doubting her, but neither did she like it. "I'll be there in a minute. Now go...before I change my mind."

Satisfied, Tye turned and trotted up the dirt path toward the kiln with Will by his side. Peg took the moment alone to ready herself, beginning to second-guess her decision despite having promised. She was twenty-nine years old – a mature woman. It would not be appropriate for her to rush to the gathering like a girl going to her first dance. She had worked hard to make a home for her and her son. A few unguarded moments could destroy what little they had. The smart thing to do would be to not go at all.

She continued arguing with herself even after she had filled a gourd with water and started down the lane the way the boys had gone. What had once been a trail through a large stand of majestic longleaf pines was now a path that meandered around the stumps of harvested trees, occasional hardwoods, and underbrush. The woodsmen had left a span of trees around the village to provide a windbreak, but the older pines – the ones that no longer produced sap from which to make quality turpentine – had been cut down to make tar, pitch, and rosin.

The smell of the kiln reached Peg long before she could see it. Smoldering pine had a distinct scent, not unpleasant, but strong and lasting. Tar kilns were simple to construct. Dig a pit on an incline, fill it with the trunks and branches of longleaf pines, and then cover it with a thick layer of dirt and sod. A fire started at the bottom of the woodpile was allowed to smolder for a week or longer. Eventually, the tar would begin to flow down a trough along the bottom of the pit and into a bucket. The job of handling the tar buckets was usually left to slaves and poor day laborers. The men who worked the tar were easy to distinguish from those who collected sap – the men who worked with tar smelled of pine smoke and always had black splotches on their hands and feet.

As she approached the crowd gathered near the kiln, Peg saw that every facet of Bath's society had come to witness the event. Plantation owners and merchants stood shoulder to shoulder with indentured servants and slaves. Several council members, a judge, and a few other officials were sprinkled throughout the crowd. Trappers, shop owners, and indentured servants stood next to small farmers, boatwrights, shopkeepers and redemptioners.

Redemptioners came from the poorest, most miserable communities in England. Their existence in the Old World had been little better than that of feral animals. Two things set them apart from the brothers and sisters they had left behind – the belief that life could be better and the willingness to bond themselves to planters and merchants for four years in exchange for passage to the New World. As with slaves, the treatment they received depended on the benevolence or brutality of their sponsor. But even those who were beaten and forced to perform backbreaking labor were far better off than they had been in England. After completing their term of service, they collected their dues and their freedom. Those who were more fortunate were sometimes even given land.

One step above slaves were the involuntary indentured servants. These were common criminals – thieves, beggars, debtors, and mental patients avoiding institutionalization – who had barely escaped the gallows. Judges in England were empowered to put common lawbreakers to death, and many did. Lenient judges allowed criminals to choose between indentured servitude or the gallows. But the prospect of trying to survive the wilderness was so terrifying that many of the criminals chose death instead of delaying what they believed was inevitable.

Pausing a moment before merging into the crowd, Peg mustered up as much of an air of nonchalance as her racing heart would allow. But for once, no one gave the fiery redhead a second glance. All eyes were on the two men facing each other in the center of a circle created by the onlookers.

Dressed in his fine clothes, it was easy to tell which man was Blyth Rader. His everyday attire was of better tailoring than the clothes any of the villagers owned. The suits he donned on Sundays were an embarrassment of overindulgence. Today he was dressed in a royal blue suit and wore a large-brimmed hat adorned with a plume of white feathers. His black boots were freshly polished; his beard and mustache neatly trimmed. In contrast to the rough-clad farmer standing in front of him, he looked like a fop.

Harboring a well-developed distaste for such dandies, Peg had avoided Rader since he had arrived in Bath a year before. Like all port towns, people were constantly coming and going. As captain of an English merchantman, he had garnered little notice at first, despite his flamboyant style. When the locals discovered he had contracted the shipyard to build a large sloop, however, they began to pay more attention to him. It seemed that the captain was as well-financed as he was clothed – and he was planning to stay in Bath for awhile.

Peg watched with a practiced eye as he took a casual stroll around his opponent, sizing him up while making broad, flaring sweeps with his rapier. The familiar burn of hot blood began pulsing through her veins.

*It's easy to strut when you are the gamecock to a farmyard of roosters with no spurs.*

"Well. Get on with it, man. The first attack is yours," Rader said.

The rube had no idea what he was doing. He gripped the sword as though it were a goad stick. His stance exposed the full front of his body. It had looked easy enough, watching from the crowd. But now that he was standing in the middle of the circle, he regretted his foolishness.

"Come on Isaac," a man from the crowd shouted.

"You can do it," another urged.

But instead of lunging forward, the man named Isaac cast his gaze past Rader and relaxed.

"I don't believe it," he said. "It's Sir Everard himself, all the way from Edenton."

Everyone in the crowd turned to look at the governor, except for Peg. Though it had only lasted an instant, she had seen fear flash through Rader's eyes. But by the time he had turned to face the governor, the fright had been replaced by a smile.

Seeing his chance, the farmer sprang toward Rader with his sword extended. Rader heard feet scuffling on the ground behind him and realized what a fool he had been. Spinning on his heels, he deflected the rube's sword at the last possible moment. In one swift motion, he sidestepped Isaac's flailing charge, tripped him, and then swatted the man's backside as he stumbled by. The farmer plowed into the ground face-first and everyone in the crowd roared with laughter. Everyone except Peg.

Rarely had she seen such quickness. Rader had realized the attack and had responded without hesitation. She would remember that. Vanity had also caused him to fall for a child's trick. She would remember that as well.

The farmer remained on the ground, stunned and embarrassed. Deciding to make the best of it, he placed his hands on his backside and called back over his shoulder to Rader, "Had enough yet?"

Again the circle of spectators laughed and some urged him to try again. But Isaac picked himself up, brushed the dirt off his clothes and slipped back into the crowd before Rader could attempt to give him another painful lesson.

"Well then, who's next?" Rader asked as he scanned the crowd for a new opponent. The men in the circle looked at their feet, not wanting to be the captain's next victim.

"Come on," he said. "We've just gotten started. Surely, there is one among you who would like to learn the manly art of fencing. Perhaps one of you aspires to be a pirate one day. You can't be a pirate if you don't know how to use a sword."

Some of the men laughed, though not as many as before. Once known as the home of Blackbeard, Rader was mocking them, and most of them knew it.

What had started out as a demonstration had turned into an arrogant display of superiority. The captain had no desire to teach, he wanted to be the cat that toyed with mice.

With no one else willing to come forward, Rader began collecting his things to leave. As he reached down to pick up the farmer's rapier he saw a newcomer appear from around the far end of the kiln. Rader had never seen the man before. He would have remembered a six-foot tall woodsman with reddish-blonde hair pulled back in the manner of an Indian. His skin was darker than most whites, but not red like that of the natives. He wore buckskins pants, a cotton shirt, and moccasins that came almost to his knees.

Oblivious to the crowd, the man was whistling a tune while leading a mule to the pit where the tar pooled. His job was to scoop up the black pitch that collected at the end of the kiln and pour it into small kegs strapped on both sides of the mule. Reaching the end of the kiln he looked up and stopped short, surprised to see half a hundred people all looking at him in silence.

"Welcome, friend," Rader said. "You're just in time."

The crowd parted enough to allow the newcomer a pathway into the circle.

"Would you care to learn a few fencing basics?" Rader asked. A ripple of laughter passed through the crowd, confusing the woodsman even more. "Come, come! It's all in good sport. You're not scared, are you? What's your name?"

"That's Asku Dare," someone from the circle said. "He don't talk much. Which is to say, he don't talk at all. But he understands what you're saying well enough."

"Well, he doesn't need to talk to fight," Rader said, never taking his eyes away from the mute named Asku. "He just needs a little encouragement."

"Come on, my good man," the captain said, sweeping his arm in a grand gesture of welcome. "There's nothing to fear, here. See, the tips are covered with cork buttons and are perfectly safe. And I can tell that you would make an excellent swordsman. Come. Join me."

"You can do it, Asku," one of his fellow kiln workers called out.

"It's all right, Asku," said another. "There ain't nobody got hurt yet."

Other men in the crowd joined in, shouting words of encouragement while making gestures for him to move closer to Rader. Asku smiled but looked from one spectator to another suspiciously.

Peg worked her way to the inside of the circle to get a better look at the newcomer. He was broad of shoulder and his eyes moved with quiet grace. Though he looked to be only four or five years her junior, he had no facial hair. That, along with his high cheekbones, suggested that he was of mixed blood. And though he was wary, his hesitation was born of instinct, not fear. He was no doubt wondering why – if it was as easy and fun as the crowd let on – were they not volunteering?

"Well, Mister Dare, what will it be?" Rader prodded. "Do you have it in you to learn a skill practiced by nobility and warriors for centuries? Or, do you see yourself...a lesser man?"

"Don't do it," Peg said to herself. "You won't have a chance."

But the woodsman's back stiffened and she knew what would happen next.

*Do brave men always have to be so stupid?*

Asku dropped the mule's reins and walked through the parted crowd toward the center of the circle.

"Excellent!" Rader said.

The crowd voiced its approval with a short burst of cheers and shouts of encouragement. As Asku came closer, Rader slid the tip of his sword under the hand guard of the rapier he had been about to pick up. With a flip of his wrist, he sent the weapon flying through the air.

Unfazed, Asku deftly caught the rapier by the handle.

Impressed by the man's quick eye and nimble hand, Rader nodded approval.

"Now then," he said, assuming the proper starting position. "Do as I do. Extend your sword with bent elbow. Stand with your legs spread apart and at an angle so as to make yourself as small a target as possible."

Asku mimicked Rader as best he could, but Peg spotted at least a dozen nuances that were either wrong or missing. She felt bad for the man, even if it was his own stupid pride that had put him in such a situation.

"Very good. Now, to advance and retreat you must move without crossing one leg past the other," he said, shuffling his feet from heel to heel to demonstrate.

"A lunge is executed like this," he said, moving his front leg forward and extending his sword toward Asku's chest.

"And you deflect your opponent's sword like this," he said, executing an exaggerated move with his sword. "Understand?"

Asku's attempts to imitate his instructor were awkward, but he was gaining confidence. The basic moves were not hard for people with coordination and speed, and he possessed both. Knowing when to move and how to set up an opponent, however, was much harder.

Again Rader nodded his approval, but the hint of a smile pulled at the corner of his mouth. Though barely perceptible, Peg saw the twitch for what it was. Rader intended to use the man for no good purpose. The woodsman was in danger.

"Very good, sir," Rader said. "Let's begin, shall we?"

The sea captain strolled around his opponent making lazy sweeps with the blade of his rapier as he considered his next move. Easing into the ready position he had demonstrated earlier, Rader lifted his rapier and nodded to the woodsman.

"Ready?"

Asku nodded.

Rader saluted with his sword then said, "Begin!"

Asku took a couple of tentative swipes at Rader's sword, testing its balance and how far he could reach. Rader batted down the jabs with ease, barely moving at all. Asku struck again, this time with more authority. Again Rader deflected the blade, then stepped back and spread his arms apart as if daring the woodsman to lung at him. Asku accepted the invitation, moving so quickly, it was as if he had been waiting for the taunt in the hope of using it to his advantage.

But Rader was just as quick and much more experienced. He blocked the jab with the bell guard of his sword just before Asku's sword tip struck his shoulder. In the same seamless motion he lunged forward, striking the center of the woodman's chest with a resounding smack. The crowd held its breath, waiting to see if the captain's blade had inflicted a wound.

Asku stepped back, rubbing the spot on his chest where Rader's point had struck. He pulled the neck of his shirt back, exposing a plump, purple welt. Some of the men in the circle chuckled while others whispered their relief. The woodsman gave the captain a wry smile as if to say, "Well, you got me good." Then, showing his grit, he came back to stand in front of the foppish captain and assumed the ready stance.

Rader studied Asku for a few moments deciding on how to execute his next attack. After lifting his sword to indicate he was ready to begin, the captain lunged before Asku finished his own salute. Once again the tip of his sword slammed into Asku with a loud thwack!

Caught off guard, Asku back-stepped as the blade struck his chest again and tripped over his own feet. He landed on his backside at the feet of several people in the circle. Embarrassed and angry, he shook off the blow and started to scramble to his feet again, but someone put a hand on his shoulder to keep him from rising. He tried to knock the hand away, but it gripped his shirt tighter. Red-faced and seething, he twisted around to grab the person's arm. When he saw that it was a woman holding him down, the rage in his eyes subsided as quickly as it had flared.

Now that she had his attention, Peg knelt beside him, pulled the stopper from her gourd and handed it to Asku. She leaned in closer to his ear as he began to drink.

"Watch the bell guard," she said, "not the tip of the sword. Whichever way his hand moves, the tip has to follow. Once you stop his blade with yours, lunge forward. Don't draw your sword back to take a swing, just lunge forward with your arm extended and guide the tip to his chest."

Asku kept his eyes locked on hers as he took another swallow of water. Peg saw his mind working as he drank, as if trying to decide whether to follow her advice. When he was done, he wiped his mouth with the back of his sleeve and then nodded.

"Go," she said, taking the gourd from his hands before his doubts grew roots. "You can do it."

Asku stood and turned to face Rader. This time the captain forwent the salute and immediately leaped toward his victim, but Asku was ready. Instead of attempting to deflect the thrust with the tip of his sword, he shifted the hilt to redirect Rader's blade away from his body. Continuing his motion, Asku lunged forward and planted the cork-covered point of his sword squarely in the middle of Rader's chest.

As one, the circle of spectators burst into howls of delight and began shouting encouragement. None of the others who had faced Rader had come close to touching him. Seeing the peacock get a taste his own medicine was far better entertainment.

Now it was Rader's turn to stumble over his own feet as he stepped back. Though he managed to save himself from falling, his opponent's "touch" had stung both his flesh and his pride. He had fenced for many years against swordsmen of great experience. He had learned from the best. It was impossible to believe that a half-wild, half-Indian novice had found a way through his defenses.

Peg could see that Rader was struggling to suppress his rage and maintain his composure. The hard line of his jaw rippled with determination and his eyes narrowed into scorching slits of white-hot hate. With a grand flourish of his rapier, he glided into the ready position – a move performed with such swiftness and exaggeration that no one realized he had removed the protective button from the sword's lethal tip – except for Peg.

Simmering in a stew of anger at Rader and fear for the woodsman, she watched as the captain feigned several attacks. Asku countered well, responding to the moves in rapid succession. His confidence growing, the woodsman went on the offensive and tried to duplicate the technique Rader used. He lunged once, and then again.

As Asku's rapier came in, the expert swordsman caught the blade with his and guided it into a wide circle. The momentum forced the woodsman to expose his front, allowing Rader to lunge in for an easy kill. By now, however, Asku knew to anticipate anything. Realizing his mistake, he twisted his body sideways and leaned back as far as he could. Rader's sword tore through the front of his shirt and came out the other side covered with bright red blood.

Peg's stomach turned hollow and she cursed under her breath. Some members of the crowd groaned while others pointed in disbelief. A few of the councilmen and town officials looked at each other, wondering if they should try to intercede, but the dark, twisted look on Rader's face gave warning that it would take more than words to stop him.

Clutching the wound with his free hand, the woodsman looked at the warm blood trickling between his fingers, clearly struggling to understand how such a thing had happened. His face was ashen and his eyes were glassy with stunned disbelief. People in the crowd were whispering to each other and pointing at the blood-wet sword.

At last Asku's gaze fell upon the naked tip of his opponent's rapier and he understood. As the realization of Rader's treachery spread across the woodsman's face, Peg knew what he was about to do. Cupping her hands around her mouth, she spoke to him in a calm, clear tone, hoping her words would reach him.

"It's an exhibition," she called out as he reached for the tip of his sword, "remember? You've proven yourself. Now withdraw."

Asku lowered his gaze, took a deep breath, then removed his fingers from the cork button. He was angry, but he wasn't a fool. He understood that this was not a battle he could win.

"Giving up, Mister Dare?" The captain laughed and threw his arms out wide in mock disbelief. "Why did I try? I should have known better than to expect a simple tar heel to have competence or courage. Indeed, I believe the women here are more brave."

A few people in the crowd laughed, but most remained silent as they waited to see how Asku would respond. 'Tar heel' was the derogatory term given to the pinewoods laborers too poor to buy shoes or thought to be too stupid to wear them. The insult was derived from the black tar that collected on their bare feet while working around the kilns.

Asku raised his eyes to meet Rader's gaze. With slow, deliberate movement, he drew the flat of his blade across the palm of his hand and removed the cork button. Behind him, Peg shook her head, lamenting the inevitable outcome.

Wasting no time, the captain moved in and out with practiced efficiency, feigning, striking, blocking and riposting. Peg's heart sank as she watched Asku's valiant efforts. Every time Rader relented, the woodsman tried to attack, but to no avail. The captain always managed to block his thrusts and slashes with the slightest of moves. The series of small strikes and stabs he delivered began to take their toll. Asku's shirt became shredded and stained with blood. Though his determination remained strong, his body grew weaker and weaker.

Soon, Peg could see that Rader was tiring of the one-sided game. In a sudden shift of tactics, the captain lunged at Asku once – twice – three times in succession. Somehow the woodsman managed to deflect the strikes, shifting backward each time the swordsman stepped toward him. But Peg knew that Rader was setting him up for a final, fatal blow.

The next move would be an artful deception employed by almost every trained swordsman who had ever drawn a blade. The captain would feign retreat to bring Asku toward him. He would then deflect, dip down and move in under his opponent's blade to make a final thrust. But as Rader drove Asku backward, the exhausted woodsman once again tripped and fell backward, this time striking the back of his head on the hard-packed ground. The rapier fell from his hand.

Rader cursed to himself but remained in place.

*Stay on the ground,* Peg thought. *Killing a defenseless man would cross a line the law would not be able to ignore. Rader knows that.*

"Come, come, Mister Dare. You're not giving up, are you? Perhaps there is tar or your backside keeping you stuck to the ground."

No one in the crowd laughed this time. They now understood the captain's intent but were helpless to stop it. As long as Asku continued to fight, he was the willing participant of what had turned into a duel, no matter how much it may have looked like a murder.

Peg held her breath as Asku struggled to overcome the grogginess. He looked about the crowd as if trying to remember how he had come to be on the ground and why everyone was looking at him. When his gaze fell on Rader, she saw recognition begin to register in his eyes.

"Or perhaps you have just run out of nerve," Rader said, "not that you tar heels are known for having such a trait."

Although the woodsman was still confused, Peg could see that the insults were working. She could see it in his eyes. As he struggled to his knees, she could stand it no longer. Moving from the crowd, she came to his side and placed a hand on his shoulder to keep him from rising.

"You're done," she said. "You've proven yourself. It's time to go home."

Peg looked in his eyes to see if he understood but saw that he was still dazed.

"Be gone, wench!" she heard Rader bark from behind her.

He had come up unnoticed as Peg knelt over Asku, placed his boot on her backside, and shoved her face-first into the dirt. Gritting her teeth, she wrenched her body around and came up on one knee to face the captain. By chance, her hand came to rest upon the hilt of Asku's sword, now hidden beneath the folds of her dress.

"You," he said in a low, ominous voice, poking the point of his rapier in her face as though it was a long finger. "You have interfered enough for one day. Now run along like a good little girl and let me finish my...exhibition. And keep your nose out of other people's business."

To emphasize his point, he extended the sword until its tip touched the end of her nose.

It had been almost nine years since Peg had felt white-hot anger. Her jaw rippled with tension as she tried to latch onto the advice she had given the young woodsman a few minutes earlier – but failed. Closing her hand around the rapier's grip, she whipped the sword around her head, knocking Rader's blade up and away from her face. Using the momentum of her swing to help bring her to her feet, she spun around to face the captain. It was a simple move, but one she had practiced many times in her youth.

As Rader brought his wayward blade back to the ready, Peg caught it with hers. Her next move was so swift and subtle that no one in the crowd fully understood what they were seeing. Somehow, Peg had liberated Rader's sword from his grasp to send it flying in a great arc. Those who watched the errant weapon fall several yards away missed Peg's follow-through. Still flowing with the move that had disarmed the captain, she stepped forward in a blur and placed the tip of her rapier on the end of his nose. The table was turned.

The crowd looked on in stunned silence. The man who had seemed unbeatable just moments before was now at the mercy of a woman, and they didn't have a clue how she had done it. With each moment that passed, the more certain it seemed that she would run her blade through the back of Rader's skull.

*No*, Peg argued with herself. *Those days are over. You can't afford to kill him even if he deserves it. You have to think of Tye.*

"I suggest you leave, Captain Rader," she said through clenched teeth. "Now. Don't bother to get your things. Someone will bring them to you later."

The defeated man's face twisted dark with hate. He started to speak, but Peg cut him off.

"No. Don't say a word. You baited that man into a fight you knew he could not win. What you intended, Captain Rader, was to commit murder. Everyone here knows it, though no one can prove what darkness was in your heart. But I know, because I know you. I know your kind. Now go, or perhaps you would like for me to give you a lesson?"

Rader mulled her words for a few moments as though trying to come to a decision.

"Now listen to me!" he said at last. "I will not–"

The rage Peg had been holding back exploded like a piked cannon. With a flick of her wrist, the sharp point of her rapier sliced through the middle of his nose. Rader clutched his hands to his face, shrieking in pain.

"You've cut me, damn you!" he said into his hands, the blood streaming between his fingers and down his arms. "You've cut my nose!"

As the realization of what she had done began to sink in, Peg's expression shifted from delicious revenge to reluctant regret. Wrath had always been her biggest failing, and now – once again – there would be a price to pay. The townspeople would begin to whisper stories about her behind her back. Those with lesser civilities would talk about her openly, though not to her face. Everything she had worked for these past eight years was crashing down around her.

*It was Rader's fault...the bastard!*

Again the rage swelled within her and she began to feel her control slipping away. Through a red haze of her rising anger and frustration she saw the soft, inviting hollow of Rader's neck. Still clutching his nose, his arms formed an inverted "V" to frame the spot under his Adam's apple. Peg placed the point of her sword against the soft skin. The bloodied captain froze, not daring even to draw breath. She stared into his eyes, relishing his fear. One short, simple jab and his life would be over.

"Mother."

Tye's voice drifted through the red haze as though from miles away.

"Mother," he said again, a little louder this time. "It's over. Let him go."

Peg let the rapier fall away from Rader's neck, though not so far that he might chance rushing her. But the sea captain had lost his interest in fighting. With his face still buried in his hands, he called for his servant to assist him. Peg watched the two warily until they were a safe distance, then knelt beside the man she had saved. His shredded shirt was so soaked with blood it was impossible to tell how many times he had been cut by Rader's sword. She examined him as well as she could but did not find any serious wounds. Once the cuts were cleaned and dressed, he would be fine, except for a few scars to remind him of his foolishness.

Asku followed every move as she inspected his wounds, accepting her effort with child-like complacency. Sensing his gaze, Peg paused to look back at him. His eyes were like none she had ever seen, as blue as the clear, azure waters of the Caribbean and as deep as an abyss.

"Thank you, ma'am. We'll take care of him from here."

Peg jumped, startled to see that two kilnsmen had come to stand next to her. Realizing how enthralled she must have appeared, her shock turned to embarrassment. Had anyone noticed? Taking a quick look around she was relieved to see that most of the crowd had already returned to their work or were heading back to town. When she turned back to talk to the kilnsmen they had already lifted Asku to his feet and were helping him back to his mule.

"Wait," she said. "You can bring him to my place. I'll tend his wounds."

The two men stopped and looked at Asku, but the young woodsman shook his head.

"Ma'am, Asku here is a private man," the larger of the two kiln workers said. "Besides, it's probably not a smart idea. People would talk...you know."

Peg thought of Tye and knew he was right. She didn't care if people gossiped about her, but she would not do anything that might cause her son to suffer teasing and shame. She also had to consider the woodsman. He might well be a pious man who would be embarrassed by village gossip. Having witnessed how badly the woodsman had handled Rader's taunts, she reluctantly accepted the kiln worker's bidding.

"All right then," she said. "But if there is any way I can help, you come fetch me. You understand?"

"Yes ma'am," the larger kilnsman said. "His camp is only about a mile from here down along the river. But we'll take good care of him, for sure."

They lifted Asku onto the mule and headed in the direction opposite of the way back to Peg's place. She watched them until they passed from sight.

"Just two miles separate us," she said to herself. The rush that came with sword fighting and the closeness of death had subsided, only to be replaced by the overpowering desire for a more basic physical need. "Just two miles. Might as well be a thousand."

"What did you say?" Tye asked.

"Nothing," she said in reply, realizing that they still had work to do before dark.

There had been a day when she would have found a way to sample the unspoken promise of such blue eyes, with no need to worry about what others might think. But this wasn't that time, and Bath wasn't that place.

# Chapter Two

PEG DID NOT GO INTO THE VILLAGE for several weeks following the incident at the kiln. It wasn't that she wanted to avoid the finger pointing and gossip, she could handle that well enough. What she wanted was to return to the obscurity she had been hiding behind before having brought so much attention upon herself. The more time that passed, the more the episode would begin to fade from their memories and the more her life would return to normal.

But time had done nothing to help her forget. The night after the confrontation she had not been able to sleep. At first, it had been regret and anger at herself that kept her awake. In taking on Rader, she had broken several promises to herself, and all of them had consequences for her and for Tye. Most of all she regretted the attention she had brought upon herself. Few women knew how to handle a sword, and fewer still who were good at it. Developing a reputation as a sword fighter was a threat to the life she had created, such as it was.

The remainder of the night was filled reliving every move, every attack, every deflection, and every word said. As the sun began to rise, she realized that what disturbed her the most was that she had loved it. She had not felt that alive in many years. Once she surrendered to that basic truth, she knew she wanted more.

That morning Peg worked with more energy and passion than her sleep-starved body should have allowed. The feeling carried her for days, and even when the frenetic energy began to subside, her spirit remained uplifted and inspired. For the first time in years she had begun to think about the future – her future – a future beyond just making a home for Tye. She knew that her life had to change. But how?

As April turned into May with no viable solution presenting itself, Peg's frustration grew with each passing day but her determination remained undaunted. Seeking a release for her anger, she focused on finishing the vegetable garden she planted each spring. The more produce she grew on her little plot next to the grain barn, the less she would need to buy at the market later. This year she had doubled the area planted, hoping that she would be able to sell a portion of her crop to bring in extra money.

Today she toiled with a rhythmic, steady purpose, digging shallow holes for pole bean seeds, trying to finish the work before the midday sun made the work intolerable. She had learned on her own that by using pole green beans instead of the bush variety she could plant corn and beans together, requiring less land and less work. The trick was to wait until the cornstalks had grown about six inches tall before planting a bean seed next to each stalk. As the corn grew taller, the bean vines would climb up the stalk. The corn would still come to tassel and throw its ears even though the bean vines would eventually cover the stalks. The plan meant twice the produce for half the work.

She was pleased with her progress. One more row, about a hundred feet long, and she could move on to other chores that needed to be done. The repetitiveness of turning the soil and planting seeds left her mind free to conceive of ways to escape her self-imposed exile. Despite the burning desire to leave as soon as possible, it was unlikely that they would be able to leave until fall. By living in the barn and keeping her life simple, she had been able to save a little money. If the weather held and the harvest was bountiful, she would have enough to buy their passage to – somewhere.

But it was the "where" that was the rub. Cities like Boston, Philadelphia or New York would give Tye access to the education he deserved, but work would be hard to find and the pay would be paltry. She also knew that living in the city would quickly grow intolerable. In addition to the masses of people living on top of each other, there were the rats and the winter cold and a loss of soul that was unacceptable. If she could not see the horizon she would lose her sanity.

It was the warmth of the islands she craved, as much as she craved life. Nothing compared to the tropical breezes and lush islands of Jamaica, the Bahamas, or Barbados. A woman could find freedom and opportunity there unlike any other place she had ever traveled. She craved that freedom again and knew that no matter where else she went, she would always look at the islands as her true home.

Peg's thoughts had drifted into languid memories of sugar cane and dark rumbullion when the handle of her hoe broke with a sudden, dry snap.

"Horse shite," she cursed under her breath, and then louder, "Tye! Tye, I need your help!"

Losing use of the hoe was more than an aggravation. She could finish the last half of the bean row by getting on her knees and using a large clam shell to dig, but the hoe had to be repaired or she would fall behind.

Tye came out of the barn where he had been cleaning and oiling the harnesses for the ox and ran to the garden.

"Ma'am?"

"Here," she said, handing him the half of the hoe with the metal blade. "Take this to Kofi and ask him to put the head on a new handle. Here's a farthing. Tell him I'll give him half a pecan pie the next time I cook, but if he balks, give him the money. Understand?"

"Yes, ma'am!" Watching the giant blacksmith working metal and fire was one of his favorite things to do – that and talking to his helper, little Briebras. Tye shoved the coin into his pocket and started running down the dirt path toward town.

She continued to watch him for a minute, wondering if she should have told him to come right back. The boy had a way of getting distracted whenever he went into town.

Tye came into Bath on King Street and cut through an empty lot to the barn on Main Street where Kofi maintained his farrier and smithing business. Built at the top of a hill, Main Street ran parallel to Bath Creek and the wharf that ran along its bank. Houses, shops, storage barns, several ordinaries, and even the jail had been built between the creek and Main Street. Kofi's barn stood on the east side of the street with more homes, shops, and various buildings.

The large double doors at the back of the barn were open, as were the two doors at the front. A slight breeze traveled through the front entrance bringing with it all the odors associated with horses, hay, iron, and hot fire. As he came through the barn's rear entry, Tye saw the well-defined silhouettes of the large African and the short French Huguenot framed by the front entryway. The two men were so absorbed in an argument – Briebras making wild gestures toward the wharf, Kofi with his arms folded under his chest – that they did not hear him approaching.

"No, no, no," Briebras said, stamping his foot. "It is not an East Indiaman. It is a Dutch fluyt. A newer one, oui, but a fluyt just the same. Even a drunken wharf rat could see the difference."

"No," the African said. "East Indiaman." His high-pitched voice belied his massive size and he spoke with a slight lisp. It was as though the two men had traded voices or were victims of a spell – the giant squeaked while the dwarf boomed.

Hearing the strange reversal of octaves, Tye almost laughed. He always had to bite his tongue when the two men spoke. Almost everyone did. It was impossible not to notice, though few men were foolish enough to laugh out loud in front of Kofi.

"Look at the stern," Briebras said. "It is smooth and round, graceful like a beautiful woman's derriere. Her bow is full like the bosoms and she is narrow at the waist like a jeune femme. She is magnifique."

Knowing full well what derrieres and bosoms were, the comparison made Tye smile.

"East Indiaman," Kofi said. The freed slave had been born in Virginia, and though English was the language he had grown up speaking, he seldom said more than two or three words at a time because his squeaky voice embarrassed him.

"C'est des conneries!" Briebras swore. "You are stupid African. You cannot tell the difference between a possum and a pig, even though you are related to the latter. You are so stupid you would try to drown a fish. You are..."

"Indiaman."

"Aaaaa...ta gueule! You drive me crazy, African. You know that? Why I work for you, I do not know. You are so mule-headed you would drive even our ami petit Tye insane. Is that not true, Tye?"

"Huh?" the boy muttered, taken off guard.

Briebras and Kofi turned to face Tye. Except for their size difference and the color of their skin, they shared an odd resemblance to one another. Both men wore the heavy, leather smithing aprons of their trade, and they wore dark shirts with the sleeves rolled up as high as they would go. Briebras was a few inches short of five-feet tall – not a true dwarf – just a very short man with large muscular arms. His short black hair swirled in tight curls, his olive skin almost as dark as the African's. He wore a small pewter cross on a strip of rawhide pulled tight around his neck to denote his Calvinist upbringing.

Kofi was about half-a-foot taller than six feet, had the short curly hair typical of his race, and wore a small, gold ring on his left ear. Both men's biceps and forearms were huge knots of muscle and sinew. Their extreme statures made it hard to guess their ages, though neither could have been much older than thirty.

"Well, what should we do with the espion petit?" Briebras asked, planting his fists on his hips. "Did your mother not tell you that it is bad manners to sneak around spying on others? Perhaps we should put you in the stock as an example to other provocateurs? What do you think, Kofi?"

"Stock," Kofi said. Crossing his huge arms, he stared at the boy. His mind was made up.

"But, but... I didn't mean any harm. I didn't even mean to sneak up on you. I mean, I wasn't sneak-."

"Aha!" Briebras interrupted. "So you admit that you were spying! The stock is too good for you. Do you know what the punishment for spying is? We hang you from your feet until your head turns purple."

The little Frenchman sprang forward, spun Tye around and held him in his vice-like arms. The boy dropped the hoe blade and struggled to break free, but the eight-year-old was no match against the powerful little blacksmith.

"But first we dip you into the hot tar and roll you in feathers so you will look like the big chicken. Then we ride you around on the rail so all can see what happens to those who spy on Briebras!"

Tye relaxed a little, beginning to realize that he was being shammed.

"Or perhaps we heat the poker and brand you on the forehead."

"No," Kofi said. Tye stopped struggling but Briebras was not yet ready to quit the game.

"But I have not even gotten to the rack," he said.

"Look," Kofi said, pointing to the wharf and the merchant ship they had been arguing about.

Briebras let the boy go and returned to stand beside his boss at the doorway. Tye joined them, his "close brush with death" already forgotten.

"Palsambleu..." Briebras swore in a hushed voice, drawing the word out so long that Tye wondered if he would run out of breath. Following their stares, he scanned the wharf looking for the cause of their amazement.

A tall woman – clothed in a fine gray dress typical of the Spanish or Portuguese – was standing at the top of a gangplank bridging the ship to the wharf. A dark lace mantilla covered her face, held in place by a large comb at the back of her head. The tall ensemble added to the woman's stature, making it difficult to judge her true height, and the veil made it impossible to tell her age, looks, the color of her eyes, or even if she wore a smile or a frown.

Every man on the wharf was staring at her. Ships from all over the world brought people to Bath, though few stayed longer than the time it took to offload their cargoes and on-load new goods. The residents were used to all manner of fashions and races of people. And while women travelers were less common, seldom did a newcomer warrant more than a glance or two.

But this woman was different. It was more than her clothes or the way she looked about the wharf as if a queen surveying her domain. If the intent of the veil was to avoid attention, it had failed miserably. Not being able to see the woman's face made people more curious, not less.

"No doubt, she is Spanish," Briebras mused.

"Portuguese," Kofi challenged.

"Look at her clothes, her bearing, the mantilla. She is Spanish, I say."

"Portuguese," Kofi said again, not bothering to defend his opinion.

Briebras glanced at Tye and rolled his eyes.

The woman remained at the top of the gangplank, scanning the wharf in search of someone or something. Tye continued to stare, trying to imagine the face behind the veil. But there was more to the boy's curiosity than the mystery of her appearance. There was an unseen quality about the woman that was far more compelling.

"Palsambleu!" Briebras said again. "Look, it is Blyth Rader."

"Rader," Kofi repeated, nodding in rare agreement.

"Where?" Tye asked, unable to find the man among all the people milling about docks.

"There," Kofi said, pointing to the southern end of the wharf.

"I can't see–" Tye bit off the last word as Kofi lifted him off the ground and sat him atop his broad shoulders.

He had just settled in when he saw the frantic sea captain emerge from the crowd and scamper up the gangplank. When he got to the gangway, Rader removed his hat with a grand flourish and bowed. The woman acknowledged his greeting with a subtle nod and held out her hand. Rader took the proffered hand in his and guided her to a carriage waiting for them on the street.

"It appears they are going to the shipyard," Briebras said as the carriage followed the road along the river. "I wonder...could she be the capitaine's benefactor?"

"That is possible," Kofi agreed.

"She does look to be a woman of means," Tye said.

"There has been much speculation at the Poisoned Oak about that ship," Briebras said, referring to one of the ordinaries on the wharf that catered to the seamen. It was the one public establishment in Bath that not only offered rooms, meals, and drink, but also boasted wood floors. "Some of the boatwrights say that it is a ship like no other they have ever built. Of course, as long as they are paid, they do not care what it's purpose may be. But now, with the arrival of the Spanish woman, we have a mystery upon a mystery."

"Portuguese," Kofi countered.

Briebras ignored him.

Tye knew of the ship as well. He and Will had slipped into the shipyard several times to see what made it so different. It had two masts and a hull, but even Tye had seen that those were the only two things about it that resembled a typical merchant ship.

"I would love to know what they are talking about at the shipyard," Briebras said. "It is a safe wager that old man Burras won't talk."

Robert Burras was the owner of the shipyard as well as its master boatwright. Shipyard matters were business and he was seldom inclined to discuss his clients with others. When it came to the work Rader had commissioned, he had been even less revealing.

"I can find out," Tye said without thinking. Kofi lifted the boy off his shoulders and placed him on the ground.

"I mean... That is to say... I know how to get into the shipyard without being seen."

"Ha!" Briebras said. "So, you are a spy. I knew it."

"I am not a spy!" Tye shot back. "I just... I hear things, that's all."

Briebras gave Kofi a glance and winked.

"Now, now, mon ami petit. We know that you are not a spy. The truth is, we have all, on occasion, overheard the conversations of others. It is, shall we say, a naturel thing. So, do you really think you can sneak...I mean...wander into the shipyard and accidentally find out what they are saying?"

"I can. I'm sure of it. Accidentally, I mean."

"Of course, of course. So...why is it you are still here?"

Tye looked at Briebras and then Kofi as if waiting for something.

"Ah," Briebras sighed. "I understand. Let me think."

He pulled at his bottom lip, mulling over the problem.

"Ah ha!" he said after a few seconds. "Mon ami. would you do us a kindness? We... That is, my boss, Kofi and I...have been wondering if the ship Capitaine Rader is having built has been launched. Monsieur Burras may be in need of some...cargo hooks and eyebolts. Yes, that's it. Would you run down to the shipyard and...look around, s'il te plaît?"

"Oh... Oh!" Tye said, adopting a French accent. "Oui, Oui! I would be most happy to see if the ship Capitaine Rader is building has been launched."

Briebras gave the boy a conspiratorial wink to seal the pact. Now, if Tye got caught he would be off the hook. With a wave of his hand, he trotted off down the same road the carriage had taken.

When he got close to the shipyard, he left the road and followed a path through the woods that allowed him to approach unseen. From the edge of the woods where the path ended, Tye surveyed the shipyard seeking the best way to cross the open site without being seen. Three ships under varying stages of construction were held upright by scaffolding next to the creek that served as the yard's wet dock. When completed, they would be launched into the water and floated downstream. A fourth ship – the one Rader had commissioned – floated high in water, securely moored to the construction site's dock. Farther up the creek, the carpenters and riggers had gathered under a shade tree to eat their mid-day meal.

Though close enough to see the ship's details, Tye wanted to be closer. Leaving the cover the woods, he darted from one hiding spot to another until he reached several stacks of decking lumber next. As he paused to catch his breath, he heard voices coming toward the ship.

Dropping to his hands and knees, he squirmed into a nook created by the stacks of lumber. The sound of hard-soled boots and shoes clacking on the ship's gangplank and down the wood dock came to a stop a few feet away.

"Your work is excellent, Mister Burras. My compliments." The voice was rough, almost hoarse, but Tye could tell it was a woman's. "I very much look forward to seeing how she sails."

Tye took a deep, silent breath, then let it out slowly. Regaining his confidence, he found a narrow gap between the stacks of decking and peeked through. Old man Burras, Captain Rader, and the Spanish woman were so close he could have reached out and touched them.

"Thank you, Doña Maria," the boatwright said, trying to peer through the veil covering her face. "I must say, I found your design to be very...inventive."

"Please Mister Burras, I'm no more Spanish that you are. I just happen to prefer Spanish fashion. I would prefer that you call me Mary."

"Of course," Burras said. "As you wish. But, if you don't mind, using your first name is a bit more informal than is our habit here in Bath. People in town might think it a bit forward, you understand. May I call you by your last name?"

The woman paused for a moment, studying the master boatwright through her veil.

"Seriously, Mister Burras," she said. "Do you really think I'm that stupid?"

Tye saw beads of sweat forming on the shipbuilder's forehead.

"You'll know my full name soon enough, as will everyone else."

"I see," Burras replied. "My apologies." Though his words were contrite, his eyes burned with a dark fire.

"Come now, Mister Burras. There's no need for us to be at odds with each other. I am paying you well for your fine work, am I not?"

"That's true enough."

"And there will be a lot more to come. If everything goes the way I plan, you will be building a lot more ships for me."

"It's not like I have a choice, though, is it?"

The woman's pause and fixed manner conveyed such darkness that Tye shuddered.

"By the way," she continued in her casual manner. "My friend in England tells me that your daughter and granddaughters are doing quite well in Portsmouth. He says that their house on...St. Ronans...St. Ronans Road is a handsome place – though, he did say that it was an older house. A bit of a fire hazard. But I'm sure they have nothing to worry about."

Tye had never before seen such fear in a man's face. His cheeks turned ashen and his lips were chalky white. The hardy old man suddenly looked frail and bowed.

"Ah, come now Mister Burras. You are a wise man and a devoted patriarch. As long as we continue to understand each other, we'll have a very profitable relationship. Do you not agree?"

"Yes," he said, all the fight had vanished from his voice.

"Very good. Now, if you don't mind, I'd like to finish looking over the ship with Captain Rader."

Old man Burras started to say something but thought better of it. Swallowing his pride, he turned and walked off toward where his workers were eating their dinner.

"My compliments," Rader said. "You certainly live up to your reputation."

Instead of replying, Mary lifted the veil so that he could see her face. Tye saw the captain was struggling not to react, but the narrowing of his eyes and furrowing of his brow betrayed his shock.

Shifting his angle, he peered through the space between the planks, desperate to see what the Spanish woman looked like. But all he could see was the back of her head and, over her shoulder, Rader's ghastly face, pale and drawn.

"Tell me, Captain Rader, do you fear me?"

A nervous laugh began to tumble from his lips, but something he saw in her face made him bite it off short. The woman named Mary grasped his bearded jaw and forced his head to the left and then to right, inspecting the gruesome appendage that had once been his nose.

"Twisty rickets, man! What the hell happened to you?"

"It... It was an accident."

"Indeed!" she laughed, releasing her grip. "What did you do, run face-first into an ax?"

"It was stupid, really. I was giving fencing instructions to the locals. Just trying to keep my skills sharp. I got careless and a woman–"

"A woman!" Mary laughed again. "My dear Captain Rader one of the reasons I sought you out is because of your reputation as a swordsman, and I don't mean with the sword between your legs. Are you telling me a provincial...an unskilled woman...did that to you? Really?"

"It was a lucky thrust," he said. "I was toying with her. I let my guard down and... Trust me, one day I will make her pay for her offense."

"My, my, Captain Rader. Seeking to revenge yourself upon a simple colonial woman? She must have made quite an impression on you. Wait. What am I saying? Of course she did. She mutilated you for life. Perhaps you should tell me her name, in case I run into her in the village. I wouldn't want to inadvertently make her angry at me lest she wants to collect my nose as a souvenir as well."

"Her name is Peg Brennan," he said through clenched teeth. "She and her son live in a barn just outside of town. She's not indentured. She's a free woman, but with no husband. She's not originally from Bath, from what I was told."

"Almost everybody who lives in Bath is not originally from Bath!" Mary shot back.

"Yes, of course. I mean, she was not with the original founders and she doesn't seem to quite fit in. The townspeople tend to treat her as some sort of odd recluse."

"So, you are telling me that a woman of no substance, standing or... Wait! Say her name again."

"Peg. Peg Brennan."

"Peg Brennan? Peg... Brennan... It seems I should know that name."

She mulled it over for a moment, finally letting go of his jaw.

"Tell me, Captain Rader, what is the color of her hair?"

"There's no forgetting that. Her hair is her most distinctive feature. It's red, like the color of a bonfire."

Her response came out as a low, rolling laugh, like a person finally understanding the gist of a joke.

"Captain... You are such a complete and utter fool. You are lucky to be alive and you have absolutely no idea why. The woman you crossed...on the day she turned sixteen she informed her fencing instructor that his services would no longer be needed. When he asked why, she told him that it was foolish to keep paying someone to teach her something she was already better at. Then he made the mistake of laughing at her. Before she was done, she had disrobed him with her sword, button by button, humiliating him before the entire town. And, having exposed him to be a man of 'little consequence,' made it impossible for him to show his face in public again."

"The woman you crossed is like the Norse berserkers of old. Once in a rage, she is unstoppable – and to tell you the truth – so completely transformed that she scares even me. But her name isn't Peg Brennan. Peg Brennan was her mother's name. Her name is Anne Bonny...and soon her name will be regret."

Tye slunk farther back into the dark crevasse of his hiding place wondering if he had heard right. Could it really be that his mother was Anne Bonny the pirate? The idea pricked his skin like a thousand needles. He knew of Anne Bonny and Mary Read, the horrid female raiders who, along with Calico Jack Rackham had terrorized merchant ships throughout the Caribbean. Everybody in Bath knew of them. Just like they knew about Edward Teach. Tye walked by the house Teach had lived in almost every day.

Each realization raised a new question. What else had his mother lied about? Who was his father? She had told him that his father was a mariner who had died in a storm before he had been born. He knew that Anne Bonny had grown up in Charles Town, raised to be a woman of society. Was it true that she had burned her father's house down in a fit of anger? Did his grandfather still live?"

Then a new thought came to him that was as incredible as it was undeniable. The Spanish woman – Mary – had to be Mary Read the piratress! Mary Read still lived!

The click-clack of shoes and boots on the dock brought Tye from his daze. A quick peek between the stacks of decking confirmed that Mary Read and Captain Rader were headed toward where old man Burras waited. But now he had a new problem. The boatwrights and riggers had finished their lunch and were coming back to work. If he didn't leave now he would be trapped. Staying low, he ran from lumber stack to pitch barrel to lumber stack in hope of making the woods before anyone saw him. But as he ran behind the last pyramid of barrels that stood between the dock and the trees, he heard one of the workers shout out.

"Hey you!" Stop!"

Abandoning all caution, Tye broke away from the barrels and rushed headlong toward the forest. Rattled by the revelations, he had forgotten about the excuse Briebras had concocted to explain why he had come to be in the shipyard.

"After him!" one of the men shouted.

"No!" old man Burras yelled to the men, shaking his head. "Let him go! It's just a boy. They're always sneaking in to look at the ships. Nothing to bother with."

Hearing the commotion, Mary Read looked over her shoulder in time to catch a glimpse of Tye as he disappeared into the woods.

"Captain Rader, did you say that this Peg Brennan has a son?"

"Aye. I did. Not more than seven or eight, I'd guess."

"Indeed," she whispered to herself. "It's just a boy."

Not having heard the master boatwright call off his men, Tye dashed headlong through the woods until he could run no more. He finally stopped beside a stream, crawled up under the sagging limbs of a cedar tree for concealment, and rested against its trunk. The only sounds to be heard were the rustling of the wind-blown boughs of the surrounding pinewoods and the gentle rippling of the stream. No one was chasing him. He was safe.

As he rested he thought about his mother and what Mary Read had said. He knew in his heart that it was all true. For as long as he could remember, he had known that his mother carried a burden. As he had grown older he had come to understand that it wasn't a feeling of misplaced blame for not taking on a man to be his father. Now that he knew who she really was, it would have been easy to believe that keeping her past a secret was the weight she carried. But he knew that wasn't the whole story either. He now understood the true cause of the distance between them – even if she didn't.

Tye thought about what he had learned for a long time, trying to decide what he would say when he saw his mother. It was well toward sunset before he could force himself to move. If he went home, he would have to talk about what he had been doing, and why it had taken so long to–

*The hoe! I forgot about the hoe!*

He rolled out from under the tree and sprinted back to town in the fading light of dusk. When he got to the barn he saw that there were three people standing by the forge. The embers illuminated the faces of Kofi and Briebras, and though the third person's back was turned to him, he knew he was in trouble.

"Tye!" Kofi said when the boy came into the circle of light.

"Dieu merci," Briebras cried. There was no mistaking his sincerity. "We were worried about you, mon ami petit. Where have you been?"

The third person turned around to face him.

"Hello, mother."

# CHAPTER THREE

PEG HAD NOT WORRIED WHEN TYE did not come home after a few hours. If the boy was taking long on his errand there had to be a good reason. The only rigid rule she had was that he must be home before dark.

But when the sun had begun to sink below the treetops, she knew he was going to break that rule for the first time. Even then, she wasn't worried. Had he been harmed in some way, someone would have come to tell her. And yet, she knew that something was keeping him from coming home, because Tye did not break rules.

Grabbing a shawl to keep warm in the cool air of the coming spring night, she hurried into town and straight to Kofi's barn. As she came closer, she saw the small Frenchman standing next to an anvil, holding something steady while the African tapped on it with a metal hammer.

"Have you seen my son," Peg asked, interrupting their work.

"Tye?" Kofi asked, caught off guard.

"Yes, of course, Tye. He was supposed to have brought a hoe for you to repair. Did he come?"

"Oui, Oui," Briebras said, pointing to the repaired tool leaning against the barn. "He gave it to us repair before we sent him to-"

Briebras stopped, realizing he had said too much.

"Sent him where? Go on."

"We... That is, I, asked him to go to the shipyard." Briebras stopped as though that was explanation enough.

"Why?" Peg prodded.

"Because...we wanted to know if the ship Capitaine Rader is building has been launched."

He stopped again.

"Why did you all of a sudden want to know whether his ship had been launched?" Growing frustration was honing a sharp edge on her words.

Briebras brushed imaginary ash off his arm, fidgeted with his leather wristbands and shrugged his shoulders. The alibi he had created for Tye did not seem as sound when actually employed.

"The Portuguese woman," Kofi said. "She came in on the East Indiaman."

"Palsambleu! The woman, she is Spanish! And the ship is a fluyt. Why is it you do not listen to-"

"Stop it!" Peg said through clenched teeth. She had witnessed their routine many times and had no patience for it now. The two men looked at their feet like chastised children. "Now, tell me what's going on."

"It was the Span... the woman from the ship that came in today," Briebras muttered, looking in every direction except toward her. "We wanted to know if she was, perhaps, the patron of the ship Rader is building. So..."

"So? Go on."

"We asked him to go to the shipyard," Kofi finished in his squeaky voice.

"You asked him to go onto someone's place of business to spy on a stranger?" Peg stared at the two blacksmiths in disbelief.

"No, no, no," Briebras said. "Not spy. We... We just thought he could look around to see if the boat was in the water. Perhaps while he was there he would, uh, learn something."

Peg was seething. Kofi and Briebras were the closest thing to friends she had. Each of them was different from the other townspeople in obvious ways. And though they had little else in common, knowing that they would always be treated differently created a natural bond.

"Tye!" Kofi said as the boy walked into the pocket of light. He was glad to see the boy, but more thankful to be off Peg's hook.

"Dieu merci," Briebras said. "We were worried about you, mon ami petit. Where have you been?"

Peg spun around to look at her son.

"Hello, mother."

The tone of his voice – like the sound a wet rag makes when dropped to the floor – purged any words of anger or disappointment she might have uttered. A sense of foreboding rushed in to fill the void.

"I know who you are," he said, letting the statement hang in the air.

Peg stared at him for the next few seconds, unable to speak. Of all the things that he could have said, she had not expected that. She had no idea what to say or even where to start. She needed time to think. Not knowing what else to do, she took Tye's hand in hers and began walking home.

Realizing that he still held the hoe, Briebras started to call out to them but thought better of it. Instead, he grasped the cross that hung around his neck and closed his eyes to pray. Though he may not have been as devout as he had been in his youth, he was still a Calvinist. Perhaps God would not fault him as long as he was not praying for himself.

# CHAPTER FOUR

WHEN PEG WOKE THE NEXT MORNING, she went to the loft door and opened it just enough to let in fresh air and the morning light. As she leaned against the door frame watching the river pass by, she tried to imagine what she would say to Tye.

Her life before Bath had been a vicious cycle of wildings, drunken binges, and bloody frenzies. She regretted everything that she could remember. The things she couldn't recall were best left unknown.

After Tye was born, the urges that had dominated her life became less compelling. For the first time since becoming a woman, she could see beyond the passions that had almost killed her. For the first time in her life, she cared about someone more than she cared about herself. Before then, she would have never been able to raise a child. And though the embers of those passions and desires still glowed within, the change had allowed her to be more like a normal woman. She did not understand why giving birth to a child had changed her, but she was certain it had saved her life.

Lost in her brooding, she didn't realize that Tye had awakened until he was standing beside her.

"How did you find out?" she asked.

"The woman...who isn't really Spanish or Portuguese...she told Captain Rader."

"But, who is she? How could a woman I've never seen know who I am?"

"She said you took your mother's name," he continued, ignoring the question. "And she knew the color of your hair."

The foreboding that had chilled her the night before embraced her again. There was only one explanation. But that explanation was an impossibility.

"I heard her say that her name is Mary," Tye said. "I suppose her to be Mary Read because she is English, and when she spoke of you, it was as if from memory. And if you are truly Anne Bonny..."

The boy's words trailed off, interrupted by the sight of Peg grasping for the door frame to keep from sliding to the floor. The impossible was not so impossible after all! Whether she had somehow escaped prison eight years ago or had come to Bath as a ghost did not matter. Either way, Mary Read would be seeking revenge.

And though that revelation was bad enough, Peg realized that was just the beginning of her problems. Despite her obvious distress, Tye had not even bothered to help her or to ask if she was all right. He had remained standing next to her, watching, but saying nothing. The damage she had done to their relationship was worse than she had feared.

"I want you to stay here today," Peg said. "I want you to feed the chickens, mind the grist mill and put the tools in order. If you finish all that, get your fishing pole and see if you can catch our dinner. I'm going into town. There are a few things I have to do...you understand?"

The boy did not answer, but Peg didn't notice. There were a thousand things to consider before she got to the village, but she knew she was making the right decision. She was not going to wait and let Mary Read find her first.

There were few places for visitors to Bath to find lodging. There was no hotel or inn. A few of the ordinaries rented rooms, mostly to seamen too drunk to return to their ships. The most logical place Mary would be staying was either the Poisoned Oak or the ship on which she had arrived. But which ship was that? At least two had arrived the day before. The easiest way to find out would be to ask Kofi and Briebras, and she wanted to talk to them anyway.

She was almost upon the Office of the Customs Collector when she stopped short. By law, every ship that traded in the region was required to declare their cargoes and pay duties on their goods in this office. During business hours, the building that housed the office was the busiest place in Bath. It was there, at the top of the brick steps leading to the front door, that Peg saw Mary Read for the first time in eight years. Though there was still a good distance between them – and her face was concealed by a veil – her stature and bearing were unmistakable. Dressing as a señora was a clever disguise for a woman who did not want to be recognized, and she seemed quite comfortable playing the role of a woman of influence.

The assistant customs collector, Kilby Bloodhoff, bowed in greeting then opened the heavy wood door, allowing her to enter the building. Bloodhoff was typical of his kind – an over-educated, pretentious, bureaucrat that the crown liked to put in such positions. They were usually young, connected and more than happy to take a salaried position in the colonies where they would execute their petty authority over people they believed were inferior. Physically, Bloodhoff was a tall, lanky fellow, prematurely balding with bad teeth and worse breath. He had only been in Bath for a month before Isaac Ottiwell, the customs collector had taken ill. Since then, Bloodhoff had run the customs office as though he were in charge, and as long as Mister Ottiwell remained sick, he was.

Though her heart was still racing, Peg continued on to the smithy instead of waiting for the two to reemerge. She wanted to learn as much as she could about Mary before confronting a woman the world believed to be dead.

When she entered the barn, she found Kofi and Briebras working on a broken carriage spring. The African was leaning on a long, oak pole, lifting the carriage's weight off its wheel while Briebras worked to remove a spring from the rear axle.

"The señora," Peg asked, not waiting for them to finish, "which ship was she on?"

Briebras gave the spring a mighty pull, breaking it free from its mount. Kofi eased his weight from the pole until the carriage frame settled back onto the mount.

"It was the *Paladin*," the Frenchman said, wiping his hands on his leather apron. "But if you have business with her, you are too late. She departed this morning."

"Departed?"

The ship had left, yet Mary Read had not been on it. That meant she intended to stay, at least for awhile. But why?

"Briebras, why did you send Tye to the shipyard, really?"

The Frenchman looked at Kofi who shrugged his shoulders.

"To see if Capitaine Rader's ship had been launched...and to discover whether the señora might be his secret benefactor."

Peg had heard about the odd ship that Rader was having built. If it really belonged to Mary Read, it would be for no good purpose. She knew Mary Read better than she knew herself, and she knew that the raven-haired vixen would not have changed her ways. She was sure of it.

"Mademoiselle?" Briebras said, interrupting her thoughts. "You are all right, no?"

"Yes, I'm...fine."

She walked to the doorway to look out over the wharf, thinking. It was good that she had not met with Mary when her blood was running hot. In her youth, she would have kept pushing ahead without weighing the consequences. Now that the two mysteries were connected – the odd ship and the señora's arrival – there was no doubt in her mind that the ship belonged to Mary Read. Peg's fear that Mary had come to Bath in search of her had no merit. That they had both ended up in the same place seemed but a coincidence. If so, all she had to do was stay clear of town until the woman left in her ship. And that she would eventually sail away was certain, because people did not build ships just to leave them moored.

"Briebras. Kofi."

"Oui?" Briebras replied for the both of them. The two men came to stand with her at the doorway.

"I would like for you to do me a favor. Let's call it compensation for the little prank you pulled with Tye yesterday."

"Oui?"

"Lots of people come to your shop here. I want you to ask questions. I want you to find out everything you can about the señora, but don't be obvious about it. People will be gossiping about her anyway. Just bring her up as a curiosity and see what people say. If you find out anything that seems important, let me know right away. Understand?"

"Yes ma'am," Kofi answered. "Fair enough."

"Good. Then I'll be going home now. I won't return to town for awhile and neither will Tye."

Peg started to walk away, but stopped and turned to look back at them.

"What I've asked you to do...it is very important. Do not let me down, my friends."

"Never!" Briebras said without pause, still wanting to make atones. "If there is anything...anything at all, we will let you know. As you said, we are camarades."

# CHAPTER FIVE

PEG SAID LITTLE TO TYE during the next few days. He didn't press for answers or explanations, and she was happy to leave well enough alone for as long as it would last. Meanwhile, she kept herself busy while waiting for word from Briebras and Kofi, but nothing she did could stop her from thinking about Mary Read.

Each morning, as soon as Tye left for school, she went to the far corner of the loft where she kept the few possessions she had been able to recover after her release from prison. Hidden behind the winter's hay, wrapped in heavy cloth, were a brass spyglass, two swords, and the clothes she had not worn since leaving prison. One of the swords was a rapier, similar to the weapon she used to split Rader's nose at the kiln. The other was a smallsword – or an épée de cour – as the French called it. Its blade formed a triangular cross-section that tapered into a sharp point. Lighter than the rapier, the smallsword was a newer, more modern weapon. Some swordsmen discounted the smallsword because of its name. Those who actually used their weapon in situations where their life was at stake, however, understood the smallsword's advantage over the heavier, more rigid rapier, and had no such qualms.

In the privacy of the loft, Peg spent several hours each day practicing with the swords. She would start with the heavier rapier until her arm fatigued, then switch to the smallsword, pushing herself until she could no longer lift her arm. Next, she would switch to using her left arm and repeat the process. It was a training regimen she had learned from her first instructor – before she had forced him to leave Charles Town.

In addition to providing balance, it gave her two additional advantages. If wounded and forced to fight using her left arm, she wouldn't be trying to do it for the first time. The second advantage was less obvious but more important. Most swordsmen never fought with their left arm – not even people who favored their left side. Being left-handed meant that you were a servant of the devil – or so the Catholic Church warned. Parents of left-handed children often forced them to favor their right side – even if it meant restraining the offending appendage until favoring their right side became second nature.

Even the best swordsmen in Europe had little or no experience facing opponents who fought with a left-forward posture. Facing a left-handed opponent rendered most of their moves ineffective unless they were able to perform the mental contortions necessary to reverse the technique. Attempting to do so during the heat of battle without ever having practiced it was impossible. An average swordsman, who had the training and guts to attempt fighting in the left-forward posture, might have a chance against a master who had never trained against such a foe.

It was shortly after one of her morning sessions that Briebras came to her with news. Peg had just finished cleaning up when the small Frenchman called to her from outside. After a week of waiting, she was anxious to hear what news he brought.

"Bonjour mon amie," Briebras said in greeting as she came outside. "I have information I think you will find interesting. Two days ago, Capitaine Rader moved his ship to the wharf behind the Poisoned Oak and sent out word that they are hiring crewmen. But before they are signed on, both he and the señora questions each man about their experience."

"That would be expected if you wanted to hire a competent crew, would it not?" she asked, beginning to wonder if the diminutive Frenchman was wasting her time.

"Oui," said Briebras. "That is true. But competent in what?"

Peg was more interested now.

"The questions that they ask, they are not only about ropes, sails, masts, and knots. They also ask about their knowledge of pistols, the cutlass, and cannons. What do you think of that, 'eh?"

Peg knew it could mean only one thing.

"Mary Read plans to go pirating," she said more to herself that Briebras.

There could be no other explanation, but saying it made the idea seem far-fetched. Few pirates roamed the Caribbean or the Gulf anymore. There were fewer still who dared to chance preying on the colonies. The Royal Navy had spent more than two decades tracking down the Brethren and had hanged them by the hundreds.

The cleansing had started eighteen years earlier when Lt. Robert Maynard killed Bath's own Edward Teach – Blackbeard – returning to Williamsburg with his severed head hanging from the bowsprit. Just two years later, when she was still Anne Bonny, Capt. Jonathan Barnet had captured Peg and Mary Read along with Calico Jack Rackham off the coast of Jamaica. Jack was tried and found guilty of pirating. After hanging him, the officials in Port Royal had hot tar poured over his body, wrapped it in chains, then stuffed into a gibbet and left to swing on Deadman's Cay.

But it wasn't until Capt. Chaloner Ogle tracked down Bartholomew Roberts off the coast of Africa a year later that the bells truly began to toll for piracy. Ogle killed Roberts, destroyed his fleet of ships, and hanged hundreds of his men. Black Bart Roberts was dead, and except for a few rogues who refused to see that the end had arrived, so was piracy.

The idea that Mary Read would return to pirating was insanity. But if she planned to make this her home port as Edward Teach had once done, then Bath would become a very dangerous place for Peg and Tye. She had to find out for certain. And though she disliked keeping her two friends in the dark about who Mary Read really was, telling them would risk exposing her own identity.

"Briebras, it seems that this woman's plans may include...illegal activities...but there may be some other explanation. I want you to keep listening. See if you can get more information."

"Oui," he replied. "The talk is, as you said, that she and the capitaine are forming a crew of pirates...but I suppose there could be another reason for the nature of their questions. We will keep listening."

"Thank you, Briebras, and be careful. I have a bad feeling about this woman."

"I share your concerns. We will let you know if we learn more."

After he had gone, Peg thought about Mary Read and what her plans might be. But in the end, the only thing that really mattered to Peg was whether Mary Read was going to leave or stay. The longer she stayed, the more likely it was that they would run into each other.

Two days later, Peg came out of the barn as she did every morning – half asleep and in need of relief. Closing the door behind her, she turned toward the privy but pulled up short to keep from walking into a man she had never seen before. They stood face to face for a moment, sizing each other up. He was tall – at least six-feet – and broad of chest. His face was dark with beard stubble and his sunken cheeks were ruddy from the sun. His clothes were those of a sailor – a motley combination that included a red linen shirt, loose-fitting breeches, a length of rope for a belt, and a dark blue thrum cap.

As the initial shock passed, Peg realized that she was unarmed and in the open. Her swords were too far away to do any good, and calling out might put Tye in danger. But as the man's eye's lingered over her body, her fear was replaced by a disgust so strong she began to tremble with anger. She knew that look and what it meant.

"No need to be startled, ma'am," he said at last, realizing that things were about to turn bad. Taking a step back, he removed his cap and held it with both hands. "Me name is 'Arry Wennell...Bos'n Wennell, if you please. An' I mean you no harm. I'm only here to deliver a message."

"A message?"

"Yes ma'am. An invitation from an ol' friend, you might say. At least, that's what she told me to say."

"And exactly who would that be?" Peg asked, though she already knew.

"I'm instructed only to say that her name is Mary. Of course, that's the only name I knows her by, so it's not like I can be givin' away any secrets or such."

Peg peered into his eyes as if she would find Mary Read's true intentions by staring harder. But in the end it didn't matter – Anne Bonny had been found.

"And the invitation?"

"Ah... She says that you are to come to the Poisoned Oak to meet with her, tonight, at four bells. I mean...that is ta say...ten o'clock. She says she'd like the pleasure of your company to talk about ol' times."

"And if I say 'no'?"

The seaman knotted his brow, not sure how to answer.

"To be 'onest with you ma'am, she didn't address such a contingency. I think she just assumed you'd be comin' regardless."

He paused for a moment as if trying to recall something important.

"Oh... I almost forgot. The lady said to tell ye, 'given a choice between the devil and the deep blue sea, she'd still take her chances with the devil,' whatever that means."

Peg smiled despite herself as a hundred memories came rushing back to her. If Mary Read had skullduggery on her mind, it was doubtful that she would have used such a personal calling card. At the same time, it was a challenge Mary knew that Anne Bonny would not be able to refuse - not if their time together had meant anything at all.

"Tell her I'll be there," Peg said, making her decision. "And tell her this...tell her that I can still kill the devil before she can."

"Yes ma'am," the sailor said, nodding his head up and down in affirmation as he committed the words to memory. Then he knotted his brow again.

"Don't try to make sense of it," Peg said. "Just give her the message."

"Yes ma'am," he said, taking a last, long look at her body before starting toward town. "Kill the devil. Got it. I'll be sure to tell her."

Peg said nothing about the encounter when Tye got back from school that afternoon. They completed their chores, cleaned up and served the evening meal as they did every evening. She had prepared a hearty corn and potato chowder, and though she went through the motions of eating, very little food passed her lips. Her stomach was a basket of snakes, turning over and in on itself. She didn't want to risk heaving her food for fear Tye would become concerned.

Already racked with guilt, the pretense of eating added to the sense of betrayal Peg felt. But telling her son what she was going to do would create more questions and more problems. She had to deal with Mary Read first, then she would explain everything – or at least everything he needed to know. There were some parts of her life she would never talk about to anybody.

After turning in for the night, Peg waited until the sound of steady breathing told her that Tye was asleep. Being careful not to wake him, she went down to the lower part of the barn and changed into clothes she had hidden earlier – the clothes she had kept from her former life. In addition to a fine, white silk shirt, she now wore black button breeches, black leather shoes, and a black velvet waistcoat that had faded to gray. Over the shirt and beneath the coat she wore a leather strap that ran from her shoulder to her hip. At the cross-section where the ends of the strap overlapped was a metal ring to which she attached her scabbard and smallsword. If she were going to reunite with her "dead" partner, she would do it on her terms – not as an inconsequential pauper living under an alias among the townspeople – but as the warrior she had once been.

A half-hour later, Peg strode past the customs collector's office and the other darkened businesses along Main Street toward the Poisoned Oak. In the dim light of a half-moon, she could see the outline of the Mary Read's new ship moored to the wharf behind the ordinary. Even in the darkness she could tell that it was special. Its hull was sleek, its masts were true, and her lines spoke of both speed and quickness. Mary Read must have done well for herself these past years to have built such a ship.

As she stepped up to the ordinary's door, Peg heard the ebb and flow of several people talking, and then a random laugh. It had been a long time since she had set foot in a tavern. Entering the ordinary meant returning to a life she had fled many years ago, even if only for this one night. Wiping her wet palms on the hips of her breeches, Peg swallowed hard and opened the latch.

What little light there was came from candles and oil lamps about the room. Half of the tables were unoccupied as most of the sailors had returned to their ships or lodging for the night. As her eyes adjusted to the dimness, she realized that the few patrons left in the tavern were all staring at her. Once again she cursed herself for not having thought things through before acting. Now she was standing in the doorway of a room full of strangers – a woman dressed like a man – with no sign of Mary Read and no plan.

What should she do? Wait? Leave? Buy herself a drink? Would they even serve a woman? The ways of Bath, after all, were a far cry from those of Jamaica.

Cursing her timidity, Peg shrugged off the doubts and summoned the boldness that had once been Anne Bonny. Acting as if she had been to the tavern a hundred times, she moved toward an empty table on the far side of the room, letting instinct guide her movements.

"Really Annie?" came a coarse, gravelly voice from the darkest corner of the room. "Weapons? You know, it's been my experience that people who look for trouble, tend to find it."

Peg gripped the pommel of her smallsword, searching the darkness for the face that went with the voice. Sitting behind a corner table, she saw the silhouette of a woman that had to be Mary Read. The black form leaned toward the next table to light a length of fatwood from a burning candle, then lit a candle on her own table. As she brought the tinder to her lips to blow out the flame, she paused. The tinder's sputtering flame cast a smoky light across her face.

Peg caught the gasp before it passed her lips. Though the right side of Mary Read's face was as beautiful and unspoiled as it had ever been, the left was a ruined, macabre approximation of its former self. A long white scar ran down from her hairline, across her eyebrow and cheek, coming to a stop just above the jawbone. Her right eye remained as it had been, a soft, inviting gray that had won Peg over at their first meeting. Her left eye was a dead, milky white orb that absorbed light instead of reflecting it.

Mary Read looked up from the tinder an instant before blowing out the flame, catching Peg's reaction. Peg knew she had been judged, and despite all her misgivings about Mary coming to Bath, hoped that she had hidden her revulsion.

"Come, Mrs. Rackham," Mary Read rasped. "Sit with me. Let's talk about old times."

Peg – as Anne Bonny – had never married Calico Jack, but they had considered themselves to be married by common consent. Mary Read had often called her "Mrs. Rackham" as playful banter, just as Peg had had called Mary "the Duchess of Wapping." The intimate reference took Peg by surprise, but she wasn't about to let her guard down. Rather than sit with her back to the room, she took the seat to Mary Read's left, an arrangement that would allow only tavern workers to approach from behind.

Mary Read gave an approving chuckle as Anne sat in the chair.

"Always the cautious one, aren't you Annie? There's nothing to fear here, Anne Bonny. We're just old friends catching up."

"How would I know what to expect?" Peg shot back, unsettled at hearing her real name. "I've never chatted with a dead woman before."

"Not as dead as you and the rest of world wanted to believe," Mary Read said, matching Peg's fire. "And not as dead as you are, living in a backwater hellhole like this."

"I did what I had to do for me and my child, something you wouldn't understand."

Mary Read held her tongue at that, peering at Anne in the dim candlelight. They held each other's gaze for a few moments, their truce on the verge of falling apart. The tension was broken when a tavern girl came to their table.

"What can I get you...ladies?" the girl asked, not sure what to make of Anne's clothing.

Though Peg had seen her many times, she had never spoken to the girl other than to say "hello." It was no secret that she was one of Edward Teach's offspring, albeit, not from any of the women he had bothered to marry. The notoriety of being Blackbeard's daughter – a fact the girl used to great benefit at the ordinary – far outweighed the disadvantages of being illegitimate.

"Clairette, be a sweet and fetch us a jug of rum and two of your short cups. Mrs...Brennan and I have a lot to discuss and we're both thirsty."

"Remind you of anybody?" Mary Read asked as the girl went to fetch their rumbullion. "Young, cocksure, ready to pluck life's pearls from the world's oysters. Desired by every man who casts his eyes upon her?"

"I hope for her sake she's a lot smarter than you and I were at that age," Peg said. They had come too close to doing battle to relax. "Good looks and wild abandon will bring her nothing but sorrow and misery unless she has a shrewd mind to go with them."

The young woman returned to place a brown jug and two small pewter cups on the table. Peg looked at the jug with the words "Kill Devil" embossed on its side.

Mary Read grasped the girl's wrist and placed a small silver coin in her hand.

"It will take a minute to make change for this," Clairette said, brushing back her golden blonde hair.

"You keep it. Just make sure you take care of me."

"I've done pretty good so far, haven't I?"

"Indeed you have," Mary Read said, letting the girl's hand slip from hers.

"Why do you call her Clairette?" Peg asked when the tavern girl had left. "That's not her name."

"Because, she is a plump grape, ripe for the picking," Mary Read said, grasping the jug. "Now, I believe you told my man Wennell that you can match my cups despite the fact that you've never done so before."

"We both know that's not true," Peg said, tiring of the back and forth about nothing. "I shouldn't have let on that I would drink with you. It was a mistake. Why don't you get to the heart of that matter and just tell me why you asked me here?"

"Annie, my dear, sweet Annie. It's been a long time since we last drank together. A lot of things have happened to the both of us. Aren't you curious?"

"Perhaps," Peg said, growing suspicious again. "But we don't have to drink to talk."

"No, no, no," Mary lamented. "It's been too long since we've killed the devil together, and who knows when we'll have another chance. If you want answers, you'll have to drink with me. One drink. One question."

Not waiting for a response, she pulled the cork from the bottle and filled the first cups. The familiar aroma of the rumbullion was more tempting than Peg would have imagined. It had been eight years since her last drink, and not once had she craved it. But as she watched the dark liquid flow from the mouth of the jug she realized how much she had missed it.

Peg took a closer look at Mary Read as she filled the second cup, the flickering candlelight alternately revealing and concealing the damage to her face. With a start, Peg wondered if she was somehow responsible for the scar. Did it happen right after she had left Spanish Town – perhaps as some sort of cruel punishment by jailers angry at having lost one of their prize captives? Or had it happened sometime later? As much as she was loath to play Mary Read's game, she had to know.

"Tell me," Peg asked, trying to mask her pity, "what happened to your face?"

"One drink...one question," Mary insisted. Raising the cup to her lips, she threw her head back and downed the rum in one swallow.

Peg looked at her cup and sighed. Distilled from fermented molasses, the taste of rum was as pleasing to her as it was strong. The first swallow would burn, but each drink after would be smoother and better than the last. Eventually, the "devil" would come to collect his due. The trick would be getting as much information out of Mary Read as possible before he arrived.

Picking up the cup, she slammed the rum down the same as Mary had done. The alcohol burned her throat like a ball of fire and then exploded in her gut.

"Now, tell me, what happened to your face?"

"It was the price I paid to get out of jail. My fever broke a few days after you left me to swing in the gibbet by myself. I pretended to be dead and they took me to the graveyard. Only, I wasn't dead yet."

Peg winced at the idea that it had been her choice to abandoned Mary. Her father had whisked her from the prison with little warning, and she had been too weak to force him to stay and help Mary. He had sworn that he was working to have her released too, but by the time she found out he was lying, they were already halfway home to Charles Town.

"You remember Thorne, the night watch?" Mary continued. "It's his body rotting in my grave. This was his parting gift to me...a wild swing of the knife that got lucky. More lucky than him, before it was over. I don't mind the scar so much, but I wish I had my eye back."

"I like it," Peg said. "It gives you character. Have you ever thought of doing the other side to match?"

Mary laughed so hard Peg was sure it would wake the whole town.

"See Annie! Only you would say something like that. God I've missed you. Not a day has passed since getting out of that stinking prison that I haven't thought about you."

Peg heard the words, but not the sentiment. Had there been a twinge of resentment in her voice?

"What happened after you escaped Jamaica?"

Instead of answering, Mary Read filled the two cups with rum. This time Peg downed hers first, wiping her mouth with the back of her hand. As Mary tipped her cup, Peg again felt the burn of the rum making its way to her stomach, but this time found it more to her liking.

"The first thing I did was to borrow some clothes from a drunken sailor in Port Royal and hired on to a galleon headed to Cuba. Six months later, we docked in Saint-Domingue, and I figured that was as good a place as any to start over. The only thing I had to offer was myself, but it didn't take long to figure out that there wasn't much demand for a one-eyed, scar-faced prostitute. Whoring didn't sit well with me anyway. Most men are pigs, and none of them was Jack Rackham. So, one night I convinced the owner of a small brothel in Cap Français that I would make a much better madam than a strumpet. He didn't want to give up ownership at first, but you know how persuasive I can be. We did much better after he was gone. I treated the girls well, expanded the business, and we made a lot of money. Enough to fund my current little venture."

This time it was Peg who took the jug of Kill Devil and filled the cups. After drinking the rum, they sat quietly for a moment while Peg reflected upon Mary Read's story. The contrast between their lives since escaping prison was stark. It had not been an easy existence for Peg, but she had been able to make her way performing honest work. The idea that Mary had prostituted herself was almost impossible to accept. Mary Read had never been subservient to anyone – it was contrary to her nature. Allowing men to use her body would have been an act of desperation. There was also no doubt that the brothel owner had awakened one morning to find Mary's dagger in his chest.

"Tell me, exactly what is the nature of this undertaking? What do you have planned, really?"

A sly smile turned up the corner of Mary's mouth as she leaned in closer to Peg.

"Oh, Annie, it is a grand venture," she said, speaking in a hushed voice. "Jack would be proud."

"It's pirating you've got planned, isn't it?" Peg asked, unable to contain herself. The rum was already having its effect on her.

"Pirating..." Mary Read repeated, letting the word hang in the air. "You might say that. The trouble with most people, even pirates, is that they think too small. What I have planned is much bigger than just looting a merchant ship here and about. I'm talking about something much bigger."

Between the two of them, Mary had always been the schemer – thinking about the next attack, the next plunder, how to get more for their stolen goods. Even with the rumbullion dulling her wits, Peg could tell by the gleam in her eye that Mary Read had a grand scheme in mind.

"Haven't you ever noticed how the inlet between Ocracoke and Portsmouth islands makes a funnel that every ship coming to North Carolina must pass through? The inlet is barely a half-mile wide. If we put a couple of 42-pound cannons on each side of the inlet, the Royal Navy could sail a hundred ships to hunt us down and they'd never make it past the inlet – we'd pick them off as they came through, one at a time. You could put a thousand pirate ships in the Pamlico Sound and there's not a damn thing they could do about it."

Peg said nothing as her imagination grasped the magnitude of the idea and took it even further.

"Remember how the buccaneers in Tortuga created their own rules? Their own state? We can do that here, Annie. We can make our own government with our own rules. We can be rulers of our own little nation and never have to bow before any man or woman again."

Peg stared at Mary Read's scarred face trying to decide if she was joking. What bothered her most wasn't that Mary was serious, but how she had slipped into saying "we."

The truth was, her plan might just work – at least for awhile. The brilliance of the scheme was its simplicity. If she could establish a haven for pirates, they would come to Bath just as they had once gathered in Tortuga.

And her timing could not be better. Most of England's ships were on the eastern side of the Atlantic where they would remain until the negotiations in Seville concluded. The navy would never expect a resurgence of piracy right under their colonial noses. If a new "Brethren of the Coast" were to form, the British would be helpless to do anything about it until the war with Spain was over for good.

"It will cost a lot to buy cannon that big," Peg said, trying to find a flaw in the plan. "How do you expect to pay for them? And how do you expect to pay for the loyalty of the pilots in Ocracoke and Portsmouth? The Outer Bankers are an independent lot. They have to be, living on barrier islands facing hurricanes and nor'easters. It will take a lot to convince them to work with a company of pirates."

Mary Read filled the cups, but Peg didn't pick hers up right away. The alcohol was taking its toll and she needed to slow down.

"With the ship I have built, I fear no ship-of-the-line and I will be able to take any prize I choose. But I want more than riches. When I left Saint-Domingue, I swore I would never bow to the will of a man again, whether it be for man's law or for a man's desires. Whatever happens to me will be of my own choosing. What about you, Anne Bonny?"

The question was simple but ran deep. Almost every time they had pulled cork from a bottle of rumbullion they had ended up talking about how, as pirates, they had fared far better than other women. But because they had both spent time pretending to be men, they also knew that men had far more freedom and opportunities. Mary had posed as her half-brother after he had died, part of her mother's ploy to bilk money from the dead boy's paternal grandmother. The ruse worked until the day the grandmother died. In need of an income, Mary continued to dress as a man and was able to find work off-limits to women. Since that time, she had seen half the world and had followed a path of her own choosing, neither of which would have been possible as a woman.

Peg, too, had spent her early life pretending to be a boy. She was born the illegitimate daughter of an Irish solicitor and one of his maidservants. Her mother had dressed her as a boy so her father could attempt to pass her off as the son of a distant relative in need of a guardian. When his wife discovered the deception, he ran off to Charles Town to escape her wrath, taking the maidservant and their daughter with him. Though she dressed as a girl for the rest of her childhood, she again donned men's clothes to be a pirate, first with her husband James Bonny, and later with Calico Jack Rackham.

Peg struggled to come up with an answer. She knew how Anne Bonny would have responded. Anne Bonny had tasted the freedom most women would never know. But the woman she had become was a different matter.

Peg finally downed the rum to numb the truth hidden in Mary Read's question.

"I'm not saying I like your plan...and I'm not saying I don't like your plan." The rum was making it hard to think straight. "But, let's assume this boat of yours is everything you say it is. Is that really going to be enough to do what you want? Will you be able to buy off the pilots?"

"I also have a map," Mary said.

"A map?"

"Yes. A map to Blackbeard's treasure on Portsmouth Island."

Peg burst out in drunken laughter.

"You've got a bloody treasure map! Well... That does it then! Why even bother to go pirating if you've got the map to Teach's hidden treasure? It must be worth a fortune...just lying there on the beach waiting for a one-eyed piratress to come along and say, 'Oh, look, Blackbeard's treasure. I think I'll scoop it up and build myself a nation of pirates with a pirate navy and have myself a bunch of little pirate babies.'"

"Shut up!" Mary Read shot back. She had forgotten how obnoxious Anne Bonny got when she was drinking. "Keep your voice down. I don't need every hayseed, chawbacon, and lubber within a hundred miles converging on Portsmouth, getting in the way. This is serious."

"Of course it is," Peg said, slurring her words. "Do you have any idea how many Blackbeard 'treasure maps' there are out there, or have you forgotten that Edward Teach lived just down the street from here? You do know that his house was burned down by people thinking they would find his treasure there, right?"

"This is different!" Mary Read said. "I got this map from Israel Hands himself in Saint-Domingue. He was in a bad way and needed help. I loaned him some money and he gave me the map as collateral. He died soon after, before he could repay me...so the map was mine to keep."

"Well, that cinches it then," Peg said throwing her hands into the air and rolling her eyes. "Israel Hands may have been Teach's first mate, but he was also a liar and a thief. Wouldn't be like him to be selling you a counterfeit map, would it?"

"Israel Hands swore to me on his deathbed that he had seen Teach draw the map with his own eyes," Mary Read shot back, glaring at Peg with her good eye. "I'm telling you, Anne, the map is real. I don't know how much the treasure is worth, but it's there, on Portsmouth Island, somewhere."

Again, there was enough truth in Mary Read's words to make Peg pause. But even in her rum-addled state, she knew there was something wrong about the whole thing.

"Tell me why," she said as she filled the cups again. She spilled as much rum on the table as made it into the cups. "Why did you come to Bath? You could have had your ship built anywhere. Why here? Why Bath?"

Peg drank her rum and waited.

"I came to Bath to reclaim that which belongs to me. When you walked away from Spanish Town, you took a part of me with you. I want it back. I want you back, too. That's why I asked you here tonight. I'm giving you this one chance to come with me. To be part of something the likes of which the world has never seen. You and me, Annie. Equal partners sharing everything. Only this time we do it our way."

Peg looked at Mary Read in disbelief. The last thing she had expected this night was to receive an invitation to be the co-ruler of a pirate nation. The words "pirate nation" and "ruler" sounded ridiculous, even in her drunken state. All of it was far-fetched and unbelievable, but even if she had been tempted to join with Mary, she knew it was impossible.

"No. I can't do it. I have a son. I have sponsil...responsibilities. Besides, you and me...we don't belong together. Not like you think. What we did was a long... was a long... a long time... ago, and..."

Mary Read watched Peg's eyes roll back as she passed out, her head crashing to the table with a solid *whack*. She had fulfilled an obligation to her past. Her sweet, crazy Annie had failed on two fronts. She had declined the invitation to reclaim their glory, and she had failed to hold her rum.

"That's it, Wennell. She's done. Take her back to her barn or whatever it is that she lives in, and don't forget to pick up my little package."

The sailor who had given Peg the message to come to the Poisoned Oak and another man stepped out of the shadows. Lifting Peg from the chair, they draped her arms over their shoulders to carry her outside. But before letting them go, Mary Read brushed the hair away from Peg's face and caressed her cheek.

"See, Anne, my dear, sweet Annie. I tried to warn you. You can't kill the devil."

The two men carried Peg out the back door, disappearing into the darkness. Mary paused to give Clairette a glance before following.

"Sorry about all the rum under my chair, love. It seems my cup had a hole in the bottom."

# CHAPTER SIX

THE EARTHY ODOR OF STRAW AND CORN HUSKS that made up the stuffing of Peg's mattress was the first thing she became aware of the next morning. She kept her eyes closed, fearing that the bright sunlight streaking in between the barn's slats would make the pounding in her head worse. The rumbling in her stomach warned that she would soon have to rise whether she was ready or not. What a fool she had been to drink with no food in her belly.

Though some details of her reunion with Mary Read were vague, she remembered the crazy scheme about a return to pirating. She also remembered being wary of Mary's demeanor, as though she was holding on to a secret. But the harder she tried to cipher it out, the harder the throbbing in her head.

Seeking to stop the pounding, she stilled her thoughts altogether. After a few minutes of reveling in the blissful silence, she began to realize things were not as they should be. Missing were the early morning sounds of the birds stirring from their nests, the crowing of their rooster, or Tye's stirrings as he did his chores. Puzzled, Peg forced her eyes open and looked toward the loft door. Though still closed, the angle of the streams of sunlight showed that it was well past dawn. She had slept half the morning away! A frantic look around the empty loft set off a wave of panic and the pounding in her head grew worse.

"Tye! Tye! Are you here? Are you outside?"

Struggling to maintain control, Peg clung to the hope that he had gone to school or was off somewhere with Will Gibbs. But in her heart, she knew it wasn't true.

Rising from the mattress, something entangled her legs and brought her crashing back to the floor. With a start, she realized that she had tripped over her smallsword, its scabbard strap still slung over her shoulder. Shifting it out the way, she tried again. Staggering down the stairs, she made it outside to the rain barrel and splashed water on her face.

The dousing revived her a little, so she leaned over and drank directly from the barrel. When the cool water hit her sour stomach, what little food she had left erupted with a vengeance. She spent the next several minutes on her hands and knees, heaving until there was nothing left to expel. Weak and trembling, she drank as much water as she could stand and then washed her face. She wasn't sure if she could make it, but she knew she had to get to the wharf. She had to find Tye.

Main Street was busy with the usual mid-morning flurry of townspeople, mariners, traders, and merchants. As she walked toward Kofi's barn, the people she passed would stop what they were doing and stare at her. It wasn't until she had almost reached the smithy that she realized she was still dressed in the masculine clothing of the night before, and with a sword dangling at her hip.

All her efforts over the years to blend in were erased in an instant. The people of Bath would never look at her the same way again. And yet, the part of her that had known a pirate's freedom soared. She had lived a lie for so long she had forgotten who she truly was. Mary Read's arrival had started a chain of events that could not be reversed. No matter what else might occur, Peg knew she could no longer be Peg Brennan. She had to be herself. She had to be Anne Bonny again.

Briebras met her at the door of the livery, his face clouded with concern. If the clothes she wore surprised him he did not show it.

"Look," he said, pointing toward the wharf behind the Poisoned Oak.

Anne glanced at the docks but saw nothing unusual. Then she realized – Mary Read's ship was gone!

"No..." she gasped. The world swirled around her.

"What is it?" Briebras asked, taking her by the hand so she wouldn't fall.

"It's Tye. She's kidnapped him. She has stolen him from me."

"Palsambleu... Mademoiselle, are you positive?"

That which had eluded Anne last night and this morning was now clear. How could she have been so blind? So stupid?

"I have to go to Ocracoke. She will anchor there for awhile. I have to go there at once."

Briebras noticed several people down the street looking in their direction, commenting to one another.

"Mon amie," Briebras pleaded. "S'il te plaît, come inside with me. People, they are looking."

"Yes," she said, forcing herself to look away from the wharf. "Let's go into the barn."

Once inside, Briebras helped her sit down on an empty keg and then brought her a piece of flatbread and a cup of water.

In between bites of bread and sips of water, Anne told Briebras everything. She told him that the señora was really Mary Read, that they had drank together at the Poisoned Oak, and how she had awakened to find Tye gone.

"But, how can you be sure she is the pirate Mary Read? And why would she take Tye?"

"Because," Peg said without pause, "my real name is Anne Bonny. And Anne Bonny is the name I will use from this day forward."

Briebras nodded at her with a knowing smile in his eyes.

"Are you not surprised?"

"Kofi and I long suspected," he said with a shrug of his shoulders. "Others in Bath have whispered their suspicion, but I think they were too scared to seek the truth. Better to let false widows lie than to rouse dead pirates. It is, after all, a town that has an uneasy partnership with buccaneers – somehow managing to embrace them at arm's length."

Though too weak and too troubled to worry about the implications, Briebras' disclosure explained why the townspeople had never accepted her.

"But you have not answered my question – why would Mary Read take Tye?"

"Because, she blames me for being left in prison. She believes I left her there to die and she wants her revenge. I thought she had come to Bath to murder me. I was ready for that but she has done a far worse thing. She has stolen the one person in the world I love. The one thing in my life that matters."

"You must help me, Briebras. I need to find a ship going east through Ocracoke Inlet as soon as possible. Who knows how long it will be before she tries to take a merchant ship. She won't risk leaving Tye behind somewhere, I'm sure of it. She will take him with her and he will be killed."

"No!" Briebras said. "She has twenty-five or thirty crewmen and she will be expecting you to come after her."

"I don't care," Anne said. "I've got to try. I won't let her take him without a fight."

"Ahhh..." Briebras countered. "I did not say that you should not try. If you are to have any chance at all, it will have to be by surprise. She will be looking for you to come on the next ship or the one after...and she would see you coming a mile away."

"What are you thinking?" she asked, dubious of any plan that did not include leaving immediately.

"Instead of sailing there directly, we can go to Portsmouth Island and walk to the inlet. Mary Read will never expect us to come that way."

"Do you know how to get us there or where to land?"

"No, but I know someone who does," he said with a hint of a smile, "and he owes you a favor."

"And who might that be?"

"Your friend, the Tar Heel."

"Asku Dare?"

"Oui. Did you not know he is from the coast? It makes no difference. He is from Cedar Island and could easily guide us. He also has a canoe."

"A canoe? It would take two or three days just to get to Cedar Island in a canoe, and we'd still have to walk to the inlet. I can't take that long. I won't take that long."

""S'il te plait, Mademoiselle. Please listen to reason. What choice do you have, really? As I said, Mary Read will be waiting for you. You cannot save Tye if you are dead."

"And as I told you, I can't wait that long. If they weigh anchor before I get there, I may never find him. I can't take that chance."

"But they cannot leave Ocracoke," Briebras said. "They are not ready. They have to load the cannons and gunpowder and cannon balls. Then they must train the crew and gather other supplies and weapons. That will take a week at least. Probably more. Not even Mary Read would attack an armed galleon with an unskilled crew."

"How do you know all this?"

"Because, Kofi told me before he left."

"Kofi's gone?"

Briebras hesitated. He had been so concerned about Anne that he had forgotten she did not know about Kofi.

"Oh, mon amie, I am afraid I have very bad news. Kofi joined the crew of her ship."

"What?"

"Oui. It is true. Capitaine Rader, he came and filled his head with talk of 'true freedom' and that stealing from the English would be small repayment for having been enslaved. He said they needed his smithing skills and were willing to give him an extra half-share if he would join them. I guess that, in the end, it was more than he could resist. He wants to use the money to buy his sister Emmie's freedom. He told me to carry on for him here, and if he were to die, the shop was mine to keep."

"I don't believe it," Anne said. "He's been a free man for years, and he's not a vengeful person."

"And yet, it is true all the same. As I said, I believe that this is more about his sister. To what lengths would you be willing to go to free your enslaved brother or sister?"

"On the other hand," he continued, his face lighting up, "this may be a good thing. He will be on board the ship with Tye, no? Trust me...no one will hurt Tye as long as Kofi is there to keep an eye on him. No one."

Anne's hopes lifted a bit at this thought. Kofi would protect the boy from harm, she was sure of that. Once they set out to sea, however, the ship would face dangers that even Kofi would not be able to shield him from. They would still have to hurry, but Briebras' arguments had been convincing.

"Are you sure Asku will go with us?"

"Oui! He understands that you saved his life, and he is the type of man who does not want to owe a debt. He will feel obligated to repay you in some way."

"Do you know where he lives?"

"Yes. His camp is by a creek that flows into the river. All we have to do is to walk downstream."

"Then let's go now," Anne said, starting toward the doors at the rear of the barn. Fewer people would see her if they used the paths behind the houses. "We may have time to do this your way, but I'll not waste one minute more than I have to."

Still weak and now hungry, Anne struggled as they followed a trail that ran along the river's edge. To her left were the thick, dark woods and all the things in it that she despised. To her right was the ever-broadening Pamlico River that flowed into the open waters of the Pamlico Sound. It was as if she were walking a tightrope. One slip and she would tumble into the forest and be forever forced to live the life of Peg Brennan. If she fell into the water, she would be swept away and die as Anne Bonny, never to see her son again.

Anne was not surprised to see that Asku lived away from the other men who worked the kiln. It also seemed fitting that his home was a simple, bark-covered wigwam built in a clearing by the water. Behind the structure were a number of animal hides in various stages of tanning. Asku Dare was a man of many skills who relied on no one but himself.

Not wanting to be mistaken as intruders, Briebras called out to announce their presence before entering the clearing. A moment later, a head of reddish-blond hair emerged from the doorway.

"Bonjour, Monsieur Dare. We have come to ask a favor of you. Do you mind if we parley a few moments?"

Asku motioned for them to sit on the ground next to a fire pit in the center of the clearing. Anne forced herself to listen in silence while Briebras explained who Mary Read was, why she had come to Bath, and that the ship old man Burras had built belonged to her. At times, Asku would nod his head to show he understood. When he knotted his brow, the small Frenchman would provide more details until he was sure that the mute woodsman grasped his meaning. Asku showed no emotion during Briebras' account of events until he explained that Peg was really Anne Bonny.

With a sharp wave of his hand, he stopped Briebras in mid-sentence, taking a moment to study Anne as if seeing her for the first time. They could see he knew of Anne Bonny's reputation. The revelation that Peg Brennan and Anne Bonny were the same person would explain how a woman could be so handy with a sword. Asku's expression made it clear that he was putting all the parts of the puzzle together.

"It is true. Peg Brennan is Anne Bonny, the pirate and the woman who saved you at the kiln."

"No," Anne said, speaking for the first time. "That is to say, not anymore. Peg Brennan no longer exists. Peg Brennan was my mother and she died many years ago. I will never use that name again."

Asku's eyes narrowed and nodded approval. They had no way to know what he was really thinking, but it was clear that the woodsman understood – the woman who had come to his aid a few weeks earlier was not the same person who sat before him now.

"We know you are from Cedar Island," Briebras said. "We ask that you take us there and on to Portsmouth Island. Mary Read will not expect us to come by land. Once we reach the inlet, we will somehow find a way to get to her ship."

"Once we reach Portsmouth Island, I will go on alone," Anne said, looking at both Briebras and Asku. "I just need you to get me there as quickly as possible. The rest I will do on my own."

They waited as Asku pondered the request, but the woodsman just stared at the red coals glowing in the fire pit.

"Did I mention that Blyth Rader is master of Mary Read's ship?" Briebras asked. "It's true. Mary Read is a shrewd woman. She knows that men who would choose to become pirates are not the kind of men who take orders from women. No offense, mademoiselle, but you know that I speak the truth. There is no doubt that Blyth Rader runs the ship, but Mary Read runs Capitaine Rader. Mary Read knows it is easier that way."

If the information about Rader influenced Asku in any way, he did not show it. Looking first at Briebras and then at Anne, he nodded agreement.

Now that his mind was made up, Asku did not wait for the others to begin making plans. Using hand gestures and pictures drawn on the ground, he told Anne and Briebras to go home, pack enough food to last six days and come back before dark. They would spend the night at his wigwam and leave before dawn.

Anne watched Asku as they worked out the details. The manner in which the young woodsman took charge gave her more confidence that Briebras' plan might actually work. By the time the men had finished working out the details, her mood had changed from desperation to guarded hopefulness. Kofi would keep Tye safe until she caught up with them, she was sure of that. Mary Read, on the other hand, would never be safe – not as long as Anne drew breath. She knew it – and so did Mary Read.

# CHAPTER SEVEN

TYE WAS SLEEPING with the soundness of the child he was when Harry Wennell and his men came into the barn sometime after midnight. What little noise they made placing his mother on her mat did nothing to rouse him. He had no awareness of their trespass until lifted from his mat and carried downstairs with a foul, meaty hand covering his mouth. Once outside, someone gagged him with a length of rope while another man bound his hands and feet. When they were done, one of the men threw him over his shoulder like a sack of grain and they hurried off toward the docks. Minutes later he was carried across a gangplank and down into the bowels of a ship.

Once below deck, they removed the ropes and shoved him into a small compartment that smelled of pitch, hewed wood, and hemp. The sound of a metal bolt sliding into place left no doubt that they had locked him in for the night. Sitting in total darkness with no hope of finding a way out, he decided that the only thing to do was to try and get some sleep until morning. But no sooner had he curled up on the floor when he heard shouts from above deck followed by the sensation of the ship moving upon the water.

A cacophony of straining masts, creaking ropes, and feet scurrying across the deck played in rhythm with the sound of water passing around the ship's hull. With a sense of dread, Tye realized his situation had turned from serious to desperate. Once the ship was on the open water, any chance of escape or being found would be lost. In a matter of hours, he would be separated from the only life he had ever known, perhaps never to return.

Springing from the floor, he felt his way to the door and tried the latch. Locked, just as he had thought. Balling his hands into fists, he was about to pound on the door and scream for help – but stopped. Nothing would be gained by going into hysterics. No one but his captors could hear him.

Sitting on the floor with his back against the bulkhead, he began to think through his predicament. The first question should have been, who was it that had kidnapped him? But he already knew the answer. Not through reason or process of elimination or a series of clues. He just knew.

So the real question was, why? The same innate ability that gave him the answer to the first question answered the second as well.

His mother had been a different person since Mary Read had come to Bath. He understood why Mary Read's arrival was a threat in that it might expose his mother's true identity. He also knew enough about Calico Jack Rackham, Mary Read, and Anne Bonny to understand that their lives would always be intertwined, but it was more than that. It wasn't until he had been able to pry information from Briebras and Kofi that he understood the darker side of the story.

They explained that some people believed his grandfather had bribed officials in Jamaica to have his mother released from prison – leaving Mary Read to die alone. Knowing that, it was easy to see why Mary would want to do his mother harm. And yet, she hadn't. Not physically. On the surface, it seemed that she had instead chosen to inflict a more lasting revenge. Instead of killing his mother, Mary Read had abducted her son, leaving Anne to spend the rest of her life wondering what had become of him.

But Tye knew that wasn't the whole truth either. He had no idea what would come next, but he resolved to face it with a stout heart. Panic and tears were the stuff of little boys, not men.

# CHAPTER EIGHT

SHORTLY AFTER SUNRISE, Harry Wennell flung open the door to Tye's room with the subtlety of a runaway cannon. Instead of startling the boy out his wits, Wennell was disappointed to find that he was awake and waiting. Rising to his feet, Tye looked the rough crewman in the eyes and said, "I demand to see Mary Read."

Wennell's mouth twisted into a sadistic smile as he looked down at the boy, but Tye refused to be intimidated. If his abductors expected to find a sobbing, cowering whelp, he was determined to disappoint them.

"As your majesty wishes," Wennell said, extending his arm toward the stairs as he bowed.

When they reached the cabin, Wennell opened the door for Tye to enter and then closed it behind him.

"Come in and sit down," Mary Read ordered, her gravelly voice barely carrying across the room. "I think it's time we got to know each other."

Stepping farther into the cabin, Tye came to stand in front of a captain's secretary behind which the woman he had first known as the Spanish Lady was sitting. Instead of the baroque attire he had seen her in before, she now wore clothes more suited for a man, though they seemed to have been sewn with a feminine hand. Gone, also, was the veil she had worn, replaced by a black-leather patch covering her left eye that did nothing to cover the ugly, white scar that ran across her forehead, brow, and cheek. It was the first time Tye had been able to see her face, and though it made a horrible sight, he managed to suppress any outward sign of revulsion.

A younger woman in similar clothes stood next to Mary Read's chair, a black bandanna covering her golden blonde hair. He recognized her as the girl from Bath believed to be one of Edward Teach's daughters, though she looked a lot different than he remembered. Placing her hand on the back of the chair, she studied him intently, as if looking for the answer to a question.

"There's no need to be afraid," Mary Read said.

"I know," Tye replied straightaway.

His boldness brought a smile to Mary Read's eye.

"I have a task for you, if you have the salt for it."

"And if I refuse?" Tye replied. He was standing ram-rod straight with his hands behind his back, his little boy's chest puffed out as though he were a small soldier.

"Oh, I don't think you will want to refuse."

"And why is that?"

"Because it has to do with your father."

For the first time since he had entered the cabin, his confidence waivered.

"This ship is named *Rackham's Revenge*, after your father, Jack Rackham. Most people knew that he was a pirate, and though no one feared him for a brute like they did Blackbeard, they followed him because of his guile. He was a very ingenious and inventive man. This ship is floating proof. It is a special ship with some unique qualities. Although I came up with a few twists of my own, most of these unusual features are of his design. If you prove yourself worthy, not only will I show you all the secrets, I will tell you everything about Calico Jack Rackham that your...that Anne Bonny never bothered to tell you."

"And how do I do that?" Tye asked. That he knew he was being baited did nothing to lessen his curiosity. Learning more about his father was a temptation he could not resist.

"I want you to go on a treasure hunt," she said, leaning back in the chair as if pleased with herself. "There are two hidden compartments somewhere on this ship, one above deck and one below. One of them contains an item that belonged to your father. The other contains a riddle. If you can find those two things and solve the riddle, then we can talk about your father."

The boy hesitated, not sure that letting her manipulate him so easily was wise. On the other hand, accepting her challenge would give him free rein of the ship. More than that, if successful, he would learn more about his father than he had ever known before.

"Where do I begin?"

"Anywhere you want. The ship is yours. I've instructed the crew to let you go anywhere you please, except for the magazine. That's off limits. There are no secrets there and it is too dangerous to be anywhere near it with candle or lamp...which you'll need to assist you in your search. Understand?"

"Yes, I understand," Tye said. He turned toward the door without asking permission to leave, then stopped to look back at the woman who would barter the knowledge of his direct lineage.

"I know what you are doing," he said. "I do want to know who my father was, but I don't think it will make me like you."

"Why is that?" Mary asked, leaning across the desk to study him closer.

"Because of her," he said, acknowledging Clairette's presence for the first time. "I don't think we will be friends as long as she is around. She's not what she appears to be."

Without waiting for a reply, he left the cabin, closing the door behind him. Mary Read stared at the closed door for a moment.

"Well, he certainly was a cheeky tyke," Clairette said, attempting to fill the awkward silence. "Who would've thought that a little boy would be such a..."

"Shut up!" Mary Read said. Then with a calmer tone, "I'm not worried about you, but I won't have you insulting him. He's...special."

"As you say," Clairette said, her voice less assured than it had been a moment before. "I didn't mean anything by it. I'm sorry. I think I'm going outside for some air. Want to join me?"

"You go ahead – I'll be out in a minute."

When Clairette didn't move right away, Mary Read looked up to an expression on the girl's face that could only be interpreted as a pout.

"It's all right, my sweet, really," she said, taking one of the girl's hands in hers. "I just need a few moments to myself."

When Clairette was gone, Mary Read went to stand by an open transom window, watching the water roll behind the stern as the ship sailed across the open waters of the Pamlico Sound. Tye's parting words had disturbed her more than she had let on. She wasn't sure if it was what he had said about Clairette, or that he had said it at all. He was nothing like she had imagined. His mind was more that of a man than a boy. She would be careful not to underestimate him, else all her work would be for naught. She had not survived this long and journeyed this far to fail. There was too much at stake.

# CHAPTER NINE

TYE SET UPON THE TASK of searching the interior of the ship using a system. Equipped with a Betty lamp and a metal marlinspike, he started below deck at the bow and began working his way to the stern. Studying every nook and cranny along the way, he searched for tell-tell gaps in the planking and panels that might betray a compartment or door. Whenever he came across anything suspicious, he poked and pried it with the marlinspike to see if it was hollow or would move. His efforts were meticulous, sometimes taking more than an hour to go over a compartment.

When he reached the center of the ship, he realized that a bulkhead he had walked by several times was not a wall at all. Studying the structure closer, he began to understand that it was actually two walls built parallel to each other and closed off at each end. Following the ship's center line, it was about thirty feet long, three feet wide, and almost six feet high, stopping short of the deck overhead. The structure was essentially a long, tall, narrow box.

Holding the lamp as high as he could, he saw two metal pulleys suspended above the box's opening. Ropes running through the pulleys dropped down inside the opening, apparently attached to something inside. Tracing the ropes in the other direction, Tye saw that they fed into the spool of the anchor capstan. The spool was flush to the overhead, attached to the capstan topside by an axle passing through the deck. Whatever was inside of the box could be raised and lowered using the same kind of mechanism used to raise and lower the ship's anchor.

*But what could it be?*

After circling around the odd, narrow box several times, Tye saw that the structure passed through the deck he was standing on and into the bilge. Certain that he was on to something, he found the bilge hatch for this section of the ship and crawled inside. Instead of finding rock or stone – the material shipbuilders most often used to create ballast – Bath's shipwright had used the one substance in the region that was both abundant and would not deteriorate over time – sand.

Crawling over to the wall, Tye dug away the damp sand around its base and held the lamp closer. What he saw did not make sense. The schooner's keel was three times wider than that of any ship he had ever seen. The width of the box was about one-third that of the keel. Tapping on the wall produced dull, thick thuds, similar to the noise that would be made by knocking on an oak bucket filled with water.

*It's not a box. It's a long, narrow well. Seawater comes inside of it from underneath the hull. The seawater doesn't spill inside the hull because the top of the well is higher than the level of the sea.*

Instead of clearing up the mystery, Tye was more confused than ever. He could not imagine what purpose a long, narrow well in the middle of a ship would serve.

*Perhaps it was some type of anchor? A pump of some sort?*

Whatever it was, it had nothing to do with his current quest. Resolving to discover its purpose later, he backed out of the bilge and resumed his search of the compartments and cargo holds.

It was well past sundown when he made it to the stern. Despite hours of poking and prodding, his efforts had turned up nothing. No longer able to deny the empty feeling in his stomach, he went to the galley only to discover that there was no cook and no fire in the brick oven. Perhaps the ship had no cook, leaving it up to each person to fend for himself. With the aid of his lamp, he found a barrel of salted pork and a wood box filled with rock-hard sea biscuits. After stuffing his pockets with both, he filled a pewter mug with water and returned to the room that had been his prison the night before.

With the aid of his lamp, this time he was able to see that the room was used to store metal parts essential to the ship's operation. Shelves along one bulkhead were loaded with various pulleys, pins, dowels, and nails. It took blacksmiths hours to make nails and they were a valuable commodity. Tye recalled that Bath's sheriff had once arrested a farmer for burning down a barn for the sole purpose of collecting the nails to reuse. He probably would have gotten away with it – had it been his barn.

Going to the far corner of the room, Tye was pleased to find that someone had left a sleeping pad and a blanket. It wasn't much, but far better than sleeping on the hard deck. He sat on the pad with his back against the bulkhead and began to eat the bread and pork he had commandeered from the galley. The sea biscuits were so hard they had to be soaked in water to make them soft enough to chew. Still, the pork was good and his stomach was soon sated.

Though tired and in need of sleep, the frustration of not finding either of the hidden compartments kept nagging at him. He kept mulling over how he had gone about the search and how his method might be flawed. He had probed every square inch of the ship below deck. The only places he had not searched were Mary's cabin – and this room!

Jumping to his feet, he shined the light on the room's bulkheads. A minute later, he found that the point where two of the bulkheads met at the back of the room were unlike any other corner he had examined that day. Rather than coming together to form a solid joint, there was a slight gap where they met. Excited, he began alternately pushing on individual boards with his hands, then prying on them with the marlinspike. When he got to a part of the back-bulkhead that supported the end of the shelves, he had to reach between them to touch the wall.

Pushing on a short section of board that finished off the end of a row, he heard a soft *snap* and the wall moved a fraction of an inch. Although the end of the shelves gave the appearance of being attached to the wall, it was a deception! They were built to support themselves, allowing the wall to move freely!

Tye gave the wall a gentle push. It moved a few inches more. With his lamp in one hand, he pushed harder, forcing the wall to swing aside revealing a small compartment.

*I found it!*

Shining the light inside, he saw a rectangular wooden box big enough to hold two flintlock pistols and their accessories. With trembling hands, he picked the box up and began to study it. Its hinged lid was engraved with a full moon in one corner, the sun in the opposite corner, and stars scattered randomly in between. Prominently carved in the middle appeared a single word – RACKHAM. A clasp on the lip secured the lid to the box's lower half. Taking a deep breath, he unhinged the clasp and opened the lid.

Instead of pistols, resting on a felt-covered interior was a triangular object of a design he had never seen before. The triangle's legs were made of rosewood and held together with brass fittings. The base of the triangle bowed outward in an arc, its face inlaid with a graduated scale made in ivory. One end of a fourth extension was attached to the triangle's apex where it could pivot, allowing its opposite end to float along the scale as a pointer or indicator.

With his heart pounding, he grasped the instrument as though it were made of crystal and lifted it from the box. Inspecting it more closely, he discovered two small mirrors. The larger of the two was attached to the floating arm where it pivoted on the apex. The second, smaller mirror was affixed to the point where the triangle's two legs met. A long, narrow telescope running the length of one of the triangle's legs was attached in a way that it was perfectly and permanently aimed at the smaller mirror.

It was a fine instrument, designed to measure – something. What, Tye had no idea. But it had once belonged to his father, and that made it the greatest treasure he had ever held in his hands. Vowing to learn its purpose as soon as possible, he placed the instrument back in the box, closed the lid, and returned it to the hidden compartment.

Pulling the wall back into place, he lay on the floor and blew out the lamp. Just before drifting off to sleep, he realized with disappointment that he still had to find the riddle. Mary Read would never explain the device's purpose until he found the riddle and solved it. Tomorrow, he would find it even if he had to dismantle the ship board by board.

As the darkness of sleep closed in upon him, he realized that he was falling into Mary Read's trap, despite his resolve not to. But now he no longer cared. Tomorrow, he would discover his father.

# CHAPTER TEN

FOR ANNE, the hardest thing about paddling a canoe was the monotony. Three strokes on the left – switch sides – three strokes on the right. On and on and on. As stupid as it seemed now, until Asku had handed her the paddle and pointed to the front of the canoe, it had not dawned on her that she would need to help. Though stronger than she was, despite his size, Briebras' short stature made it hard for him to paddle without leaning far to each side and risk tipping the canoe. And though he sat in the middle doing nothing, Anne noted that he at least had the good sense not to speak unless he had something relevant to say.

Her night at Asku's wigwam had been filled with fitful dreams of Tye, suffering at Mary Read's hands, forever sailing just beyond reach. When the time to leave finally arrived, she was the first to gather her things and load them into the canoe. Though it was still dark, the openness of the river framed on either side by the woods provided enough contrast to start their journey toward the sound. For the first time since Mary Read had taken Tye, Anne was able to breathe again.

When sunrise came, she was able to see the fine craftsmanship of Asku's canoe. Though made from a bald cypress tree like most dugouts, Asku had the advantage of using metal hand tools – saws, chisels, and planes – to form and finish his canoe. Indians used little more than fire and sharp shells or rocks. He also had used steam to soften the upper half of the wood, allowing cross planks to be inserted at the craft's middle section, giving it sleeker lines, a wider midsection, and more stability.

To her surprise, the canoe glided over the water much faster than she had imagined possible. The trip to Cedar Island would not take as long as she had feared – two days at the most – a realization that lifted her spirits and erased the fatigue caused by lack of sleep. Briebras' plan was working.

By noon they entered the sound and then headed in a southwesterly direction, following the general contour of the mainland. Once in awhile they would stop to drink water or eat a few strips of jerky or dried fruit, then resume the rhythmic paddling. Because she sat in the front and did not have the stamina for long periods of fast paddling, Anne set the tempo. Sitting at the back, Asku matched her strokes' timing and power, keeping the craft traveling in a straight line.

As the day got warmer the work got harder, forcing them to break for water more often. At times Anne felt like they were paddling in place, not moving forward at all. Even though she knew it was an illusion created by the openness of the sound, it still drove her mad. At about four o'clock they reached a wooded peninsula that offered shade from the afternoon sun and shelter for the night.

"Why stop now?" Anne demanded to know when Asku pointed toward a clearing and turned the canoe. Despite being on the verge of exhaustion, she wanted to keep going.

"Crossing the open sound in the dark is too dangerous," Briebras answered. "If a storm or clouds were to come, we would lose sight of the stars and end up going in circles. And you know, canoes are not made for open waters. Anything stronger than a shower could make waves that would sink us."

"But–"

"S'il te plaît," Briebras said, cutting her off. "We cannot help Tye if we are exhausted...or dead. We must all rest."

She knew that they would not change their minds so she stopped trying – but she didn't like it. When they beached the canoe, she saw that Asku had not picked their campsite at random. Set back just beyond the tree line he showed them a lean-to and a fire pit made of oyster shells. The little spit of land that he had brought them to was a well-used stopping point for anyone traveling the sound. Anne guessed that Asku's people had used the campsite for many years and probably by the Indians before them.

Working together, it only took a few minutes to put the camp in order, shoring up the lean-to and clearing away storm debris that had collected since the site's last use. When they were done, Asku used hand motions to indicate that he was going to hunt for fresh game and leave them to build a fire. Because Briebras was long-used to building fires for the forge, Anne left him to that task while she began walking the shoreline in search of driftwood.

She returned a few minutes later to dump an armful of sun-bleached limbs and knots beside Briebras who already had a small flame burning. Going back for more, she wandered farther from the camp this time, coming upon a small stream of fresh water flowing into the sound. A well-worn game trail along the stream made her wonder if the hunting on this side of the spit might be more productive than the side Asku was on. She had followed the path for only a couple of minutes when she found herself standing in front of a small, freshwater pond surrounded by several majestic cypress trees, their gnarled knee-roots planted deep into the water, their limbs dripping with huge clumps of gray moss.

The air beneath the arboreal canopy was cool and fresh, the water clear and tempting. It was certain that over the years, hundreds of people had stood on this same small patch of ground gently sloping into the water. No doubt, almost all of them had done what she was about to do. The water was too inviting and the day had been long, hot, and hard. The urge to relax and release the stress of the past few days was too much to resist.

A minute later she waded into the pond, her clothes dropped in a heap at the water's edge. The sandy bottom felt good to her feet as she waded in far enough to sit down where the water could cover everything except her head. After wetting her face, she leaned back to rest the weight of her upper body on her elbows. Closing her eyes, she drank in the soothing warmth from a shaft of sunlight that had found its way through a hole in the canopy to land on her face.

The lack of sleep, warm sun on her skin, and soothing water soon lulled her into a state that was more asleep than awake. She had not intended to abandon her wood gathering. She had only wanted to bathe long enough to wash the day's exertions from her body. But the birds around her made sweet sounds as they searched the trees and brush for seeds and berries. On occasion, one would land at the water's edge on the far side of the pond to splash around, taking a bath of its own.

Lost among the hushed cacophony was a soft rustling of grass followed by a faint splash as a serpentine torso began to twist and twine its way through the water. And though the rippling grew more distinct as it drew closer and closer to where Anne rested, her fatigue had conspired with the serenity to dull her senses and arrest her defenses.

Too late, she opened her eyes. Even then, the image that filled her view made no sense – a gaping maw of white cotton topped by dark round orbs with catlike pupils. It wasn't until the next instant, when the dark, thick-bodied reptile closed its eyes and unsheathed its curved fangs to strike her in the face that Anne realized her peril. In a blur of fear-driven instinct, Anne tried to twist her head away, but she knew it was too late. As his triangular-shaped head arched downward toward her neck, a feathered shaft blossomed in its mouth, driving the deadly water moccasin away from Anne and under the water, pinning it to the pond's sandy bottom. As the snake thrashed about in a death convulsion, wrapping and unwrapping its body around the arrow's shaft, Anne bolted out of the pond and began to throw on her clothes.

She did not have to look to know it was Asku's arrow that had saved her. Nor did she have to look around to know that she was still in danger. The first moccasin's thrashing had alerted others. As she finished pulling on her shirt, Anne heard splashes from the far side of the pond followed by the unmistakable sound of thick, serpentine bodies undulating through the water at a rapid pace.

Grabbing her pants, she glanced at the water to see how much time she had. As the second cottonmouth exited the pond, another one of Asku's arrows pinned it to the ground. A third snake slithered from the water to take its place. Anne had one leg in her pants now, but lost balance as she attempted to slip in the other. To save herself from falling to the ground, she threw her bare leg behind her, planting it toward the oncoming viper. As she struggled to regain her balance, she felt a sharp stabbing on her right calf – then another and another. Looking down, she saw that the moccasin had wrapped itself around her leg and was now high enough to sink its fangs into her thigh.

Anne watched, helpless, as the snake reared back to strike again, but Asku swooped in at the last second to grab the serpent just below its head and pulled it from Anne's bleeding leg. With the moccasin winding itself around his arm, Asku grabbed his hunting knife and sliced through the snake's body where it protruded below his fist. The contorting length of muscle and flesh unwound itself from his arm and fell to the ground. Shoving the blade through the snake's jaw, he used the knife to catapult the head across the pond.

Liquid heat surged through Anne's body as the poisonous venom coursed through her veins. Time was slowing to a crawl. With detached interest, she saw that her long blouse was still unbuttoned and her pants were piled around her ankles. Though too lightheaded to be embarrassed, she knew she should cover herself. Bending over to pull up her pants, her face flushed hot and large beads of perspiration appeared on her forehead. Then she saw that her calf was swollen to almost twice its normal size. The skin around the puncture wounds had turned purple and red.

The sight of the grotesque wounds brought on more dizziness. Waves of nausea rose from her stomach and her throat tightened. A coppery, metallic taste filled her mouth and she began to gag. For the second time in two days she fell to her hands and knees, heaving. What little food she had managed to eat since the first purging now lay in a puddle of puke before her.

As if watching from a distance, she saw Asku collect a handful of moss and begin covering the wounds on her leg. It was too late to stop the poison from spreading through her body, but the damaged flesh posed a bigger problem. If not treated quickly, the skin around the wounds could die, giving her a slow, ghastly death.

Anne was only vaguely aware of being carried through the woods and back to the campsite. She tried to fight the poison the way a drunk struggles to act sober, but to no avail. By the time Asku laid her under the lean-to she was numb except for a constant tingling throughout her body. The sound of Briebras' frantic voice came to her as if from a distance, wanting to know what had happened. It was the last thing she heard before slipping into dark oblivion.

# CHAPTER ELEVEN

TYE WAS ROUSED from a night of restless sleep by the rhythmic chanting of crewmen pushing on capstan bars to raise anchor. Then came shouts from Captain Rader directing other men to release optimal sheets of canvas from specific sections of the masts based on the morning's wind conditions. *Rackham's Revenge* – like all ships negotiating the waters of the Pamlico – could only sail during daylight when a spotter in the rigging could look for shallows. Although the silt bottom wasn't likely to cause damage to the hull, a sudden stop would wreak havoc with anything not battened down, and it would take a rising tide to free her again.

Hurrying topside, Tye looked toward the east and saw the distant outline of the chain of narrow islands that formed the barrier between the inland waters and the ocean. The previous day's light winds had made for slow sailing, forcing them to anchor some five miles from Ocracoke where the shallows were more plentiful and harder to navigate. Once they were within a mile or two of the island they would have to take a pilot on board to guide them through the ever-changing channels.

Surveying the deck, Tye saw Mary Read and the young cozener she had called Clairette, standing near the bowsprit, looking toward the islands. That meant that their cabin was empty and he could search it unobserved. But he would have to hurry, as the wind was beginning to pick up and it would not take long to reach Ocracoke. He might not have another opportunity to search the cabin with no one around to look over his shoulder.

Focused on the setting of the sails, neither Mary Read or the rest of the crew saw Tye slip into the cabin. Upon entering, he assessed the layout with a more critical eye than the day before when facing his abductor for the first time. Rather than an austere, functional room, the cabin was well decorated with drawings, paintings, and curiosities and of every type imaginable. Such opulence was unusual aboard seafaring vessels because of their fragility, but all of these items had been mounted or displayed in a way that would prevent them from being tossed about in rough seas. Their presence was not an impulsive afterthought, but a well-designed blend of the practical and the extravagant.

In addition to a chart table next to the starboard hull, the cabin was furnished with several plush chairs and small, ornate tables arranged on a fine carpet. Across the room, where the hull met the stern to make a corner, was a large bed covered with fine linens and piled high with pillows. Next to it was an area that had been left open, absent any furnishings or obstructions whatsoever. Why, Tye had no idea. That was a mystery that would have to be solved later. Right now he had a more important matter to address.

Starting at the doorway, he began testing suspect boards and suspicious-looking gaps with the marlinspike as he had done the day before. About a half-hour had passed when he came to an ornate, oval-shaped, full-length mirror fastened tight to the bulkhead. Most of the mirrors Tye had seen were highly polished disks of metal. Only once before had he seen a real mirror made of glass laid over a tin and mercury compound backing. And never had he seen one large enough to reflect a full-grown person's entire body.

Being able to see his whole self so clearly for the first time was too compelling to ignore. After spending several minutes making faces at himself he began watching his hands and arms to see how they moved. Next, he tried to see how far he could turn his body while continuing to keep his head oriented on the mirror so that he could see what he looked like from behind – almost as if a dog chasing his tail.

What intrigued him most was the idea that mirrors reversed things from side-to-side, but not top to bottom. He asked himself, why was it that, in the reflection, his left arm magically was a right arm on his reflection self, but his head remained at the top rather than reversing itself to become the bottom? It was a silly thought, but there was just enough logic in the riddle to entertain him for a few more minutes. His actions were more like a student of science conducting experiments than a child spellbound by a simple curiosity.

Retrieving a clay ointment jar from the chart table, Tye held it up to the mirror, looking at how its painted designs reversed direction in the reflection, giving the porcelain a similar but oddly different appearance. As he rotated the jar in his hand, it slipped from his fingers. A desperate attempt to grab the jar before it hit the deck only managed to bat it back up into the air. As it came down he reached for it again, this time knocking it back toward the mirror. With a panicked leap, he sprang across the cabin, stretching his arms as far as he could as he landed full-length on the deck. To his astonishment, the clay jar landed safely in his cupped hands.

Taking in a deep breath, he began to stand but pulled up short. Just inches from his face he noticed that the head of a wood dowel holding the bottom of the mirror to the bulkhead was not quite flush with the frame. Jumping up, he returned the jar to the chart table and turned back to study the dowel at the top of the mirror.

He was right! The top pin was a small axle or pivot point upon which the heavy mirror could swing. Dropping to his knees, he used the marlinspike to pry the dowel from its hole then pushed the mirror to his right. To his delight, hidden behind the mirror about waist high, was a small compartment. Inside the compartment was an envelope with his name written in large swooping letters. He retrieved the envelope then allowed the mirror to swing back into place.

After replacing the dowel, he broke the seal on the envelope and removed a single sheet of brown, deckle-edged paper. There was no personal message, only ten short lines written with the same sweeping hand as that on the envelope.

Shakespeare said,

> *If you prick us, do we not bleed?*
> *If you tickle us, do we not laugh?*
> *If you poison us, do we not die?*
> *And if you wrong us, shall we not revenge?*
> *I say, that in an upside-down world,*
> *Revenge can sometimes be as the shark.*
> *Sometimes she can be as the humpback whale.*
> *Find that which makes this true,*
> *Then you will know the truth about Revenge.*

Though not what he had expected, Tye brushed off his disappointment. He loved riddles, and this one seemed a dandy. Was it the whales and sharks that were upside down? What did that mean? Or was it the world? That didn't make sense. And what did whales and sharks have to do with revenge?

Perplexed but not discouraged, he sat down with his back against the bulkhead and retrieved a bit of dried pork from his pocket he had saved from the night before. He read the words over and over again as he nibbled on the salty meat, trying to make out a common thread that might help him understand.

The repetition of reading the lilting words in rhythm with the ship's gentle rocking proved too relaxing for a boy that had not slept well the past two nights. Tye did not realize he had fallen asleep until he heard the latch on the cabin door move. Startled, he stuffed the riddle and its envelope into the front of his shirt as he scrambled across the floor, hiding behind a large chest next to the chart table. He would have been caught had the person at the door not paused for a moment.

"Yes," Clairette called from the half-opened door. "The new one. The old one has the cracked lens."

Tye held his breath as the girl walked across the room to a built-in rack next to the chart table. Though she was just a few feet away, the table blocked her view of his hiding place. But then his gaze fell upon the mirror on the opposite side of the chest and his flesh flushed hot with panic. His view of Clairette's reflection in the mirror was unobstructed, which meant that if she looked toward the mirror, she would see him as clearly as he saw her. He might as well be standing in the middle of the cabin dancing a jig.

Petrified, he watched the reflection of the former tavern girl retrieve a bright, brass telescope from the chart rack and turn back toward the door. Sweat broke out on his forehead when she stopped for a moment to look at herself in the mirror. Moving first one way and then the other to study her profile, she had only to shift her gaze an inch or two and he would be caught.

"Clairette!" Mary Read shouted from outside. "Move quick. I need that spyglass, now!"

It wasn't until he heard the telltale click of the door latch falling into place that Tye was able to breathe again. Scooting over to sit against the wall, he wiped the sweat from his forehead with the back of his sleeve, pleased with himself. By Mary Read's order, he had the run of the ship. But Clairette was a different matter. The less she knew about his business, the better. His innate ability to read people was growing stronger, and it was telling him that everything about Clairette was wrong.

With the tension of the moment fading away, he became more aware of the sounds from outside. Rader was ordering the men to shorten sail and the ship was beginning to slow as if making a tack. If he could get a good look at where they were going, he might be better able to plan an escape. Remembering that Clairette had spoken of two telescopes, Tye went to the chart rack. Nested in between several charts was an old, dented long glass made of dull brass. Removing the scope from the rack, he studied it and found that the lens in the larger, objective end was indeed cracked. Still, it might be worth a try. If the ship was tacking, he might have one chance to see what lie ahead.

Stepping over to the window, he trained the glass as far forward as he could and saw a small boat coming toward them. Pulling the telescope open, he held it up to his eye and saw – nothing. Only a hint of light made its way through the length of the telescope. A cracked lens wasn't the only thing wrong with the glass.

Frustrated, Tye shook the long glass hoping to dislodge whatever was blocking the view. As he did, he felt something shifting inside. It wasn't a hard object, like a piece of glass lens, and the movement was very subtle. But it was enough to catch Tye's attention.

Flipping the scope around, he saw that a metal ring, screwed into the end of the telescope's tube, held the lens place. Gripping the scope with one hand, he tried to turn the ring but it wouldn't budge. Undaunted, he placed the telescope between his legs, gripped it with his thighs, and twisted the ring with both hands as hard as he could.

Success! The ring broke free from its seat. With a few quick twists, he removed the ring and cracked lens to peer inside the tube. Nestled within the hollow space there appeared to be a rolled-up document of some sort. Tye inserted two fingers into the tube and plucked the obstruction from its nest.

The document was a parchment of the highest quality and marked with words and images. Excited, he unrolled the thin calfskin out on the chart table, taking care not to tear or damage it in any way. Etched on its surface in heavy ink was a map showing the point where two islands came together to form an inlet. In the void that was the Atlantic Ocean, there was a block of words that Tye was sure were meant to convince the reader he was looking at an authentic treasure map. Beneath the stanza in bold, joined-up writing was the name Edward Teach.

Tye's excitement waned as fast as it had waxed. He had heard about such maps. Under the signature was a large, hand-drawn image of a black flag with a white, horned skeleton. With one hand, the skeleton was piercing a bleeding red heart with a spear. In his other hand, he waved an hourglass in the air as though to say, "Time is up." The image was a depiction of Teach's flag – his Jolly Roger – meant to serve as the map's seal of authenticity.

Tye smiled at the thought. It was a nice touch. Something most fakers would not have included.

The two islands weren't shown in their entirety – only the first three or four miles from where they met to form the inlet. But he had seen enough maps and charts to know they were the Outer Banks islands on which the twin villages of Portsmouth and Ocracoke had been built. And though the mapmaker had not attempted to show every building on the islands, several small squares sketched in the appropriate areas depicted the villages. Other than the boxes, there was little else drawn on the Ocracoke Island portion of the map. But on the Portsmouth section, in one of the many coves cutting into the sound-side of the island, was a box with nothing else around it. Below the box were the words, "Jack's Home." In the open space beside it where the sound waters lay was a set of instructions listing landmarks and the number of paces to make. A final sentence of four words told where to dig.

The stories and rumors of maps made by Edward Teach showing where he had buried treasure were so prevalent in Bath that they had become a community joke. Merchants would often refuse patrons who tried to make purchases with the hand-written bills North Carolina used for currency because they were easily counterfeited. "As worthless as a Blackbeard treasure map" had become a popular refrain by the merchants. Two or three of Bath's less honest residents regularly sold treasure maps to drunken mariners who patronized the ordinaries. And there was hardly a boy in Bath – including Tye – who hadn't made a treasure map of his own while pretending to be a brethren of the coast. Bath, after all, had been the home of the most ill-famed pirate ever known.

Then a new idea forced its way into his thinking.

*This ship was built for pirating! That's why it looks so different from the other boats Ol' Man Burras has built. Mary Read had been a piratress once before and plans to be once again. That has to be it.*

The logical, adult-minded Tye understood that choosing such a path was folly, but the boy he still was embraced it without reservation. Then a new thought occurred to him, one that came back to the idea of finding out who he really was. *Both my father and mother were pirates. Not even Clairette can claim to have been born of two pirates!*

He was the child of a union unlike any that had come before. And while it might not have been the birth story he would have wished for himself, it was his. It was who he was and would always be.

With a shudder of excitement, another thought washed over him in a wave of understanding. *This is what she really wanted me to discover. Everything else is secondary. But why? Other than being an accident of my birth, why would that be important for me to know?*

Sensing that the ship was coming to a stop, Tye rolled up the map, slid it back into the long glass's large tube, and spun the ring back on. As he returned the damaged telescope to its slot in the chart rack he heard Rader order the men to set the sails again. *Rackham's Revenge* had taken a pilot on board to guide the ship through the winding channel toward the inlet. It was time to leave.

No longer feeling the need for stealth, he left the cabin without looking around to see who might be watching. Returning to the storage closet that served as his quarters, he stayed only long enough to secure the riddle in the secret compartment with the box he had found. A few moments later he was topside again, scurrying up the foremast's shroud in hope of gaining a better view of where they were headed.

Perching himself far above the deck, he was able to see for miles around. Never had he beheld such a view of the world. They were close enough to the barrier islands that he could make out the buildings and homes dotting the sound side of Ocracoke and Portsmouth. He could even see the channel to the ocean and the potato patch of choppy water where the waves met the outgoing tidewaters.

Turning to look behind and below him, he first saw Harry Wennell at the helm standing next to a leathery-faced pilot giving directions. Looking far beyond the pilot's boat tethered to the stern, he thought he could see a faint line of trees on the western horizon where the mainland and his home should be. Without a long glass, he couldn't be sure if it was land or an illusion. The Pamlico Sound was so vast, at times it seemed as open as the ocean.

Turning his gaze toward the bow, he saw Mary Read, Clairette and Blyth Rader standing together, taking turns looking through the spyglass. Judging by the way they were focused on the northern island, Tye guessed that they were headed toward Ocracoke.

He considered jumping overboard to escape if they got close to land, but the idea wasn't practical. Ocracoke was a small island with few places to hide, and half the people who lived there had once been pirates or were related to former pirates. With sanctuary an unlikely option, the idea of riddles, treasure maps, and pirate ships became more enticing. Unless he could return home, he would rather stay and learn about his father.

A seagull soaring toward the ship let loose a shrill cry as if to signal that it was time for the boy to leave his perch. Regaining his footing on the shroud's ratlines, he worked his way down to the gunnel.

"Good morning," Mary Read said as he dropped to the deck. Looking up, he had to shade his eyes and squint, as the morning sun was directly behind her. "Did you enjoy the view?"

"Yes, ma'am," he replied.

"And how is your search progressing?"

"Very well, ma'am. I've found the box and I have the riddle. I don't know what the instrument in it is...just that it has something to do with the heavens and measuring the stars. And I haven't had time to solve the riddle, but I'm sure I can figure it out, given more time."

"Really?" she said. "Well then, here's what's going to happen today. In less than an hour we are going to dock on the leeward side of Ocracoke to take on water, food and...some other supplies. You will stay in your quarters until I give the word, at which time you will come to my cabin with the box you found. Understand?"

"Am I still a prisoner?"

"No," she said, choosing her words carefully. "As of now you are my guest, but it is my responsibility to protect you from harm, so you will have to do as I say for the time being...for your own good of course."

"I see," he said without protest, though his tone revealed that he wasn't totally convinced.

"Tye, I brought you here for several reasons, the most important being to tell you about your father. By now, I think you understand that I am one of only two people alive who can do that properly, and the other person apparently doesn't want you to know. I also think you understand that my heart is true in this matter."

Not waiting for a reply, she went back to rejoin Rader and Clairette at the bow. Despite having been banished to his room, he began to accept that the decision to stay truly was his. He wasn't being locked up and no one was assigned to watch him. It would be an easy matter to escape, if he wanted. Now that it was his decision to make, the pendulum had swung to the side of wanting to stay. For as long as he could remember, he had wondered who his father was and why he had left them. At least now, he knew that his father's absence hadn't been a case of abandonment. If it had not been for Mary Read, he wouldn't even know that.

The truth was, he liked Mary Read a great deal. Despite her hard edges and coarse exterior, her directness and honesty resonated with his sense of how people should be. No pretensions. No facades. Only raw, unblemished truth. Other than his mother, she was the only person who had ever talked to him as though he were an adult.

Though he loved his mother and missed her, he harbored a measure of resentment for what she had done. She had deceived him about who she was and who his father had been, creating a giant hole in his self-identity. That void would not have existed had his mother been honest with him, and it burned like salt rubbed into a life-long wound.

The more he thought about it, the starker the contrast became. His mother had always seemed lost. Bath was their home, but neither of them had many friends. Even worse, she had accepted a life of menial labor, little better off than a slave. He was old enough to understand that his mother was an attractive woman and would have made someone a fine wife. But suitors had never found a way to penetrate the tough skin that "Peg Brennan" had grown. And now even the name he had always known her by stood as a wall between them, a lie reminding him of all the other lies.

Mary Read, on the other hand, had purpose. She was a force unlike any man or woman he had ever known. She commanded men and ships and moved through life knowing exactly where she was going. There was nothing ordinary about her. She walked different, talked different and looked more different than any sojourner who had ever made port in Bath. Before the patch covering her dead eye and the wicked scar, she had been a woman of beauty. And yet, she was still beautiful to anyone who could see past the ravage done to her face.

Arriving at his room, he sat in the doorway to take advantage of the light filtering through from above. Taking the brown paper from his shirt, he read the riddle over and over, trying to make sense of it. He knew almost nothing about Shakespeare's writings, but the lines from *The Merchant of Venice* seemed out of place and pointless.

*Or were they?*

As he had heard the story, the encounter between Rackham's *William* and Barnet's *Snow-Tyger* had been a farce as compared to Blackbeard's final battle. Barnet had come upon the *William* in the dead of night while anchored at Jamaica's Negril Bay. Rackham and his crew had been drunk and Barnet had closed on the pirates before they knew they had been found.

Barnet had called out for the pirates to surrender, but Mary Read awakened the crew while Anne Bonny took to the swivel gun and fired on the *Snow-Tyger*. Grabbing an ax, Mary cut the anchor line to set the *William* adrift. The handful of crewmen sober enough to make it above deck scurried aloft and dropped as much canvas as they could to put distance between the two ships.

But the escape was short-lived. Barnet closed in as dawn broke and fired a volley of cannonballs into the *William*. Fearing for their lives, the few men who had come topside scurried below to the safety of the hold, leaving Anne and Mary to fend for themselves. True to her reputation, Anne Bonny had become a woman possessed, screaming obscenities and vowing to kill every member of the crew herself. But it was Mary Read who calmly fired her pistols into the darkness of the hold, killing two of the men and even wounding the still-drunk Jack Rackham.

In the end, only Anne and Mary had remained on deck to face Barnet's boarding party, and it still took them an hour to subdue the piratresses. Standing with their backs to the bow and wielding cutlasses, the two women defended their ground as if repelling a demon horde flooding through the gates of hell. But Captain Jonathan Barnet was a smart man. Rather than have his men rush the two women in an assault, he had them mimic a tactic employed by wolves. While most of the men held back, two or three others would initiate cautious attacks against the women. When those tired, another two or three with fresh arms would take their place. As the women grew tired from the constant nipping, the attackers closed in, never allowing them a moment's rest.

Though their skill with the sword had not failed them, their bodies could not go on forever. Drenched with sweat and leaning shoulder to shoulder, their legs could no longer hold them upright. Sinking to the deck in a sopping heap of wilted flesh and matted hair, they managed a few last swipes as the wolf pack closed in. Exhausted and no longer able to raise their swords, the boarders finally took them captive.

Tye considered every aspect of the story, but could not find any detail in it that would be motivation for revenge – at least not between his mother and Mary Read. As he began to pore over the riddle again, the sounds of Rader barking orders and crewmen scrambling on the deck interrupted his thoughts. A minute later a wooden thud shuddered through the hull and the ship came to a stop. *Rackham's Revenge* had docked at Ocracoke.

*That's it!* Tye realized. *The second part of the riddle is about 'Revenge' the ship. That 'Revenge' is spelled with a capital letter. The 'revenge' in Shakespeare's verse is lowercase.*

He still didn't know how the revenge Shakespeare wrote about might be relevant, but he was sure the answer to the riddle's second part rested within the ship itself. Heartened by the discovery, he read the words with new insight.

> *I say, that in an upside-down world,*
> *Revenge can sometimes be as the shark.*
> *Sometimes she can be as the humpback whale.*
> *Find that which makes this true,*
> *Then you will know the truth about Revenge.*

He had no idea how the *Revenge* could be both a shark and a whale, but he was certain that he was close to solving the riddle. Breaking the verse down into its separate parts, he tried to visualize the difference between sharks and whales. Sharks were fish and breathed through gills. Whales were mammals and breathed with lungs. That may have been the most obvious difference between the two, but Tye could not see how breathing would have anything to do with the ship.

There had to be another difference – perhaps something in their appearance. Taking his marlinspike, he etched the outline of a whale on the room's blank wall and studied it for a minute. Then he drew the outline of a shark and compared the two. The difference was obvious.

*Surely it can't be that simple,* he thought. *A shark has a fin on its back that cuts through the water when it is on the attack. A humpback whale has no fin to speak of. But the 'Revenge' does not have a fin; and what good would a fin sticking out from the deck into the air be to a ship?*

Despite the contradiction, he was sure he was on the right track. Looking back at the riddle, he studied the line that said, "...in an upside-down world." He visualized the ship as if rolled over by a huge wave, but could not imagine how that would serve any good purpose.

*Perhaps it wasn't the ship, but the shark and the whale that should be upside down.* He looked at the images he had carved into the wall, tilting his head to try and better imagine them turned over. A whale's back looks a lot like the hull of a ship. So does a shark's, except for the fin.

Once again, he believed himself to be on the right track. He had never seen a ship with a fin protruding from its hull, but instinctively understood how one could help a ship remain stable. *But I saw the 'Revenge' being built, and I know it does not–*

A long, loud, rolling rumble above his head interrupted his thinking. At first he wondered if a sudden storm might have appeared, but the rumbling continued moving across the deck above until finally coming to a stop near the stern on the port side. A few minutes later, the noise started again, this time stopping close to the bow on the starboard side.

Although he could not imagine what was causing the sound, the lack of yelling and panic from the crew made it apparent that there was no danger. Unable to see what they were doing made his skin itch with anticipation. Once again, life aboard *Rackham's Revenge* was proving to be a hundred times more interesting than anything he had experienced in Bath.

"All right, boy!" Clairette's voice called from the hatch above. "Mary says it's time for you to go to her cabin."

"Coming!" Tye shouted back. He folded the paper up and placed it back in its envelope and returned the riddle to the hidden compartment, grabbed the wood case and bounded up the stairs. As he emerged from the hatch, he saw some of the crew were just beginning to pull on a set of ropes running through a block and tackle rig attached to a six-pounder fixed to its carriage.

"Heave...! Heave...! Heave...!" Bos'n Wennell said in a steady beat. Each time he said the word "heave," the men pulled on the rope as one and the cannon moved another foot toward the bow.

Slowing his pace, Tye surveyed the deck as he walked toward the cabin. Now that he knew what had caused the thunder, he also understood that they were placing each new cannon in a spot that would spread the balance of weight evenly around the ship. But, looking toward the stern, he couldn't find any sign of the first cannon that had been brought aboard. *What had they done with them?*

His question was answered when he entered Mary's cabin. The area of her quarters that had been left free of furnishings now housed a cannon pointing toward the stern's bulkhead. Looking closer, he saw that the barrel was inches away from gun-port hatches built so seamlessly into the structure that they were invisible to the casual glance. Visualizing the deck outside the cabin, he realized that similar hatches ran along both sides of the ship. Old Man Burras had done a masterful job disguising the ship's true purpose.

"So, what is it that you have found?" Mary Read asked. Tye jumped despite himself. She had been sitting so still he had not noticed her behind the chart table.

"It is a fine instrument of some type," Tye said. "I don't know what it is, but I am sure that it measures something and that it once belonged to my father."

"Indeed. Well, bring it here and let's take a look at it, then."

Tye placed the box on the table and opened the lid. Using both hands, Mary Read removed the instrument from the box and held it in front of her where they could both see it.

"It's called a reflecting quadrant," she said, admiring it as though it was a work of art. "Some people have come to call it an octant. Edmond Halley of the science vessel *Paramour* presented it to your father as a gift when he was barely eighteen."

"What does it do? How does it work? How did my father know Sir Halley?" He stopped as quickly as he started, overwhelmed by the number of thoughts flooding into his mind.

Mary Read lowered the octant a few inches to look at Tye.

"What about the riddle?" she asked.

"The riddle?

"Our agreement was that I would tell you about your father if you found the items and solved the riddle."

"Oh, yes...the riddle. It's about the ship, isn't it?" he hedged, hoping her expression would confirm his theory. Mary Read narrowed her eye but revealed nothing.

A thousand images of the places he had seen during his exploration of the ship rushed through Tye's mind as though flipping through the pages of a book of drawings. *The bow – sail room – storerooms – cargo hold – bilge – galley – orlop – well... The well!* "*In an upside-down world, Revenge can sometimes be as the shark.*" And then he knew.

"In the center of the ship is a well," he said, exciting at having steered into the answer. "But it is as much a scabbard as it is a well, as it holds a large fin...a retractable keel, that is. The ropes running to the capstan are used to lower and raise."

"And when would such a thing be needed?"

Tye thought for a moment, formulating a theory on the quick.

"To steady the ship...when she's running full sail...and in deep water. And when the keel is sheathed, the ship can navigate shallow waters!"

The last words came out in a rush as he put all the pieces together.

Mary Read held Tye's gaze, allowing the hint of a smile. The rumble of another cannon rolling into place resonated through the ship.

"And why would anyone want a ship that is faster and more elusive than any other ship on the ocean?"

"For pirating, of course," he said without hesitating.

"You already knew?" she asked, surprised. "And it doesn't bother you?"

"No ma'am. It's the only thing that makes sense."

"I was going to tell you, eventually," she said, placing the octant back in its case. "But first, I wanted you to learn what it means to be a pirate."

"Isn't it what it appears to be?" he asked, suspicious now. "Aren't pirates just thieves in ships who steal from others?"

"There is that," she said, "I cannot lie. But that's why I wanted you to learn more before we discussed my...past...and that of your father's. What I wanted you to learn is that there can be nobleness in being a pirate. I want you to understand that the only, truly free people in the world were those who do not have to bow before kings or any other swayer. I want you to know the value of being the master of yourself."

She paused just as the ship's movement allowed the mid-morning sunlight to stream through the window. From where Tye stood it looked as though her wild, flowing locks had turned into shining swirls of jet-black flames. Though obvious she was disappointed at his having leaped ahead of some timeline she had established, it was just as clear that he had impressed her with all that he'd accomplished the past two days. Not only did her respect make him proud, the idea that her opinion mattered so much confirmed his beliefs about her. She challenged him like no one ever had before, and he had succeeded beyond expectation. Euphoria grew inside him like a wildfire, and he wanted more.

"Your father once told me that he first left his home in Jamaica as a shaveling to work the islands – Hispaniola, Saint Croix, and the like...on a small cargo sloop. Jack happened upon Sir Edmond Halley and the Paramour while they were anchored at St. Christopher's. Halley and the crew were sick with nervous fever and in desperate need of water. Every day for a week, your father rowed out to their ship with fresh kegs of spring water. No one else on the island would do it because they were too scared...too afraid they might catch the fever."

"At the end of the week, the crew was recovered enough to sail again, but not before Halley gave Jack the octant and taught him how to navigate with it. Sir Halley told him it was one of the first such instruments ever made by a great man of science named John Hadley. I'm told there are newer, better ones these days, but I kept this one...for you."

Leaning forward, Mary Read took the octant out of the case again and placed into Tye's hands.

"Jack said the day Sir Halley gave him this instrument his life changed forever. He said, 'Any man can pilot a boat by following the shoreline. And a man who sailed by dead reckoning was a man destined to be lost. But a man who could navigate a ship across the ocean by the sun and the stars...well, that man could rule the seas.' And for a few years, before he died, that's exactly what he did, at least in his own small way. Without the knowledge to navigate, he would have been just another pirate. But with it, he became captain of his own ship."

"How does it work?" Tye whispered, holding the octant in his hands as though it was a relic.

"Point it toward the window and look at the horizon through the little telescope. The small mirror reflects the horizon. The large mirror is the index. Because the swing arm is at zero degrees, you should see one image of the horizon. Now, slowly move the swing arm. You will see half the image begin to move until you see the top of the window frame. When the window frame comes to rest upon the water, stop and look at where the swing arm pointer has come to rest upon the scale. What does it show?"

"It shows 44 degrees."

"Then that's the angle between the earth and the top of the window. If you were outside you would use it to measure the distance between the horizon and the sun, the moon or the North Star."

"But, how does that tell you where you are?"

"It's...involved. Mathematics. It took me months to learn."

He kept looking at her as though she had not replied. That it was "involved" did not bother him in the least.

"It's based on the science of earth rotation and the position of the heavenly bodies," she continued, conceding to his stubbornness. "Finding a latitude is hard enough. Once you determine the angle of the sun, you make calculations to determine your first plot point. Longitude is much harder still. Not only do you have to make similar calculations, you have to know the exact time of day it is in Greenwich when it's exactly noon where you are at that moment. And that would..."

"...require an accurate chronometer," Tye finished.

"Twisty rickets, boy! How in the great blue did you know that?"

"I spend a lot of time on the docks and I sometimes do errands at the ordinaries. Almost every ship's captain and navigator I've overheard talking have complained about the difficulty of determining longitude and the need for an accurate chronometer. Most navigators depend on dead reckoning. Others use the Sully chronometer, but only for a week. Two at most. After that, it loses or gains so much time it's no more accurate than a sundial...or so they say."

"Well then, just damn," she said. "Is there anything you don't know at least something about?"

"I don't know how to navigate. It is my expectation that you will teach me."

As Mary Read's face shifted from growing admiration to emerging understanding, Tye wondered how it must feel for her to realize that she was now the one who was being led.

# CHAPTER TWELVE

AS THE NIGHT PASSED, Anne alternated between restless sleep, fevered bouts of sweating, and vomiting. Briebras and Asku took turns cleaning the bile from her face and applying damp cloths to her forehead when the fever spiked. Long before daybreak, Asku carried her to the canoe and placed her upon their sleeping mats relocated from the lean-to. Though Anne sometimes drifted into consciousness, she was oblivious to the dark clouds gathering from the west and the whitecaps created by the growing wind. Nor did she stay lucid long enough to register the apprehension on Asku's face as it grew deeper and more foreboding.

Instead of trying to help with the paddling, Briebras took to bailing out the cresting wave water with a hollowed-out gourd. What started as a task carried out every half hour soon increased to every ten minutes. By noon, Briebras was bailing water almost non-stop. Though a small man, he was also a blacksmith used to working hard for long stretches. Few men of bigger stature would have been able to match his endurance.

When the cool rain began to fall, Anne roused from unconsciousness long enough to see how dire their circumstances were becoming. The white caps were cresting the rails and the choppy waves sometimes came close to rolling them over. If not for Briebras' constant bailing, their little canoe would have gone down long ago.

From where she rested, Anne could see Asku battling to keep the canoe upright and moving forward while the sound of Briebras scooping up water maintained a constant rhythm behind her head. Not only had she caused their situation, she was now unable to help them survive. She tried to sit up, but her body refused to bend to her will. As the venom-induced darkness returned to claim her consciousness, the last thing she saw was the resolve on Asku's face that gave her hope. If it were at all possible for them to survive, he would find a way.

Anne remained unconscious as they passed between a small island and a marshy peninsula jutting out from the mainland. Although the peninsula blocked some of the wind, the rain now fell in blinding torrents.

"Let's find shelter on the mainland!" Briebras shouted. Asku shook his head and nodded toward Anne who remained lifeless despite the rain cascading over her face. The message was clear. If they were going to save Anne's life, they needed more than shelter. They had to find help.

Once they passed the island it took two more grueling hours of paddling across the open water before they entered a protected cove between two spits of land on the western end of Cedar Island. The downpour slacked off to a steady rain and, at last, Briebras was able to take a break from bailing. When they were well into the bay he began to see evidence of the people who lived in Asku's little community.

The village did not appear to have a central area, just a random scattering of buildings here and there. The houses were a mix of shacks, huts, and buildings constructed from whatever materials might be available. Some were close to the water while others were farther inland, perhaps a delineation between those who fished and those who farmed.

The rain continued as they paddled to the innermost recess of the bay. The clouds, still thick and threatening, were bringing an early end to the daylight.

Darkness would soon be upon them. It had been hours since Anne had opened her eyes. If not for an occasional moan, she may well have been dead.

At last, Asku steered the canoe toward one of the small shacks set back from the waterline just far enough to avoid the high tides. When the canoe slid to a stop, Briebras rose to jump over the side. Instead, his numb legs buckled and he crashed to his knees. Learning from Briebras' mistake, Asku stretched his legs out before attempting to stand. When he felt the numbness begin to subside, he helped Briebras ashore and then pulled the canoe out of the water.

Anne did not open her eyes or make a sound when Asku picked her up. As he carried her up to the cabin, Briebras followed behind, wondering whose home it was they were going to and whether it was already too late for Anne. Instead of knocking when they came to the door, Asku reached under Anne, still cradled in his arms, and deftly opened the latch. Inside, a middle-aged woman with graying hair sat at a table reading a book by the flame of a rush lamp.

"Asku?" the startled woman said in disbelief as she stood.

"Mother," Asku answered.

"Palsambleu!" Briebras said in a hoarse whisper.

# CHAPTER THIRTEEN

DESPITE THE DIMNESS of the light seeping through the crack beneath his door when Tye awakened, he sensed that dawn had long since passed. Hurrying topside, a blast of angry wind buffeted him about, making it hard to steady his feet. Above him an ominous sky laden with black clouds proceeded to dowse him with a steady drizzle. With still more and darker clouds closing in, there would be no work completed above deck this day.

Returning below, he found most of the crew busy splicing rope, patching sails, and performing similar tasks that could be done with little light. Taking advantage of the relative quiet, Tye began making his way to the section where the smithing tools were stored in hope of finding Kofi.

He had seen the big man several times during his search of the ship, but only in passing. The first time he had come upon the blacksmith, fortune had been in his favor. The former slave was on deck, forming links to make a chain for the knipple shot. Tye had watched him lift the heavy smithing hammer with his huge arm, then smash it down upon a red-hot section of iron rod strategically held in place on the anvil's shaping horn with metal tongs. Though he had almost blurted out Kofi's name, he realized just in time that his friend was now part of the crew. While greeting Kofi was not likely to cause harm, his gut had told him to keep their friendship a secret from the rest of the men.

"Pay me no mind, sir," he had said as he passed the blacksmith on his way to the bow. "I perform a task given to me by the ship's owner, Mary Read, and, though my actions may appear odd, I assure you that I will not interfere with your work."

Having received the order to let "the boy" have run of the ship, Kofi would not have been surprised to see Tye. Rather than respond to the greeting, he gave the lad a nod that conveyed both familiarity and caution.

They saw each other a few more times as Tye moved about the ship in search of the hidden compartments. On each occasion, Kofi held his gaze long enough that Tye knew the blacksmith was keeping an eye on him, but not so long that anyone would suspect they knew each other. Now, while the crew was lulled by the rocking boat, the dim lighting, and the banality of their tasks, Tye was determined to talk to his friend.

The compartment that held the smithing stores was near the bow. The only room farther forward than that was the head with its seats of ease. When he entered the compartment, Tye held his Betty lamp high, looked around as best he could, but saw no one. Disappointed, he started back the way he had come.

"Wait," someone whispered.

Tye recognized Kofi's squeaky voice but was still unable to see him.

"Sit down, there, in the passageway. We talk. If anyone comes, we stop."

Pressing his back against the bulkhead, Tye slid down until he was seated on the deck with his legs stretched out in front of him.

"You must try to get away, as soon as possible."

"I can't," Tye said, keeping his voice low.

"Why?" Tye saw a dull flash of white in the far corner of the room, just a few inches higher than the deck. "Mary Read, she is..."

"Mary Read is bad hoodoo. You need to leave. She cannot be trusted."

Tye saw Kofi now, or rather his faint outline and an occasional flash of white from his teeth when he spoke. He was lying on the deck under a shelf where many of the smithing tools were stored. Tye supposed it was where he slept.

"I don't trust her. But she is teaching me about my father, Jack Rackham."

"Do not believe her. She lies."

"No! She knows too much about my father. I have his octant! And she is going to teach me how to use it."

"She is using the octant as a shiny stone to distract you. She wants your soul."

"I know her better than you think. Besides, I want to learn how to navigate...and I want to learn about my father. Would you not want to learn about your father if you had the chance?"

Even in the darkness, Tye knew that the question had struck home. Kofi had been separated from his father and mother as an infant.

"Do not trust her."

"I don't. I won't. But, Kofi, if you do not trust her, why are you here?"

"Not for you to know."

"What?"

"It is better you do not know. It is enough to say that I am here to make chains and to fix metal parts that are broken. That is all you need to know."

"You're not a pirate," Tye said. "You don't belong here any more than I do. You're up to something. I know it. Why did you join this crew?"

Before Kofi could respond, a shout from amidships traveled through the hull to their compartment.

"Tye! Tye Rackham! Where you be, lad! Mary Read wants you in her cabin, now!"

"Rackham? Is that what they call you now?"

"Yes. No! I mean, I am Jack Rackham's son, but they've never used that name before. I've never used that name."

"What would your mother say if she knew they called you Rackham instead of Brennan?"

The question angered Tye.

"My surname isn't Brennan. My true surname is Rackham, and if it wasn't for Mary Read I wouldn't know my real name and I wouldn't know who my father was."

"Tye Rackham!" The crewman was closer now, and Tye recognized the voice as being Harry Wennell's.

"Go! Go now! They must not see us together."

"Here sir!" Tye shouted over his shoulder to Wennell. "I'm on my way!"

"I'll be back," he whispered to Kofi, "We'll talk more then."

"Do not trust her," Kofi warned again as Tye disappeared into the ship's gloomy belly.

Forced to cross the open deck in the downpour to fetch the boy, Bos'n Wennell was soaked to the bone and in a foul mood.

"Here," he snapped, throwing the boy a hooded cloak. Unable to see in the dim light, the heavy garment hit Tye square in the face. "Put that on an' go to the whore's cabin, an' be quick about it. I don't want her claws into me any deeper than they already are."

"She's not a whore!"

Wennell scowled at the boy with a cocked eyebrow.

"Aye.... Got a likin' for her, do ya? No doubt she was a beauty in her day, but her face is a bit wicked now to be inspiring lusty thoughts in a pup the likes of you."

"Shut your filthy mouth. If she heard you talking about her that way she'd cut your tongue out...or worse."

"Har! That might be, lad. But you ain't her, and you better not tell her. What's it to you anyway?"

"She was a friend of my father."

"Really? An' who might your father be?"

"Was," Tye corrected. "My father was John Rackham."

"John Rackham? Wait. You don't mean Calico Jack Rackham, do ya?"

"Indeed, I do."

Blyth Rader had not told Wennell or the rest of the crew why they were kidnapping the boy, but they all knew that the Spanish lady was really Mary Read and that, for some reason, she had it in for the boy's mother. Even in the dim light, Tye could see the man's demeanor changing as he began to understand the truth about the two women and the boy.

"I...I was just makin' a joke. You understand. I meant no harm. You won't tell her...will you? Here, let me help you with that cloak, Master Rackham."

Tye made no comment as the mangled-mouthed bos'n opened the oversize garment for him. He was beginning to understand how saying the right words at the right time could be a powerful weapon.

"Oh, an' be sure to take your octant. She said she's going to start learnin' you how to navigate. Would you like me to fetch it for ya?"

"No. It belonged to my father, and no one but me will handle it. Understand?" Tye threw the last part in to see how the bos'n would respond – a test of his newfound power.

"As you wish," Wennell said, conceding to the boy's will. But Tye was already halfway down the passageway to the closet that served as his quarters.

A few minutes later, he entered Mary Read's cabin without knocking, the octant case clutched tightly beneath the protection of his cloak. Sheets of rain blew in as he struggled to close the door with his free hand. When the door's latch slid into place, he turned to see his navigation teacher standing by the chart table.

"Come in, Tye." The dampness in the air muffled some of the roughness in Mary Read's voice, giving it a quality similar to that of a bone passing through a meat grinder. "I see you had the good sense to keep the box covered. Good! That tells me you already understand the first rule of navigation – always protect your octant, no matter what. And if it ever comes time to abandon ship, your first priority, beyond all else, is to secure the instrument in that case. If you make it to a longboat and are lost in the middle of the ocean, you can sail within a few miles of land and never know it. But with an octant and the skill to navigate, you can save yourself and all those who travel with you. The knowledge I am going to pass on to you – if you master it – will give you power and leverage you will be able to use for the rest of your life. Do you understand what I'm saying?"

Not having moved since entering the room, a small puddle of rainwater dripping from his cloak had formed around his feet. Placing the octant case on the chart table, he slid out of the heavy garment and hung it on a hook next to the door.

"I've been wondering," he said.

"Yes?"

"Why are you doing this?"

"Teaching you how to navigate?"

"No. I mean, why are you being kind to me? It's not your nature."

"Tell me, what do you think you know about my nature?"

"More than your crew does...but I think they will find out soon enough."

"Really? And why is that?"

"Because, soon they will have to make a choice. They will have to decide whether to follow you or Rader. Right now, they're siding more with you. They like the idea of being with a legend...a legend they believe has been resurrected from hell. But Rader is working on them with poisoned words and promises. He tells them that you wouldn't be here if it weren't for him. He tells them that, when anything goes wrong, it's because of a decision you made. But when anything goes right, he takes the credit. Most of all, he tells them that the grand plans you have are really his ideas that you stole, and if they really want to be rich, they'll do away with you."

He paused for a moment, letting the words sink in.

"Of course, if they knew you at all, they would shun Rader like a leper and throw him overboard."

"That may be true," she said, "but how the hell would you know?"

"Because I know you. I was there when you threatened ol' man Burras with his daughter's life. And I was there when you squeezed Rader so hard with your stare he nearly soiled his pants. But even if I hadn't been, I would know your nature. It's written on your face so deep even the scar can't hide it. It lives in your walk and oozes from your pores. You wear it about your person as if it were a cape - a large handbill made of cloth - proclaiming, 'I give no quarter!'"

"You can see all that?"

"As clear as the grit from the street that chafed you in your youth and the blood you had to let to survive. The crew that mutinies on you will learn in hard terms what I see plain."

"You see a lot, don't you? That is to say, you see things most people don't." Tye shrugged.

"I don't know what others see. I don't know if they can't see, or if they don't know how. But yes, I guess it to be true. I only know that I see these things as clear as you see me standing here."

"How did you learn about Rader and the crew?"

"It wasn't hard. Remember, I spent a good bit of time poking in the nooks and crannies down below, getting down in the dark spaces. Many were the times that some of the men would start to talking, not knowing I was but a few feet away. It didn't take long to learn which way the wind was blowing."

"I see."

"So, what's the answer?" he asked.

"What do you mean?"

"Why are you being nice to me? I know you want me to like you, what with the stories about my father and giving me his octant. But why?"

There came a rustling from the darkest corner of the cabin, but Tye could not hear it. The Hollow's bone rattle was meant only for Mary Read's ears, warning her to be straight with the boy.

"Did your mother ever tell you where you were born? No. Of course she didn't. You know why? Because no mother wants to tell her child he drew his first breath in a prison surrounded by the stench of reprobates, sodomites, and every stripe of degenerate imaginable. It was in a filthy shite hole of a prison and the worst imaginable place for a mother to birth a child. And if your mother never told you that, then there was no reason for her to have told you that there were two babies born in that stinking Spanish Town prison...one to your mother and one to me! The only thing is, one was born pink and warm and the other was born cold and still."

SsssshhhhWHAM!!!

A short, stooped man entering the cabin unannounced had lost his grip on the handle, allowing the door to slam against the wall. Loose parchments swirled about the room until the man was able to force the door shut again.

"Sorry to be late," he said, removing his cloak and hanging it next to Tye's. "I lost track of time, what with it being so dark."

His voice was tinged with the cracking that comes with age. His hands were browned and weathered, and his hair was almost white. When he turned, Tye saw that his face was as chapped as his hands, like an old tanned hide, too long without oil or salve. His movements were slow and deliberate, but his blue eyes were full of life. He might not yet have been considered old – but was knocking on its door.

"Pardon me, ma'am," he said upon seeing the cross look on Mary Read's face, "you did want me to come here, didn't you?"

"Yes, I did." Her anger at being interrupted began to wane. "Did you remember to bring your tape?"

"Ah! Yes ma'am. Indeed I did. It's right here in me mending bag." The aging seaman patted the top of a small leather pouch resting on his hip, held in place by a shoulder strap running across the front and back of his torso. As he pulled the flap open, Tye saw that he was missing the last two digits of his right hand.

"Mister Peppers is our sailmaker, among other things," Mary Read said as the man fished around in his bag for the measuring tape. "He patches canvas, sews garments and is known to stitch a crewman now and then, or so I'm told. Is that right Mister Peppers?"

"More true than I care to recall...at least that last part. I can sew just about anything, but I can't stitch a severed arm or leg back on. That would be a nice trick, for sure. I can only keep them from bleeding to death."

Finding the tape, he placed the bag out of the way and gestured for Tye to hold his arms out. Though a little wary, Tye did as instructed.

"If you're going to be a part of this ship, I can't have you running about looking like that," Mary Read said as the sailmaker-turned-tailor continued taking Tye's measurements."

"Looking like...what?" Tye considered his shirt and breeches as if seeing them for the first time. "What's wrong with my clothes?"

"They make you look like a chawbacon. Those rags aren't fit for the son of Jack Rackham. Your father was known for the clothes he wore. Well, his clothes and his pirating. It wouldn't be right if you didn't do him proud by living up to his image."

Hearing the name "Jack Rackham," the sailmaker paused for a half moment before resuming his work, hoping his hesitation had passed unnoticed.

"Don't you need to be writing down those measurements, Mister Peppers?"

"No ma'am. Numbers and names stick in me head, they do. No need to write them down. 'Sides, I got nothin' to write them down with."

A minute later, he placed the tape back in his bag, pulled his cloak back on and turned to Mary Read.

"Shouldn't take but a couple a days, ma'am. I'll be back with his new habiliments as soon as I'm done...everything according to your specifications, of course."

As the weathered sailmaker vacated the cabin, Mary Read nodded to a stool behind the chart table next to hers, an invitation for Tye to take a seat. As he climbed onto the perch, Mary flipped a chart over to its blank side, revealing a simple depiction she had drawn of the earth, the sun, and the moon.

"Figuring out latitude is easy. All you need to know is the altitude of the sun at noon and, with the aid of astrological tables..." she paused, reaching behind her to pull a reference book from the chart rack and opening it to a random page of logarithms, "...what the sun's declination for that day of year is, and then you can figure out what the latitude is."

Tye scanned the tables on the open pages of the book. Instead of seeing what they meant, he began to feel their meaning.

"Longitude is a whole different bailiwick. To figure out longitude, you have to know exactly what time it is at a fixed point...like Greenwich...and exactly what time it is where you are. Finding the local time based on true noon isn't so hard...it's figuring the exact time in Greenwich that's a poser."

"That's why the captains complain about not having an accurate chronometer," Tye said, jumping ahead.

"True. Clock pendulums don't work correctly aboard ships. With all the swaying to and fro, it's nigh impossible to keep accurate time with a clock."

"So...how do you get Greenwich time?"

"That's the chafe. You can put ashore and do the calculations. But that won't work when you're in the middle of the ocean and there's no land to be found. And a marine chronometer will work for a week or two, but after that, they go all helter-skelter, either speeding up or slowing down because of the temperature and humidity changes or the constant rocking of the boat."

"Well then, how do you determine longitude?"

"Lunar distances."

"But I thought that was one of the ways to determine latitude?"

"Not exactly. The altitude of the moon will give you the latitude. Lunar distancing is the science of predicting the angular distance between the moon and the sun, the moon and a planet, or even the moon and a specific star."

"I see! If you know where the moon is in terms of its revolution around the earth, and the distance between the moon and a given star or planet, then you can determine longitude. Right?"

"That's it! And if you have a chronometer, you can reset it and carry on a few more weeks without having to take another lunar calculation for time."

"Now," Mary continued, "look at these logarithms for a few minutes and tell me how you think those calculations reflect the moon's movements. I need to talk to Rader about signing on more crewmen from Ocracoke and Portsmouth while we're here."

"The table is broken down in fifteen-degree increments," Tye said before she got halfway to the door. "I think they are set up that way because the earth rotates 360 degrees each day...so it travels 15 degrees each hour. Yes! That's it, I'm sure."

"That's...amazing," Mary Read said. "It took me several days to understand how that works. If your talents extend to trigonometry, you will be navigating in no time.

Brushing off her meeting with Rader, she began walking Tye through some simple equations and astrological measurements with the octant. He grasped the material so quickly, Mary soon jumped into explaining trigonometric functions and how to apply them.

"Have you ever heard of Robert Boyle, Christopher Wren, or Francis Bacon," she asked after he'd successfully completed several made-up sightings.

"Bacon, of course," he said. "I know Boyle's Law, but I've not studied it. I've not heard of Wren."

"Wren was known as the best geometer in Europe and rebuilt London's churches after the Great Fire. But do you know what these men had in common? They were all prodigies. Geniuses. Savants. Do you know what a savant is?"

Tye looked at her but did not volunteer the answer.

"Of course you do. Your aptitude for mathematics, your ability to read people, and your uncanny intuition make for a potent combination. But living in Bath...you must have been desperate for knowledge."

Tye sensed that this time, her praise was part of her effort to gain his trust. And if he was honest with himself, he had to concede that it was working.

"Anne must know that you are special," she continued. "And yet, she chose to remain in Bath, a stagnant port town whose biggest contributions to the world thus far are pirates, pitch, and churls with tar on their feet. Why, I don't know. But you've never been given the opportunity you deserve to learn and to grow. I'm going to change that...if you'll let me."

# PART TWO

## CHAPTER FOURTEEN

ANNE AWAKENED MID-MORNING of the second day lying on a soft mattress filled with goose down. She had no recollection of Asku's mother applying damp cloths to cool her burning body or swallowing a vile concoction of medicinal herbs every few hours. Nor did she recall the torment caused by the venomous snakebites or that she had broken fever during the past night.

Instead of returning all at once, her senses crept back to her like an early morning mist lifting from a meadow. The first awareness she had was through touch. A sheet so soft and fine of weave pressed against her skin, she wondered if she might have awakened beneath a death shroud. She had forgotten how exquisite fine linen could be.

Her hearing returned next as the subtle sound of hard wood rolling back and forth on hard wood came from close by. It was steady and rhythmic, the familiar sound of – someone in a rocking chair. Someone was sitting next to the bed, watching over her.

A more subtle sound came from a far corner of the room, sneaking in between the pauses of the rocking chair. It was a soft, occasional rustling, similar to that made by the fluttering thrust of a small bird's wing. Though it was a familiar sound, Anne was unable to place it.

Distinct, familiar aromas associated with cooking came next, prompting memories of her childhood in Charles Town and of many pleasant hours spent in the kitchen of her father's plantation. The smell of fresh baked bread and perhaps a soup or stew filled the room.

The pleasant awakening within her nose triggered a less pleasing awareness that her tongue retained a foul metallic taste left by – something. Her mouth felt gritty and dry, and her tongue laid inside it like sun-parched driftwood. She would have to have water before she could speak, and she was now aware of the incredible emptiness in her stomach. She had never been so hungry in her life.

Forcing her eyes to open just enough to see, Anne began to take stock of her surroundings. Her bed was butted up against a corner of the room; a footstool sitting close its head. A little farther away she saw a woman in her mid-forties sitting in the chair. Despite her steady rocking motion, she appeared to be sound asleep. A scattered memory flashed through her mind. She had seen the woman before, perhaps when they had first arrived. There was something about the woman that was important to know – she just couldn't bring it back into focus.

Then she remembered the water moccasins and the bites. The woman in the chair – whose dark skin and bent nose spoke of an Indian bloodline – must have taken care of her.

Sitting at a small table across the room she saw Briebras reading a large book. As he lifted one of its huge, thick paper leaves and let it fall upon the others that preceded it, she again heard the other sound she had been unable to recognize – the simple turning of a book's page.

Satisfied that she was in a safe place, Anne's mind was free to note the various aches and pains inflicting her body. Her neck was stiff and the entire right side of her body tingled with numbness. Her right calf had begun to itch with such intensity that, once realized, had to be scratched.

Lifting her arm from the bed, she began to reach toward for her lower leg.

"Stop!" the woman ordered. Anne froze. "Don't you be messing with my cures. If you knock the maggots off, the sores won't heal."

"Maggots!" Anne said, jerking her hand away.

"Yes," the woman said as she rose from the chair to look at Anne's leg. "Maggots. They're eating away the dead skin around the bite holes, otherwise, mort-a-facation will set in. You wouldn't want that, take my word for it."

Anne had seen sores mortify before. One of the pirates on the *William* had been bitten by a spider just below the ankle. A week later, the meat on his foot had fallen away. In two weeks, the only thing left below the knee was bone. Sometime during the third week, he died.

"It's about time you woke up. I was getting worn out washing and feeding you. I was starting to believe you were playing opossum, just so you wouldn't have to do it your own self."

The woman's accent was familiar to Anne – a mixture of English West Country brogue and Gaeilge. It was akin to the Bristol accent of many pirates, but with a trill that was totally different. Though the pilots and fishermen of Portsmouth and Ocracoke who came to Bath to trade spoke in a similar way, it had never occurred to her that other Outer Bankers shared the unique accent.

Anne shifted her gaze to Briebras who was watching from the corner, a big grin fixed on his face. Any hope that he would rescue her from the awkward situation vanished. He was enjoying her misery far too much.

"My name is Ona," the woman said, taking mercy on her. "Ona Dare. Don't laugh. Ona is short for Winona. I'm Asku's mum...him what brought you here."

"His mother? Anne repeated, still trying to find her bearings. "I didn't know he had a mother."

The woman chuckled as she moved toward the fireplace.

"Everyone's got a mum, girl, even folks what live on Cedar Island."

"Oh...yes. Of course. I didn't... I mean..."

"It's all right. I know what you meant. Asku's not one for volunteering information about himself. What I want you to do right now is to rest, let the medicine do its work, and get your energy back. You're going to need it."

The effort to make sense of things was taxing, and Anne was happy to let the conversation wane. Closing her eyes, she took a moment of quiet, trying to find a second wind. As she rested, she began to realize that the sheet covered only the part of her body from her neck to her knees. The lower parts of her legs were left exposed to allow the maggots to do their work.

Still too weak to worry about the propriety of the situation, she dismissed any concerns about modesty. More compelling at the moment was the need to shift her weight around. She had been lying in one place for too long. Making sure no one was watching, she pushed herself up so that she could rest her back against the wall at the head of the bed. The effort was exhausting, but the change brought a flood of relief. It also reawakened the incredible craving in her belly. She had to eat something. Anything.

As if reading her mind, Asku's mother turned from fireplace and returned to Anne's bed with a bowl.

"Here," she said, placing the bowl and a wood spoon on the footstool. "It's chicken soup. More broth than chicken, really. But there's a little meat in there, too. One thing we have plenty of around here is chickens, though it sometimes takes awhile to catch them. Most of them run free. But this one was a laying hen I kept out back."

"You shouldn't have," Anne said, though she took the bowl and began spooning the soup into her mouth.

"Not at all," Ona said. "She stopped laying eggs about a week ago, so her time was up. Asku will catch another one to replace it."

With a pang of guilt, Anne realized that she had forgotten to ask about the man who had saved her life. Vague memories of his silhouette outlined against the dark sky as he sat at the back of the canoe came back to her in flashes. As she spooned the soup into her grateful mouth, she tried to recall all that had happened.

Asku would have had to paddle the canoe through the storm for hours to make it across the sound. And Briebras must have bailed water endlessly to keep them from sinking. Her moments of consciousness had been few and fleeting, but she remembered enough to know that she owed her life to both men. Any debt to her that Asku may have felt because of the incident at the kiln was repaid in full. If anything, she now owed him, a truth that aggravated her but could not be denied. Piled on top of that realization was the selfish hope that this new, unwanted obligation would not interfere with her quest to save – *Tye!*

The reason she had come to be here in the first place shouted at her through muddled thoughts. She had to get up! She had to continue on to Portsmouth Island before it was too late. How long had she been here?

"Where are my clothes?" Anne demanded, placing the bowl on the stool and twisting around to sit on the edge of the bed. Gathering the sheet around her, she planted her feet on the floor and tried to stand. Blood rushed from her head. Her legs gave way and she crashed back onto the bed. Briebras and the woman rushed to help, but Anne tried to fight them off until overcome by the dizziness.

"What's goin' on?" boomed a voice Anne had never heard before.

She glanced across the room to see the new arrival as Briebras and Ona helped her lie down again. To her surprise, the person standing in the doorway with his bow in one hand and a brace of rabbits in the other was a man she knew well.

"Asku?" she asked, confused. "Why... How... You can talk?"

"Of course he can talk," Ona chuckled, shaking her head. "What is it with you mainers that makes you all so gullible?"

"Mainers?"

"Mainlanders," Asku said, his words brined with the same odd brogue as his mother. "People from the mainland. Someone who's not a Banker... umm... not from the Outer Banks, that is to say."

Though it was strange to hear Asku's speaking, Anne found his voice to be both strong and assured.

"Why did you pretend to be a mute?"

"It's an old Indian trick," Ona said, chuckling again. She was down on her hands and knees, retrieving the wiggling maggots that had fallen from Anne's leg. "It's like hiding in plain sight."

"It's true," Asku said. "People think that because you can't talk, you can't hear either. You'd be surprised at the things people say around a mute, even though he's standing right there."

"But why do it at all?"

Instead of answering, Asku looked at his mother. Having collected all of the little white larvae she could find, she rose from the floor, cupping them in her hand. She looked at Asku then back to Anne, trying to make a decision. When she looked back at Asku again, he nodded to her.

"It's not that we don't like mainers," Ona said. "And it ain't nothing personal, you understand. It's just that we've made it here on our own for a long time. A very long time. When outsiders come 'round, eventually they want to know exactly how long. When we give them the answer, they either call us liars or act as if we're mad. So, mostly we just keep to ourselves. Now lay down again so I can put these maggots back on your wounds."

Rather than clearing things up, Anne was more confused than ever.

Asku picked up where his mother had left off.

"What my mum is trying to say is, that by pretending to be a mute on the mainland, I don't have to explain to anybody where I'm from. And I don't have to worry about getting mad at somebody for calling me a liar. It's just easier that way."

"I still don't understand," Anne said, trying to ignore the sensation of having the disgusting maggots crawling around on her leg. "What is it about telling people you are from Cedar Island that would make them be that way?"

"You might as well go ahead and tell her," Ona said, with a shrug, "now that you let half the cat out of the bag."

Asku leaned his bow against the wall and hung the rabbits on a hook next to the door.

"It's not about Cedar Island as much as it's about us. About who we are. How we came to be here."

"Ah..." Anne sighed, sensing that she was, at last, about to hear the answer to the riddle that was Cedar Island. "Please, tell me, just how long have you been here?"

"How long?" Asku repeated, searching for the right words. "We were here before there were people in Bath. We were here before the merchant ships started coming through Ocracoke Inlet and we were here before there were people in what you call Virginia. We've always been here."

"That doesn't make any sense," Anne said. "Colonists didn't start coming to the Carolinas until about fifty years ago." She paused. "It doesn't make any sense, unless... you're all Indians."

She started to laugh but stopped when she saw Asku and Ona exchange another look. Their expressions told her she had stumbled onto something.

"That's almost right," Asku said. "We are partly from the Hatteras tribe of the Algonquian, and part English. The English part started about 140 years ago."

"But, there weren't any English colonies here that long ago."

Asku or Ona watched her without speaking, waiting.

"No..." she gasped at last. "It can't be. They were all lost, never to be found again. John White said they were all killed. Maybe by Indians – maybe by the Spanish. I mean, he wouldn't have just abandoned them."

"And yet, here we are," Asku said.

"John White!" Ona said. She turned her head and spit on the floor. "John White was a coward and a fool. Quit looking because he lost a couple of men in a search party sent ashore to find our people. Of course, they didn't know that at the time, it's what they pieced together many years later. But those original colonists didn't go nowhere. They were here the whole time, right where he had left them back in 1587."

"I find that to be a bit hard to believe," Anne said, quickly adding, "No offense. I mean, how could White have missed a whole island when he came back to look for your people? And what about Roanoke Island? They say that's where the colony was."

"He only missed it by about a hundred miles," Asku said. "Think about it. You've seen the coast from the ocean. Standing aboard ship, it all looks pretty much the same. Just a bunch of sand, sea oats, an' scrub brush. Hard to tell one part from any other. Now keep in mind, from the ocean, Roanoke is an island that sits behind a barrier island. So is Cedar Island. You've got to go through a channel and go behind the barrier islands into the sound waters to get to either one of them."

"During the three years between the time White left and when he returned, there were several hurricanes," he continued. "The channels that cut through the barrier islands change all the time. New ones open and old ones close. White would have been trying to find Raleigh's colony based on the location of the channels, and that's where he went wrong."

"What happened," Ona interrupted, "is that he went to the wrong island and sent a few men ashore to find us...I mean, our ancestors. After two in the search party got killed by Tuscarora, he gave up looking. And that's the long and short of it."

"Our people," Asku said, picking up the story again, "our English ancestors kept waiting for White or someone from Raleigh's company to return, but none ever did. So they had to make it on their own. Many adopted the ways of the Hatteras Indians, and many of the Indians adopted the ways of our people. After awhile, nobody really cared where they had originally come from. They were all good people, what did it matter? Most of us who live on Cedar Island can trace our families back to both Indian and English blood."

A hundred questions flashed through Anne's mind, but a new thought rose above all others.

"Dare!" she said, staring at Asku. "Asku Dare? No, it can't be. Are you saying that you are related to Virginia Dare?"

"'Her Hatteras name was Winona-Ska," Asku. "Roughly translated, it means 'First of the White,' meaning that she was revered by the Hatteras as first-born among the white people – not 'White Doe' as some of the mainers like to claim. Our Hatteras ancestors understood that being the first white person born in their world made her a special person. When she grew up she was wooed by both white men and red men, a fact that speaks to her beauty and status. That she chose Chief Okisko as her husband should tell you a lot about the closeness shared by our two people, and about who we are today."

"But, still," Anne protested. "The Lost Colony? This is it? It's been here the whole time?"

"It is true, mon ami," Briebras said. After helping with Anne, he had returned to the table and the book he had been reading. "That is, if we are to believe this Bible."

"Bible?" Anne asked, unable to understand how Bible verses could prove their claim.

"Oui," Briebras said. "It is a Bishops' Bible, not the Geneva Bible the Puritans favor. On the first page, which originally was blank, appear the handwritten names 'John White' and 'Tomasyn Cooper,' and a notation showing that they were married in 1566. According to this, they had two children, 'Thomas' and 'Elyoner.' Thomas died when he was still very young, and Elyoner married Ananias Dare in 1583. The last entry is; 'Virginia Dare, born on the 18th Day of August in the Year of our Lord 1587.'"

"And look," Briebras said, holding the heavy book up in the air so Anne could see the aging yellow pages from her bed. "In the back of the Bible, someone wrote the names of all 114 men, women, and children who stayed with the colony instead of returning to England with White. This is magnifique!"

"Is it true?" Anne asked. They had no reason to lie, but – the Roanoke colonists, found? "Are the notes in the Bible true?"

"Don't know for sure," Ona said. "I mean, I didn't know what was in there till your small friend just told us. We...that is, everybody on Cedar Island...lost the skill to read letters after taking up with the Hatteras. You see, most of the older folks died of sickness or were killed. The younger children what lived never had a chance to learn, and the older ones forgot what they had learned because there were no books to read. My family held on to the Bible because it's sacred. They knew that God somehow lives in it, and somehow our ancestors do too. I guess you just proved that."

It was an incredible story, and the Bible entries made for compelling evidence. Having seen many coastlines from the sea, the theory that John White had returned through the wrong channel made sense to Anne. Without any distinguishing natural formations or man-made structures to use as landmarks, White's ship could have spent weeks trying to find the same channel – a channel that may well have ceased to exist, thanks to the hurricanes.

"I believe you," she said. The comment sounded odd, even to her. Her thoughts were scattered, shooting off in one direction and then another.

Her eyelids were beginning to weigh heavy now, as though she had been drinking rumbullion. The food in her stomach and her fatigue were forcing her to succumb to a healing slumber. But her thoughts turned back to Tye, and she resisted.

"Now," she said, moving her hands as though to push herself up from the bed. "I've got to...go to...Tye. I will go to him. I...just need...to...rest...my..."

Despite the urgency to resume the journey, nature would not be denied. Anne fell asleep the moment her head came to rest on the mattress.

"Well, I reckon she'll be quiet till the morn," Ona said as she inspected Anne's leg. "And I think we can get rid of these little fellows now, they've done their job."

"We won't be able to keep her from leaving tomorrow," Asku said, watching his mother remove the maggots from Anne's snakebites.

"And will you be heading out with her?"

"Yes," he said without defending why or making excuses. "I will go with her."

"You know, I'll bet you could use some help," she said. "You should take Birdman with you."

"Blood and hounds, mum! His name is Dyonis. And you'd be doing him a favor by calling him by that name what you gave him when he was born."

"I know what his Christian name is!" Ona said. "And don't be cursin' at me! If he wants to be called Birdman, I got no reason to deny him such a small thing. What harm does it do?"

"We've talked about this before. Dyonis should be treated like a regular person. You treat him like he's a little boy."

"If you're going to attempt to get her boy off that boat, wouldn't it be a big help to know what the moon and the tides are doing? You know Birdman knows those things."

"I also know he could just as easily take off after a butterfly or try to adopt a sea turtle," Asku said.

"He's your brother, and he's not an idiot. He's just different, that's all."

"If we both go, there's a good chance that one of us won't come back. Maybe both of us. You still sure you want me to take him?"

His mother paused and drew in a deep breath.

"I know it wasn't easy growing up with Dyonis," she said. "When you were a little boy you two were best friends, probably because you were the same age, at least in terms of how you acted. When you got older, he followed you everywhere instead of the other way around, the way it usually is with brothers. But that's not why I'm asking you to take him now."

"The reason I want you to take him is because I can't stand the thought of what would happen if you don't come back. He's pretty much lost when you go on your trips to the mainland as it is. But if he thought you were never coming back..."

She paused to collect her thoughts, searching for the right words.

"I know you think I've done him wrong, the way I treat him sometimes. And you probably think that losing him would be too much for me. As much as it would break my heart to lose either of you, the idea of watching him suffer for the rest of his life, not understanding why you don't come back...I couldn't live with that."

Her eyes had turned watery. A moment more and there would be tears.

"I'll go get him, then," Asku said.

Picking up his bow he turned to Briebras. "It'll take me about an hour. When I get back, we'll pack everything we need for the trip. I figure we should take enough food and water for two days. Anything after that we'll have to get in Portsmouth or Ocracoke...or Mary Read's ship. We'll leave first thing tomorrow."

# CHAPTER FIFTEEN

ANNE OPENED HER EYES to the startling sight of a strange man standing over her, his face mere inches from her own. Though his closeness was a bit disturbing, she somehow sensed that he was not a threat. He had beautiful gray eyes set above high cheekbones, much like Asku's. His nose was similar to Ona's, though the crook was much more pronounced. He wore a hood pulled tight around his head making his nose stand out more than it might have otherwise. Had she not just learned about the origins of the people of Cedar Island, she would have believed this man was an Indian.

"Very pretty," he said as he grasped one of her long, red tresses of hair between his thumb and forefinger, savoring its softness. "Very, very pretty. Pretty, like the red robin. Do you like robins?" His eyes grew wider. "I love robins. Very pretty."

The odd greeting made Anne smile despite the awkward circumstance.

"Yes, I like robins. They are very pretty."

"Robins eat worms," the man explained. "Robins have red breasts and wake up early to catch the worms."

"Indeed they do," Anne said. "You, sir, are a very smart man."

The compliment brought a smile to his face.

"I like her, mum," he said, though he continued to stare at Anne. "She's nice. Very nice."

"I told you you would like her," Ona said from across the room. "Now come on and eat your breakfast."

"We're having chicken an' biscuits," the man said. "I like chickens. Chickens lay one egg every thirty-six hours. That's four an' a half eggs a week. Twenty eggs a month. Two hundred and forty-three eggs a year. Do you like chickens?"

"I do like chickens, thank you very much."

"Then let's eat. We have a long way to go today. A half-mile on foot. Two miles by boat. Fourteen miles up the beach. That's sixteen an' half miles."

"I'd love to," Anne said, raising her voice, "but I need to have my clothes first."

"Clothes are right there on the footstool at the head of the bed," Ona said. "Dyonis... I mean, Birdman, go outside with your brother and his little friend so Mrs. Bonny can get dressed."

"Yes, mum."

He continued to look at Anne in fascination as he backed his way to the door. Once he had moved a few feet away, she saw that the hood covering his head was covered with feathers – the same colorful, parrot feathers she collected in Bath. As he turned to go out the door the cloak – entirely adorned with feathers – flared out behind him. Combined with his bent nose, high cheekbones, and piercing eyes, he looked as though he were a human bird.

"Hurry up!" he said as he closed the door. "I'm hungry."

With only Ona left in the room, Anne got out of bed and began to dress.

"He's Asku's brother?" Anne asked as she slipped on her shirt.

"Yes, his older brother," Ona said as she placed food on the table Briebras had sat at the day before. "Not hard to tell, is it."

"I see you in both of them. They are special men. You must be proud."

Ona stopped for a moment and her faced turned dark. For a moment, Anne wondered if she had said something wrong. Perhaps Ona had mistaken the comment as some sort of insult.

"Dyonis is filled with spirits," Ona said, letting whatever had angered her to pass. "Good spirits, spirits of nature – but spirits just the same. Asku is full of himself, but he's a good man as well. Yes, I'm proud of them both."

"Now, you tell me something," Ona said. "What does the shameless piratress Anne Bonny want with my Asku?"

The abruptness of the question was like a red cape waved in front of Anne's bull temper, but she recognized Ona was only looking out for her son.

"Shameless?" Anne asked in mock surprise. "I thought I was notorious."

Ona didn't laugh or smile.

"I used to be the pirate Anne Bonny," she continued, dropping the attempt at humor. "Now I'm just a mother who's desperate to save her son. I was in need of a favor and Asku owed me one. He's paid me back and then some. I don't expect him to go any farther if that's what you are worried about. If he can just take me across to Portsmouth Island, I'll go the rest of the way on my own. Any hold I had over him is done."

Ona weighed Anne's words for a few seconds then smiled.

"Asku said you were special. But let's be honest, sweetie...you an' I both know that the hold you have on him goes far beyond whatever was owed. He's going with you. I couldn't stop him if I tried."

The comment surprised Anne. She had been too worried about Tye and too immersed in the search to find him to think about Asku. There had been a moment back at his wigwam – when she first saw his eyes again – but the thought had been fleeting and her need to find Tye unrelenting. If Asku had feelings for her, it was not because she had invited them.

"Oh, come now, Anne Bonny," Ona said, seeing the look on her face. "You don't expect me to believe that a worldly woman such as yourself can't see that the boy is in love with you?"

Anne looked across the room at Ona, not sure what to say.

"Well, I'll be," Ona sighed. "You really didn't know, did you?"

"But...why?" Anne asked, denying the obvious. "How? There's been... I mean, we've not even spent time alone together."

"Really?" Ona chastened. "I'm not sayin' he's ready to die for you...although, come to think of it, he did already risk his life for you. What I'm saying is that he's on your trail like a dog on the hunt, and I don't mean for game. He's hoping for a chance to find out if you've noticed him and if you might be open to getting to know him. In other words, he's standing on the edge of the cliff. Whether he falls off the edge or not depends on what you do."

Anne searched her memory, recalling certain glances and comments Asku had made since she had sought his help. She had been so absorbed in her pain and desperation that she had missed their significance, but in looking back, could not be denied.

The revelation made her both angry and annoyed. She did not want the distraction of deflecting Asku's attentions and cursed herself for agreeing to Briebras' damnable plan. If she had followed her first instinct – to hop an outgoing ship and sail directly to Ocracoke – snakes would not have bitten her, she would not have wasted several days traveling and recuperating, and, one way or another she would have settled her score with Mary Read.

Now she was stuck traveling with people she did not want to be with and dealing with distractions that might keep her from finding Tye in time. Rather than gratitude, the only thing she felt at this moment was a deep, gnawing desire to get the hell off Cedar Island and on her way to Portsmouth.

"Why me?" Anne asked, unable to veil her exasperation. "What does he see in me?"

"Well now, that's the question, isn't it? Can't say as I know for certain, but I think I have a pretty good idea. You see, Asku's not like most men. He's a handsome lad and has attracted girls all his life, but he's looking for something more. He wants a woman that's his equal – or his better. For some reason, he thinks you might be that woman."

"And exactly what is it that would make him want such a woman," Anne asked, though she was sure she knew the answer.

Once again, Ona gave her a dark look as if trying to judge the sentiment behind the comment.

"I didn't teach him to want someone like me, if that's what you're thinking," Ona said. "He's his own man...and a good one at that. I'll not apologize for setting a good example."

"I know what it's like," Anne said as she sat on the footstool to pull her shoes on, "to fear for the life of your son. I promise you, I had no idea that he was thinking that way about me. If I had it to do over again, I would go after Mary Read on my own and none of this would have happened. But I can't, and right now the only thing I want to do is get to Tye as fast as I can. Because if I don't, I fear I may lose him forever. And if your son...if Asku...sees fit to help me, then I'm going to thank my lucky stars and let him, because I'm going to need all the help I can get. You understand, don't you?"

"Aye, indeed I do," Ona said. "I expect I would feel the same way, were I in your place. Just one thing...you watch his back. You hear?"

The two women looked at each other, recognizing a bond forged by the mutual fear that no mother should outlive her child.

"Come an' get it, boys!" Ona called.

# CHAPTER SIXTEEN

THE MIDDAY SUN BEAT DOWN on the four wayfarers as they maintained a steady pace on the hard-packed sand close to the surf. But as the sun had risen, so had the breeze coming off the cool ocean water, turning what might have been a trudge into an easy march. If the weather remained in their favor, they would complete the fourteen-mile hike to Portsmouth Village well before nightfall.

They traveled in single file, Asku leading the way, followed by Anne and Briebras. Dyonis spent most of the time falling behind to look at conch shells or debris washed up on the beach, and then scurrying to catch up with the others. In addition to the water gourds slung over their shoulders, each person carried a weapon. Asku was armed with his bow and arrows as well as a musket. Anne had her sword and knife while Briebras carried two flintlock pistols. Dyonis had an old musketoon slung over his shoulder, loaded but with its flint removed. His instructions were to carry the weapon and give it to one of the others should trouble start, a job he accepted with great pride and satisfaction.

Having devoured her breakfast – the first real food she had eaten in days – Anne had been rejuvenated. In addition to being renourished, her body had benefited from the full day's rest forced on her by Ona's medicine. She felt better now than she had in a week.

As they were eating breakfast, Anne had noticed that Dyonis wore a braided leather cord around his neck with a carriage watch attached on the end. More than a watch, it was a small work of art. A thin ring of gold circled its silver champlevé dial and its face was engraved with a bird at the top, a mask on the bottom, and foliage throughout. Arabic numerals ran around the outer edge of the dial where the minute hand swept and Roman numerals ran inside those for the hour hand. Watches made of silver and gold were expensive – that this one included a minute hand made it a valuable timepiece. Anne couldn't help but wonder how Dyonis had come to possess it and whether he even knew how to tell time.

They left Ona's home as soon as they had finished eating. Anne thanked Asku's mother and accepted a parting gift of food wrapped in a cloth before stepping outside. Ona hugged Dyonis goodbye first, then Asku, giving Anne one long, last look as she did so, as if to say, "I expect you to take care of my boys. Bring them back to me."

Before striking out, Asku and Dyonis had gone to one of the several large, scrubby bushes planted around the shack, each stripping off a handful of dark green, needle-like leaves. Crushing the tiny leaves in their hands, they massaged the extracted oil onto their faces and other exposed areas of skin.

"Try it," Asku said. "It's sea dew. It will help keep the mosquitoes off. Be sure to save a handful for later, they can get awful bad."

"Mosquitoes are bad at dawn," Dyonis added. "Mosquitoes are bad at dusk. Mosquitoes bite and suck blood. Bats eat mosquitoes."

Anne and Briebras stripped the tiny leaves off the stems as the brothers had done and began crushing them in their palms. Anne sniffed her hands and recognized the piney lemony odor.

"Rosemary," she said, savoring the smell. She had used the herb many times, but only as a seasoning.

"I also have some bear fat mixed with goldenseal in my pack," Asku said. "It works even better, but it stinks to high heaven. We don't want to use that unless we have to. Trust me."

When they had finished rubbing themselves with the rosemary, they resumed the journey that had begun in Bath five days earlier. Though it had begun by crossing Cedar Island on foot – with Asku and Dyonis carrying the canoe above their heads – once in the water, it did not take long to paddle to Portsmouth Island. A few minutes after landing and securing the canoe, they had traversed the width of the narrow barrier island and headed northeast, following the beach toward Portsmouth.

On several occasions they saw the sails of a merchant ship following the coastline, and each time they took cover in the dunes so no one would spot them. They were most concerned about the ships that came up behind them from the southwest because they were most likely to pass through Ocracoke Inlet. If they anchored there and crewman made mention of seeing a group of armed people walking on the beach, word might somehow make it to Mary Read or one of her crew. But they also hid from any small boats that came their way regardless of what direction they were sailing, as they were most likely local fishermen who would eventually return to one of the inlet's two villages.

Asku was first to spot the newest set of sails headed toward them from the northeast. With a wave and a warning shout to the others, they once again took cover behind the dunes. As she had with the previous sightings, Anne retrieved the spyglass from her pack and trained it on the approaching ship.

What Anne saw through the glass this time startled her. The ship coming toward them was a beautiful two-masted schooner. Unlike any she had seen before, this ship did not have a rectangular sail atop its foremast nor did it have the typical horizontal yard arm – or cross spar – that would have held the square canvas. In its place was a second boom-and-gaff combination similar to the ones on the lower part of the fore and main masts. This type of rigging was simpler to trim and required fewer crewmen to operate. It also meant that the sails were far larger than those of square-riggers.

Anne had never seen a ship with so much canvas billowing in the wind. It was as if her crew had captured huge white clouds and lashed them to the masts. She was sure the boat was flying every square inch of sail she had, taking advantage of the moderate but steady wind blowing from the east.

Anne's heart raced with awe. She knew ships, and she knew that this one was special. Moving the spyglass down from the sails, she saw that the bow was also different. Schooners were known for their sleek, narrow prow. While the lower part of the bow on this ship maintained that standard, the upper area at the main deck flared out, allowing more deck space around the bowsprit.

By every possible measure, its craftsmanship and design were incredible, the work of a master. What shipyard could have built such a magnificent boat? From what country did it hail? There was no way of knowing because the ship did not fly a flag.

"There are forward-facing gun ports on either side of the bowsprit," Asku said.

"You can see that from here?" Anne asked.

"No. I heard Daniel Williams, Old Man Burras' head carpenter, talking about it. That there is Mary Read's ship, I'm sure of it. I saw it at the shipyard as it was being built, and I saw it as it sailed down river when she left Bath."

Anne lowered the glass and looked at Asku, remembering the faint outline of the ship she had seen docked at the Poisoned Oak. If it was Mary's ship, the flared bow and unique rigging were refinements intended to create tactical advantages, not aesthetics.

"Like I told you," Asku said, tapping a finger to his ear, "folks forget that a mute can hear."

Anne nodded and then resumed studying the schooner through the long glass. This time she focused on the bow, just below the point where the bowsprit ran into the interior of the ship. Asku was right. On either side of the bowsprit were two open gun ports, each with a cannon ready to be pulled into place.

"You one-eyed, scar-faced whore," Anne said under her breath. "You stole my idea!"

"What do you mean?" Asku asked.

"It was one of the things we used to talk about when we broke out the rumbullion. We were always looking for an edge, asking 'what if' questions. One of the ideas I came up with was flaring out the main deck at the bow so as to allow two cannon to be placed on either side of the bowsprit."

"Why hasn't that been done before?" Asku kept his eyes on the schooner, hoping to make out more details as it drew closer.

"The bows were too narrow. Makes the ship front heavy. Nobody thought it would work. Take your pick. Many ships have swivel guns at the bow, but nothing like the two cannons she has mounted."

"But, this ship does not seem to be bow heavy," Asku said. "She schoons the water on even keel."

"Look at the gun ports on the side of the ship when she goes by," Anne said as looked at them through the glass. "You'll see that there are six ports on the side, but the one nearest the bow is empty. It's the same on the port side. Leaving those two cannons off allows for the added weight of the two forward-facing cannon. The weight is evenly distributed. That was my idea as well."

"What about the bow pitch? Won't it be hard to shoot accurately?"

"Not if she's using the rest of my idea," Anne said. She lowered the spyglass and turned to look at Asku.

"The notion was to take two large cannon, as big as a ship could handle without turning it into a water plow. Place them at the bow, load them with two balls chained together, and fire them at the same time."

"Palsambleu!" Briebras said. "That makes sense! Now I know why they wanted Kofi."

"That's right," Anne said. "They need a blacksmith who can forge chain links and attach each end to the cannon balls. Knipple shot isn't new, but it's never been used like this, I assure you."

If Mary had incorporated those elements into the ship's design, it was likely it included others they had once imagined. Things that would make it a formidable raider.

"A ship! A ship!" Dyonis shouted, interrupting Anne's musing. The feathers covering his cloak shimmered in the breeze, adding the illusion of flight to his bird-like appearance.

"Yes, it's a ship," Asku said. "We know. Now stay down an' keep quiet."

"No! Another ship!"

They all turned to look to in the direction Asku's brother was pointing. Coming toward them from the south was a sleek-looking brig working against the wind, tacking to maintain its northerly heading. In a few minutes, it would have to alter course or risk running aground. Anne realized that the ship's captain wasn't piloting the ship toward them, but was trying to put the brig on a line to intercept Mary's schooner. But why?

A quick look through the spyglass answered that question – the ship was running a Union Flag on its jack staff. The brig was an English warship, perhaps the only vessel left patrolling the area. Its captain intended to force the undeclared schooner to heave-to so as to determine its business.

As Mary Read's ship drew closer to their position, they watched the crew attach a large red cloth to the pennant line and run it up to its highest point. As the huge flag unfurled, Anne felt the chill of a dark truth pull at her soul. Despite the damp, clammy heat that she had endured most of the day, she shivered.

There was no subtlety to Mary Read. There never had been. The flag she now raised was the biggest standard Anne had ever seen – at least a third of the height of the main mast and nearly half as long as the ship itself. And once seen, no man, woman or child would ever forget the threat it conveyed. Forsaking the black adopted by pirates in more recent times, Mary had resurrected the color used by pirates of an earlier day – blood red. In the middle of its expansive field was a scowling white skull floating above the familiar crossbones seen on almost every pirate flag flown in the past hundred years.

The Mary she knew was the type of woman who would make sure no one mistook her for some other Brethren of the Coast. Eight years ago, she had clawed her way out of hell's cellar and had struggled for almost a third of her life to reclaim a place among the most feared. Now that she was back, it was clear that she intended to make certain everyone knew who she was and that they would once again fear her name.

To that end, just in case the size and the color weren't enough, she had added a personal touch to the giant banner now snapping in the wind. On the outside third of the flag were three black hearts, evenly spaced from top to bottom. While the lower two were unblemished and perfect in shape, the top heart had a dagger buried in it almost to the hilt.

Anne stared in silence, too stunned to speak her thoughts. While the images on the flag would evoke terror in the stoutest sailor, there were but three people in the world who could possibly know what those symbols represented – and one of them was dead.

Now that the English ship recognized the danger, its crew scrambled about the brig's deck and rigging, making the preparations to fire their cannon and to repel boarders. Anne swung her glass back to the schooner to see what they were doing with the two bow guns. The bow cannon on the port side was already loaded with a ball, the attached chain running out of the gun's short, stubby tube. A crewman on the starboard side was leaning out of the porthole, reaching under the bowsprit with a pike, its sharp spearhead replaced with an iron hook. A crewman on the port side slipped the last link at the end of the chain over the hook and the crewman with the pike pulled the chain into the starboard side porthole. Anne could not see what they were doing, but knew that Kofi would be waiting with a single, white-hot iron link that would be used to connect the last link of the chain to a second cannonball. Once the link was pounded closed, he would douse it with cool water and the gun crew would load the newly connected ball into the starboard cannon. Sure enough, a minute later Anne watched the pirates roll both cannon forward into firing position, the chain connecting their two cannonballs hanging free below the bowsprit.

The captain of the brig was doing what any good commander would do in the same situation. At any moment he would begin a tack to his starboard, turning the ship away from the beach. The shift of direction would bring his port guns to bear on the schooner. As each of the brig's ten port-side guns aligned with Mary Read's ship, they would fire a 6-pound cannon ball at its bow. If just one of them hit her ship at the waterline, the battle would be done.

The brig was now close enough they could hear someone aboard shout the order to begin the tack. The sound triggered a thought in Anne's head that made her heart stop. With so much going on she had forgotten about Tye! Was he aboard Mary Read's ship?

Sweeping the spyglass across the schooner's deck, she searched for her son while praying that she would not see him. Though farther out on the water than the brig, Mary Read's ship was now right off the beach from where they stood. When her glass came to the ship's wheel, she froze.

Standing left of the helmsman was Blyth Rader. Still dressed in dandy clothes and foppish hat, he was barking out commands. To the right of the helmsman and farther behind, stood Mary Read, her long raven hair flying wild about her face. In addition to readopting the attire worn in her former pirating days, she now wore a black patch over her dead white eye. And next to her was a shorter crewman Anne had never seen before, wearing a red bandanna atop his head.

To Anne's relief, she did not see Tye. If he was on board, at least he was below deck, hopefully in the ship's rear quarter where there was relative safety. Perhaps Tye had been left back at Portsmouth, or Ocracoke, or wherever it was they were anchoring. But Anne knew better than to dare hope for anything so optimistic when it came to Mary Read.

Still looking through the long glass, Anne saw the crewman with the red bandanna lean over to say something to Mary Read. When the crewman turned back to look toward the brig, Anne was both surprised and amused to see that it was not a man at all, but Clairette, the girl who had served them at the Poisoned Oak.

The tremendous boom of two cannons discharging in perfect unison rolled across the water to where they watched. The command to fire had been given at the exact moment the two ships' bows were about to align. Had the shot come a few seconds later, the brig would have completed its tack and fired its own cannons. Instead, the group on the beach heard the mighty whoosh of two cannonballs linked by chain as they spun like a horizontal pinwheel from Mary Read's ship toward the brig. The chain hit the ship's bowsprit with such power that it sheared the oak spar, taking out the staysail and jib rigging with it.

Continuing on its path, the chain sliced through the bodies of at least a dozen crewmen who never knew what had hit them. The front third of the ship erupted into a gory explosion of blood, intestines, and disembodied heads. Though the foremast held strong when the chain hit it, the two cannonballs began orbiting the upright spar in opposite directions, obliterating everything in the knipple's increasingly rapid and ever-shortening path. Rigging, sails, and crewmen were mowed down, sent sprawling into the sea, or smashed against the gunnels. Blood flowed from the scuppers like crimson seawater.

Because the chain had severed the bowsprit near its base, the rigging above the path of the knipple remained attached to the top of the foresail. When the bowsprit fell into the water on the ship's starboard side, its sails acted like an anchor, causing the brig to dip and spin on its nose. Though four port-side gun crews aft of the mainsail had survived the carnage, any chance of accurately firing on the schooner was lost. Only the gun closest to the stern attempted to fire, its cannonball traveling so far off its mark the crew on Mary Read's ship sent up a loud cheer that turned into laughter.

By the time the schooner reached the English ship, its bow was facing south, the opposite direction it had originally been traveling. The brig had spun around one hundred and eighty degrees, and now both ships were pointing in the same direction. The English vessel was dead in the water.

Rader brought the schooner up along the brig's starboard side prepared to release a broadside into the crippled ship, but its crew was finished. Her captain – before being killed by the knipple shot – had moved most of his men to the port side and readied only the port cannons, as that was where he expected to dictate the engagement. The few crewmen left alive were still on the opposite side of the ship, and none of the starboard cannon were loaded. Rader ordered his men to strike sail, allowing the schooner to drift up to the brig. Grappling hooks were thrown over the brig's gunny rail unopposed and Mary's crew began drawing the two ships together.

Anne's heart sank as she surveyed the devastation through her spyglass. A frantic signalman on the brig was retrieving the ship's jack. Next to him stood a junior officer ready to hand the signalman a white flag. The British sailors were surrendering to a ship of pirates who had just won their first victory. Anne wanted to scream a warning to them – to tell them that they must fight. But even if they could hear her, she knew it was too late.

She continued watching through the glass as, one by one, the English sailors crumpled lifeless to the deck, like puppets having their strings cut by invisible scissors. And each time the macabre sight was followed a moment later by the popping of a musket being fired from Mary Read's ship – the sound of the kill shot catching up to what she had just seen.

Asku, Briebras, and Dyonis did not need a spyglass to know what the puffs of smoke meant. The pirates were methodically picking off the remaining sailors despite their attempts to surrender. When there were no crewmen left standing topside, the pirates went below deck, hunted down the few remaining souls and murdered them as well.

"They killed them all," Briebras said, unable to believe what had just happened. "Every last man. The whole battle did not last twenty minutes."

"Seventeen minutes," Dyonis said, holding up his carriage watch as proof.

"One man still lives!" Anne said, still watching through her long glass. She began describing the events as they played out on the two ships. "It's...someone in a red coat. A soldier. They've bound his arms behind his back and walked him across a plank to the schooner. Rader is saying something to him."

"Rader," Briebras echoed, snorting at the name.

"Yes, Rader. It may be Mary Read's ship, but he's running it for her, or so it would seem."

"Now the red coat is saying something," Anne continued, "and not being too meek about it, from what I can tell. I think he's cursing Ra– Damn! He just spit in Rader's face. Blyth Rader pulled out his pistol and is holding it to the poor fool's head!"

From their position behind the dunes, Anne and her three companions had not missed a moment of the battle or the massacre it had become. Anne steadied herself on one knee to look through the spyglass while Asku, Briebras, and Dyonis huddled closer to hear her running description of the scene.

"Mary Read is saying something to Rader, trying to get him stop, I think," Anne continued. "He's lowered the pistol some, but he's hesitating. Now she's yelling at him. She snatched the pistol from him and..."

The three men beside her were able to see a puff of smoke followed by the man in the red coat pitching backward and falling over the rail. The sound of the gunshot reached them about the same time the man hit the water.

"She murdered him," Anne said. "She kicked him in the gut and blew his brains out. Rader is seething. They're arguing and the crew looks to be getting uneasy...no doubt beginning to pick sides. I think Rader is mad because he was knocked down a peg and the crew knows–"

"Damn!" Anne said again, cutting herself off. "Mary pulled another pistol from...I don't know where...and is pointing it at Rader. Rader doesn't like that at all. More words being exchanged. Rader is laughing now...but it's a hollow laugh, I can tell that even from here. More talking. Now he's removed his hat and making one of his foppish bows. Mary's walking away and Rader is shouting out orders. The crew is moving, but slow to it. Looks like they're starting to make repairs to the brig's mainmast rigging while others are throwing bodies in the water. Taking the brig as a prize or making her the first addition to Mary's fleet would be my guess."

An hour later the two ships hoisted sail, tacking away from the coast on a heading that would eventually give them the wind to pass through Ocracoke Inlet. As the two ships made their turn away from the beach, Anne continued studying them through her spyglass. The first ship to present its stern toward shore was the brig, its precise letters spelling out the name "HMS *Hazard.*" The well-armed ship would make a formidable addition to Mary's fleet.

When the schooner turned to follow, its huge red flag of black hearts and white bones caught the wind, billowing out in full glory as if to taunt Anne. She cursed it and she cursed Mary Read for designing it – not for what it symbolized, but because it made such an excellent Jolly Roger. Like everything about her return to pirating, it was perfect.

Moving the glass for a final scan of the aft deck, she was able to read the name painted on the schooner's stern for the first time – delivering a final kick to her gut. Painted in bold white letters outlined by a black and gold border were the words, "RACKHAM'S REVENGE."

Staring at the name in numbed silence, a thousand memories raced through Anne's mind. More than her lover, Calico Jack Rackham had been the only truly decent man she had ever known. They would have been husband and wife, had she not still been married to spurious James Bonny. Though strong enough to manhandle her, Jack understood that brutality would have been the quickest and surest way to lose her. He had instinctively known that she wanted to partner with strength, not be subjugated by it.

Mary Read had been a welcome interruption in their journey – and intoxicating diversion they had both embraced. From the moment she had first seen the raven-haired hellion fighting on the deck of a Dutch merchant ship they had taken, Anne had been drawn to her. Although the ship's sailors had given up at once, Mary had fought Jack's crew with rapier and main-gauche until they cornered her at the bow – not a man among them realizing that it was a woman holding them at bay. But Anne knew. She had known it that first instant, and it had amused her that no one else did. And then, with thirty men ready to pounce on her, Mary lowered her weapons, raised her head, and laughed as though she had just been told the best and bawdiest joke ever told. Jack's pirates stopped in their place and began looking at each other, wondering how such a young fellow, facing imminent death, could find the situation so humorous.

That was the moment that she had fallen in love with Mary Read. Not in a lustful way – that would come later. Anne had, at last, met a woman who was her equal. A woman who loved life as much, and feared death as little, as she did. A kindred spirit.

All it had taken to save Mary's life was a whispered plea in Jack's ear. "Look at him Jack. He's got half the crew cowering in their boots an' the other half-frozen in awe. We can always use a man like that. Give him the pirate's option."

Rackham, conceding Anne's wisdom, offered the warrior with blinding speed and cool resolve the choice of joining their crew or being the recipient of the ball packed tight in the barrel of his pistol. After taking an exaggerated bow, the "man" looked Jack in the eye, smiled, and said," My name is Mark Read, and I would gladly become a member of your crew, but only if afforded three shares of any and all treasure we come to liberate."

Jack and the rest of the crew had laughed at that. As captain, he was entitled to only two shares.

"Come now," Mark had replied with a look of indignation so authentic that Anne had almost believed it was real. Sweeping his rapier in a wide arc before him, Mark said, "Look! Do you not see me standing here, holding more than two dozen of your men at bay? Is a warrior like that not worth three shares?"

Jack had paused before answering. He had been both amused and wary of such bravado from a man in no position to barter. With his men watching him so closely, he had to handle the situation deftly or it would not play well with them later.

"I'll make you a deal," he had said. "If you can defeat all of these men, then I'll give you three shares. Agreed?"

Mark had thrown his head back and let out another hardy laugh.

"I have a counter offer. You let me have a share-and-a-half of all booty and I'll let all your men live. That's a half share less than a captain and a half more than the scurvy goats you have here get. That way, we can both be happy."

The pirates had laughed at first but stopped short when they saw the earnest look in Mark's eyes. If the man could be taken so easily, he would already be dead. They understood that it was impossible for him to defeat them all, but they also knew that a good number of them were sure to die in the process.

Jack had returned the smile. Mark Read's counter offer was the one he had hoped for.

"Well then, let's leave it to the crew. What do you say, men? Do we let this young but capable warrior have one-and-a-half shares...or do we take him down and throw him in the ocean for the sharks? What say you?"

The crew's bloodlust had waned during the pause in the fighting. The "man" who stood before them had already killed several of their mates and wounded several more. Those who stood closest to Mark Read knew that they were the most likely to die if the fighting resumed.

"Seems to me we're goin' to need another pair of hands to replace all the mates he's already killed," one of the crewmen had said.

"Aye, said another. "We've given others the chance to swear allegiance and become members of the crew. An' this one's a screamer, that's for sure."

"Anyone opposed," Jack had asked, knowing there would be none. "Well then, it looks like Mark Read here is our newest member of the crew."

That had been the beginning, Anne remembered. Later, Jack began to wonder why she was spending so much time with the new crewman. Eventually he discovered what she had known all along, that "Mark" was in truth a woman. Soon, the three of them were spending all their private time together, not as a triangle of lovers, but as like-minded associates committed to a mutual descent into debauchery. Anne had never tried to understand the exact nature or their unnatural union, but at no time had she ever felt that Mary was a threat to her relationship with Jack.

Now, seeing Jack's name on the transom of Mary Read's schooner, she began to wonder if she should have. The one thing that was clear to her was that Mary Read was driven - not by greed - but by a lust for power and revenge.

Movement on the deck caught Anne's eye and she leveled her long glass on the source of motion. A small man leaning against the gunny rail was looking back toward where the sharks were feeding on the bodies floating in the water. Though the ship was more distant now, she was able to see that he wore a tricorne hat and flamboyant waistcoat with a shirt and breeches made of calico - the exact type of clothes that Jack had worn!

But it wasn't until a tall black man came to stand beside the man in calico did she understand what she was seeing. The African had to be Kofi, and the contrast between him and the shorter fellow made it clear that he was not a man at all, but a boy dressed as a man. It was Tye!

Dropping the spyglass, Anne screamed Tye's name and began running toward the water, shedding her weapons and coat as she ran. She was knee deep in the breakers before Asku caught up to her. As he struggled to pull her back to the beach, Anne cursed and kicked him while trying to bite his arm wrapped tight around her chest. Her violent exertions caused Asku to lose his footing. Together they fell forward into an oncoming wave. When they resurfaced, Anne stared at Asku with eyes of fire.

"You can't stop me!" she screamed, shaking her head in defiance. "I will not be denied."

"But you can't swim all the way to the ship," Asku shouted back at her.

"The hell I can't!" she said. "She's changing him! She's turning him into a monster. I have to go to him. I have to save him!"

"And you will," Asku said, grasping her by the shoulders to look into her eyes. "But we stick to the plan."

"The plan?"

"Yes, the plan. We will continue on to Portsmouth Village and find a way to board her ship. That's where they are headed now. It has to be. They are returning to Ocracoke Inlet where they will anchor. We will save Tye, but you have to trust me."

Rather than restoring calm, Anne's expression shifted from uncontrolled frenzy into a seething contortion of restrained rage.

"I trust you," she said. Her words were so full of choler that Asku released his grip on her shoulders. "BUT...I...DON'T...CARE. That is my son on that...that profane vessel from hell. I'll do anything to get him back. ANYTHING. And I'll kill any man who stands in my way. You best remember that before you try to stop me again."

Anne saw both hurt and anger on his face but didn't care. Tye's life was the only thing that mattered.

"Have it your way, then," he said, releasing his grip on her shoulders. "Go on. Be my guest. But I doubt you'll make it past the sharks."

"Oh...," Anne said, the foolishness of her actions finally beginning to sink in. "Yes. The sharks."

They stared at each other, each trying to determine where the other now stood.

"SHARK!" Dyonis yelled from the beach.

Still waist deep in the water, Anne and Asku looked at Dyonis.

"Yes," Asku shouted. "We know about the sharks."

"SHARK!" Dyonis yelled again, pointing in the direction where the two ships had come together. A huge dorsal fin was cutting through the water, closing in on a man swimming as hard as he could toward shore. Somehow, one of the crewmen had survived.

"Give me the musket!" Asku shouted to his brother as he and Anne waded back toward shore.

"He'll never make it," Anne said, looking back over her shoulder.

Dyonis, breathing hard from running to dunes where Asku had left the musket and back, handed the weapon to his brother as he exited the water.

"There's still a chance," Asku said.

Raising the gun to his shoulder, he took aim, then squeezed the trigger. First came the distinctive clink of flint striking the metal frizzen, followed by the whoosh of black powder igniting in the flashpan that in turn burned through the barrel's touchhole to ignite the main charge with an explosive roar. The round ball whistled through the air and over the water to strike the small, exposed patch of flesh below the shark's dorsal fin. A trail of blood began to stream into the water behind him, but the shark sped ahead unfazed.

Asku reached to his side for the powder horn only to realize that it was back behind the dunes. There wasn't enough time to retrieve it and reload before the shark reached the swimmer. All they could do now was watch the inevitable.

As it passed through the thin, top water of a swell, they were able to see the fourteen-foot shark with tiger-like stripes open its cavernous mouth. From nowhere, two smaller sharks hot on the trail of blood, hit the tiger shark at the same time. The water turned frothy white, then dark red, as the three beasts tore at each other.

While the frenzy continued just a few feet away, the man who had escaped death managed to reach knee-deep water and was crawling through the turbulent shore breakers. Handing his musket to Dyonis, Asku ran to the man's side and helped him onto the beach. Upon reaching the dunes, Asku propped him up against a steep bank of sand as Briebras handed him a water gourd.

Anne studied the newcomer as he drank. Still wearing his red coat, she saw that he was the man that Mary Read had shot and shoved into the water. Though not as tall as Asku, he was of a stockier, more powerful build. His straight, neatly trimmed hair was coal black and flecked with gray. Some of the black discharge from Mary Read's pistol that had not washed away ran down the left side of his chiseled face, making it difficult to judge his age. Scars and pit marks littered the side of his face she could see clearly, perhaps cicatrix from the battlefields upon which he had waged war. Despite his disfigurements, she knew that some would call him a handsome man.

"Thank you," he gasped, still trying to catch his breath. Though still winded, his exacting English came across clear and precise. "I guess I owe you my life."

"The marksman with the keen eye and steady hand is Monsieur Asku Dare," Briebras said, glancing toward his friend.

"Then, I thank you, Mister Dare," he said, nodding his head in substitution for a bow.

Though it had been subtle, Anne saw the newcomer use the brief gesture to make a quick assessment of Asku.

"Just be thankful that he is a better shot than Mary Read, the virago who left you for the sharks," Briebras said.

"Mary Read?" the soldier asked, though Anne thought it sounded more like a tactical probe than a question. "Mary Read died almost nine years ago, after the good Captain Barnet of the *Snow-Tyger* captured her and that other whore, Anne Bonny. Mary Read died in prison and Anne Bonny...well, nobody seems to know for sure what happened to that scourge. I think, however, that it would be a safe gamble that she was hanged as was befitting her sentence as a pirate and a murderer."

"I'll take that wager," Anne said. "Anne Bonny might well have been a pirate and, on occasion, a murderer of some who more or less deserved it. But I'm sure she would take great offense at being called a whore."

Anne had been standing behind the others who stepped aside when she spoke. This time, the male clothing she wore did nothing to conceal her gender. The soaking-wet blouse clinging tightly to her torso left no doubt that she was a woman.

"And who might you be?" the man asked without making it sound like a challenge.

"Don't you know?" she replied. "You seem to consider yourself an expert on the subject of notorious women and whores, though I suspect you have much more experience with the latter."

"Am I that transparent?" the man asked, feigning indignation. "As a company commander in the Admiral's only standing regiment of marines, I'm afraid I have to confess that my knowledge of notorious women is an occupational mandate. As a gentleman, I'm not at liberty to discuss my depth of knowledge or the nature of my association with whores. As a man who appreciates the limitless abilities of both, I can only say that I believe you to be one or the other. And as much as God has already smiled upon me this day, I pray for my own gratuitous reasons that you are both."

Anne felt her face flush red with anger at the implied insult, then relaxed, realizing that he was both denigrating himself and paying her a compliment – one warrior to another. In the wisp of a second, he had correctly assessed her character and formed a reply that was both playful and taunting, a quality that brought back a torrent of memories of her beloved Jack Rackham.

"Allow me to introduce myself," the marine said, taking advantage of the opening created by his clever turn of words. "My name is Major Samuel Gant, formerly of His Majesty's Coldstream Regiment of Foot Guards in the regular Army and, as I alluded to previously, now an officer of good standing in the Admiral's marines."

He paused for a moment to look out toward the ocean where the pirates had usurped his ship.

"That is to say, I was in good standing until about an hour ago. Now...I'm the lone survivor of a massacre that claimed more than a hundred lives, twelve of them damn fine marines. I seriously doubt that a military court will see my 'miraculous' survival as anything other than an act of cowardice."

When he looked back at the others, their faces betrayed nothing.

"It was the knipple shot," he began, reliving the battle in his mind's eye. "What a bloody, spinning horror that damned thing was. I was standing amidships when the chain caught the foremast. The ball that swept across the port side caught a seaman square in the chest. The poor bastard's body flew twenty feet across the deck and hit me dead on. The force of the impact flung me into the gunny rail and knocked me out."

He raised his hand to the back of his head, searching for a bump beneath his hair with his fingers.

"When I came to, the pirates had already taken over the ship and were pitching bodies overboard. They didn't know I was still alive until they lifted the dead sailor off me."

"Why didn't they just kill you then, like they did the others?" asked Asku.

"Indeed, my friend. That's the queer thing. I don't know why they made a show of it. Perhaps it was because I was the last officer left to kill. What I know is that when they hauled me across that plank to their ship, I kept thinking, 'Not like this. Not without having fired a shot or drawn a drop of blood.' After all the times I had nearly been killed in battle, I refused to believe that it would end like that, with my arms tied behind my back!"

"The man whose face you spit in, Blythe Rader, what was it that he said to you," Anne asked, recalling the confrontation she had witnessed through her long glass.

The tone of her voice – hollow and veiled – caught Gant off guard. He turned to look at her face, but the sun was sitting just above her left shoulder, blinding him. As he shifted his position so her head would block the brightness, Anne leaned the opposite way, denying him the shade that would allow him a clear look at her face.

"Ahhh... That was a strange thing," he answered. "This Rader fellow was ranting about how the Royal Navy had been a thorn in his side for as long as he could remember. That it had cost him several fortunes and was part of the reason he had become a pirate."

"Is that why you spit in his face?" Anne asked.

The lines of Gant's face contorted into a sneer of disgust.

"No. He said that the marines were nothing but derelicts that couldn't make it in the army...and weren't fit for anything other than servicing sailors. That's when I spit in his face. When he pulled his pistol on me, I thought for sure I was done. Then, that raven-haired demoness stepped up, told him that he talked too much and was setting a bad example for the others by taking so long to kill me off. That's when she snatched the pistol from him, kicked me in the gut and shot me. Or, at least tried to. I don't know how she missed, standing as close as she was."

"The next thing I know, I'm hitting the ocean and wondering whether I would get my hands free before my breath ran out. Fortunately for me, they had done a poor job with the knot, probably because they didn't think I would be around long enough for it to matter. I managed to get my boots off and was about to shed my coat when the sharks started tearing into the corpses. It's amazing how fast a man can swim while wearing a full coat when there are sharks about."

"Sharks are big and have sharp teeth," a new voice said from above.

Gant leaned to his side and tilted his head back to see Dyonis perched above him atop the same dune. Squatting on his heels with feather-covered arms wrapped around his knees, Asku's older brother looked like a multi-colored vulture waiting for his next meal to die off.

"They are indeed!" Gant said a little too loud. "As it would seem, are the birds hereabouts. Tell me my feathered friend, are you a migratory fowl or is this your permanent territory?"

Confused by the question, Dyonis cocked his head to look down at the marine then back to Asku as if asking for help.

"He wants to know if you are like a duck flying south for the winter or like the Osprey that stays to fish the waters year-round," Asku said.

Dyonis's expression changed as he began to understand and then started to laugh.

"I'm not a bird," he said, drawing out the last word in a singsong lilt of exasperation. "I am a birdMAN. I can't fly at all!"

"Indeed!" Gant said. It was clear that he did understand, or at least, understood enough. "Well, I for one, am happy to know that you won't be flying away and leaving us. The services of a bird man are always a welcome asset to have on an...expedition?"

Anne knew he was fishing for information. They doubtless made an odd-looking group – a white man who appeared to be an Indian, a diminutive Frenchman who looked like a shrunken version of a circus strongman, a woman dressed as a man, and a man who looked like and believed himself to be part bird. What such a collection of odd people would be doing on a deserted beach would be hard for anyone to fathom.

When no one volunteered an answer to his implied question, he continued.

"I know that we're on Portsmouth Island and that Portsmouth Village is several miles north of here. And if I recall correctly, Cedar Island to the south, on the sound-side of the island. If you don't mind my asking...and not that I should want to question the good fortune of my rescue...how is it that you came to be here, in the middle of nowhere?"

Asku and Briebras turned to look at Anne. It was her quest. It was her choice whether to reveal their purpose.

"We are on our way to Portsmouth Village to rescue my son," Anne said, deciding there was no reason to be evasive and too driven to care. "Mary Read kidnapped him from me some five days ago in Bath and I intend to take him back."

"I see," Gant said. "So we're back to the Mary Read story." Again, he shifted his position, trying to put Anne between him and the sun. Again, Anne leaned to the opposite side, denying him the shade he sought. "Tell me, why is it that you are so sure it is Mary Read the dead piratress who stole your son?

"Because, I'm Anne Bonny."

Anne knew he couldn't see her face – he didn't have to. The conviction in her voice hung in the air between them the way the executioner's ax hovers over the neck of the condemned right before taking the fatal swing. The wild, crimson hair waving about her head. The male attire she wore with comfortable familiarity. An exterior as hard as the steel she wore on her hip.

"I see," Gant said again, clearing his throat like a man who realized he had just escaped death for the third time within a half an hour – because he had. "Given who you are. And given that you know your son's abductor better than anyone. I'm sure you realize that your chances of making it out alive aren't worth a tinker's damn? You just witnessed for yourself the wanton carnage her motley collection of assassins visited upon my former mates."

He paused for a moment as he appraised each of three men with her.

"Do you honestly believe that you can persevere where a whole crew of seasoned warriors failed – with just these three men? No offense."

"I do," Anne said. "Whether you think so or not, major, I don't really care. I will have my son back and I will hang Mary Read's head from the bowsprit of her own ship."

"I'm sorry you lost your shipmates," she continued. "And I'm sorry that we can't take you back to Cedar Island. But if you walk about ten miles south, you'll see where our footprints cut across to the other side of the island where you will find our canoe. Feel free to take it and cross the sound to Cedar Island. The people there will take care of you."

"No thank you," Gant replied.

"What do you mean?"

"I'm going with you," he replied. "That is, if you'll have me."

"I don't understand, Major Gant. A minute ago you implied that we will all die if we continue...and now you want to join us?"

"The way I see it, I don't really have a choice. If I go back, I will eventually have to explain how I came to be the sole survivor of a pirate massacre. I will be accused of either being a coward, or worse, colluding with pirates. If I go with you, I may find a way to redeem myself. Perhaps reclaim the *Hazard*. Perhaps kill or capture Mary Read. That would–"

"Mary is mine!" Anne said. "You're welcome to come with us, but don't forget that. I will have my vengeance on Mary Read. You can have your ship. You can kill Rader and anybody else on the crew. You can do anything you feel you need to do to reclaim your name. But Mary Read is mine. Understand?"

"I do," he conceded. "And I pity the woman once you find her."

"Save your pity. She reaps nothing but that which she has sown."

"Asku," she called, though she kept her eyes on Gant, "how much farther to Portsmouth Village?"

"Four, maybe five miles."

"Then now is a good time to move. I want to be as close to the village as we dare get by dark. How long will it be before sunset?"

"About three hours," Asku said.

"Three hours and twenty-two minutes," Dyonis said, looking at his watch, though the timekeeper in his head was far more accurate than the watch he wore around his neck.

"That gives us plenty of time to get there, eat, and get some rest before dark," Anne said, calculating the time and distance in her head. She paused for a moment, thinking.

"What is it?" Asku asked.

"We need to know the tides," she said. "Once we get to the village, we can steal a boat to get to Mary's ship. There will be pilot boats and fishing boats aplenty for the taking. But if we get caught in an ebb or flow tide, we'll have to work harder to get there and make more noise rowing. Do you have any idea what the tide will be?"

Asku smiled.

"I have a tide chart," he said.

"You do! Where?"

"There," he said, nodding toward Dyonis.

Anne looked at Dyonis, still perched atop the dune. She didn't understand.

Asku chuckled and then called to his brother.

"Dyonis. What time were the tides at the inlet today?"

"That's easy," he said. "High tides were at 1:50 a.m. That means morning. And 2:40 p.m. That means after noon. The low tides were 7:56 a.m. and 9:16 p.m. Some days...some days only have three tides."

"And tomorrow?" Asku prompted.

"The first tide tomorrow is the high tide," Dyonis said, "at 3:01 a.m. That's one minute after three in the morning."

"How close does he usually come to getting it right?" Anne asked.

Asku's expression reflected mock annoyance and surprise.

"He's spot on, every time."

"Of course," Anne said, finding a new appreciation for Dyonis's talents. "All right then, everybody grab your gear and let's go. The sooner we get to Portsmouth the more sleep we get before the high tide."

Making sure the long glass was secured, Anne collected her weapons, picked up her water gourds and started walking up the beach. They had been walking for less than a half hour when Gant noticed that Dyonis was no longer with them.

"Where is the Birdman?" he asked.

"It's not 'the' bird man," Asku corrected. "It's 'Birdman.' He likes to be called Birdman."

"My apologies," Gant said. "I can see he's a smart fellow...that thing with tides and all...but, do you think it's a good idea for him to be out there, by himself?"

Asku smiled.

"Dyonis has been known to disappear for days at a time. I know he seems strange to you and says funny things, but he is very smart, in his own way. He can take care of himself."

It was still well before nightfall when Anne noticed that the terrain was beginning to change. There were now frequent breaks in the dunes where channels of runoff and overwash from the ocean had broken through. Through the gaps, she saw marsh grasses beyond the dunes where the island widened out to provide structure to the inlet that separated Portsmouth and Ocracoke Islands.

"How far are we from the village, now," Anne asked, stopping to survey their surroundings.

"A half mile," Asku said. "Maybe less."

"This is close enough then," she said. "Where should we sleep?"

"At the foot of the dunes, on the ocean side. I don't think anybody will be walking down the beach this time of day, and the mosquitoes will be hell on the sound side once the wind settles."

"All right," she said, walking through the soft sand to drop her gear in front of a large dune. "It's about half past 6 o'clock, so we'll each take watch for two hours. Asku, you take the first watch, Major Gant the second, Briebras third, and I'll take the last. I'll be waking everyone up at 2:30, so get some rest while you can."

"Do you have a plan?" Gant asked.

"Of course I have a plan," she said as she rolled her coat up to make a pillow. "We're going to steal a boat, row out to *Rackham's Revenge*, kill Mary Read and bring Tye back."

"Just like that?" the marine asked in disbelief.

"Yes. Just like that."

"Don't you think it will be a little hard to get on board the ship without anybody noticing? I mean, there's bound to be a watch."

"Maybe," she replied. "The way I figure it, they've just won a major victory over a highly-trained English crew and taken their ship as a prize. I suspect that right about now the crew has gone through at least one barrel of rumbullion and started on a second. By the time we get to the *Revenge*, the entire crew will be dead drunk. Any of the bastards left on deck will be easy to dispatch. We can lock the rest of the crew below while they sleep and then take care of Mary."

Gant thought it over for a minute, then shrugged his shoulders.

"Damn good plan," he said, taking off his coat to make a pillow of his own. "I'll be taking my turn at sleep now. And, by the way, thanks again for saving my life today."

"Save it," Anne said, already half-asleep. "You might not thank me come the morrow."

# CHAPTER SEVENTEEN

THE VIEW THROUGH THE GUN PORT was limited, but Tye reasoned that it was better than no view at all. Hidden inside a nest of ropes hanging off a belaying-pin rack, he clutched his new tricorne hat against his chest, praying that neither it nor the red and black calico he now wore would be fouled in the coming battle. Mister Peppers had done a wizard's job of tailoring the coat and breeches and had thrown in a white shirt to go with it, finishing them in time to be donned on the *Revenge's* first outing at sea.

What had started out to be a quick test of ship and crew, had turned into an opportunity served to Mary Read on a chafing dish. No sooner had they cleared the inlet than the lookout spotted the English ship's tops'l peeking above the horizon to the south. When they were close enough to determine that it was a warship, Rader had bristled. Seeing that he was about to order the crew to turn the ship about to make a run for it, she had stopped him. Despite the bloodlust in her eyes, Rader made a desperate attempt to talk her out of attacking. During their heated exchange, Tye had strolled across the deck with as much casualness as he could muster, then taking his position of concealment next to the bow's port cannon.

From this vantage point, he would be able to stay clear of the port-side gun crew when it came time for them to load powder and ball into the stubby cannon and roll it into position. As long as he didn't move from his nook or poke his head higher than the gunwale, it was unlikely that Mary Read would spot him and send him back to his storage closet quarters.

A few feet across the deck, Kofi crouched in front of the bow's starboard cannon, waiting for the free end of the knipple-shot chain. To the right of the blacksmith sat an iron box filled with burning coal, its embers radiating red-white heat as he pumped the small bellows affixed to side base. To the left of the small kiln stood a wiry, hunched-backed seaman cradling an eight-pound cannonball with an iron ring. Every time the ship see-sawed across a swell, the old salt staggered like the drunken sailor he no doubt was at times, struggling to maintain his balance and his grasp on the ball. Strategically placed between Kofi and the kiln, a small anvil and a bucket of water lay waiting to help him perform metalsmithing alchemy.

"Threadin' the needle!" yelled the gun crew's captain who stood next to the bow's starboard gun port.

A crewman leaning out of the port yanked a hooked pike through the opening and began backstepping toward the cannon, dragging the free end of the chain with him. Coming to a stop on the far side of the anvil, he positioned the last ring of the chain on its flat surface. As Kofi fished the final chain link from the coals with metal tongs, the man with the cannonball positioned it so that its embedded ring and the end of the chain were an inch apart.

In a swirl of practiced motion, Kofi slipped the open gap of the red-hot link inside both the final link of the chain and the cannonball's ring. Holding the link in position with the tongs, the African deftly picked up his hammer with his free hand. With a resounding...*CHAANNGGG*...of metal slamming against pliable metal, the link was closed. Kofi grabbed the bucket and poured water over the closed link, producing a loud hiss of steam. His task complete, he closed the metal lid on the portable kiln to prevent sparks from flying away and cleared the area. By the time he settled into the same sort of nook Tye had found on the opposite side of the deck, the gun crew had loaded the ball and wheeled the stubby gun into place.

Tye knew he should be scared, but so many things were happening at one time, fear found no room to surface. *Rackham's Revenge* flew atop the water with a speed he had not known was possible. Above him, yards and yards of white canvas harnessed the power of the wind, multiplying it as though it were the force of a hurricane, pushing the ship toward its adversary like a bird of prey.

Time moved in a blur, his mind able to grasp only brief images here and there. As the ship rose and fell on the swells, his view changed from sky to horizon to water, and back again in reverse order. His eye followed the line of the bowsprit as though it was a pointing finger, and for a moment, it directed his gaze toward the beach, an unbroken terrain of sand dunes and sea oats. Then the ship rose with a new swell and then he could see the sky. As the ship passed the plane of the horizon on its downward track, this time the bowsprit pointed to the oncoming British brig bearing down on them. Men were about to die.

"Fire!" Mary Read yelled with a grainy howl. Captain Rader was supposed to have given the command, but sensing that he was going to miss the timing she could not restrain herself.

"KABOOOM!!!" The two cannons roared in unison.

The concussion hit Tye in the chest like a giant hand, slapping him back into his nest of ropes. Though he had become used to the noise cannon make when the crew had practiced their timing, he had not experienced the powerful, rolling backwash of compressed air at close range. By the time he was able to gather his senses, the knipple chain had passed through the brig's bowsprit and was cutting down men on the deck the way a scythe slices through wheat. For a few moments, a pinkish mist of volatilized blood filled the air above the brig's deck, covering the horrific scene in an absurd veil of pastel.

During the next half hour, he remained pressed against the gunwale nook as tight as a barnacle latched upon a barge's hull. The howls of victory, wails of anguish and pleas for mercy threaded themselves into an aural blanket of infinite despair. The sea was revealing itself to be a two-sided tapestry. This was the dark side, countering the sense of "coming home" he had experienced with the harsh reality of a hell on earth.

As the legato-paced nightmare continued to unfold, Tye's gaze traveled across the deck to where Kofi remained ensconced within his starboard-side sanctuary. The black man's eyes locked on Tye's. The calmness in his expression was like an anchor, holding the world steady despite the storm raging about them.

Now, Tye began to see everything all at once and in great detail. Acts of horrific carnage that should have affected him deeply played out before him with no more consequence than the impaling of a worm on a fishing hook. He felt neither revulsion nor satisfaction. The words pleasure, pain, sadness, joy, fear, and valor held no relevance or meaning connected to what he was experiencing. He was watching from afar – a detached and impartial observer to a moment that was no more or less important than all such moments that had occurred throughout history. For an instant, all the secrets of the universe were revealed to him, taunting him just beyond his ability to comprehend. And then – like an oyster snapping its shell closed to protect the pearl within – the window was gone.

As the world around him began to move at normal speed, Tye realized that he was not breathing. With a mighty gasp, he inhaled all the air his lungs would allow. Exhaled. Then again, and again.

Looking about the two ships, he struggled to understand what had taken place. Amidships, Mary Read and Blyth Rader were standing in front of a soldier wearing a red coat, asking him questions. The soldier smiled at Rader – though Tye saw it wasn't a friendly smile – then spit in Rader's face. Within the span of a heartbeat, Rader whipped a pistol from his waist sash, cocked it, and positioned the muzzle on the soldier's forehead. Every man on deck stopped what he was doing to see what would happen next.

"Wait!" Mary Read ordered as she came to stand beside the two men. "The final kill is mine."

Rader wiped the spittle from his face with the inside sleeve of his free arm without taking his eyes off the man in the red coat.

"He has dishonored me," Rader said through clenched teeth. "I must have ven–"

"Remember your place, Mister Rader," Mary Read ordered. Tye noticed that she had not used his title of captain. "What's more important, your vengeance or my sponsorship?"

Rader began to lower his weapon but stopped. The eyes of his men bore down on him with the weight of a cannon.

"The men..." Rader seethed, his words seasoned venom. "They are watching me."

"Damn it, man!" she said, snatching the pistol from his hand and shoving him aside. "This is the proper way to dispatch a Royal Marine."

Tye watched in disbelief as Mary Read pointed the flintlock at the man's head and pulled the trigger. The weapon discharged into his face, snapping his head back. In the same instant, she planted her foot in his gut and shoved him over the rail.

"Enough lollygagging!" she said to the crew as she turned away, tossing the empty pistol to Clairette. "Captain Rader, let's get these ships back to Ocracoke before it turns dark. Bos'n Wennell, do you think you can get the brig repaired enough to sail her back to port?"

"Yes ma'am!" the knurl-toothed sailor nearly sang out. The order implied that he would get to skipper the captured ship.

"No!" Rader said. "You may well be the sponsor, but I am the captain of this ship, and I will not give orders that we have not discussed beforehand."

Tye held his breath, waiting to hear Mary Read's reply. She had left Rader no room to save face with the crew. In the euphoria of their victory, she had reverted to her natural inclination to take charge. In doing so, she had not only compromised the man's stature with the crew, she had created a standoff where neither of them had a way out without appearing subservient to the other.

"Is that so, Mister Rader?" Reaching inside the sleeve of her blouse as she stepped forward, Mary whipped out a small pistol and pressed it against the man's temple. "Order Bos'n Wennell to take five men over to the *Hazard*, repair her rigging and sail her back to port."

Instead of showing fear, Rader laughed, made a sweeping bow with his hat.

"Bos'n Wennell."

"Cap'n?"

"Take some men over to the *Hazard* and ready her for sail."

"Aye, cap'n!

Rader's eyes remained fixed on Mary Read's as the men around them returned to their tasks. Rather than one of them having won the exchange, it had been a draw. She had forced the captain to acquiesce to her will, an act which the crew would allow a measure of respect. Rader, on the other hand, had shown panache in the face of death, an act that would also resonate well with the crew.

"Clairette, take a couple of men and fetch a keg of rumbullion from the *Hazard*. She may not have much treasure, but the Royal Navy always carries rum to make grog. We'll be celebrating well tonight."

The crewmen standing within earshot of Mary Read shouted their approval, and news of the coming victory celebration rippled out to the rest of the men. The tension was immediately forgotten by the crew.

Tye watched Mary Read with new eyes as she strolled back to her cabin, not giving a jot about the man she had murdered just moments ago. Brutal death was a common occurrence on the frontier, and Tye had grown a thick skin to its frequent occurrence. The coldness with which Mary Read had committed murder, however, was different. Never before had he seen such disregard for human life first hand. It did not seem possible that this was the same Mary Read who had spent hours teaching him the secrets of the octant.

When she was no longer in sight, Tye hurried to lean over the gunwale to look for the man who had just been shot. Below him, dozens of sharks feeding on the corpses of dead sailors had turned the water into a pink froth. If the man had somehow survived being shot, there was little chance he had made it past the churning swarm of killers finishing what the pirates had started.

He continued watching the beasts even after the two ships hoisted sail and the pirates began to withdraw from the scene of their bloody victory. His thoughts ricocheted from one stark memory to the next and then the next with dizzying speed. He struggled to make sense of it all, to sort out the good from the bad. To discern that which was relevant from that which was not.

"People, they think death is the opposite of life," Kofi said as he put his hand on the boy's shoulder. Tye stiffened for a moment, trying not to let on that the blacksmith's shrill voice had startled him. "Not true. Death...is the opposite of birth. They are both beginnings. They are both endings. We exist in both."

"Kofi..." Tye asked, "Is it bad to not fear death? I mean, I didn't like watching those men die, but the fighting...it was beautiful."

As Kofi searched for an answer, Tye saw a puff of smoke – like that made by a musket – rise from the beach close to where their sea battle had taken place. They were too far away now to tell for sure, but it looked like there were people on the beach. Perhaps locals who wanted to know what the cannon fire had been about.

"I knew a man, long ago," Kofi said. "A true African. He taught me a proverb that said, 'To God, all things are good, all things are beautiful, and all things are just...it is only men who see the world as good and bad, beautiful and ugly, just, and unjust.'"

"What does that mean?"

"I do not know, exactly...but I think what you saw today, you saw through the eyes of God."

# CHAPTER EIGHTEEN

ASKU ONLY HAD TO SHAKE GANT ONCE to rouse the marine from his slumber. The major's dark eyes shot open, wild with confusion. His hands flailed about the ground in desperate search of a weapon. Looking around in a panic, his darting eyes fell upon the pirate woman and the bantam-sized Frenchman sitting next to the small campfire he had started during his watch. With a sigh of relief, he remembered where he was.

Anne, who was using the fire's light to go over their weapons one final time paused until she was sure that Gant was all right, then went back to what she had been doing. Beside her, resting on a plank she'd found, were the pistols Briebras had carried the day before.

"We leave in five minutes," she said as she finished loading the musketoon. "There's food in the bag if your stomach can hold it. And water in the gourd, there. Now's the time to eat and drink...it could be awhile before we get another opportunity."

"What about weapons?" he asked.

"Here, this one's for you," she said, tossing him one of the pistols. "Don't fire it unless you have to. Until such a time occurs, use it as a club."

"Of course," he said as he looked over the weapon. "How will we get to where we need to go?"

"There are likely to be fishermen along the channel at the inlet, so we can't follow the shoreline anymore. We are going to have to cut through the marsh. We have the light of a three-quarters moon and Asku has traveled here before, so we should do all right."

"But, I have no shoes! There are oyster shells below the mud surface. My feet will be turned into a bloody pulp."

But as he turned to pick up his coat, he saw three pairs of military-style boots placed in a neat row just above the spot his head had rested.

"You can thank Dyonis for those," Anne said without looking at him. "Apparently, he waited until a few of your men washed ashore...or the parts that still had feet on them...and relieved them of their boots. I'm sure he figured out that you needed them more than they did."

"But, why three pairs?"

"Because he doesn't know what size you wear," Asku answered from the darkness beyond the firelight. "Pretty thorough and clever for an imbecile, wouldn't you say."

"Of course, I was an idiot to doubt him," Gant said. Grabbing the boot closest to him he began pulling it on. "Where is he? I'd like to thank him."

"Don't know. Out there...somewhere. I reckon he's watching. Or maybe he's sleeping."

"I hope he'll be all right," Gant said, looking out into the darkness.

Asku didn't answer this time. If his brother's absence bothered him, he didn't show it.

"The mosquitoes will be as thick as fog," he said, pulling out his pouch of bear fat and goldenseal. "Everybody better put some of this on, or else you'll come running from the marsh screaming like a banshee."

Scooping out a palm full with two fingers, he handed the pouch to Anne and began smearing the goo on his face and other areas of exposed flesh. Following Asku's lead, Anne used her fingers to dig out some of the paste then tossed the pouch to Briebras. The Frenchman opened the pouch wide, stuck his nose in the opening and took a whiff.

"Putain de merde!" Briebras said, jerking his nose away from the bag. "The smell...it would make a dung beetle puke! The mosquito that would land on this would do so only because of a desire to commit suicide."

Holding the pouch at arm's length, he fished out a share and passed the open bag to Major Gant. Taking a deep breath, he rubbed the repellent with both hands then began smearing it into his exposed skin. Forewarned, Gant took pains to avoid breathing in the putrid concoction while applying it to his face and the back of his hands.

"What about Dyonis?" Anne asked.

"Don't worry about him," Asku said, "he has his own."

"All right then," she said, nodding for Asku to lead the way. "It's time."

The well-worn path through the marsh was not as treacherous as Anne had feared, but the dense cloud of mosquitoes that enveloped them was as Asku said it would be. The trail they followed was elevated a few inches above the boggy water that served as a hatchery for the unrelenting pests. And though the bear-fat kept most of the mosquitoes off their exposed flesh, the tiny beasts swarmed so thick that the four intruders began inhaling dozens of the nasty biters through their mouths or noses with each breath. Swatting at them was like swatting at the mist, but they did so anyway – a futile gesture humoring the illusion of having control over a relentless assault that would otherwise drive them mad.

Aided only by the moonlight, they stumbled along the path for what seemed an eternity. At last, upon arriving at the outer edge of the slough, they rushed out of the tall grass and into open ground, gasping for air.

Rather than return to the horror of the marsh and its mosquito horde for concealment, Anne dropped to one knee, motioning for the others to do the same. To their left, she could see the gray outlines of the village, its shacks and shanties dark and quiet. A ribbon of white to their right was the sandy bank of the channel, disappearing into the night where it would eventually turn southward to become the oceanfront. Straight in front of her, the dark silhouettes of almost half-a-hundred boats floated at anchor upon the sound.

There were fishing boats, pilot boats, pack boats and several merchant ships waiting for the morning light, either to be guided through the channel out to the ocean or to resume sailing to Bath. The glow from a few random lanterns or candles speckled the blackness on the other side of the channel, reminding her that the village of Ocracoke was a short mile away.

"There!" she said in a hushed voice. "Those two large shapes farther back from the other boats, closer to Ocracoke. They've got to be the *Hazard* and *Rackham's Revenge.*"

"Oui," Briebras said. "I think the closer one is the *Revenge.* There are no lanterns burning on the other boat and there are at least two on the near one."

"That makes sense," Anne said. "The men on the *Hazard* would have gone over to the *Revenge* to join in the celebration. I'll wager there's not a sober man among them."

"We have to find a boat, quick," Asku said. "The tide is starting to turn."

Rising from her knee, Anne began walking toward a collection of rickety, rough-hewn docks extending out into the sound. Asku held back for a moment, allowing the other two men to fall in behind her first. While the others searched for a boat, he watched to make sure no early risers surprised them. One shout of alarm and the whole village would be upon them before they even got started.

Spotting a small boat at the end of the dock that would do, Anne stepped over its gunwale and untied the bowline. Briebras followed, then Gant, who took the rower's seat and began placing the heavy oars into the oarlocks. Seeing that they had gone undiscovered, Asku joined them. Untying the stern line, he pushed the boat away from the dock and jumped in.

As Gant pulled on the oars, Anne began to question her choice. The craft she had selected was a pilot boat, meant to carry one man to ships waiting for a local waterman to pilot them through the ever-shifting channel between the two islands. While capable of carrying two when needed, the weight of three-and-a-half people was taxing it to its limit, riding so low that its gunwale rode mere inches above the water. Even a small breeze would put the small vessel in danger of sinking.

"Head for the one with the lanterns still burning," Anne whispered, praying that the calm would hold. "If it's the *Revenge*, her bowsprit will still be intact. Now, no more talking from here on out."

As their boat glided closer to the dark, lurking hull, Anne felt the familiar rush of imminent battle surge through her veins, heightening her senses. Although Gant rowed with great skill, she heard the slight slapping of the oar blades on the water's surface as though they were musket shots. And now that her sense of smell had grown accustomed to the bear fat, she was able to smell the stagnant pongs of a ship in still air. The organic aromas of tar, pitch, hemp, and canvas mingled with the collective reek of the pirates' body odors.

Aided by the light of a three-quarter moon and faint ship's lanterns, Anne saw the deck of the *Revenge* illuminated in sharp hues of black and gray. Salt in the air from the brackish sound waters mixed with the copper taste in her mouth that always surfaced when she was about to face death. When they were close enough to see the ship's bowsprit confirming that it was the *Revenge*, every nerve in her body stood at attention.

This is what it means to be alive. This is what I was born to do.

The realization was both intoxicating and sobering. The voice of reason she had worked so hard to nurture since Tye's birth struggled to maintain control over the berserker's rage building within her. Succumbing to her nature could end up proving deadly to Tye. The thought sent a cold shiver through her body.

Shaking off the distraction, she focused on the thick, taut line attached to the ship's anchor now within her reach. It was time to act.

Grasping the coarse rope at the highest point she could reach, Anne threw her legs over the line in crisscrossed fashion and began climbing up like an upside-down inchworm. When she reached the hawse pipe she paused to look down. Briebras was close behind and would soon catch up. Gant was clutching the line and about to follow. She had to hurry or they might all be caught in the open with no way to escape.

Still hanging on to the anchor line with one hand and the lip of the anchor line hole with the other, Anne searched for another handhold that would put her in reach of the gunwale. In disbelief, she realized that the modified bow put the cathead and any other potential handhold out of reach. With a wave of anger, she realized she was stuck! After having traveled for days and barely escaping death, she was going to fall two feet short of making it to the deck!

Sensing that Briebras had reached her heels, she decided to make one desperate lunge at the gunwale. If she missed, she would fall into the water. The splash would rouse the ship's crew and they would all be captured – or worse.

The risks be damned! I'll not be this close just to give up.

Letting her legs drop from the rope, she turned herself around to face the ship. With two hard kicks, she propelled herself up toward the rail with all her might.

For one long, agonizing second she hung from the rail by her fingertips – her purchase too weak to pull herself up and too precarious to last. As she felt her feeble grasp begin to give way, she dug her fingernails into the wood rail, cursing her luck. For the first time since setting out to save Tye, the idea that she might fail flashed through Anne's mind.

In a final protest, her nails made a distinct scratching sound as the weight of her body pulled her over the side. But in the same instant, an invisible force snatched her wrist, arresting her plunge. Fire tore through her shoulder. The sudden stop had almost wrenched her arm from its socket. For a moment, she dangled in the air, suspended above the dark, inky water. She then began to rise without effort, as if she were a child's kite caught in a lofting breeze. Looking up, outlined against the light gray sky illuminated by the moon, she saw a huge black face with two pure white eyes topped by a shiny bald head looking down at her.

*Kofi!*

The African lifted her over the rail and set her down on the deck, then held a finger to his lips warning her to keep silent. Turning back to the gunwale, he helped Briebras, Gant, and Asku onto the ship in secession. Once they were all on board, he motioned for them to gather closer. As they started to bring their heads together, Kofi recoiled back a step in disgust.

"You...stink," he said in a high-pitched whisper, then placing a hand over his mouth as if in fear of heaving.

"It repels the mosquitoes," Briebras said in feigned indignation, continuing their running banter as though they had never been separated.

"And every other living creature that God created," Kofi countered. "Except, perhaps, for flies and maggots. Tomorrow the flies will think that a whale has washed up on the beach and will carry you away, little man."

"Better to smell like a dead whale than to..."

"Shut up, you idiots!" Anne yelled as loud as whispering would allow.

Kofi and Briebras averted their eyes. Banter was a habit they could ill afford.

"Who's this?" Kofi asked, nodding toward the marine.

"His name is Gant," Anne whispered. "He's the marine Mary shot and shoved over the side yesterday. He's come along to exact a little revenge of his own, if he can."

Kofi looked the newcomer over as best he could in the dim light.

"What about you?" Anne asked, unable to mask her own doubts. "Why are you helping us? Are you with us, or against us?"

Kofi looked at Anne as though his feelings were hurt.

"Ahhh...Mon amie," Briebras said before his friend could respond. "You are not the only one who has been practicing the art of subterfuge. We knew that your friend Mary Read was up to no good and that she intended you a harm – but we did not know what or how. Kofi joined with the crew to find out what they were up to. There is more...but now is not the time."

"Indeed," Anne echoed. "Now is not the time."

"Where is the scar-faced whore now?" she asked Kofi, her bloodlust starting to rise. Her darker heart was pounding like one of his hammers against an anvil, testing the restraint she had fought so hard to maintain.

"In her cabin," Kofi said, his squeaky voice barely audible. "The crew is below deck, dead drunk. Forward and main hatches...wedged shut."

"All of them?" she asked. "And they left you on watch?"

"Yes," Kofi answered to both questions, chopping off his sentences as he always did. "Except for the booby hatch where the sails are stored."

"Kofi does not imbibe," Briebras pointed out as explanation as to why he alone would be left on watch.

"Of course not," Anne said, daring to believe that they had a chance. "And where is Tye?"

"Captain's cabin."

Anne felt the hammer in her heart begin to pound again. The stage was set. She knew all that she needed to know.

"Let's go then," she said, turning toward the ship's stern. Tye was only a few dozen feet away. She felt his presence in her bones.

When she came to the door of the cabin she saw faint lantern light spilling out from the gap at the bottom. Pressing her ear against the door, she listened for sounds indicating that those inside were awake. Satisfied that all was still, she turned to the others.

"This is it," she said, drawing the pistol from her belt.

Lifting the latch, she gave the door a gentle shove. The hinge-pins let out long, high-pitched wail that would have wakened a sober person – but nothing within stirred. A lit hurricane lamp sitting on a table in the center of the cabin and the muted glow of the moon shining through transom windows provided more light than she had expected. On the opposite side the room, she saw an ornate, wood-framed bed butted up against the bulkhead. Two people covered by sheets were fast asleep, lying on their sides, oblivious to the intruders. Within the next breath, Anne was on the other side of the room – the barrel of her pistol pointed at the back of the larger person's head. Asku and the others formed a semi-circle around the bed

"Wake up!" Anne said, no longer bothering to whisper. "I've come to reclaim my son. Pray that I don't find him hurt in any way."

Instead of jumping up in shock, Mary Read rolled over on her back and looked at Anne with a look of mock surprise. Her raven hair splashed wildly behind her in perfect contrast to the white bed linen.

"Oh, my," she said in her rasping voice. "Clairette, look who's come to pay us a visit."

The blonde-haired tavern girl from the Poisoned Oak turned over to reveal her face and looked at Anne.

"It's about damned time," she said. "I was about to fall asleep for real."

Anne knew something was wrong, but nothing was going to dissuade her now.

"Where is Tye? Where is my son?"

"Your son..." Mary answered, drawing out her words, "...is safe, which is more than I can say for you."

"That's a bold statement, considering I have the pistol." Her reply conveyed much more confidence than she felt.

"True, my dear Anne. You have the pistol, but I have the spring."

"The spring?"

"Yes, the spring to my trap. Captain Rader! Now, if you please."

All at once, half-a-dozen crewmen erupted from concealed places about the cabin while at the same time another group of men poured in through the door. The crackle of more than a dozen flintlock pistols being cocked filled the room. Taking a look around, Anne saw there were at least two pistols trained on her and each of her friends. Fighting their way out was not an option.

Clairette jumped out of bed, revealing a pistol of her own. Mary threw the sheet back and stood next to the headboard, unarmed. Rather than wearing nightclothes, the two women were fully dressed and ready to fight.

Anne turned her head, giving Kofi a hard, hateful stare, her eyes accusing him of betrayal. Kofi met her stare with an expression and slight shrug that declared both his innocence and his confusion. He was as surprised as anyone.

"I must say, I'm rather disappointed," Rader said, strolling into the cabin. Several crewmen came forward to collect their weapons as he continued. "I was expecting you to put up more of a fight. Perhaps Anne Bonny the legend is just that, a legend. The real person seems to be a bit lacking."

The urge to smash Rader's smirking face with her fist was almost more than she could resist.

"That may be true," Anne replied, "but it was you who was lacking the day I bested you at the kiln. It makes a woman wonder in what other areas you fall short."

Rader's smirk morphed into a disgusted frown as he raised his hand to his disfigured nose.

"You got lucky," he said, cutting his eyes to either side to see if his men had caught his reflexive gesture. "Had I known who you really were, I would not have let my guard down."

"That would have been a great loss for the world," Anne countered.

"What do you mean?" Rader asked, taking the bait.

"I would wager that the circus would pay you well to be 'the man with the cauliflower nose' in a side show."

Blyth Rader's expression turned black as pitch, fueled by the hatred that had been festering for weeks. Summoning the speed he had revealed during their first encounter, a foot-long Scottish dirk appeared in his hand as if by magic. Its double-edged blade created a streak of light that mimicked a lightning bolt as he whipped the weapon's sharp, symmetrical point under Anne's chin. A drop of blood oozed out from where the knifepoint pressed against the soft flesh then trickled down the blade. With slight effort, Rader could have forced the dirk through the underside of Anne's jaw past the back of her throat and into her brain.

"Stop!" Mary Read ordered. The tone of her voice pierced through the cloud of Rader's hatred as she glared at him with her good eye. "I didn't set this up just to have her skewered like a pig."

Instead of removing the dirk from Anne's throat, Rader cocked an eyebrow and shifted his gaze to Mary.

"And if I don't?"

Rader's defiance did not come as a total surprise to Mary Read. The tension between them had been growing with each passing day

"In that case, I'm afraid my friend, Clairette, will be forced to demonstrate her skill with the pistol," she said.

Taking the cue, the tavern girl shifted the barrel of her flintlock away from Anne and aimed it at Rader's head. Though still in her teens, her manner was nothing but one of total confidence. The blood of her pirate father ran true through her veins.

Despite the certainty of his predicament, Rader gave no indication that he was about to surrender to Mary Read's authority.

"Give it up, Rader," she ordered again. "You've got no more cards to play."

At that, Rader's face transformed from a look of defiance into a knowing smile of self-satisfaction. Mary Read had made a terrible miscalculation.

"Are you sure about that?" he asked, looking first at Mary and then at Clairette.

Clairette brought her pistol to bear on Mary Read standing on the other side of the bed.

"I'm sorry," Clairette said, peering over the pistol barrel. "It's been fun being with you. It truly has. But there are some things a man has to offer that you simply aren't...equipped to provide. And I'm a woman what has needs."

It was the first time Anne had ever seen Mary Read at a loss for words. Her response was to stare at Clairette – her face a blank slate, conveying neither surprise nor anger or even disbelief. Had it not been for the dirk jabbed into her throat, Anne would have laughed.

"What about the map?" Rader asked.

"She never showed me where it's hidden, and I've searched the entire cabin ten times over," Clairette said. "I'd wager a gold coin that it ain't hidden in here, but it's got to be on this boat, somewhere."

"No matter," Rader said. "I'll take great pleasure in making her talk. I only hope she doesn't give in too quickly."

"No!" Clairette said. "You promised you wouldn't hurt her."

"And you promised that you would find the map!" Rader said. "I've spent the past two years of my life taking orders from this mutilated, vainglorious hag and living in that hell hole called Bath so that I could take possession of Israel Hand's map. I'll not walk away now, empty-handed. One way or another, she will tell me where the map is, that I promise."

Anne burst out laughing despite the dirk.

"All this! For a stupid treasure map? You cannot be serious. Hey! I have some magic beans in my pocket. If I give them to you, will you let us all go?"

A few of Rader's crew chuckled at the joke despite themselves. Others looked at each other, wondering if Rader had bought them off with a false promise of treasure.

His anger renewed, Rader stepped in closer to Anne, his bulbous nose almost touching her cheek.

"Shut up, or I'll..." He stopped in mid-sentence, jumped back a few feet and then buried his mouth and nose into the sleeve of his coat. "Mother of Hell you stink! What grotty dunnykin have you been wallowing in?"

Now that he was aware of the rancid bear fat concoction, he realized that the odor was all around him. A cautious whiff of Asku confirmed his suspicion – all four of the would-be raiders stank like rotting corpses. With the tension dampened, the rest of Rader's crew was able to take their first deep breath since the encounter had begun. The smell of the foul ointment permeated the cabin. Several of the men struggled to keep from gagging.

"Wennell," Rader called out, his voice muffled by the coat sleeve. "Take these four out on the deck and have some of the men wash these dregs down with seawater. Use turpentine to remove the smell if you have to."

"Aye," the bos'n answered. Anne recognized him as the sailor who had come to her home to deliver Mary's invitation to join her at the Poisoned Oak. "I'll do it. But I expect an extra coin for me and me mates for taking on such a stinkin' job."

"Coin?" Rader replied, striking on an idea. "I'll pay your fee...but you'll have to take it from Mary Read and her friend here."

"Beggin' your pardon, cap'n?"

Rader raised an eyebrow, glanced at the two women, then shifted his eyes as if looking below decks.

"Oh...," Wennell said at last. "Well, I won't have any shortage of volunteers for this job, that's for certain."

"Just be sure to bring the scar-faced hag back in one piece when you're done. It won't take long to make her tell where the map is once I get her back, but I do need her back alive and able to talk."

"Thank you, cap'n," Wennell said, looking at the two women with lewd intent.

"What about the dwarf and these other two?"

"I am NOT a dwarf, you rotten-toothed son of a sow!" Briebras said.

Wennell started toward the Frenchman to give him a backhand but changed his mind when he got close enough to smell the bear fat.

"Take him down below when he's clean and chain him to the African," Rader said. "It won't hurt to have two blacksmiths. Put the tar heel and the other man in chains as well. We may be able to trade them to the Indians as slaves or sell them to a merchant ship as crewmen."

Looking at Clairette now, he added, "Don't disturb me until mid-morning. I'll be...trying out my new cabin."

Although Clairette's expression did not change, Anne saw that the girl could not bring herself to look at Mary Read.

With their pistols still cocked and ready to fire, Wennell and several of the crew shoved Kofi, Mary, and the four intruders out of the cabin and onto the deck. While two of the men escorted the African below deck, Anne and the rest of her foul-smelling band were shoved up against the gunwale between the ship's fore and main masts.

"Here," Wennell said, kicking a deck bucket toward Asku. "Do the little man first."

Asku tossed the bucket over the side. When it was full, he pulled the bucket back up by its retrieval line and poured the brackish sound water on top of Briebras' head."

"That's good enough," Wennell said, eager to move on to Anne. "I really don't care if you have to stew in your own stink, as long as you ain't around me."

Using his pistol, he pointed to two of his men and ordered them to take Briebras below deck.

"Well, get on with it!" Wennell said to Asku. "Do the Redcoat next."

As Asku lowered the bucket again, Wennell turned his attention to Anne and Mary Read.

"I think the only way to do this right is for you to take your clothes off and have your friend here scrub you down real nice and proper with a brush and some soap. In fact, there ain't no reason why Miss Read here couldn't use a bath, too. To my way of thinking, watching you two scrub each other down would be damn fine entertainment."

"Wennell," Mary Read said, rubbing her left brow just above her eye patch. She waited for him to respond.

"Aye?"

"If you so much as touch me...or her...I'll slice off your little willy and feed it to the fish."

Wennell and the crewmen remaining on the deck burst into laughter. But when he paused to catch his breath, the dead calm of her face made him draw up short. Any doubts he might have that she would do exactly what she promised if given the chance, vanished.

"Enough!" Wennell said, waving at his men to be silent.

"Now then, Miss Read," he said, taking hold of Mary's chin with his free hand, "seeing as how I'm touching you, how do you propose doing such an awful deed as you have vowed?"

"Trust me," she managed to mutter, "one day I'll find you, and for however much longer you live, you'll do so as something less than a man."

With all eyes on Mary Read, Asku tested the weight of the full bucket unobserved. If he grasped the handle with both hands and swung as hard as he could, it would make an acceptable weapon.

"No," Wennell said. "I have a better idea. After you an' me have a little fun, I'm going to take you back to Cap'n Rader an' help him whip the location of that map out of our hide. An' when that's done, I'm going to loan you out to the crew for a few days. When they tire of taking turns with a used up, scar-faced bawd, you're goin' to have a little accident one night an' fall overboard when we are far out on the ocean. A fittin' end to a would-be piratress, wouldn't you say?"

Out of the corner of her eye, Anne saw Asku tighten his grip around the bucket's handle. If she moved fast enough, she could grab Wennell's wrist and twist in a way that would bring him to his knees. If she could snatch his pistol – and if the others attacked at the same–

"SSSKKKKKKKRRRRREEEEEEEEEE!!!"

An ear-splitting shriek shattered the night like the scream of a giant eagle swooping down from the sky. From the other side of the ship, the lower boom on the foresail swept across the deck, entering the circle of lantern light too quickly for the disoriented group of pirates and captors to react. Riding atop the boom with his arms extended from his sides like the wings of a raptor stood

Dyonis. With his feathered cape flowing wildly around him and his hawkish face reflecting the light in an eerie scowl, the pirates thought that one of hell's demons had lighted upon them.

"SSSKKKKKKRRRREEEEEEEEEE!!!" Dyonis screamed again as the boom plowed over the pirates and then the others. The sweeping spar knocked Wennell and several of his men to the deck, the impact causing one man to fire his flintlock into the air. As Anne, Mary, Asku, Gant and two of the pirates fell over the side into the water, Dyonis jumped from the boom, grabbed the lantern and flung it into the sound. The ship's exterior was plunged into darkness. When Anne and the others surfaced, they heard the ship's crew scrambling about the deck, some screaming in terror as they tried to escape the horrific, winged beast seemingly released from the bowels of hell.

Anne was first to reach the pilot boat, still secured to the anchor line. As she flung her leg over the side, one of the crewmen in the water grabbed her. With a desperate heave, she flung herself into the boat, landing on her back. As the man pulled himself up over the rail, she kicked him in the face as hard as she could. The brittle sound of facial bone shattering beneath her boot heel was followed by the sailor's shrill wail that continued even after his head slipped beneath the water.

Gant climbed aboard as Anne freed the boat from the anchor line, almost flipping them over as his body slid over the gunwale. By the time the marine had placed the oars back into the locks, Asku had scrambled into the boat over the transom. Even as he steadied himself, he began scanning the schooner for any sign of Dyonis. Although their little boat was drifting farther away from the *Revenge* and farther into the darkness, Anne saw that the second crewman who had fallen overboard had grabbed hold of the ship's anchor line. There was no sign of Mary Read, perhaps having been knocked unconscious in the fall or even drowned.

The boat made a violent roll on its port side, nearly dumping Anne into the water again. Spinning around in her seat, she saw a hand grasping the rail less than a foot away. Then another hand shot out of the darkness to grasp the rail, nearly pulling the gunwale below the waterline. Reacting on instinct, Anne and the two men leaned in the opposite direction, raising the rail a few inches. As the side of the boat rolled back toward the starboard, the motion pulled Mary Read out of the water, her face peering at Anne from over the rail.

"Well, Annie," she asked in her grating voice, "are you going to let me drown like a wharf rat, or will you help an old friend in need?"

Anne stared at her in disbelief. After all of the hell the woman had put her through, she dared to call upon their dead friendship for help?

"No," Anne said without a hint of misgiving. "You can sleep with the fishes tonight, Mary Read."

Anne drew her leg up, ready to stomp on Mary's hands.

"I know where Rader will take Little Jack!" Mary Read said.

Anne froze. That Mary Read was calling her son "Little Jack" made her sick to her stomach and mad as hell. Worse still, if she killed Mary she might lose Tye forever.

"Kill her...or don't," Gant said, still stretching his body out. "One way or the other, we've got to right this damned boat, now!"

Cursing the conundrum she could not win, Anne extended her hand toward Mary Read.

"Take it," she said, not trying to hide her disgust.

Mary Read's lips turned into a crooked little smile as she grasped Anne's hand. As Anne pulled her into the boat, Asku and Gant shifted their weight back to center to keep the boat level.

"Now, turn this thing around," Asku said. "We've got to go back an' get my brother."

"His brother?" Mary Read asked.

Instead of replying, Gant pulled hard on one oar and pushed on the other, making the boat turn within space of its own length. Then, as he started to row the boat toward the schooner, several crewmen emerged from below deck holding up lanterns. A moment later, a half-dressed Rader emerged from his cabin carrying a lamp of his own in one hand and a pistol in the other. Perched on the gunwale, illuminated by the lanterns, stood Dyonis – his wing-like arms spread wide, screeching at the men on the deck. The crew had formed a semi-circle around him, some pointing while others cowered, still not sure whether they were facing man or beast.

"Get him, you fools!" Rader screamed.

Seeing that his luck was about to run out, Dyonis whirled around to leap into the water – but his foot slipped on the gunwale. One of the quicker crewmen leaped across the space between them, grabbing Dyonis around his lower legs. Then another man grabbed the back of his cape as a third clubbed him over the head with a belaying pin. Stunned, Dyonis fell back into the throng of pirates.

"Faster," Asku shouted upon seeing his brother dragged down. At the same time, the crewman in the water clutching the anchor line began shouting to the men above and pointing toward the pilot boat.

"Quiet!" Rader said to the men who were shouting profanities as they beat Asku's brother with their fists and feet. "I said be quiet!"

At last the crew paused to look at Rader. This time, they all heard the shouts.

"Down here!" the man in the water cried out. "They're down here...coming back!"

As one, Rader and his men crowded along the gunwale, straining to see through the darkness.

"There they are!" Rader shouted. "About fifty yards straight out."

"I don't see them," the crewman standing next to him said. "Where are they?"

"Right...there..." Rader said, using his pistol to point toward the boat.

"I still don't see them, cap'n."

"There!" Rader said again, then fired his pistol at the boat.

The shot ball splashed harmlessly into the water ten feet in front of the pilot boat, but now the entire crew could spot them.

"Keep rowing," Asku yelled, refusing to leave his brother behind.

In answer, a dozen pistol shots rang out from the schooner in rapid succession followed by the shrill whistle of the pistol balls as they flew all around. Again, Gant muscled the boat into a hard turn, then began to pull on the oars with all the strength he could muster. It was too dark and they were too far away from the schooner for the pistols to be of much concern, but it would be a different matter if they broke out the long guns.

"I said go back to the ship," Asku repeated, rising from his seat. "I will throw you out of this boat if you don't turn around right now."

"Don't be a dullard, man," Gant said, maintaining his calm.

"I don't give a damn if they start to fire at us with cannon, I'll not be leaving my brother to that lot. I promised I'd bring him home, safe, and that's exactly what I intend to do."

"We won't get within fifty feet of the ship, and even if we did, there's no way we could make it to the deck alive," Gant argued.

"I don't care," Asku repeated. "I'll die before I go home without Dyonis. Now, turn around."

"We'll come back for him," Anne said. "But right now you've got to sit–"

A staccato volley of more than a dozen pistols drowned out her words. Pistol balls whizzed all about them. Asku crashed to the bottom of the boat without even a groan – the bulk of his body falling in a heap against the port-side hull. The sudden shift in weight dipped the little boat's rail beneath the surface allowing several gallons of water to flood in. Stretching his body over to starboard side as far as he could, Gant was able to bring the rail back above the waterline, but could not return to a sitting position.

"Move him to the centerline!" the marine ordered, keeping his body extended as counterbalance.

Mary Read sprang from her seat next to Anne, climbing over Gant to the reach the back of the boat. Taking pains to stay on the opposite side of the centerline to keep from adding her weight to Asku's, she passed by Gant close enough for him to see the details of her face in the dim light. Their eyes met for an instant – two disfigured warriors, one who had almost killed the other. The next moment she was in the back of the boat, pulling Asku away from the hull. Gant shifted his weight back to center accordingly.

"He's still alive!" Mary Read called out.

Sitting with her back against the transom, she pulled his unconscious body toward her as best she could and placed his head in her lap. The warm wetness of blood stuck to her fingers.

"He took a shot to the head," she said to the others. "Can't tell how bad."

While Mary had been struggling with Asku, Gant had resumed rowing the boat toward the inlet that passed between the two islands. Their only chance was to put as much distance between them and the *Revenge* as they could. As they caught the outgoing current, the orange-yellow glow of dawn was beginning to reveal itself out over the ocean. Gant used the swiftness of the ebbing tide to help them cross the mile to Ocracoke Island. In a few more minutes they would either have to put ashore or ride the current through the channel into the open ocean.

"Row to that sand flat," Anne said, pointing to an area of the inlet's beach exposed by the outgoing tide. "We'll have to take our chances on land. We'd be sitting ducks out on the ocean."

As the bow of the pilot boat skidded into the mixture of sand and mud, Anne jumped out with the bowline. Digging her heels into the muck, the stern of the boat continued to swing around, following the strong outflow of water. Dropping the oars and scrambling over the side, Gant grabbed the bowline and helped Anne pull the boat farther up on the bank.

Once the boat was secure, Gant went to the stern, and with Mary Read's help, lifted Asku over the rail and laid him on the beach next to the water. Tearing off the sleeve of her blouse, Anne soaked it in the water and began to clean his wound. As she wiped away the clotted blood from his hair he began to stir, then opened his eyes. The musket ball had only grazed him.

"Where are we?"

"On Ocracoke, just off the inlet...and we've got to get moving."

"Ocracoke? Dyonis! Where is Dyonis?"

"He's still on the *Revenge*."

"We've got to go back and get him. I gave my word."

"I know," Anne said. "And we will. But right now we have to get off this beach. It's a good bet that Rader sent some of his men after us. We need to get out of the open and find cover. It will be full light soon."

After tying the sleeve around Asku's head as a makeshift bandage, Gant helped Anne lift him to his feet. He was unsteady but able to stand on his own.

"We need to scuttle the boat," Anne said. "We'll follow the shoreline and walk in the water so as not to leave footprints. If they don't see the boat, they may think we took our chances out on the ocean."

Gant returned to the boat and picked up one of the oars. Holding it handle-side down, he drove it into the center of the hull at its weakest point. After striking the same spot several more times, one of the boards separated from the frame. Together, Anne, Mary Read, and Gant pushed the boat into the swift moving channel waters and watched it for a moment to make sure it was sinking. Asku came to stand beside them, still dazed, but able to walk on his own.

"Time to go," Anne said, seeing that the boat was lower in the water. "Stay at least ankle deep in the water. We'll follow the shoreline until it becomes light, then cross the open beach into the dunes."

Anne kept looking back over her shoulder as they walked but saw no sign of Rader's men. They sun's crown was cresting the horizon now. It was a race to put as much distance between them and the inlet as they could before crossing the beach to the dunes. Walking across the sand meant leaving footprints that could give them away. She hoped that the pirates would stick to water and keep looking for them on the ocean, but there was no certainty that they would not look on land at the same time. It depended on how badly Rader wanted to track them down.

When the sun began to clear the horizon they could wait no longer. But for once, luck was with them. Just as she was about to turn inland, Anne spotted footprints coming from the dunes to the water's edge and back again, made not just by one person, but by dozens. This was where the villagers accessed the beach to fish and to collect debris from shipwrecks. As long as the four fugitives traveled over the same ground, their footprints would be indistinguishable from all the others.

"This way," Anne said, pointing toward a break between the dunes where all the footprints converged.

Anne quickened her pace so much the others had to hurry to catch up to her. As she passed between two dunes forming the passageway inland, a large, gray-bearded man wearing a broad-brimmed black hat and long coat emerged from the shadows. Stopping in the middle of the path, he placed his fists on his hips, blocking her way. She reached for the hilt of her sword but it was gone. She had forgotten that Rader's men had taken their weapons. She was defenseless.

"I've been waiting for you," he said.

"Why would you be waiting for us?" Anne challenged, looking around to see if there were others with him. It seemed impossible that Rader's men could have traveled to this part of the island so quickly. Perhaps the foppish captain had somehow signaled crewmen in the village to look for them on the beach.

"Because you need me help," the man said. "Now, you can all shilly-shally here if you want, but I think it best you come with me...while you still can."

Anne wasn't sure whether the last comment was a warning or a threat, but she could see that he was a dangerous man. He stood well over six-feet tall and his chest was as big as a firkin. His fists, still planted on his hips, were the size of four-pound cannonballs, and his nose looked to be broken in at least two different places.

"And what if we don't want to come with you?" Gant asked.

Asku came to stand next to them, but Anne doubted that he was recovered enough to be much help should they have to fight their way past the big man.

"Then you can take your chances on the beach or you can rot in hell for all I care," the man said. "I'm offering you refuge...one brethren to another. A professional courtesy, you might say. But I ain't gonna force you to take it. It's up to you. Now, I'm taking my leave. You can follow me or not."

With that, he turned and began walking along the sandy path between the dunes toward the island's interior.

"I vote we follow him," Mary Read said as she moved past the others, not waiting to see if they would follow.

Anne looked at Asku and Gant, still not sure if it was the smart thing to do.

"Judging by the bulges beneath his coat, I'd say he has at least four pistols on his person," Gant said. "If he wanted us dead, we'd be dead."

Having made his decision, he fell in behind Mary.

"He did say he's a pirate," Asku pointed out. "He must be a screamer from the old days."

Anne knew that after Maynard beheaded Edward Teach, he had rounded up the surviving crewmen and tried them in Charles Town where they were hanged. But everyone living in the area knew that the pirates who had battled Maynard on the ocean made up only about half the lot that followed Blackbeard. At least a hundred more were scattered about Ocracoke and Portsmouth villages, where they had been waiting to commandeer more ships and make them part of Teach's fleet.

Anne almost shuddered at the thought. The man who had come to lead them away from the beach, undoubtedly, was one of Blackbeard's forgotten crew.

# CHAPTER NINETEEN

HAVING VEERED OFF THE MAIN PATH, the route they followed wound its way through a maze of   sea oats, scrub pines, and farther inland, scatterings of live oaks and myrtle bushes.   Anne's misgivings and anger increased with each step they took.

The source of her misgivings was the huge man leading their column. There was no doubt that he was of the brethren, as he had claimed, so it made little sense that he had come to the aid of strangers. If he was helping them, it wasn't out of kindness – it was because he wanted something. She had known his kind all of her life, and she knew that he would expect something in return for any favors he granted.

Even the roundabout trek they were taking was cause for concern. It was obvious that the graybeard's intent was to avoid something. Not as clear was whether he was trying to keep other people from seeing them, or if he was trying to keep them from knowing where they were going.

The source of her anger was the raven-haired piratress and former bawd who had once been her friend. Not only had she stolen her son and put him in danger of his life, she had clothed him in calico and had turned him into a dwarf-sized duplicate of his father. But it wasn't the clothes by themselves that made Anne angry. It was the realization that, if Mary Read was trying to turn Tye into a young Calico Jack, it meant that she had told him about his father and the things he had done. It had been Anne's desire to keep the details of those dark days as vague as possible. Even after shedding her persona as Peg, she had decided that Tye would keep the name, Brennan. Having a notorious criminal's name was a burden no young man should have to endure.

*Mary Read had no doubt ruined that too, stealing away his innocence as surely as she had stolen him away from me. Yet, there she is, following the graybeard as though she were sauntering around the lawn of an English castle.*

The path ended in a clearing behind a large house facing the sound – they had traversed the breadth of the island. On the right side of the open area, about halfway between them and the house, was a large barn. Leading them to the barn instead of the house, the graybeard opened one of its double doors and hurried them inside.

"Stay inside here. The hay is fresh and there be no horses here, only two goats and a cow. I'll be back in awhile."

"Wait," Anne said as he turned to leave. "Why are we here? Why are you helping us?"

The grizzled Ocracoker paused before shutting the door. He studied Anne for a minute as if sizing her up. As he gave Mary Read the same measured look, it struck Anne that he was comparing the two women he saw with the stories about them that had grown over the years.

*But...how could he know who we really are?* she wondered.

"You'll be safe as long as no one knows you're here. I give you me word. Now, rest your bones."

With that, he closed the door and slid a board into place to lock them in.

"What the hell?" Asku exclaimed, rushing to the doors. "We're locked in!"

"Take it easy," Gant said. "It wouldn't take two minutes to work that crossbar out of joint. He probably just wants to make sure the doors stay closed should anyone happen by."

"That may be," Anne said, "but it doesn't explain why he's helping us."

"I think the expression, 'don't look a gift horse in the mouth,' works pretty good here," Mary Read said as she moved about the barn looking for a good place to lie down.

"We're wasting time," Asku said as he rubbed the bandage covering the wound on his head. "They have my brother and I won't abandon him."

"They also have Tye...and Briebras and Kofi," Anne snapped. "But we need a plan and we need help. There are fifty of them and they are sitting in the middle of the sound. Sneaking up on them will be impossible, now."

"Sixty-seven," Mary Read said from the other end of the bay. She was peering into the next to last stall on the left side of the barn. Next to it was the corner stall and the two goats the graybeard had mentioned. The cow was in the corner stall on the opposite side of the barn. "Between the *Revenge* and the *Hazard*, there are sixty-seven men and more being recruited. A damn good start, I'd say."

Having finished her inspection, she began turning to face the others. As she did, Gant's hand closed around her neck and he slammed her against the wood post that formed the stall's opening.

"There were forty-five souls on the *Hazard*," Gant said, his face almost touching hers. He held a pitchfork under her chin while keeping her jammed against the beam with his other hand. "I would have been the forty-sixth if your shot had been true. You are a pirate and a murderer who deserves to hang for what you did to my mates. But I'm thinking that hanging will be too long coming. Give me one good reason why I shouldn't pin you to the wall like an insect right now?"

Mary Read looked him in the eyes without flinching and smiled. In a slow deliberate motion, she grasped one of the pitchfork's tines and pushed the deadly tool down away from her neck.

"If you did that, you wouldn't be able to thank me properly," she said.

"Thank you? Thank you for what?"

"For saving your life, of course. You know better than anyone that I don't miss at point-blank range."

"Maybe so, but you damn near burned half my face off, firing that thing so close to my head. And what about the sharks?"

"Would you have preferred I let Rader blow your craggy-face to bits?" she asked as she reached behind his head to pull him closer.

"Well...you do have a point," he admitted. Instead of resisting her embrace, the marine pulled her hard against his body and kissed her full on the mouth. It wasn't a kiss of desire or passion. It was the partial reclamation on a marker. When he felt her body start to relax, he backed off a few inches to stare into her good eye again, not yet ready to let the matter rest. "Still, they were good men. Somebody will have to pay."

"I won't apologize for killing the ones who died during the initial row," she said as though they were bartering trade goods. "As for the men who were slaughtered after that, that was Rader's doing. You can make him pay, if I don't kill him first."

She paused, and then added with a wry smile, "If you feel like you're still owed something after that, maybe we can negotiate some sort of trade."

"Damn it!" Anne said. "I knew it. I knew the moment he opened his mouth on the beach there was more to him than he was saying. Something about him just didn't sit right."

Asku kept looking back and forth, from Anne to Mary Read, trying to understand.

"Are they...lovers?" he asked.

"Lovers?" Mary Read said. "Once upon a time, in Saint-Domingue, we were lovers. But now we're mostly just business partners. Mostly."

"What business would that be?" Anne asked, her anger growing. "The business of killing and slaughtering?"

"It wasn't supposed to be that way!" Mary Read said. "I wanted to take the crewmen who survived the initial sweep of the deck alive. Convince as many as possible to swear allegiance to ship and crew. Any that refused would have been put on an island north of here."

"So, what happened?" Anne asked, unconvinced.

"Rader. He had the crew so worked up, that by the time I realized a slaughter was on, it was too late. Their blood lust had to be sated."

"How does he fit in?" Anne asked, nodding at Gant.

"Sam was going to keep me informed as to the *Hazard*'s general whereabouts. That didn't work out so well. The *Hazard* came this way before we were ready. I nearly peed my breeches when we spotted her yesterday. But what a victory it was! *Rackham's Revenge* is a beauty, isn't she?"

The comment struck Anne as so absurd, she was unable to speak.

"Everything I told you on the beach was true," Gant said, taking up the story. "It's strange to say, but if it hadn't been for the knipple shot knocking that sailor into me, I would have been killed early on. By the time the pirates found me and brought me to, I was the only one left alive. When they stood me up in front of Rader's ugly, split-nosed face, I was sure my luck had run its path. And then Mary appeared, in all her handsome glory...to sear half my face off and to kick my arse overboard into a school of sharks."

"If I had stopped Rader, he would have figured out that he is not...or was not...the partner he thought he was. If he had found out that you knew more about my plans than he did, both our lives would have been on a short fuse."

"Your life IS on a short fuse," Anne said, planting herself in front of her former friend. Gant stepped back, giving the two women room to face off. "The reason you're still alive is because of Tye. Make no mistake, Mary Read, you get to live only as long as I know my son is alive and unharmed...and as long as I still believe you can take me to him. At any time should one of those conditions no longer be true, you will no longer take breath."

"You're threatening me?" Mary lashed back, matching Anne's vitriol with her own. "You're angry because a friend betrayed you and left you with nothing but a desperate hope that things would be all right? How do you think I felt, watching you and your father walk out of that cell in Spanish Town? How do you think I felt, sitting there alone, waiting for you, day after day, hoping you'd come back for me? You promised. YOU PROMISED you would come back. And I believed you. Even after that greasy hog of a night watchman told me that you and your father had sailed away without so much as a goodbye, I believed you. I told myself that it had to be a ruse...a trick you had created to make Governor Lawes believe you had left but were going to double back and free me. You lied to me, Anne Bonny, and you betrayed me. I could steal a hundred sons away from you and it wouldn't come close to repaying me for what you did!"

The hate and bitterness lacing Mary Read's words had no effect on Anne. The two women were as powder kegs on the verge of exploding.

"Wait!" Asku said, holding his hand up to signal for quiet. "I hear something." Returning to the double doors, he peered through the cracks for a moment. "Someone's coming!"

As Asku backed up to where the others were standing, the barn doors swung open with a whoosh. The graybeard walked to the center of the bay with four of the roughest-looking brigands Anne had ever seen. Each of them was on the cusp of middle-age, only slightly younger than the graybeard who led them.

"Peppers?" Mary Read said, recognizing the sailmaker who had tailored Tye's suit. "What are you..."

Her question trailed off with the sudden understanding that it was he who had told the graybeard about them.

"So, what's your game?" she asked, turning her attention back to the graybeard. "You gave your word that you would do no harm to us."

"And none will," he said, "as long as we can come to an agreement."

"What kind of an agreement," Anne asked before Mary Read had the chance. She didn't like the idea that Mary knew more about what was going on than she did.

"We help you get your ship back as long as we get the map," the graybeard said.

"What!" Anne said. "You're after her stupid map? What is this place, the spawning ground for village idiots? Honest to God, Mary Read, if harm has come to Tye all because of your damned, stupid map...I swear by St. Michael's bells, I will–"

"Silence!" the graybeard said. "Now. I don't know exactly where it be, but I'm dead sure that it's on your ship and not your person. You didn't have time to collect it from its hiding place and you didn't come all this way and get this close to the treasure to have not brought it with you on the ship."

"What is this map everyone keeps talking about?" Asku nearly shouted. "What treasure?"

"The map to Blackbeard's buried treasure, of course," Anne said, rolling her eyes. "Mary has it, they want it, and all of them actually believe it's real."

"Trust me, it's real," the graybeard said. "An' I promise you, it shows exactly where the treasure be buried, or me name isn't William Scarlette."

"William Scarlette?" Anne laughed. "That's rich. Will Scarlette was killed by Lieutenant Maynard along with Blackbeard. You're a fraud!"

Leaning closer to Mary Read, Gant asked, "Who the hell is Will Scarlette?"

"Bloody Bill Scarlette," she said. "Him and Israel Hands were Teach's lieutenants."

The graybeard came closer to Anne, taking a long look down the length of her body and up again, stopping his gaze at her breasts. Anne felt her flesh draw tight as though trying to shrink away from his leering stare.

"Make no mistake," he said before raising his eyes to meet hers. "I'm as real as those kettledrums you have stuffed in your shirt, an' I'm just as alive as Mary Read an' Anne Bonny be."

Asku took a step forward but stopped short as all four of the men behind the graybeard pointed their pistols at him.

"Settle down, pup," Scarlette said. "I ain't interested in your woman. "It's the map I want."

"This is insane," Anne said. Already exasperated, the comment about being Asku's woman was beginning to stoke her rage. "There are dozens of such maps circulating between the mariners who travel these waters. I've seen three of them myself. What makes you think this one happens to be real?"

The graybeard gave Anne's breasts a final look of appreciation and then stepped back so that they could all see his face.

"Because, I took it from Anders Pellicane...the poor bastard what made it for Teach...after I put a pistol ball in his heart."

"What," Anne said, not sure what to believe at this point. "Why did you kill him?"

"That was my job, that's all. When Maynard showed up in the *Ranger* and her sister sloop *Jane*, Teach an' most of the rest of us were ashore. Just after dark, Teach had Pellicane an' two other men take a small boat out. With them, they took every man's share of booty from the past year and buried it. When they were done, Pellicane killed the other men and made a map so Teach would know where to find it after the battle with Maynard."

The graybeard paused for a moment to make sure they were following his story. Grabbing an empty crate, he stood it on end and sat down. As he did, his coat spread open to reveal the pistols Gant had spotted earlier. His men remained standing, forming a half-circle behind him.

"Teach told Pellicane to make the map and give it to me as insurance, you know, in case Pellicane got killed. That way, one of us was bound to survive, an' either I could lead the survivors back to the chest by followin' the map, or Pellicane could take them there by memory. But Teach was as mean as he was greedy. He didn't want nobody knowing where the treasure be excepting him. So he told me to kill Pellicane once I had the map, and for me not to look at it lest I wanted to forfeit my own life."

"And how is it that you came to lose it?" Anne asked, trying to find a hole in his story.

"Israel Hands! The conniving, slimy eel hit me over me head when I wasn't lookin' an' took it from me. Then him an' a handful of other cowards fled, leaving me for dead. After Maynard killed Teach, Hands was captured along with the others hiding out in Bath. They let the traitorous bastard go free after he witnessed against his mates at the trial in Williamsburg."

"Are you saying that Israel Hands had the map on his person when he got captured in Bath and was able to keep it hidden the whole time he was awaiting trial...and nobody discovered he had it?"

Scarlette gave her a foul look.

"No, I'm sayin' that he hid it here afore fleeing to Bath. We know he came back to Ocracoke after the trial, but he only had time to get the map. We ran him off afore he had time to look for the treasure."

"How do you know that?" Anne asked. There was enough detail in his story that she was beginning to believe there might be something to it.

"Because, if he had lingered two minutes longer than he did, me an' me mates would have snared the scurvy-riddled bag of pus and peeled off his skin. We followed him for awhile, like a shiver of tiger sharks after a whale calf, but lost him in Bermuda. I don't know where he went after that, but I know for certain that he never got a chance to come back to Ocracoke. We was watchin' an' waitin'.'"

"And what makes you so sure I came in possession of the map?" Mary Read asked.

Scarlette gave her a burning stare, then smiled

"Because of me spies, like Sailmaker Peppers here. Loyal men of the brethren workin' with me to recover their due. You see, I survived bein' captured because I didn't come to until after the battle. I never made it back to the *Adventure*. The crews from Teach's other ships had no taste for pirating after the affair, what with half of them having seen Blackbeard's head dangling from Maynard's bowsprit. Most of them eventually ended up here or across the channel in Portsmouth because of the treasure, figurin' it would turn up some day."

"Your mistake was lettin' Rader in on the secret," he continued. "The man may be quick with a blade, but he's a regular talkin' magpie when he's been drinkin'...an' he did a lot of that in Bath whilst waitin' for *Rackham's Revenge* to be finished. Yeah, we know you've got the map what Israel Hands stole from me. An' we intend to get it back, one way or another."

"Now," he said, rising from his seat, "I'm tired of talkin'. Do we have a deal or not? your map for our help. All you have to do is say 'yes' an' drink a toast from Blackbeard's cup to seal the deal. After that, we can get to the business of killin' your man Rader and retrieving our properties."

Mary Read stared back at the graybeard but gave no sign that she was going to agree. The longer the silence lingered, the more the tension in the room grew. Scarlette's men fidgeted with the hammers of their pistols while Asku and Gant took quick glances about the bay for potential weapons.

"Tell him it's a deal!" Anne demanded, unable to fathom why Mary was hesitating. "You told me yourself you have the map. I don't care if it's real or not. If we get the *Revenge* back, we get Tye back. Tell him you'll show him where the damn map is."

"What's it gonna' be?" Scarlette demanded, his patience run out.

Mary Read looked at Anne and back at Scarlette, still struggling to make a decision.

"GOD DAMN IT, MARY!" Anne screamed, grabbing the woman by the front of her blouse. "Tell him it's a deal or I'll kill you myself, right now, with my bare hands."

Mary looked at Anne, her face pale and blank. Long seconds ticked by before she answered in a stilted, grating voice that could barely be heard.

"...deal..."

Everyone in the room relaxed a little, except for Anne, who continued to stare at Mary in disbelief. The raven-haired piratress was shaken, a state in which Anne had never before seen her. It may have been years since they had spent time together, and their once-strong bond had dissolved like zinc in acid, but she could still read her former friend like a sea chart. At first, she had assumed it was a reluctance to give up the map and the treasure it promised. But now she saw it wasn't greed that had caused her former friend to balk, it was something much more ominous. Bewilderment having replaced her anger, she released her grip from Mary's blouse.

"You made a wise decision," Scarlette said with a wave of his arm. "But it ain't a deal until we drink the toast." As he continued to talk, two men entered the barn carrying buckets of fresh water and a basket of food. After placing them in the middle of the bay, the men left, followed by Peppers and the rest of the crew.

"Here's some victuals to hold you over," Scarlette said as he started to follow. "Someone will come to fetch you after dark. Just remember, until then...until we drink...our partnership ain't binding. If you try to leave, I'll consider it a breach of trust and one of you will forfeit your life."

After the door closed and they heard the crossbar slide into place, Mary Read shambled to the crate Scarlette had used as a chair and plopped down on it, weak and drained. Her skin was ashen. Asku and Gant now began to see what Anne already knew – Mary Read was horror struck.

"What is it?" Anne asked, hoping to find a clue by looking into Mary's eye. "What is it you know that we don't?"

Mary Read looked up at Anne, her face clouded in turmoil.

"It's...it's the devil's bidding," she said. Her words came out thick and slow.

"What?" Anne asked. Seeing the unflappable Mary Read nearly paralyzed by fear made her skin tingle with dread. "What are you talking about?"

"That man. Don't you know who he is?

Anne started to answer that she didn't, but Mary cut her off.

"We have to leave! Now!"

"What the hell?" Gant said in a hushed voice. "Get a hold of yourself, woman. You're not making any sense."

Instead of bringing calm, Gant's words only agitated her more.

"You don't understand," she said, emphasizing each word. "You don't know about the cup."

"No," Anne said. "I don't. Tell me."

"Of course, you don't know," she said, taking a deep breath. "You haven't been living with pirates and all manner of outlaws like I have these past years. The cup Bloody Bill Scarlette said we must drink from...it is reputed to be of evil origins. Some say that if you drink from it and intend treachery to the brethren, you will go insane. Others say that the concoction you drink from it conjures up the Blackbeard's ghost and that it will it take over your body if you ever betray the brethren. Others tell tales of men dropping dead just from taking one little sip, simply because they were weak of constitution."

As she went on, Anne began to remember how talk of ghosts, goblins and witches had been topics that made Mary Read uncomfortable.

"I don't understand," Anne said. "I've seen you face down a dozen men without batting an eye. I've seen you lead boarding parties over the gunwale and into a hail of musket fire as though you were taking a stroll by the lake. I've seen you shake hands with the Reaper just so you could spit in his face. But until this day, I've never seen you show fear. I don't believe that a woman who can do all that could be so frightened by talk of ghosts and goblins."

"Maybe that's because you've never actually seen one," Mary replied, her voice all at once clear and strong. "It's true. I'm not ashamed to admit it. I've seen a ghost. The Hollow, I call it, because it's never quite really there. It appeared in our cell several times after you left. The damn spirit followed me to Saint-Domingue and it followed me here. I saw it in my cabin just a few days ago. So DO NOT DOUBT ME when I tell you that ghosts are real."

Silence settled over the barn as they each considered the veracity of Mary Read's story and the unholy contract that they were about to enter into. Science had brought much enlightenment during the past century, but the fears associated with the supernatural were real and no farther away than the darkest corner of a room or an unfamiliar bump in the night. If Mary Read said she could see ghosts, there was no reason to doubt her.

"This cup you speak of, from where did it come?" Asku asked.

A tortured smile spread across Mary Read's face, savoring the answer before sharing it with the others.

"I don't know for certain. The pirates that speak of it, but have never seen it, say that it belonged to Blackbeard and that it was forged in hell. The ones who have seen it have been sworn to secrecy and won't say. They just look at each other in a knowing way, as if to say, 'You wouldn't believe me even if I told you.' All I know with certainty is that no matter how drunk they get, or how much money they're offered, they won't betray their oath."

# CHAPTER TWENTY

TYE HAD BEEN AWAKENED by the unnerving sounds of men being led below deck and of chains rattling as they were being shackled. It was then that he discovered his door had been locked from the outside. His status had changed from that of passenger to prisoner. The series of screeches, shouts, and gunfire above deck that followed had been even more unsettling. When the commotion stopped and the clatter of footsteps came toward his room, he had huddled down against the back wall and waited.

A moment later the door had opened and the room was flooded with a rush of light from several lanterns, blinding him. After dropping a body on the floor the door had been slammed shut, throwing the compartment into darkness again. During the flash of illumination, Tye had only been able to see that the body was that of a man with a sharp, hooked nose and a bald head.

Now, still hunkered down against the wall, he heard the man moan and realized that he wasn't dead, just unconscious. Crawling over to him, he felt about until he touched the man's head and discovered that something warm and sticky seemed to be covering his entire face. He was bleeding. More feeling about revealed that the man wasn't really bald but was wearing some sort of hood. Fearing that the head covering might be hiding a wound, he pulled it back. Blood began gushing out over his hands so profusely, even in the darkness Tye could tell that he would quickly bleed out if something wasn't done.

Moving as fast he could, Tye found his canteen and a cloth and hurried back to the injured man. Removing his new coat, he rolled it up and placed it under the man's head. Next, he dampened the cloth, found the wound, and pressed the cloth against it.

He didn't know much about treating injuries, but he knew that applying pressure would clot the wound and stop the flow of blood. Making himself as comfortable as possible, he sat next to the man and held the bandage in place, hoping that the aid he was giving would work.

Tye awakened with the jolt of surprise that comes with the realization that sleep had come unbidden. Remembering the hooded man, he realized that his hand no longer rested on his forehead. A quick feel about the area revealed that the man was no longer within arm's reach. Stilling his breath, he ceased all movement and listened.

There! Against the back wall. He made out the faint sound of someone taking irregular gasps of air, the way a person trying to hide would do.

"Are you all right?" Tye asked.

"Are you a pirate?" the stranger countered. Though his voice was that of a man, his tone was like that of a child's.

"No. I'm not. I was kidnapped from my home in Bath and have been aboard this ship for a week now."

"So...you're a kid? I mean, you'd have to be a kid to be kidnapped, right?"

Tye considered the question for a moment.

"Yes, I am," he answered. Trusting his instincts, he continued. "Are you a man?"

"Yes. I am Birdman."

"A bird man? I've never met a bird man, before. Are there others like you?"

"No. I'm not 'a' bird man. I am BIRDMAN." Then, with a touch of sadness, "I am the only one...and I am no more."

"No more? What do you mean?"

"The pirates...they plucked me. I no longer have my beautiful feathers. Whoever heard of a bird without feathers?"

"You have...I mean, had...feathers?"

"Yes. Beautiful feathers I borrowed from my friends, the parrots."

"How do you borrow feathers?" Tye asked. The more they talked, the more he understood that the man was of a simple nature.

"Oh, I have to borrow them. I could never keep them. That would be stealing. I pick up the feathers they leave on the ground and keep them on my cape. The parrots can have them back any time they ask."

"I see. You truly are a man of the birds. Perhaps when we get out of here we can find you some new feathers and make you Birdman again."

"Really?" the newcomer asked, shuffling across the floor until he was next to Tye. "Thank you. You're not a pirate. You're too nice."

"You're welcome," Tye said, feeling for the man's arm. "Here, shake my hand. My name is Tye Brennan."

"Oh," he sighed. "My name is Dyonis Dare. I thought you might be the boy they took from that pretty robin, Anne Bonny. His name is Tye, too."

"What? Are you saying mother is using her real name?"

"I don't understand," Dyonis said.

"It's...complicated. It's sort of like when a woman gets married and her last name changes. But this is different. Just...trust me. The woman you speak of...Anne Bonny...she's my mother."

"All right," Dyonis said, though it was obvious he still didn't understand.

"Tell me, when did you last see my mother...Anne Bonny?"

"Three hours and fifteen minutes ago, as she was falling over the side of the ship."

"She was here! On this ship! Why did she fall overboard?"

"I knocked her off when I rode the boom across the..."

"You knocked her overboard! Why? Was she hurt?

"It was an accident," Dyonis said. "I didn't mean to. The men pirates had her and the lady pirate and they were going to hurt them."

"Wait. Why were they going to hurt Mary Read? Did they mutiny?"

"I don't know what mootinee means, but I think the other pirates decided that they did not like her anymore."

"Where is she now?"

Dyonis hesitated, scared that his answer would rouse the boy's alarm again.

"She fell overboard, too, with Anne Bon- Your mother. But they were both all right the last time I saw them. They were in a small boat heading to shore with the other two."

"What other two?"

"The major man and my brother, Asku."

"Of course," Tye said, beginning to understand. "Asku is your brother. I forgot that his last name is Dare, too. But who is this major you speak of?"

"He is the military man that Mary Read shot, but didn't. The sharks would have eaten him had it not been for Asku. I found boots for him to wear."

Tye continued asking his new friend questions until he knew the whole story, from how his mother had been bitten by a snake up until the moment Dyonis saw them escaping into the darkness.

"After they caught me, they hit me, kicked me and pulled my feathers off. Then they threw me down here with you. I don't like it here. It's too dark."

"I'm sorry," Tye said. "I have a Betty lamp, but no way to light it."

"I have a flint," Dyonis said, reaching into a pocket sewn inside his cape.

A few minutes later, Tye looked at the man for the first time by the light of the small oil lamp and was struck by how much he did, indeed, resemble a bird. Not one that sported a beautiful plumage, but more like an overly large fledgling, newly hatched from its egg. Except for a few broken and scragglylooking feathers, his cape had been picked clean.

"I wonder what time it is?" Tye asked, hoping that his stare had not lingered too long.

"It's eight thirty-seven a.m.," Dyonis replied. "The a.m. comes from Latin. It means ante meridiem, which means before midday."

"How do you do that?"

"Do what?

"How do you keep track of time like you do?"

"Oh...I have a carriage watch. That is to say...I had a carriage watch. One of the pirates took it from me. It was such a beautiful watch."

"So how do you know what time it is now?"

"It just stays in my head, like the months of the year, the days of the week, when the moon is full and when the tides are high and low. When to reap and when to sow. I learned how long it takes for a minute to pass, and how long it takes for an hour to pass by watching the watch. I said 'watching the watch.' That's funny. But it slows down after awhile. If you don't wind it up every hour, it falls behind. Every morning when I wake up, I have to wind it up and reset it."

Tye was beginning to understand that Dyonis was a lot like his friend Will Gibbs, only more so. He wondered at how Dyonis did not know what "mutiny" meant, but understood that "a.m." came from a Latin term and even understood its application. He also suspected that, like Will, some people feared him because he was so different. Perhaps it was this deep-rooted aversion of the unusual that had kept the pirates from killing Dyonis outright. The difference between that which was unnatural and that which was supernatural was sometimes hard to distinguish. Sailors, being the superstitious lot that they were, had spared Asku's brother because they feared what he might be.

The sound of someone sliding the bolt on the door interrupted his thoughts. A moment later it swung open with a crash and several men rushed in. Without giving reason or cause, one man bodily carried Tye while two others dragged Dyonis along behind. As they traversed the open deck, Tye saw that the ship was under light sail, following the channel that flowed on the sound side of an island, probably Portsmouth Island.

Once inside the captain's cabin, Tye and Dyonis were forced to stand in front of the chart table while their guards fell back to block the doorway. On the opposite side of the table stood Blyth Rader and another crewman Tye recognized as Curlee Leathers. Leather's eyes were two opaque orbs of black floating in sinewy, beast-like sockets. Though they seemed to lack the spark of life, they weren't like a dead man's eyes. It was as though they sucked light out of the air, adding sinister intent to his already freakish form. Across the room, Clairette huddled on the bed with her back pressed against the hull, trying to make herself inconspicuous.

With his hands locked behind his back, Rader looked out of the port-side transom windows, watching the sand and brush of the barrier island pass by as the ship followed the flow of the channel. Curlee Leathers, a thick-boned, dark-skinned, brute of a fellow, stared at Tye and Dyonis as though he were a minion of the devil.

"Clairette," Rader called without looking toward her. The tavern girl cringed at the sound of his voice. "Go find a pot to wash or some clothes to scrub."

Clairette slid off the bed, shirking as she started to the door. Though she tried to hide her face as she passed by, Tye saw that her right eye was shiny-black and her lips were puffy and bruised. Their gaze met only for a moment, but Tye saw shame and pleading in her eyes.

"Tell me Master Brennan," Rader said when she was gone from the room, "or should I say...Master Rackham? What should I do with you and this...fellow...who fancies himself to be some kind of bird?"

Without Mary Read to protect him, Tye knew that he was in a very bad position. Rader still hated his mother for what she had done to him. How could he not? Every time he looked into a mirror or pool of water, the reflection that looked back at him was that of a once handsome man whose nose now looked like an overripe, scuppernong grape stomped into a plank floor. If he were not careful, the hate Rader harbored for his mother was one wrong comment away from being unleashed upon him.

"I have skills, Captain Rader. Navigation skills. I can help you find your way across the open sea, and I can help you avoid seafaring authorities, whether they be English, Spanish or French."

Rader stiffened but continued to look out the window. Having already made up his mind to hold the boy to lure in his mother, the question had been rhetorical. It had not occurred to him that the boy had any actual value beyond serving as bait.

"Ah...that's right. I had forgotten that Mary Read taught you how to use the octant and the celestial tables. But tell me...why would you do that? Why would you help me, even if I thought you could navigate properly?"

"For a trade."

"A trade?" Rader mocked, turning away from the window to face them. "What do you propose to trade?"

"I will be your navigator in exchange for the safety of myself and my new friend. We will receive the same rations as the rest of the crew. And...we each get a half-share of any plunder the *Revenge* takes."

He threw the last part in as an afterthought, hoping bravado would show that he should be taken seriously. Mary Read had been the only other person on *Rackham's Revenge* who understood the science and mathematics of navigation. Without a navigator, Rader would be forced to follow the shoreline or attempt to dead reckon his way across open waters. Both practices were filled with peril. Following the shore in this area ran the risk of running aground on shoals created by the confluence of currents off the capes. Dead reckoning was a term that described both the "art" of sailing by compass, speed, and wild guesses – and the likely outcome of using the method.

Rader stared at the boy with a caustic mix of disbelief, rage and grudging respect then began to chuckle.

"Well, I'll give you this, boy. If you navigate half as well as you negotiate, you'll make a damn fine navigator. You're already a pirate. Must be in your blood."

"All right, then" he continued, "I accept your trade. But only for as long you demonstrate actual skills to navigate. If you run us aground or get us lost...I'll kill you...your mother be damned. And the deal only applies to you, not the...bird."

"No. It's both of us or neither," Tye said. "I need him."

"For what?" Rader said in disbelief.

"My home," Dyonis said, speaking for the first time. Everyone in the room looked at him, trying to understand.

"What about your home?" Rader asked, angry at having been interrupted.

"That's Cedar Island," Dyonis said, pointing through the transom window on the starboard side of the cabin. Until now, no one had noticed that the ship was approaching the point where Portsmouth Island and the sound-side land mass of Cedar Island closed-in to be within two miles of each other. "My home is on the other side of the island where I live with my brother, Asku."

"Don't!" Tye warned, realizing too late that Dyonis did not know about the bad blood between his brother and Rader.

"Indeed," Rader replied, raising an eyebrow. Until now, he had not known that it was Asku's brother – this crazy bird man standing before him – who was responsible for freeing the three people in the world he most hated. "Would you like to sail by? Say hello to a few friends, perhaps."

"Oh, yes! Please. Mum would be surprised!"

"Master Leathers, would you be a good fellow? Go ask the helmsman to change course and take us to the other side of this island, please."

"Aye, cap'n. It would be me pleasure."

Tye winced at the conspiratorial tone the two men were using. Their forced politeness veiled dark intent.

"I don't know how this bird-thing imbecile could possibly be of help to you," Rader said, as his first mate left the room. "But know this. Because of him, I lost Mary Read. Mary Read is the only person who knows where Teach's treasure map is. She didn't tell Clairette, of that I'm sure. And I've already gone over every inch of this cabin looking for it, but it's not here."

He paused for a moment to pull out one of the telescopes stored in the chart rack. Extending its tube to full length, he pointed it toward Cedar Island and peered through its eyepiece. When he saw that its lens was cracked, he closed it with a snap and cursed.

"You went over every inch of this ship, didn't you," he said, still holding the collapsed long glass. "Did you find it?"

Tye shook his head but was unable to tear his eyes away from the glass.

"Baaah! Of course you didn't. She wouldn't have sent you on a search that would have revealed the location of her precious map. I'm beginning to believe that it's not hidden anywhere on this boat."

He returned the broken long glass to its storage place and picked up the newer one. Opening it, he began surveying Cedar Island's shoreline.

"It makes no matter. Bos'n Wennell will find her and bring her to me. She'll tell me where it is eventually, and I'll have a fine time making her. In the meantime, your fool friend here is responsible. Both he and his tar heel brother are due retribution. But, if you insist that he is necessary to aid you in your navigations, then I'm afraid I must find another way to satiate my vengeance...at least for awhile."

Lowering the telescope, he took a quick glance out of the port-side windows then looked back at Cedar Island.

"Ah... I see the helmsman is changing course. Let's go topside, shall we?"

A few minutes later, they were all standing on deck as the ship dropped anchor at the mouth of the bay leading to the Dare's home. Even with its shallow draft, the *Revenge* drew too much water to enter this cove.

"That's it!" Dyonis said, pointing to his home, a small shack nestled in the trees a half-mile away. Other than a wisp of smoke curling out of the chimney, there were no signs of life.

"Master Leathers," Rader called. "I believe the range of our four-pounders was said to be in excess of four-thousand yards. That would put the Dare cabin well within our range, would it not?"

"That it would, cap'n."

"Well then, I think this is an excellent opportunity to see whether they live up to their billing. I'll give you a pint of rum if you can hit it on the first shot...a half pint if you hit it with the second."

"No!" Tye cried out. "Don't do it!"

Dyonis watched the gun crew with detached curiosity, unable to comprehend what the result of their practiced movements was about to yield.

"Leathers was our master gunner before he became my first mate," Rader continued, ignoring Tye's plea. "He's quite good."

"But, there might be someone inside," Tye said.

"Ready Master Leathers?"

"Aye!"

"At your ready."

"Fire!" Leathers yelled.

The cannon roared and everyone on deck looked toward the cabin, waiting...waiting... waiting... Instead of hitting the Dare home, the four-pound ball swooshed a few feet over its roof, plopping into the soft, island soil having caused no damage.

"Awww... So close, Mister Leathers. Try again!"

"Nooooooooo!" Dyonis screamed, now able to understand the threat he had brought to his home. He rushed toward Leathers, but one of the gun's crewmen jabbed him in the gut with the butt end of a bore swab, doubling him over. As he tried to regain his air, another crewman hit him over the head with a belaying pin.

"Please," Tye begged. "He's an innocent and was only trying to protect his brother. He did not act with malice toward you."

"And what about his brother?" Rader snarled, staring down at the boy.

Tye tried to look Rader in the eyes, but his gaze could not focus beyond the fiend's mutilated snout. The disgusting thing loomed between them, an impregnable rampant, repelling any logical argument that Tye could construct.

"Ready!" Leathers said.

"On your mark, Master Leathers."

"Fire!"

Again, the men on deck followed the ball as it flew through the air, watching...waiting. A moment later they saw the small structure implode from the force of the solid iron ball smashing through its front wall. By the time the sounds of the initial impact traveled back across the water to their ears, the outer walls of the building were falling in on each other, followed by the roof.

The men on deck cheered while Leather's gun crew slapped each other on the back. Having regained his senses, Dyonis used the gunwale to pull himself up and peer at the rubble that had once been his home.

"Mum..."

# CHAPTER TWENTY-ONE

"THERE'S ANOTHER ONE," Asku called back over his shoulder to the others, then resumed peering through the space between the two doors. "That makes at least seventeen. I wonder what this Scarlette blighter is up to?"

"I suppose we'll find out soon enough," Mary Read said, stretching her arms above her head. "It's almost dark."

After filling their bellies with the food Scarlette left, they had scattered to different areas of the barn and spent the rest of the day sleeping. Alerted by the sound of men making their way past the barn to the graybeard's house, Asku had started keeping track of new arrivals while the others continued sleeping. One by one they had come, a procession of rough-clad brigands, armed with every sort of weapon imaginable, moving with the stealth of wanted men.

"Bloody Bill Scarlette," Gant said. "What kind of a name is that?"

"It's the name Stede Bonnet gave him after a little tavern incident down Nassau way," Mary Read said. "Will Scarlette was Bonnet's first mate before he and the rest of the crew deserted Bonnet to join with Blackbeard. Seems they thought the 'Gentlemen Pirate' was too much of a gentleman for their liking. After they saw Teach's butchery and how effective it was, it's no wonder."

"Where does the 'Bloody' part come from?"

"Oh," she said with a chortle. "That might be the only honest thing he earned in his life. One night he's leaving the tavern after a stiff bout of drinking with his mates, and in walks a fresh mullet from Charles Vane's ship, *Ranger*. Scarlette hated Vane and everything associated with him, since it was Vane who had cheated him out of a good share of plunder. This aspiring young sea dog spies Scarlette and blows out a greeting for everyone in the room to hear. 'Why, hello Will Scarlette! A long way from Sherwood Forest, aren't you? Where's Robin Hood an' the rest of your band of merry men?' Scarlette hated it whenever someone joked about his name that way, and he had been spoiling to pay Vane back for years. Mixed together with a night of rummin' and, well, it was a bad move on the young lubber's part. Scarlette took his cutlass and proceeded to carve him up into chum. After hacking off the man's hands and feet, he began taking 'a pound of flesh' for each pound of booty Vane had stolen. But he did it slowly, and by the time the man finally died, blood coated Scarlette from cap to boot."

Asku saw two men leave the house and start toward the barn. One carried a lantern and both had pistols stuck in their waistbands.

"They're coming," Asku interrupted, bringing an end to the story.

A moment later, the doors swung open and two of the men who had been with Scarlette earlier came inside.

"The cap'n says it's time," the man holding the lantern said. He lifted the light up so he could see their faces better. "Come with us."

The entrance to the house opened into a large room lighted by a mix of oil lamps and candles. A huge, hardwood table in the center of the room gave it the appearance of a banquet hall similar to the ones found in castles. Seated around the table and along the walls were at least two dozen gritty men, all of whom stared at the newcomers with looks of suspicion and menace. After latching the door, the two escorts directed the newcomers to take seats at the center of the table and then broke away to claim chairs for themselves along the wall. Without any warning, all of the oil lamps were doused, leaving only the dim, dancing flames of the candles. Anne and Asku sat on one side of the table facing Mary Read and Gant on the other – waiting.

With a sudden whoosh that snapped the taut silence, a door on the far side of the hall flew open and Sailmaker Peppers entered the room.

"ON YOUR FEET!" he yelled.

The sound of chairs scraping the wood floor filled the room as everyone stood. When it fell quiet again, Will Scarlette stepped through the doorway holding a large, silver cup with both hands. The air in the room moved ahead of him as he walked, causing the candle flames to spit and sputter. The wicked shadows they created danced upon the gray walls. Taking the position of authority at the head of the table, he held the cup up high above his head.

"DEATH TO SPOTSWOOD!" he said. His deep voice – honed with a sharp edge of visceral hate – resonated throughout the hall.

"DEATH TO SPOTSWOOD!" all of the men repeated in unison.

Anne gritted her teeth, the abruptness of the imprecate setting her volatile nerves on edge. Mary Read shivered and pressed her thighs together tighter for fear of losing her water.

As governor of Virginia, it was Alexander Spotswood who had funded Lieutenant Maynard's expedition to hunt down Blackbeard and kill him – an act detested not only by the brethren but also by those who had governed the state at the time. The colony's officials had profited handsomely for looking the other way and providing Teach a safe harbor from which to launch his raids. In truth, the entire colony had benefited from the arrangement, as it was mainly North Carolina's port towns where Teach had sold the goods he stole from merchant ships, and at a much lower price than they would have fetched otherwise. Most of North Carolina's merchants – and all of the pirates – still detested Spotswood as just another British, powder-wigged interloper who had exceeded his authority and had impugned their colony's autonomy. The matter of their own reputations was not an issue, given that they were already beneath contempt.

Lowering the silver cup, Scarlette first looked around the room at his mates and then upon each of the newcomers.

"I've called you here to enter into a contract, if we all be in agreement. Aye, a contract that will give us back the treasure what Israel Hands would have stolen from us had he had his way."

The men began chattering to each other in excitement.

"Silence!" Scarlette ordered. When the rumbling died down, he continued.

"As you all know, Israel Hands stole the map what shows where our rightful fortunes be buried. Well, I'm here to tell you that I know where the map be, an' that we can get it back if you still want it."

Again, the men broke into a dozen different conversations, some calling out questions. This time, Scarlette remained silent until the commotion collapsed under its own weight. Placing the cup on a ring designed to keep it from rolling on its rounded bottom, he pulled back his coat to reveal a half-dozen pistols.

"If interrupted again, I'll be forced to exercise me executive authority and make an example of one of you. Am I clear?"

Some of the men pushed back into their seats, attempting to become less visible while others nodded affirmation.

"The two ladies gracing us with their presence tonight be Mary Read an' Anne Bonny."

Despite the warning, a couple of the men gasped in disbelief. Scarlette cocked his eye at the closest one, letting him know that he had almost won the "I want to be the dead example" lottery.

"I don't really know who the Red Coat an' the Indian be, an' it don't matter. They're all together, an' what one knows, they all know. So, they all agree to the contract...or there won't be one."

Ann, Mary Read, Gant, and Asku sat in their seats like watch springs, wound tight and on the verge of breaking. The implication was clear – if any one of the four outsiders refused to agree to Scarlette's conditions, they were all dead. And they had yet to learn what would be demanded of them.

"Until a day ago, Mary Read here was in possession of the map Anders Pellicane made the night he buried the treasure for Blackbeard. But last night, Mary Read lost her ship...an' the map still be hidden there."

Some of the men shifted in their seats but resisted the urge to speak out. The riches that had eluded them for so long were almost within their grasp.

"Now, afore I go on, it's only proper that our guests commit their fortunes to us in the same manner we have committed our fortunes to each other."

Once again, Scarlette turned his focus on the four newcomers.

"Understand, anyone who breaks the oath is breakin' a sacred vow. And all others who are of Blackbeard's body are duty-bound to take their revenge upon the oath breaker by takin' the traitor's life."

"Hear! Hear!" the men shouted, as was in keeping with the ritual.

Lifting the cup from the table and once again holding it up toward the ceiling, the graybeard recited words he had said a hundred times before.

"Know you all that he who drinks from this cup is bound by Blackbeard's blood an' body to never tell of what you have seen or heard this night, not even on the gallows. BECAUSE IF ONE OF US HANGS...!"

"...WE ALL HANG TOGETHER!" the men shouted back.

Raising the cup to his lips, Scarlette tipped it toward his mouth and took a long swallow. When he had taken his fill, he passed it to the man sitting to his right. As he did, Anne was able to see details of the odd-shaped bowl that had been hidden by the darkness.

*It's a human skull! They were affirming the oath and their agreement by drinking from Blackbeard's evacuated cranium.*

Anne felt her stomach beginning to churn as she watched the cup make its way around the table. Knowing that she was about to drink from a dead man's skull was repulsive enough. Knowing that it was a part of Blackbeard's mutilated body made her want to hurl. Across the table, she saw that Mary Read's face was ashen, her eyes transfixed on the skull. Instead of disgust, the raven-haired piratress was in the grip of sheer terror.

Anne had never feared bumps in the night, but drinking some unknown, foul concoction from the skull of a man she had known when he was alive was different. The liquid she was about to drink was in a vessel that once contained Edward Teach's sick, sadistic brain. If spirits did exist, it was likely that they maintained a connection to their earthly remains. Drinking from the skull would bring her closer to the afterworld than she cared to be. Such a thing had to be an affront to God – and that couldn't be good.

"Your turn," Scarlette grunted. "What will it be?"

Anne turned to see the man next to her was holding Blackbeard's last known remains mere inches from her face. The aroma of its contents assaulted her nose, her stomach recoiled with renewed protest. With her eyes beginning to water, she sucked in another deep breath of air for fear of passing out. The second whiff of the nasty concoction was, to her surprise, not nearly as disgusting as the first. This time she thought she could detect the familiar odors of corn liquor, blackberry wine, the musky scent of mushrooms, and...blood?

Pushing the thought from her mind, she grasped the hideous bowl, pressed its cold, silver-coated rim to her lips, and tipped it. A wave of the dark liquid flowed into her mouth more quickly than she had anticipated. The vile drink burned its way down her throat and into her stomach, crashing into the bile that was already on the verge of spewing forth.

She began coughing in a violent fit and one of the pirates behind her grabbed the skull to make sure its precious contents weren't spilled. The men about the room began poking each other with their elbows, laughing with satisfaction. Burying her face into the crook of her arm, Anne tried to stave the flood of snot issuing from her nose while at the same time suppressing the urge to heave. As she struggled to recover, the pirate behind her handed the skull to Asku.

Resisting the urge to fling the ghastly thing on the floor, the woodsman looked at the liquid rippling in the skeletal bowl as if he were holding a nest of snakes. With all eyes in the room watching him, he followed Anne's example and took a swallow.

How he was able to suppress any outward indication of his revulsion, Anne didn't know, but he made look as if he hadn't drunk anything worse than a cup of water. With a triumphant glint his eye, he smiled and passed the skull to the next man.

As the bone cup made its way around the table, Anne watched Mary Read with growing trepidation. After each man took a swallow, the bowl was passed on to the next. The closer it moved toward Mary, the more obvious her fear and dread became. Once again, Anne was struck by how Mary Read's stone-solid resolve was crumbling. But even as she had the thought, she realized it was wrong. With sudden insight, she understood that Mary's collapse didn't stem from a fear of the unknown, it was because she knew something that they didn't.

When it was Gant's turn, he took the skull without hesitation, placed it to his lips and downed the swill before his sense of smell could sabotage his stomach. Nodding approval, he took another hard swallow and then turned to pass the bowl. For the first time that evening, the pirates conceded a measure of respectful winks and grunts of approval.

Mary Read was now a pasty-white approximation of her true self. Any hopes she may have had that the "cup" was an empty legend were completely dashed. Now it was her turn to take the dead thing in her hands and place it to her lips.

"Damnation," Gant said. "Take the cup and drink. It's no worse than the piss and vinegar you used to serve in your whorehouse."

Anne watched Mary Read drowning in a whirlpool of panic, helpless to do a thing to help her. Anne could see by the look on her face that there was no way in hell she was going to drink from Blackbeard's dead and once rancid head. Everyone else kept their eyes on Mary Read, waiting to see what she would do.

It was only because she knew Mary so well that Anne was able to see something in her eyes begin to change...and somehow she knew. Mary was looking at the Hollow. She stole a quick glance over her shoulder but saw nothing. But Mary did. Somewhere across the room, hidden in the shadows, the Hollow had made itself known to her. Mary squinted her eyes, no doubt trying to see that which did not want to be seen. It's formless face appearing and reappearing in the shifting spaces of dark and light created by the men as they altered their stances and moved their arms in gesture.

Oblivious to the stares of the men about the room, Anne watched Mary's visage begin to thaw from its frozen stupor. Almost as if magic, she could see a strange calm wash over Mary, freeing her mind from the debilitating panic that was about to cost them their lives. Then, with a distinct nod that had to have been directed to the Hollow, she was back.

"Take it!" Gant said, his face twisted with desperation. If she failed to drink, they were all dead.

When at last she turned to look at him, the panic in her face was gone, replaced by her usual air of total confidence. Grabbing the skull, she brought it to her mouth and took a deep swallow. The Hollow's quiet grace had removed both its foul smell and taste.

After the rest of the men in the room had taken a swig from the skull, Scarlette took a second swallow and placed it back on the table.

"Every man what drank from the cup is now bound to the other for the duration of our venture," he said. "Any man – or woman – what breaks the bond, forfeits his life an' will answer to Edward Teach in the dark belly of the beast."

"And what, exactly, is our venture?" asked one of the men from across the room.

"Didn't I tell you?" Scarlette laughed. "We chase down that popinjay Rader, take over *Rackham's Revenge* and recover the map that will take us to our rightful property...easier than a walk on the beach at low tide."

# CHAPTER TWENTY-TWO

"PLEASE, MISTER BIRDMAN," Tye said. "I need your help."

Diffused light filtering through the cargo hatch and into the doorway of their storage-room quarters gave Dyonis's skin a dull, ghostly look. He sat cross-legged on the deck with his elbows on his knees, his head resting in the palms of his hands. His natural exuberance - usually as flamboyant as his cape of feathers - had turned into an aura of dark despair. His perpetual chirping of useless facts had ceased altogether, not having spoken since Rader's destruction of the Dare's home earlier in the day.

"Captain Rader says it's time for us to pay our due, and I can't do it without you. The water runs shallow here, and we need to know when it will be high tide or risk grounding when we cross the bar. You have to tell me when the flow will peak. You said you know the tides, remember?"

Long after losing sight of his home, Dyonis had clung to the rail, looking back toward the wreckage, hoping for a sign that his mother survived. Despite his vigilance, the only thing he had seen was a growing cloud of smoke rising above the pines where the shack had stood.

Once they were back in the channel, the ship had resumed its southwesterly course toward Cape Lookout in search of an inlet to access the ocean. The farther they sailed away from his home, the deeper Dyonis had retreated within himself. When the *Revenge* dropped anchor a half-mile from the inlet just north of the cape, Tye had pried the gawky man's hands from the gunwale and led him down the hatchway steps to their room to escape Rader's stares and cutting remarks. Slumping to the floor, Dyonis had sat in the same position for several hours without talking or looking up.

Now, crouching to his knees in front of Dyonis, Tye placed his hands on the man's shoulders attempting to reassure him. He had to get Dyonis to speak, not only because of the immediate concern, but also for fear that his new friend would retreat into a shell from which he would never return.

"Look," Tye said, reaching inside of his shirt. "I've pinched some of the crew for the feathers they stole from you. It's not much, but it's a start."

Dyonis looked up for a moment to see the handful of parrot feathers, smiled as he began to reach for them, then stopped. His grin faded as quickly as it had appeared and he returned his head to its sullen perch upon his hands.

"Come on, Mister Birdman. If you help me, I promise that when we get back, I'll help you gather more feathers and we'll fix your fine cloak as good as new. What do you say?"

Dyonis laid on his side, pulling himself into an even tighter ball of despair.

The gesture tore at Tye's heart. He was desperate to appease Rader and keep him pacified, but attempting to bribe Dyonis with the feathers had been a shameful act.

"Here," he said, placing the feathers beside Dyonis. "These are yours. Take them. And when we get back to Bath, I'll help you get all the feathers you want...no matter what."

Rising from the deck, Tye started toward the door. He had no idea when high tide would be, but he had to tell Rader something. He would guess a time based on the tides he had observed at Ocracoke and hope for the best. It wasn't much of a plan, but it was the best he could do. It would have to be, because he knew he would never try to manipulate Asku's brother ever again.

"Seven-fourteen," Dyonis said.

"What? What did you say?" Tye asked.

Instead of looking at Tye, Dyonis picked up the feathers and began to inspect them one at a time.

"Tick...tick...tick... High tide at Cape Lookout is twenty-six minutes before high tide at Ocracoke. The next high tide here will be at seven-fourteen P M. Count the minutes. It will be seven-fourteen in twenty-seven minutes. Better raise anchor, quick, tick...tick...tick..."

With that, he laid the feathers on the floor, turned his back toward the boy and balled up again.

As he dashed up the steps to tell Rader they needed to hurry, Tye considered Dyonis's fleeting moment of awareness. If he could not find a way to help Birdman find his way back from despair, there was little doubt that Rader would murder them both.

# CHAPTER TWENTY-THREE

IF HAVING THE POWER to order men about was intoxicating, Harry Wennell had become Lord of Rumbullion. Not only did he have a crew to command, fortune had made him the captain of a warship and its full complement of cannon. The capacity to hold sway over the life and death of those about him was finally and gloriously his. He was now a force to be reckoned with, and he had all intentions of wielding the full weight of that power at every opportunity.

A day-and-a-half of presiding over his small repair crew had confirmed what he had always known – that given the chance, he could become the stripe of captain that would accomplish great things. Despite his thin crew, he had already replaced the *Hazard*'s bowsprit, repaired her rigging, and made her seaworthy. True, he had been a strict captain thus far, and his men already knew that he was not going to tolerate idlers. But he had also been a benevolent commander, giving them all double rations of rum instead of grog.

Well on his way to fulfilling his orders to bolster the *Hazard*'s crew with experienced watermen and brigands from the twin villages, he would soon join Rader in Charles Town. The crew had grumbled when he had gone ashore to seek out new recruits in Ocracoke's ordinaries while leaving them on board to make repairs, but they had wisely done so under their breath and not to his face.

Even the recruiting had gone well. Many more locals than expected had promised to come out to the *Hazard* first thing in the morning. Rader's victory over the experienced British crew had spread through the village like a runaway ship fire. And Wennell's loud, boastful promises of gold and treasure had proven to be a powerful siren to the island's weather-beaten fishermen and pilots.

But it wasn't until Wennell found himself in an ordinary called the Cockle and Bulrush that he stumbled on to one of command's better benefits. Being captain of a ship, he discovered, was a powerful amatory to the higher quality vixens that frequented taverns. From the moment he had entered the establishment until he had downed the last drop of rum, the wenches had fawned over him as if he was the Prince of Wales. The more attention he received, and the more he drank, the more right and just it seemed that he should enjoy life's pleasures. He had, after all, earned every sweet morsel.

The proof of his deservedness rested on either side of him in his captain's bunk. The dark-haired lass on his right, Merriam, had turned out to be an aggressive trollop, constantly demanding his attention and insisting that he promise to bring her a fat ruby. Even when asleep, she had clung to him as if she had won a grand prize that no one would wrest from her grasp. Sadie – or was it Katie – sleeping peacefully on his left, had not stirred in at least an hour, no doubt worn out from her exertions. Wennell had seen right away that the sweet, blonde-haired lass was new to the world of tavern trolling, but what she had lacked in experience she had more than made up for with enthusiasm.

Both of his new lady friends smelled of stale rum, tobacco, salt air, perspiration, and an abundance of sickly-sweet perfume. Still, the two women had been the best of the lot, and their long night of debauchery had surpassed his wildest imaginings. Alas, despite the desire to prolong such pleasures for a day, Harry Wennell knew he had to take care of business or reckon with Blyth Rader's wrath.

Even then, he would have remained in bed awhile longer had it not been for the fullness of his bladder. Rousing the women from their sleep, he hurried them to don their clothes and ushered them onto the deck with such haste they wondered if the ship might be on fire. As soon as his two conquests had descended the rope ladder and settled their bums into a waiting shore boat, Wennell rushed to the open gangway. Freeing his engorged member from his trousers he began arcing a stream into the waters below.

As the course of his release passed beyond the point of jaw-clenching pain and into the exquisite pleasure of sweet relief, Wennell began surveying his surroundings with the eye of a newly-crowned monarch. Across the water sat Ocracoke, the small village that had welcomed him with the respect and admiration befitting his new station. And there, in the small boat already on its way back to the village, were the two adoring women who had kept him company through the night – an indulgence he intended to repeat as soon as possible. Looking about, he saw the deck of his ship crowded with at least twenty new recruits – men from the taverns making good on their promises to join the crew this morning. Several of them eyed him with curiosity, wondering at what might have prompted their new captain to demonstrate how piss proud he was instead of using the private facility in his cabin.

The truth was, Wennell had forgotten that a captain did not have to take his turn at the head like a regular crewman. His cabin boasted its own head. Turning his attention back to the vista before him, he planted his hands on his hips and proceeded with nature's calling like a dog marking his territory.

As the last few drops fell to the water below, a swift glint of sunlight on steel streaked through the air, down and across the front of Wennell's body. In the same instant, he felt a quick tug at his groin followed by a strange, but not altogether unpleasant, sensation. It was as though he had been relieved of a burden of which he had never before been aware. Curious, he looked down to see what could have caused the unfamiliar feeling and, just in the nick of time, saw a meaty tube of pale flesh bounce off the hull with a dull thump before splatting on the water's surface.

The rubbery length of tissue bobbed about the dark, green water, a hint of blood trailing from its severed end. It remained visible for a few moments, mocking its former owner – tantalizingly close, yet agonizingly far away. Then, adding absolute insult to unimaginable injury, a splash of silver shot up from the depths of the water, snatched the pallid sea cucumber from the surface with its sharp, pointy teeth, and disappeared back into the darkness from which it had sprung.

"What a pity," Anne said. "Seems a little early for the mackerel to be running. But honestly, I don't think it would have mattered anyway."

Still dazed by the undeniable truth of his amputation and the absolute refusal to accept it, Harry Wennell looked for the person that went with the voice. Both hands were now clasped over the bloody nub that had once been his manhood.

Anne – who was leaning over the gunwale as though trying to spot the fish that had absconded with his pride – looked up and peered at him with mock sympathy.

"I told you what I would do if you touched me," Mary Read said, grinding the words out with more Wapping-parish burr than she had allowed in many years.

Wennell spun around to see the woman standing just inches away, glaring at him with her one eye. A drop of blood collected on the tip of her cutlass and fell to the deck, leaving a splatter of red next to her boot.

To everyone on deck watching the scene play out, the person facing Wennell appeared to be a man. Both Anne and Mary had dressed themselves to blend in with the recruits that had come aboard that morning. Wearing Monmouth caps to hide their hair, their faces darkened with soot to mimic fresh beards, and garbed in motley ensembles of linen shirts, waistcoats, breeches, and sashes, the two women would have passed as men in any gathering of commoners.

"Why are you just standing there?" Wennell groaned, looking at his crew scattered about the deck. "Kill them!"

But as his eyes darted from one crew member to the next, he began to realize the bitter truth of his predicament. Far outnumbered by newcomers, each member of his crew was boxed in by at least two of the new men. Anchored next to the wheel where he could observe the open deck stood a tall, gray-bearded man wearing a tricorn hat, a long coat, and the air of command. Harry Wennell's first command was over.

Anne watched with odd detachment, wondering what Mary would do next. She had fulfilled her vow, but would she kill the man outright?

"Ah...whill...kkhill...eew!" Wennell vowed, his words mangled by an ache that had started in his back teeth and spread throughout his jaw and throat.

Stumbling forward, he reached out to put his hands around Mary Read's neck. Mary's cutlass came up in a blur, its point intercepting Wennell's assault long before his fingers could find the soft flesh of her throat.

"Kill me?" Mary Read challenged. "You're going to kill...me?"

With each sentence she advanced another step, the point of her cutlass forcing the bos'n to take a corresponding step back. "You'll not be killing anyone this day, Harry Wennell. In truth, I'm trying to decide whether it will be you who dies."

Wennell now stood teetering at the edge of the gangway. One more step back and he would fall into the sound. If he tried to stand fast, Mary Read would run him through

"I have an idea," Mary Read said, eyeing the blood stain on the front of Wennell's breeches. "Let's let the sharks decide whether you live or die."

Extending her cutlass with just enough force to inflict pain, Wennell did the only thing he could do and still live. The would-be captain hit the cool, brackish water square on his back, knocking the wind from his lungs. He broke surface a few moments later, oblivious to everything about him, swallowing air in desperate gulps. He was alive, but he had to regain his breath and try to make shore before the sharks detected the blood seeping from his wound.

Mary Read stood at the gangway, watching the gnarl-toothed reiver only long enough to see that he still lived. It didn't matter whether he made it to the island. The revenge that been exacted would haunt Harry Wennell for the rest of his life, however long that might be.

Deftly sheathing her cutlass, she gave Scarlette a nod.

"Listen here, fishies!" the tall graybeard said so all could hear. "This ship an' all upon her now belongs to Bloody Bill Scarlette. You men what signed on with Blyth Rader have a choice – either sail with me and the rest of Blackbeard's Order...or leave now. If you stay, you get a share of any new booty taken from this day forward. If you leave, then you can eke out your miserable existence any way you see fit."

Listening to Scarlette's coarse sales pitch from her spot by the gunwale, Anne wondered if the long-suffering bastard would really allow Rader's men to live should they decline his offer. As long as they remained they did not pose a threat. If any of them returned to shore, the chances were good that they would tip Scarlette's hand to the authorities – either by accident or by aim. By Anne's estimation, she doubted that the grizzled pirate had managed to survive this long by making such stupid mistakes.

"What do you mean, 'new' booty?" one of the crewmen challenged.

The man had dark skin, like that of a Spaniard, though it was doubtful even Scarlette's dregs would have tolerated a diego. His hair was pulled back and tightly braided into a long ponytail, giving him a stark, severe appearance.

Of Harry Wennell's five crewmen, this one appeared to be the most intelligent. Anne recognized him as one of the transient mariners who had haunted Bath's wharf before signing on with Rader. He moved with the assuredness of an experienced seaman and some of his clothing hinted of having once served in the king's navy. Judging by the way he had asked the question, there was no doubt he had come to the same conclusion Anne had regarding the consequences of making a wrong decision.

"Aye," Scarlette said. "Me an' me crew, we have claim to treasure already taken but...misplaced. We intend to reclaim it. That belongs to us. If you help us to find it, we'll pay wages, fair, but full shares of that booty belong to us."

"Seems evenhanded enough," the man said, making the only choice that afforded any real chance of living.

"And the rest of you?" Scarlette challenged.

The other four members of Wennell's crew looked around the deck, taking note of the odds against them.

**234**

"I got no other place to be," one of them muttered, giving himself up to fate. The three other men nodded agreement.

"It's settled then," Scarlette said. Then turning to look down at Mary Read over the crook of his broken nose, "All right, lass. Which way?"

"Follow the deep water behind Portsmouth Isle, the same course Rader took. They're heading south."

"Why not take to the sea an' cut them off as they come out an inlet?" he challenged.

"Because, we have no idea which inlet they'll come out of or when. Better to follow their path and come up behind them than to override our head and end up finding ourselves in front of them and their cannon."

"Aye," he said with a nod of respect. "That makes sense to me."

"Prepare the tops'l," he shouted to the men waiting in the rigging. The command to weigh anchor followed and crewmen at the capstan put their backs into the push bars. A few minutes later the brig eased into the channel where the tidewaters flowed behind the barrier island.

Trusting his helmsman's ability to keep the *Hazard* in the deep water, Scarlette wasted no time putting the ship in order. The two women – being women – would take the captain's cabin, shutting the door on any bad ideas the rest of the men might have before they could arise. They might be his mates, but they were still men. He would take the quarters set aside for the ship's junior officers for himself. Everybody else was on their own.

Knowing how the ship was laid out, Gant signaled for Asku to follow and claimed the quarters that had been his. It was a small cabin, cramped for two men, but an arrangement that allowed Asku and Gant to watch each other's back. They may all now be brethren of Blackbeard's wormy skull, but neither man was ready to trust in Scarlette's men. The rest of the crew would bunk below deck or sleep in the open if they preferred.

As the ship followed the meandering course of the channel, Asku began wondering about the ship, looking for materials to make a new bow and arrows. Anne and Mary Read were close to the stern, engaged in a serious but civil discussion as they began to pass between the island of Asku's birth and the barrier island protecting it. Though still dressed as men, they had washed their faces, let their hair fall loose and belted their blouses in a way that left no doubt as to their gender.

A few feet away, Bloody Bill Scarlette stood next to his helmsman, surveying the water ahead for hazards and sudden turns in the channel. The mid-morning sun promised that the day would be a hot one, but he was pleased that the breeze was steady and favored their heading. Though the brim of his hat made it difficult to see his face, anyone glancing his way would have little trouble noticing the smile he wore. It had been many years since he had sailed a true ship, and he was enjoying it to full advantage.

"Asku! Asku Dare!"

About two-hundred feet off the starboard bow two men in an anchored skiff were waving at the ship, trying to get his attention. Asku recognized them as Henry Cage and his son, Drexel.

"Came back just in time," the elder Cage yelled as the *Hazard* drew closer. His dark brown face was dried and cracked like leather having gone too long without proper oiling. Although Drexel was only a few years older than Asku, the weathering he had endured while helping his father eke out an existence on the sound waters made him appear middle-aged.

"How so?" Asku called back, his hands cupped around his mouth.

"You mean...you didn't know?" It was Drexel who yelled back this time. "It's a good thing we happened to see you, then. It's your mum. She's in a bad way." His voice grew softer as the ship drew next to the skiff. "You better go to her now, before it's too late."

"Reef the tops'l and drop anchor!" Anne ordered as she hurried to Asku's side. All the men on deck and in the rigging looked at her and then at Scarlette, trying to decide whether to comply.

Scarlette was about to tell the men to belay Anne's order when Mary Read came up beside him.

"Let them go or they'll both jump overboard," she said, her coarse voice pelting his ears like pebbles bouncing off a metal drum, "I can see it in their faces."

The graybeard hesitated, weighing his options.

"It's his mother, man. You can't expect his oath to you to outweigh dedication to his mother. And if they go, so do I."

The muscles in Scarlette's jaw grew taut as he considered his options. He could do without the other two, but he needed her. Mary Read had him by the small hairs.

"You heard the woman!" he said. "Reef the tops'l and drop anchor!" Then to Asku and Anne, "You have two hours. Don't be making me wait a minute longer."

The two fishermen freed their boat from his anchoring and maneuvered their skiff alongside the ship as it came to a stop, allowing Asku and Anne to cross over. Instead of setting a course that would take them to the Dare's home on the far side of the island, they sailed directly into Cedar Island Bay and the cluster of shacks and huts that was the island's closest thing to a town square.

"They took Ona to the Gurkin's place," Drexel said as his father piloted the skiff toward a stretch of sand where several fishing boats were beached. "She was burnt pretty bad, and...well...just prepare yourself, you hear?"

By the time the skiff's bow slid onto the sandy incline, the Cages had told what little they knew about the attack. In the same Cockney-like accent of the Dares, they learned that the *Revenge* had leveled Ona's home without warning or provocation. Ona had been trapped inside when hot embers from the cooking hearth set the razed building on fire. Neighbors had pulled her out of the blaze, but not before most of her body had been burned. They had taken her to Gerald Gurkin's home, the only house on the island big enough to boast a spare room and an extra bed where she could be attended. Leandra Gurkin – Gerald's wife – and Ona had grown up together and were lifelong friends.

As they approached the cottage they were met with a long wail of agony in a voice that could only have belonged to Ona Dare.

"Mum!" Asku shouted, bursting into the Gurkin home without knocking. Not seeing anyone in the main room, he called to her again. "Where are you, Mum? It's me, Asku!"

"In here," a man's voice called through a doorway on the other side of the room.

Asku and Anne dashed into the room to find Gerald and Leandra standing next to the bed where Ona rested. The middle-aged man wore a dark coat over rough clothes befitting a man whose life had been spent working the waters. His wife wore a cotton dress, its long sleeves soaked dark from having wiped the perspiration from her forehead countless times. Their expressions reflected the hopelessness conveyed in Ona Dare's pitiful cries.

Despite the Cages' warnings and the wails of pain, neither Anne or Asku were prepared to see the charred, raw mass of human flesh writhing on the bed before him. Although a sheet covered the right half of her body, the other half was exposed. The crinkled, oozing tissue that remained was either too moist or too brittle to place cloth or bandage on it. The left side of her head had also been burned, leaving a small lump of deformed pulp where her ear had once been. The side of her face was a series of sagging, red ripples of skin, and her hair looked like short, crinkled sprigs of singed corn silk.

"A beam fell and pinned her to the floor," Gerald said, shaking his head. Leandra continued to wipe the unburned side of Ona's forehead with a damp cloth in the futile attempt to comfort her friend. "By the time they got to her it was too late. The shack...the wood...it was old and dry and it burned fast. It's a miracle she's still with us. I think the only thing that kept her alive this long was the hope of seeing you and Dyonis."

"Who would do such a thing?" Leandra asked as she continued her nursing. "What could she have done to deserve this?"

Anne watched as Asku struggled to speak, but failed. She could see the unbearable grief and overwhelming guilt written across his face. His mother was about to die, murdered by Blyth Rader in an act of revenge for things he and Dyonis had done. It was clear that Asku blamed himself for his mother's death.

"Asku...." His mother's faint voice jolted him back. "Askuwheteau ...is that you?"

Asku went to his mother's side and grasped her hand.

"Yes, mum, it's me, Asku. I'm here to take care of you now."

Ona tried to smile but grimaced instead.

"Where is your brother, Asku? Where is Dyonis?"

He tried to swallow, but the knot in his throat was so hardened it was impossible.

"Is he...alive?"

Asku's delay in responding had been as much an answer as any words he could have spoken.

"Yes. He is...with the boy...Anne Bonny's son."

"Is that true?" she wheezed. "And where...is the boy?"

Again, Asku attempted to answer but no words came.

"It's true, as far as we know," Anne said. "But now Blyth Rader has both of them. They are sailing south and we are giving chase."

"I see," Ona said.

She closed her tired eyes for a moment and sighed. Then, as she tried to take a deep breath, a series of tremors took control her body. When they subsided, she strained to look at Asku through slitted eyelids. She began to speak but her voice failed to carry across the short distance between them. Leaning in closer, Asku placed his ear to her lips.

"My body...is just a vessel...for my soul. Do not wait...to bury...me. Find...Dyonis."

"But, you're not-"

"No!" she said. Then she reached up to grab his arm. "You've been a good son...Asku. Now you...must find your... brother. Bring him home."

Her body jolted then stiffened as every muscle began to spasm at the same time. Life left in a final, long exhale. Then her body relaxed, no longer tortured by the pain of her burns.

Everyone in the room remained silent, trying to accept the fact of Ona Dare's death. Finally, Asku pulled the sheet across his mother's body to cover her nakedness.

"What did she say?" Anne asked, placing a hand on Asku's arm.

"We're wasting time," Asku said, and then left the room.

"Asku!" Anne called out. But he was already outside and walking down the path back to the skiff.

"It's all right," Gerald said. "He knows we'll take care of Ona. There's only one thing on his mind, now...to find his brother. They are the only two of their line left, at least on this side of the ocean. And Asku is the only family left to watch after his brother. I think you know what I mean."

"Thank you," she said, realizing that this was what Ona had wanted – that she had been giving Asku permission to leave for the sake of his brother.

She caught up to Asku at the beach where the Cages were waiting next to their boat. As she approached, she could see that the two men already knew that Ona had died. Asku's face had told them everything they needed to know, so they neither greeted him nor asked about her condition, letting silence show their respect.

"I need for one of you to come with us," Asku said, without the usual island small talk. "We'll be passing through the channel down south and need a pilot."

"Take Drex," Henry said. "He knows the channels better than anybody, accept me, and I ain't got the time to give up right now. Drex will get you across the bar safe, have no doubts."

Once back aboard the *Hazard*, they resumed their southerly course between the islands with the Gurkin's skiff in tow. When they approached the inlet that Rader had passed through, Drexel told the helmsman to ignore it and continue following the channel running behind the cape.

"That's a new inlet," he said. "I don't think it's deep enough for this brig to pass. There's another inlet on the other side of Cape Lookout. It's been there for many years and runs good an' deep. We'll pass there."

It was getting late in the afternoon and the tide was low when they reached the more southern inlet. If they attempted to pass now, there was a good chance they would either run out of light or run aground. Not willing to take the chance, Scarlette decided to anchor in the sound's calm waters for the night and wait till dawn to leave.

Making use of the light they had left, Gant took some of the crew to the stern where he taught them how to load and fire the muskets his men had once used. Other crewmen practiced loading and aiming the cannon, a process most of them had not attempted in many years. Taking up a position near the mainmast and out of the way, Anne and Mary Read looked on while Scarlette – standing between two cannon – walked several gun crews through the steps.

Neither of the two women realized that Asku was standing next to them until he spoke Anne's name. Turning to him, she was surprised to see that he held two cutlasses confiscated from the ship's armory.

"Teach me," he said, presenting one of the swords to her, hilt first.

"Well, well, well..." Mary Read cracked. "The woodsman wants to be a swordsman. And he has no pride about learning from a woman. Once again, you've found a rare man indeed, Anne Bonny. One day you must tell me how you do that."

Anne ignored the comment, focusing on Asku instead. Sadly, she no longer saw the traces of innocence and nonchalance that had made him so disarming. A determined seriousness had erased his easy-going attitude. He was all business now, and his business was murdering Blythe Rader.

Taking the sword, Anne led Asku to an open area of deck away from the drilling gun crews and began showing him the basics of swordsmanship. Once he was able to assume a proper stance and understand why it was important, she showed him how to attack, thrust, parry, and riposte. Forcing him to repeat the moves over and over, he soon began demonstrating a modicum of skill, convincing Anne that he had the agility and natural talent to become a competent fighter. She also knew that it would be a long time for him to become anywhere near as good as Rader.

The sun was beginning to dip below the horizon before she allowed him to attempt actual fencing. Asku had proven to be an excellent student, asking questions about the things he did not understand and focusing on Anne's instructions with an intensity she had never seen. He absorbed every word she uttered as though his life depended on them. Asku soon became so adept at attacking that Anne found herself having to call upon ever more advanced skills to deflect his thrusts and lunges. He was also becoming too confident.

Initiating their next engagement, Asku advanced, executing a series of short thrusts before making a decisive lunge intended to touch Anne's midsection. Having watched him attempt the move several times already, Anne recognized his strategy and slid aside, leaving him to stab the empty space she had occupied an instant before. Adding insult to injury, Anne stuck out her foot and tripped him, sending him sprawling to the deck. The crew, who only moments before had ceased their own training to watch, roared with laughter.

"In ferro veritas!" Anne said, holding her sword up to salute Asku's efforts. And then with a sweeping bow, she translated, "In the sword is truth."

Asku scowled at her, no doubt righteously peeved that she had embarrassed him in front of the other men. But she gave him a coy smile and he seemed to understand that it was a lesson she had given him, not humiliation.

"Thank you," he said. "I hope I am not the worst student you've ever had."

"You'll do," she said without embellishment. His nod told her that he took the comment as praise, as had been her intention.

With the show over and darkness full upon them, everyone headed to the galley where they hoped a decent meal awaited them.

"You do realize that he will never learn enough to hold his own against Rader by the time we catch up to the bastard," Mary Read said when the others had gone below.

"I have no intention of letting him fight Rader," Anne said. They may have called a truce in their little feud, but she had no desire to make small talk.

"Then why are you wasting your time?"

"Because, it gives him something to think about instead of his kidnapped brother or his dead mother. Besides, I need the practice, for I fully intend for it to be me who kills Rader."

"Not if I have anything to do with it!" Mary shot back with a rare surge of anger. "He mutinied on me and took my ship. I'll pith Rader at the back of his skull and use his body parts for shark chum, while he's still alive."

"And after that, we'll have some unfinished business to take care of," Anne said, refusing to let her forget their feud.

"Awwww...Annie. You just don't understand, do you?"

"Oh, I understand well enough. You stole my son and now his life is in danger. I'll never forget that, and I'll never let you forget it either."

With that, she turned and went below to find the galley, leaving Mary Read to wonder what type of revenge she might one day have to face.

# CHAPTER TWENTY-FOUR

THE MEAL HAD BEEN FISH STEW, heavily peppered and thickened with wild rice. Both fresh and filling, it was much better than their usual fare. With their bellies full, most of the men chose to take advantage of the cool night air and found places to sleep topside. Gant, still wary of his new partners, sought out the familiar surroundings of his room. Needing time alone, Asku, found a secluded place at the bow where he could stretch out with his back resting against the bowsprit.

After having their fill, both Anne and Mary Read retreated to their cabin, intent on being well-rested for the challenges that would come on the morrow. By the light of a gimble lamp next to the captain's washstand, Anne filled the stand's basin with fresh water and took off her clothes to bathe. Aware of Mary Read's eyes following her as she rubbed a soapy sponge over her body, Anne made haste of the cleansing. It was the first time the two of them had been alone since Jamaica – if being in a prison surrounded by dozens of other prisoners in nearby cells could be considered alone – and it made her uncomfortable.

That revelation lead to another, one that – for reasons she could not quite grasp – disturbed her even more. Anne had not truly been alone with another adult in eight years. It was infuriating that Mary Read, of all people, would be sharing her bed. Fate was having a grand time, mocking her for being such a fool. She had wasted nearly a decade of her life trying to be something that she wasn't, only to find herself right back where she had left off.

When she was done, Anne dumped the basin of dirty water out of the transom window, slipped into a ruffled shirt that had belonged to the ship's captain, and climbed into bed. Taking Anne's place at the washstand, Mary Read removed the leather patch covering her eye and began filling the basin with fresh water. Anne turned on her side to face the hull. It was bad enough that she had to be with the woman who had stolen her son and then lost him to the one man in the world who most hated her – she'd be damned if she would subject herself to the spectacle of Mary Read's nakedness.

"You know," Mary said as she rubbed soap into the dampened sponge. "There was a time when you were eager to look at me. Was that so long ago?"

Surprised by Mary's directness, Anne clutched the cover tight against her chest, dreading what words might come next. Whatever affections they had shared and longings they had explored were long since gone. Like the brief eruption of mist created by a wave crashing on the shore, those days had been fleeting, even if glorious.

But Anne was wide awake now, her yearning desire to sleep usurped by a swirl of unwanted emotions and memories competing for attention. As her eyes darted about in frustration, her gaze fell upon a glass pane in the transom's window. With a start, she realized that she could see Mary's reflection. Warm light from the gimble lantern danced playfully across Mary Read's smooth, white skin, accenting the curves of her naked body and casting shadows suggesting mysteries to which Anne had once known the answers. Her sable hair, set free to cascade over her bare shoulders, shimmered with half-remembered wantonness.

Anne continued watching despite herself, enthralled by the liquescent beauty of Mary Read's bathing. She felt a pang of disappointment when Mary's form disappeared from view as she bent over to sponge her legs and thighs. But her disquiet turned to self-rebuke when Mary rose again, accepting the truth that she wanted to see more.

Oblivious to Anne's voyeurism, Mary wrung out the sponge, wet it again, applied more soap and resumed her cleansing.

"What happened to you, Annie? You were the wild one. Sure, I knew how to fight and put on a good show. But that was just well-acted bravado. It was you who always threw caution to the wind, never hesitating to attack when the time was right, and somehow always being right about having done it. We were mates, Annie, you an' me... as much as any man and woman ever was."

Mary's movements slowed as she continued to talk, perhaps distracted by the memories of their days together. The momentary reverie created the illusion that her hands were lingering on her nether region in a lustful way, inciting a hot flash to pass through Anne. When Mary's hands mercifully moved up to her belly, Anne realized that she had stopped breathing.

Aggravated with herself, she inhaled as quietly as she could and prayed that Mary would not hear. She knew she should just close her eyes and go to sleep, but watching Mary's softly lit reflection in the window made her feel as though she was looking on from afar, from a protected place where her actions could not be discovered. It was an indulgence she was not yet ready to relinquish.

"Even when Jack had you brought to his cell – his last request – you knew where your heart lay and you gave no quarter. 'If you had fought like a man, you needn't be hanged like a dog,' you told him. God, what magnificent truth you spoke, Annie! Our lives would have been much different had we been able to rouse the crew – those drunken bastards – and Jack was no better than they were."

Mary paused for a moment, staring at her reflection as if looking for answers to questions that she had never thought about until now. Again, she rinsed out the sponge then lifted one breast to clean the delicate flesh underneath and then did the other.

Still the clandestine observer, Anne followed every move, submitting herself to a slow, carnal torture that tested her resolve – and her sanity. Pent up desires too-long denied screamed for release. Perspiration on her temple pooled together to form a drop that ran across her cheek, under her chin, and down her neck.

Mary Read laughed softly. Fearing that she had been caught staring, Anne's attention snapped back into focus.

"Do you remember that stupid tribade that testified against us at the trial? What was her name... Doris... Dodie...? Something like that. The ungrateful manatee. I should have let you kill her like you wanted after we looted her pathetic little canoe. And a fine thanks we got, too, for allowing her to live."

Dropping the sponge into the basin, she cupped her breasts in both hands, lifting and pushing them together, making them appear as though squeezed into a corset. Twisting her body to view her profile from each side, she shrugged her shoulders in a "not bad, given the years" verdict.

"Do you remember how she witnessed us?" she continued. And then in a mocking voice, "'I knew they was women, your lordship, by the largeness of their breasts.' All those years pretending to be a man, and what good did it do? Done in by the testimony of a woman who should've been on her knees thanking us for her life."

Finished with her musings – and receiving no encouragement to go on – Mary let her breasts fall free and resumed her bathing. When she was done, she toweled herself off and put on one of the captain's shirts as Anne had done. She then blew out the lantern's flame and slipped under the cover. Moving as close to Anne as she could without touching, she raised up on one elbow and leaned over to whisper in her ear.

"I know you're awake, Annie. Did you enjoy the show?"

Anne felt a rush of heat and was thankful that Mary Read could not see her red face. Her body remembered things her mind struggled to suppress, and for a moment she teetered on the edge of surrender. No matter how much she wanted to give in, she could not forgive the wrong Mary Read had committed against Tye.

"Don't worry, sweetie. I'll not be throwing myself at you. What would be the fun in that? I want you to come to me on your own accord. And come to me you will, as surely as the Caribbean wind blows warm and fair. Because, no matter what you've told yourself, you can't deny who you are any more than I can. We are the same, my sweet Annie. You and me, we are the same."

# CHAPTER TWENTY-FIVE

TYE LOOKED AT THE WATCH resting in the palm of his hand, impressed by its excellent craftsmanship and detail. Though he knew it was Dyonis's watch, he had yet to possess it. The braided leather cord running through the timepiece's metal ring was tied together behind the neck of the sleeping crewman named Oliver Cullen who wore it. Even if he could reach the knot, he was sure it was too intricate to undo without rousing the man. Nor could he slip the cord over his head, unless he shifted into a different position.

Tye had been keeping an eye on the black-haired Bermudian since noticing Dyonis's watch hanging around his neck. Given that he was missing a chunk of flesh from his cheek that left cheekbone, jawbone, and half of his teeth exposed, he was an easy man to spot. The hideous cutlass wound had given rise to two nicknames. One was "Skullen," the name the crew called him to his face, and the other was "Cull the Skull," the one they used when they did not think he could hear them.

After dark, Tye had kept as close to the man as he dared until he picked out a spot on deck to sleep. Now, by the dim light of the stars and moon, he crouched over Skullen with the watch in his hand, trying to figure out how to recover the timepiece without waking him.

In a sudden jolt, Skullen sat up in his bunk and thrust his head within an inch of touching the boy. The Bermudian clutched at his face as though he were in agonizing pain, reliving in a dream the moment he had lost his left cheek. His eyebrows arched so high it seemed that they would leap from his face. His eyes bulged so much Tye thought they would pop out of their sockets. Foul breath poured from his perpetually wheezing mouth.

Then, as suddenly as it had started, the wild display was over. Skullen closed his eyes and fell back on his mat, sound asleep. His eyes may have been open, but he had never really been awake.

Motivated by the shock of nearly being caught, a new idea leaped into his mind. Retrieving the marlinspike from the outseam of his breeches where he kept it, he used the narrow tip to open a gap in the metal link through which the leather cord passed and removed the watch. Now, instead of thinking that someone had stolen it from him, Skullen would believe that the watch had fallen off the cord on its own.

When he got back to his room, he could see by the light of the Betty lamp that Dyonis was in much the same state as he had been since the incident at Cedar Island - curled up in a ball on the floor. Settling down beside him, Tye gave Dyonis a soft shove and told him to sit up.

"I have something for you," he said. "Something that belongs to you."

Curiosity getting the better of him, Dyonis sat up to see what it might be.

"I took it from one of the pirates. I had to leave the cord, but...well here. This belongs to you."

Rather than take the watch, Dyonis stared at the thing in Tye's hand as though afraid to touch it.

"It is your watch, isn't it?" Tye asked, afraid that he may have kicked a hornet's nest for no reason.

Cautiously, Dyonis took the watch and studied it, turning it over and over, looking at it from every angle. Then he held it to his ear for a moment to listen to the machine's inner workings. A tear formed in the corner of his eye and ran down his cheek.

"Yes," he said at last, clasping both hands around the watch and clutching it to his heart.

Tye studied him for a moment, looking for signs of normalcy – whatever that might be for a man who believed himself to be a bird.

"Here," he said, holding out some dried meat and bread wrapped in a cloth. "You need to eat and drink. I have water, too."

Dyonis gave him a blank stare, and for a moment Tye feared that he was about to withdraw again.

"I need your help, Dyonis...Birdman. I need a man who can keep time. Accurate time. Can you do that? Can you keep time for me?"

Tye saw a hint of life coming back to Dyonis's expression. His eyes drifted for a moment as though trying to make a decision.

"Tick...tick...tick..." he replied. "Birdman is no more. I am Timekeeper. I will keep the time. I like keeping time. Tick...tick...tick..."

Tye thought he understood. Adopting a new persona was a transition Dyonis had to make to separate himself from the trauma he had suffered. Being stripped of his feathers had stripped him of his dignity. Without his feathers, all he had left was shame. And the only way to remove that shame was to create a new cloak, one that could never be taken away.

"Thank you," Tye said, placing his hand on Dyonis's shoulder. "You will have a very important task. I will need for you to be the clock of England."

Dyonis looked at him, confused.

"Don't worry, I'll explain later. In the meantime, I have some good news. I've been talking to Briebras. He and Kofi – the darkie that was trying to help the night you knocked my mum and the others overboard – are chained together, but otherwise free to move about the ship to do their work. They know you are here and we are...working together to find a way off the ship."

The last part wasn't entirely true. They had only gotten as far as agreeing to create a plan. They hadn't had an opportunity yet to actually come up with any. Tye wasn't sure how far Dyonis had come back from his depression and just wanted to give him hope for now.

"Rader told me that we are sailing to Charles Town. I'm not sure what he intends to do, but I know it is something dangerous. Once we are close to land or in the harbor there will be many opportunities to escape...but we must make ready."

"Tick...tick...tick..." Dyonis replied, still holding the watch close. "It is 12:07 a.m. That means ante meridiem."

"Seven minutes after twelve? I'm late! You make an excellent timekeeper, Dyonis."

"I keep time. I am Timekeeper."

"And now it is time for you to sleep," the boy said, rising to leave. "Tomorrow I have much to teach you, and you need to rest. I know you haven't been sleeping. Promise me you will sleep tonight."

"I promise. I promise I will eat. And then I will sleep. But, where are you going?"

"I have to see someone."

"Is he a pirate?"

"Not exactly. Just someone who needs a friend. I need to go now, all right?"

"All right. But you'll come back, won't you?"

"Yes," Tye said as he left the room. "I won't be long. Now, go to sleep."

"Tye..."

"Yes?"

"Thank you."

"You're welcome," he replied. Then with a smile he added, "Timekeeper."

Hurrying topside again, Tye stopped at the hatch and scanned the deck. They were supposed to have met at the capstan at midnight, but he only saw the silhouette of the night watch standing near the bow. It was a dangerous game they were playing, one that could easily turn around and bite them both. The failure to show up could mean several things, almost all of them bad. But it could also mean that his help was needed now more than ever.

Movement caught his attention and he spotted a slight figure huddled up against the capstan. Taking a deep breath, he scooted across the deck to the large round winch, keeping low and quiet.

"Hello," he whispered.

When she did not reply, his heart sank. Things must be getting worse, despite his efforts.

"Clairette, are you all right?"

Rather than answer, the blonde-haired girl brought her hands to her face and began to sobbing silently. Tye watched with helpless frustration as Clairette took in great breaths of air, endured the spasm of a restrained wail, and then start the process over again.

"Did he hit you again?"

Clairette struggled to regain her composure, then moved her hands away from her face.

The hideous ruin she revealed startled Tye. Even in the dim light he could see that one of her eyes was black and swollen shut. The entire left side of her face was bruised, and her lips were split in several places. He could see dried blood under her nose and it looked like it might be broken. The shock he felt gave way to anger. For the first time in his young life, he felt the fire of rage course through his veins. This was at least the third time that Rader had beaten her. Each time she came away more withdrawn.

"You've got to get away," Tye said, taking one of her hands into his.

"But how? You said that last time. Have you seen any way for me to escape? When we were close to land, he watched me every minute or locked me in the cabin. Now we are too far away to swim for it. I... I don't think I can take much more."

"No," Tye said. "Don't give up. We'll be close to land again, soon. And if that doesn't work, there will be other chances. I promise. But you can't give up."

Clairette looked at the sky, resting the back of her head against the capstan. A tear ran down her cheek and she sighed in despair.

It was an unlikely friendship, but one that had budded quickly after Tye had brought her water and cleaned her cuts a few days before. Since that first night they had talked several times, albeit briefly. It was clear that the realization she was not alone had lifted her spirits at first. But now, Tye saw that she believed nothing was going to change – that there would be no escaping Rader's brutality.

"You'd better go before he sees us together," she said.

"I don't care if he–"

"No. Don't. If I have any chance at all, it rests with you."

Tye's heart stilled a moment as Clairette placed her hand on his cheek, her eyes filled with both gratitude and reluctant acceptance of the inevitable. The moonlight flirted with the curves of her face, invoking the likeness of La Tour's Repentant Magdalene. The heart of the man that Tye would become ached to be more than the boy he was.

"You are a sweet lad, and I thank you for what you have done. You're...different...in a good way. Smarter than I could ever hope to be. I made a big mistake and now I'm paying for it. If you want to help me, don't give him an excuse to break his agreement with you. As long as you are free to roam the ship, I have hope."

Tye struggled to reply. Her words were convincing, but the gruesome collage of bloody cuts, welts, and scabs that was Clairette's face spoke to him in a different way. If only he were older, bigger – there would be nothing to consider. He would have already killed Rader, or died in the attempt. But she was right. Her only chance – their only chance – was to outwit Rader. If he could somehow manage to arrange Rader's demise in the process, then so much the better.

"Stay away from him," Tye said, "as much as you can. And promise me that you won't give up. You can't give up."

"I promise," she said, conceding a slight smile. "Now, be off before the piper comes for his due. I'll be all right. I will."

"Swear it!"

"I swear."

Tye took her hand again and squeezed it hard. He had no idea what he was going to do, but he wanted to leave her with the belief that anything was possible.

On the way back to his quarters he began to feel the heavy burden of responsibility he carried on his small shoulders. First, there was Kofi and Briebras. The ship would soon be nearing Charles Town, yet he was still trying to figure out a way to help them. He needed to find a way to have their shackles removed, so that if things went bad, they might be able to save themselves. He was also sure that Clairette was on her last leg, despite her promise. She was saying the right things, but she was saying them for his sake. Her eyes could not lie.

And then there was Dyonis. Asku's brother seemed to be recovering, but there was no way to be sure how much he would embrace his new identity, much less his new task. Tye felt fairly confident that he could keep them all alive - at least for awhile - if Dyonis could keep Greenwich time in his head. As far as creating a plan that would allow everyone to escape Rader and *Rackham's Revenge* - he had no idea.

As he settled down next to the already slumbering Dyonis for the night, he had one final thought. Unless she was dead, his mother was out there - somewhere - trying to find him."

# CHAPTER TWENTY-SIX

ANNE WAKENED WITH A START, jolted from her restless slumber by explosive thunder peeling across the sound. Gale-force winds tore through the ship's rigging as bolts of lightning blasted light into the cabin in an irregular but unrelenting tempo. Though it was still the dark of night, she was sure the ship was moving. Something was terribly wrong.

It had taken Anne hours to fall asleep. Sabotaged by Mary Read's evocative manipulations, she had lain in bed damning her raven-haired tormentor for putting her in such an agitated state. Mary Read had reentered her life hell-bent on revenge, and in taking Tye, she had exacted her toll. So why was she now acting like nothing had ever come between them, that the water was no longer poisoned? Did she consider the matter settled? The debt paid?

None of it made sense. Beyond confusing, it was maddening. All Anne wanted at this point was to recover Tye and be done with Mary Read and this pirate nonsense. While she would never go back to the life she had in Bath, she was even less inclined to associate with the likes of Mary Read. There had to be a third way, and she would find it.

But now there was a more immediate concern. If the *Hazard* was adrift then they were in danger of being swept out to sea, or worse, running aground on a sandbar to be battered into pieces by the waves. Turning to wake Mary, she found only the disheveled spot on the sheet where the woman had slept. A flash of lightning illuminated the room, revealing that the cabin was empty. Mary's absence ramped up Anne's concern and she began to wonder how bad things were.

Not bothering to dress, Anne ran onto the deck wearing only her make-do nightshirt. A blast of wind and pelting rain stopped her in mid-stride. As she struggled to regain her balance, another bolt of lightning blasted through the darkness only a few hundred yards away. The thunder that followed shook Anne to the bone, but it was what she saw in the flash that made her shiver.

Mary Read stood at the ship's helm, the wind thrashing her long, soaking-wet hair about her head like small black whips lashing out at the storm. Her arms strained against the wheel as she fought to gain control of the ship. Having broken free of its anchor, the *Hazard* was drifting sideways, caught in the flow of water passing through the inlet on the ebbing tide. Beyond the inlet lay a maze of shoals and sandbars, ready to snatch the ship's hull by the keel and hold her down for the merciless breakers to finish off.

Grabbing onto anything that wouldn't move, Anne pulled herself along the deck toward Mary Read. Another flash confirmed her fear – they were the only two people on deck, and the shoals were drawing ever closer. At the same moment, Mary Read turned and saw that she was no longer alone.

"GO TO THE BOWSPRIT!" she shouted above the howling wind. "SET THE JIB!"

Anne nodded understanding and began fighting her way through the wind and rain. Without forward motion to drive the ship faster than the current, the rudder was having little effect. The jib was the only sail that Anne might be able to manage by herself.

As she pulled herself along, Anne continued scanning the deck for Asku, Gant, Scarlette – anybody. Where were they? Had they gone ashore? For what? Food? Water? But why at night? And why all of them? Nothing made sense.

Reaching the bow, she threw her leg over the sprit, and with the water tossing violently below, she began to inch her way up the spar to the outermost lashing. Each time the bow lifted, she scooted a few more inches forward. When the bow dipped toward the churning water, she held on with all her strength. Reaching the sail's head, the lightning flashes revealed that the halyard was still secure. At the same moment, the bow tracked downward and the bowsprit crashed into a large swell. Anne dug her fingernails into the canvas and held on for all she was worth. The bow blasted through the surge with Anne soaked to the bone. The bowsprit was trying to live up to its nickname – widowmaker – but still hung on.

Untying the outer lashing, she began to inch her way backward toward the deck. Despite the wind's fury and the relentless assault of the roiling water, Anne managed to untie each lashing to release the canvas. In short time, she made it back to the relative safety of the bow, but her work was only half done. Each time the bow dipped, the sagging folds of the unfurled sail plunged into the water. If the sail opened even a little, the water would snag it and rip it from the sprit.

Scrambling to the foremast, Anne grabbed the halyard and pulled the line hand-over-hand as fast as she could. A blast of wind hit the rising sail, blowing the sheet open with such force it exploded into the night air. The sudden unfurling ripped the halyard through Anne's hands, burning her palms and fingers before mercifully coming to a halt. Taking advantage of the wind's lull, she cleated off the halyard and collapsed in a heap against the foremast.

Her chest rose and fell in great heaves as she struggled to find her breath. The rain beating on her face was part heaven, part hell – revitalizing and torturous at the same time. Peering out over the bow, the lightning's onslaught revealed that the jib was flying free and fair, her sheets somehow finding the proper trim on their own as if by providence. Beneath her, she sensed the water begin sliding past the hull as the sail pulled the ship at a clip faster than the current. Looking back toward the stern, she saw a smile spread across

Mary Read's face during the flashes of lightning as the rudder began to bite the water. The brig was beginning to straighten.

Crawling back to the bow, Anne pulled herself up far enough to see over the gunnel and into the darkness. Each time the lightning ripped across the sky, she tried to determine their position and any dangers ahead. They were almost in the throat of the channel, about to pass between the two points of land through which the water flowed. Very much different from the channel at Ocracoke, the inlet Drexel had brought them to was deep but dangerously narrow. So close was the ship's passage that a stone thrown to either side would have landed on sand.

The lightning held off for a moment – and a moment more. Anne held her breath waiting for the next flash, desperate to know their progress. At last, a jagged line of light tore through the blackness, striking the water mere yards from the bow. Enveloped by the concussion, Anne felt the teeth in the back of her mouth rattle and was vaguely aware that she may have lost her water. Dazed, every detail of the inlet floated before her, seared into the back of her eyes by a light brighter than the sun. The image began to drift away, merging into the dark, but not before the fading imprint revealed a new danger. A hundred yards ahead, the channel took a hard turn to starboard and then completed its flow into the ocean. If they continued on their present course, they were sure to run aground.

Cupping her hands around her mouth, Anne shouted as loud as she could, but the wind obliterated the words long before they reached Mary Read. Rising to her feet, she pushed away from the gunwale and staggered back to the foremast.

"HARD A STARBOARD!" she yelled again. Again, the wind drove her words into oblivion. Mary Read stared at Anne from the aft, her face knotted in confusion.

With time running out, Anne leaned against the foremast for balance. With her arms free, she began to pantomime the act of pulling on the wheel followed by frantic pointing to her left.

Mary's look of confusion morphed into understanding and she leaned into the wheel with all her might. The rudder took hold and the bow began to turn with all the urgency of a glacier flow. But as the brig's speed increased, so did the angle of the deck. As the ship leaned hard to starboard, the two women struggled to keep their balance while looking down to see the point passing by the rail just a few feet away. Anne held her breath while the ship slowly completed its turn, passing so close to the spit of land it seemed as though she could have easily leaped from the deck onto the sand.

And then they were through. Turning the wheel to straighten course, Mary Read piloted the ship out of the channel and into the open water. As the brig moved farther from shore, the two women rested in place at opposite ends of the deck. The torrent of rain began to subside into a downpour and the buffeting wind became a hard, steady blow. Though the heart of the storm had passed, its trailing edge continued to unleash great lightning bolts upon the ocean's surface.

Still resting against the foremast, Anne stared at Mary Read during each flash. Like Anne, she had not had time to put on clothes and wore only the shirt she had commandeered from the captain's locker. Rivulets of water streamed around her face, her hair matted wet against her cheeks and chest. She stood at the wheel, strong and undaunted, as though there had never been any danger.

Anne continued watching as Mary Read scanned the horizon beyond the bow. When their eyes finally met, Anne refused to look away. For the first time since coming out on the deck, she realized that Mary was wearing her eye patch. *The crazy vixen had taken the time to satisfy her vanity before venturing out into the teeth of the storm.* Anne found the absurdity of the indulgence somehow reassuring, a remembrance of better times when they had been friends. Her resolve to hate Mary gave a little, and she cursed her weakness.

Anne felt her body respond as Mary Read continued caressing her with her gaze. Anne realized, that like Mary's, her drenched blouse was plastered against her body by the wind. Turned translucent by the rain, it was as though Mary wore nothing at all. Low resonances from the thunder vibrated through the ship's hull and into her core. She shivered.

Anne had covered half the distance between them before realizing that she had left the security of the foremast. Her legs moved by their own volition, bringing her ever closer to the helm. Mary stood behind the ship's wheel, watching impatiently as she took each step.

When she reached the helm, Anne slid around the wheel and Mary turned to face her. They stood so close that their wind-whipped hair tangled together like dark snakes. Several moments passed as the now distant flashes of light played upon their faces, two women standing eye to eye – equals in stature, resolve, and passion.

A final lightning bolt created by a gap in the breaking clouds razed the invisible barrier that held them apart. Like water rushing from a broken dam, they came together in desperate embrace. Their first hungry kiss unleashed a torrent of desire, their lips pressing together with bruising consummation. Anne reveled in the sensation of their embrace, the firm roundness of their breasts and bellies and thighs settling into welcoming niches long left unfilled. Heat surged through her body, a forge of need stoked ever higher by the bellows of desire.

Mary placed her hands on Anne's face and guided her head back, forcing an end to their kiss. Anne stared at Mary Read, her mouth pleading for more, but at the same time, her eyes were demanding answers. Mary looked back at Anne, her face revealing nothing but the deep, burning ache that consumed her.

"Mary..." Anne whispered, her lips brushing Mary Read's. Closing her eyes, she gasped and whispered again, this time imploring, "Mary... My Duchess... I want–"

"Anne." The emphatic call cut through her stupor like a knife shredding through the canvas of a beautiful Furini.

"Anne!" Mary Read said again, this time more demanding. "Wake up! Are you going to sleep the day away?"

"What... What happened? Where are we?"

"About ten miles southwest of Cape Lookout. Asku's mate piloted us through the inlet and cut loose to go home about an hour ago."

"What about the storm? The crew?"

"The crew is close-hauled and spoiling for trouble – and the only storm to speak of is the one brewing inside Bloody Bill Scarlette. I pity the bugger that lights his fuse."

Anne looked around the room as she tried to right herself. The restless state Mary Read had put her in the night before had kept her awake for hours. The whole episode with the storm and the channel had been nothing but a dream invented during a bout of exhausted sleep, conjured up by Mary Read's unabashed baiting.

Awake now, she turned her attention back to Mary Read standing next to their bed with her arms crossed like a mother who had caught her child in a lie. Anne felt her face flush hot, realizing that Mary knew more than she was letting on.

"You better get dressed and come out on deck. There's a whole day ahead and I think the men...all of the men...are growing impatient. You do know that every man on board lusts for you, right?"

"No...no I... What?" The comment threw Anne off kilter.

"It's true. But, that was always the way of it, and you know it. Oh, I had my fair share of admirers, and am glad for it. But there aren't many willing to look past this scar and the dead eye I earned in Spanish Town. I'm at peace with that. But you're a handsome woman, Anne Brennan Bonny Rackham, so don't be pretending that you're not. It's not becoming of you...and we both know better."

Mary opened the door and started out to the deck.

"Anne..." she said, pausing for a moment.

"Yes?"

"I want you, too."

And then she was gone.

# CHAPTER TWENTY-SEVEN

"NOW WHAT TIME IS IT?"

"In England or here?"

"In Greenwich, England," Tye shot back, trying not to show his frustration. "I only need for you to know the time in Greenwich. Whenever I ask you the time, just give me Greenwich time. You've got to remember that."

"But, I know both," Dyonis said, beaming. "I am Timekeeper!"

Dispirited, Tye plopped down on the soft sand, propped his elbows on his knees and placed his face in his palms. If responsibilities were stones, his bag was full and his shoulders were suffering under the burden. Both mentally and physically exhausted, he allowed his mind a few minutes to wander.

They had set up a field table about a hundred feet from the waterline where he could rest his octant and scribble out his calculations by lantern light. The outline of *Rackham's Revenge* - anchored about a hundred yards beyond the tidal sandbar - was clearly visible in the moonlight. The air was still and thick with humidity. Reduced to ripples, the surf made so little noise it didn't even drown out the crickets.

Behind them stood Curlee Leathers and the two crewmen who had rowed them ashore, eliminating any thoughts the two might have of making a dash for the brush. Even if Tye and Dyonis managed to escape, the island was so small it would be impossible to evade their captors for long. But Tye had no intention of trying to get away, not with his friends still on board the *Revenge*.

A thousand thoughts swirled around inside his head. How would he get them all free at the same time? How could he protect Clairette from that bastard, Blyth Rader? Were his calculations truly correct? And how in God's name was he going to teach Dyonis to give him only Greenwich time? The little boy that he still was wanted to cry, but the responsibility he shouldered would not allow it. There was too much to do and too many people depending on him.

Earlier in the day, Rader had piloted the schooner past the inlet to Charles Town's harbor, giving the pirate captain the opportunity to take stock of the heavily laden merchant ships and affording Tye a chance to see the target they would be shooting for later. Once past the inlet, they continued following the shoreline until dropping anchor at this small island nestled in the mouth of the Edisto River.

After setting up his station, Tye spent the afternoon taking sightings, checking the tables and performing calculations to determine the exact astrological time for their location. Then he did the same for Greenwich, England. The mathematics involved were far beyond the fundamentals Mary Read had taught him. Sometimes the progressions came to him quickly, following a natural order that he understood without explanation. At other times he invented formulas to come up with solutions, and sometimes he just made a wild-ass guess based on instinct.

Once he thought he had worked it all out, Tye used the coachman's watch to show Dyonis the time in England. To Tye's surprise, Dyonis grasped the concept right away and matched his calculations to the second. Tye repeated the test twice more, and each time his calculations and Dyonis's internal clock were in accordance.

Then came the snag. The boy had assumed that once Dyonis's internal clock was reset to Greenwich time, that would be the only clock in his head. He realized now – given how Dyonis was able to track local time while simultaneously calculating tides at any given point along the Outer Banks – he should have known better. Indeed, Dyonis's ability to keep various times seemed limitless. It was as if the man was not keeping time at all, but was somehow in harmony with the temporal universe around him, feeling time rather than tracking it.

"Which one?" Dyonis asked again.

Tye didn't have to look at Asku's brother to know that he was clutching the coachman's watch. Dyonis didn't need the watch to keep track of time, he had learned the proper lengths of seconds, minutes, and hours long ago. Tye suspected he held on to it much the same way a child clings to a blanket or a doll for security. It was a connection to his past, a reminder of his family and his home.

But Birdman was gone forever. Not only had Dyonis shed his plucked cape, he had somehow managed to alter his appearance as though he were a human chameleon. When Tye first saw Dyonis in his new garb – scrounged up from who-knew-where – he understood that Dyonis was embracing his new persona. The brown, straight-lined clothes he now wore made him appear taller and more narrow. Without the tight-fitting hood of the cape covering his head, Dyonis's face appeared rounder. The mustache he was growing was narrow and pointed at the ends like the hands on a clock. Tye was convinced that in a few days, Dyonis would be able to stand against the wall and pass himself off as a grandfather clock. All he needed was for someone to add Roman numerals to his face.

Then a new thought occurred to him. Although his mind had strayed from the problem at hand, his subconscious had continued struggling for a solution. It was so simple, he felt stupid for not having thought of it right away.

"Dyonis, from now on I will tell you how I want the time so that there is no confusion, all right?"

Dyonis's expression showed that he wasn't sure.

"Here, let's try it...give me Greenwich time."

"Nine fifty-seven A M," he said without hesitating. A smile spread across his face as he began to understand.

"Cracking good!" Tye said as he picked up his octant.

By the light of the lantern, he made a few sightings and scribbled them down on a slate with a piece of chalk. Dyonis watched with curiosity as the boy made calculations at a feverish pace, using both sides of the slate.

"Yes!" he shouted. The sound of his voice stirred some of the birds roosting in the nearby marsh for a moment before settling down again. "We've done it, Dyonis! I have our longitude!"

"Longitude!" Dyonis echoed, joining in the celebration. Though he understood what the word meant, he had no idea why it was important to his young friend. But seeing Tye happy made him feel good.

"It's 'bout time," Curlee Leathers said, his deep voice cutting off their celebration. "The mosquitoes are eatin' me alive and Cap'n Rader will be wantin' to know if you can hold up your end of the bargain. Now pack it all in an' let's head back to the ship."

A short time later, Tye was standing on the schooner's deck, his octant secured under his arm, looking up at Blyth Rader. Light from the ship's lanterns played tag with the darkness, dashing back and forth across Rader's face in an eerie dance. The fluid movement of the shadows made his mutilated nose seem to pulse as though it were an evil, living thing, moving on its own volition.

Placing his arms behind his back, Rader bent over slightly and looked at the boy in expectation. A breeze stirred the tufts of feathers on his hat.

"Well?" he asked.

"I can do it."

Everyone on deck remained silent as Rader studied the boy, trying to decide whether to believe him or not. A few moments passed before he straightened up to peer down at the boy over his deformed nose.

"All right," he said to his men while continuing to stare at Tye. "At dawn, we sail due east over the horizon. From there we prepare the cannon, sharpen our swords, and load our muskets with fresh powder. After sunset, young

Master Tye will navigate us into the harbor as pretty as you please and we will take the town while it sleeps."

"Aye!" several of the men shouted in approval. Excited conversations broke out across the deck, then died as quickly as they had begun.

"What about the *Hazard*?" the first mate asked.

Charles Town was a fortified settlement, the only city in North America the English had deemed necessary to enclose with a wall. The original plan included using both ships and relied upon deception. Only a madman or a genius would try to take the city with one ship.

"That's the beauty of it," Rader said, at last turning away from Tye to face his men. "We don't need the *Hazard*, now. We'll make it to the dock under the cover of darkness and walk into town as if they had given us the key to the gate. Once they realize we're there, it will be too late. The *Hazard* will close the inlet as soon as they arrive, but we don't need them to cover our rear, we'll have command and control of their cannons. The harbor and everything in it will be ours."

"Sail through the inlet to Charles Town harbor in the middle of the night?"

"That's right," Rader said, stiffening. "For all we know, the *Hazard* won't be here for days, or even a week or more. What I do know is that the longer we sit here the more likely it is that someone will see us and start to ask questions. It's been years since there's been any real threat of piracy and the people of Charles Town have gotten lazy, but they're not stupid. If we go in now they won't suspect anything is awry until it's too late for them to stop us. If we wait, we're all likely to be hanged. And I, for one, have no intention of hanging."

"But...sail through the inlet...at night?" Leathers said again. "'How?"

"With this..." Tye answered, holding up his octant. He had no desire to help Rader, but he knew they would have a much better chance of escaping if they were in the harbor than if they were on the ocean. "...and with my calculations. I have devised a way to navigate that can determine within a hundred feet where on the Earth we are located."

Leathers stared at the boy, his brow creased into a knot. For a moment, Tye thought he was either going to laugh or give him the back of his hand.

"Tell me, little minnow, exactly what do you know about navigation?"

"To start with, I know geodetics, cartography, trigonometry, angular measurement, and lunar distance," Tye shot back without missing a beat. "What do you know about navigation?"

Several of the crew chuckled and even Rader smiled. Leathers' smirk changed into a look of disbelief and then defeat.

"There you have it," Rader said, shutting off any further objections. "It will be light in a couple of hours and the wind should soon be stirring. I want sails set with the first breath of air and be beyond the horizon with all haste. Am I clear?"

"Aye, cap'n," Leathers said, and then began shouting orders to the crew.

Turning back to look down at Tye, Rader's smile disappeared as quickly as it had emerged.

"You keep your wits about you when you're under fire, I'll concede that. But do not confuse my benevolence with weakness. If you fail to hit that inlet, you and your walking, talking, chronometer friend will be shark food. Understand?"

Tye nodded but did not avert his eyes from Rader's. He did not fear Rader's threats. He was more concerned about what the man wasn't saying. Tye had bartered his safety and that of Dyonis in exchange for his navigation skills. Once they were safely in Charles Town Harbor, there were no guarantees Rader would still need those skills. Tye knew what a conundrum was, and understood that he was in one. To survive, he had to successfully navigate the inlet at night. Navigating the inlet might also hasten his death. It was yet another stone added to his burden.

Blyth Rader returned to the helm without further comment, leaving Tye and Dyonis free to rest until night came again. Rest, however, was the last thing on Tye's mind. He had to make sure that Kofi and Briebras could be freed from their ankle chain when it came time to escape, and he had to let Clairette know how to tell when they were going to make their move. But first, he needed to go to his room and make sure his equipment was ready and that he had everything he needed to make his calculations. If he failed to guide *Rackham's Revenge* through the inlet, all of his efforts would be for naught.

Once below deck, he saw light coming from beneath the door to his storeroom quarters. Dyonis was following behind him, so it had to be someone who did not belong there...and then he knew. Dashing across the last few feet, he flung open the door and searched the dimly lit room for Clairette.

"Shut the door!" Kofi hissed in his squeaky voice from the back of the room.

Tye hurried Dyonis inside and closed the door. Clairette was sitting in the far corner, her back against the bulkhead and her legs extended in front of her like a rag doll's. Briebras was kneeling beside her, gingerly wiping blood from her cheek with a damp cloth. Although he whispered soothing words to her in French, she stared off into the distance as though unaware. Kofi stood as far from Briebras as his ankle chain would allow, ready to defend the bloodied girl if they were discovered by Rader or one of the crew.

"What happened?" Tye asked, regretting the words even as they left his mouth.

"Her skull, I think he may have cracked it," Briebras said, answering the question he knew Tye meant to ask. "I fear that she may have a concussion."

Briebras turned to look at Tye and froze.

"Palsambleu! Mon ami petit, are you all right?"

Rather than the round, soft visage of a boy, Tye's face had become taut and gray. His eyes were red from sleepless nights and fatigue. His pupils were dark and lifeless. Captivity was affecting Tye's emotional state, and the physical change that went with it was startling.

"I'm glad you're here," Tye said, shrugging off Briebras' concern. "We'll be going to Charles Town in the dark of tomorrow's morn. We need to be ready to make our escape. We must all be ready."

"I am not sure," Briebras said. "I think Mademoiselle Clairette will be all right, but she can take little more abuse. I fear for her life."

"He is done with me for tonight," Clairette whispered through cracked lips. "He will not look for me again until nightfall."

Tye went to Clairette and took her hand in his.

"Clairette, if...if there is a battle, will you be able to break away from Rader and make a run for it? Can you?"

It took Clairette so long to answer, Tye began to wonder if she had heard him. Finally, she looked down at her hand cradled in his as though to make sure he was still there.

"Do not worry about me. I will do what must be done."

Tye and Briebras exchanged a look, wondering if she was speaking truthfully or just telling Tye what he wanted to hear.

"I thought Rader was waiting for the *Hazard*," Kofi said to end the awkward silence.

"Well, that was the original plan. Rader was going to have us lay low until Wennell and his crew caught up. Then, together, we were going to sail to Charles Town's harbor pretending to be merchant ships. Wennell and the *Hazard* would anchor near the inlet while Rader would continue on to the wharf. When the customs collector came by to inspect their cargo they were going take him hostage. Unsuspecting ships would be allowed to enter the harbor to be looted at the pirates' leisure, but no ships would be allowed to leave."

"I do not understand," Briebras said. "Holding one man might keep the militia at bay for awhile, but they would not surrender the entire town in exchange for one life."

"Rader knows that," Clairette said, rallying from her stupor. "He also planned to have several of his men go into the village and kidnap the first two or three white children they came upon...the more prominent their families the better. Once they had the children on board the *Revenge*, they were going to force the town leaders to do their bidding."

"It's true," Tye said, keeping his eye on Clairette as he took over. "But now, he...we...will sail into the harbor under cover of darkness. Rader plans to take the governor and his family hostage and take over the city before they even know they have been invaded."

"Ahhh... I see," Briebras said. "If they have the town, they have the cannons along the wall and bastions. With such powerful cannon, they can prevent any ships from leaving or entering."

"That's not the sum of it," Tye continued. "I heard Rader say that it will be a simple matter to convince many of the seamen from the merchant ships to join them. He plans on taking over one or two ships in the harbor and have those men guard the inlet. If that works, the *Hazard* will be free to do his bidding elsewhere."

"Oui, it is a very good plan," Briebras said, contemplating the ramifications. "Rader will be able to loot the town and all the ships in the harbor before their militia can do anything to stop him. In two days, he will have accumulated unimaginable riches."

A dry, sardonic laugh rolled past Clairette's bruised lips.

"You underestimate Rader," she said. "But then, we all did. Not only does he plan to loot the city, he intends to turn it into a pirate fortress. It may have been Mary Read's idea, but Rader has not let that fact keep him from embracing it as though it were his own. The difference will be the way in which he will control them. Where Mary Read would have used iron will and threats to manage the villagers...Blyth Rader will employ abject fear and torture."

"But the Royal Navy, it is the most powerful force in the world," Briebras said. "Once they learn pirates have taken over–"

"You still don't understand," Clairette said, cutting him off. "Britain and Spain have a truce, that's true, but King George cannot afford to scatter his navy...not yet. The truce could fall apart in an instant if the diegos think they have an advantage. Rader plans to commandeer all of the most seaworthy craft in the harbor and any new ones that arrive and convert them into warships. Crews that don't join him will be threatened and tortured into taking the pirate oath, as will the slaves."

"How can you know this?" Tye challenged.

"Because of this!" Clairette snapped.

Leaning into the full light, she pulled her hair back. For the first time since entering the room Tye could see the beaten, swollen pulp her face had become. He caught his gasp in time, but his expression betrayed the horror he felt. Clairette was almost unrecognizable. The damage Rader had inflicted on her earlier paled in comparison to his latest work.

"And because when he talks to his mate he is no more concerned about talking with me in the room than if I were a dog...which, in truth, is what I have become. Mark my words, if he's not stopped he will bring hell upon the people of Charles Town and any who run afoul of his ambitions."

Exhausted by the outburst, she let her hair fall around her face again and leaned back against the wall. No one spoke for several minutes, numbed by the audacity and scope of Rader's ambitions. Having sensed the evil residing in Rader from the beginning, Tye had no doubts that Clairette spoke the truth. He also realized that – more than ever – their best chance of escaping would be shortly after guiding the ship through the channel. Once Rader carried out his plans and secured Charles Town, there would be no reason to keep any of them alive.

"Can you get out of your shackles?" he asked.

"Yes," Kofi said without elaborating.

"Oui," Briebras said. "We could have been rid of them long ago, but it would do no good, for we have nowhere to go. Two strikes of the hammer on a cold chisel...*CHING-CHING*...and the shackles are no more."

"Clairette, are you sure you can you be ready to leave at a moment's notice?" Tye asked for the second time. "Can you watch for Briebras and Kofi and join with them?"

"I will do what must be done," she said without looking up.

"Listen closely to me, all of you. I do not have a plan. I only know that Rader intends to enter the city while it's dark. There will have to be moments when no one is watching us. Whenever that moment comes, we take whatever opportunity is afforded...whether it is jumping over the side and swimming to shore or running through town to alert the night watch. We stick together and we help each other no matter what may occur. Agree?"

"What about Dyonis?" Briebras asked.

"He will be with me, always. And when it is time, he will follow me. Right, Dyonis?"

"When the time is right, I will be right...because I am Timekeeper."

Tye had come to trust his instincts and abilities so much that it did not occur to him that the others might balk at being led by an eight-year-old boy. And none of them did.

"Briebras, you and Kofi need to go now. Clairette can stay here for as long as she feels it is safe for her to do so. Everyone must sleep as much as they can. Once we make a break for it, we may have to keep going for a long time."

"And you, mon petit ami? Do you not need rest as well?"

The boy looked at the Frenchman for a moment as though confused. Tye had not allowed himself to think about his own well-being. Briebras' question was like a secret password, opening the floodgates of exhaustion he had unconsciously been holding back.

"No. I...must go over my...calculations." He wavered for a moment as though he might collapse, but managed to roll onto his makeshift bedding in a heap instead. "I just need to close my eyes. Just for a min..."

His voice trailed off as the inevitability of sleep claimed him at last. Clairette moved from her corner to sit next to him, lifting his head enough to for her to scoot underneath so that it would rest on her lap. Dyonis laid on his mat while Briebras and Kofi tightened the rags they had wrapped around their chain to muffle its noise. When they left the room, Clairette was stroking Tye's hair over his forehead and along his temple – staring off into the nothingness as though looking for the life she once believed she would have.

# CHAPTER TWENTY-EIGHT

ANNE REMAINED STILL AS STONE as she watched a dark orange cat emerge from the *Hazard*'s inner sanctums into the dim light of breaking dawn. Crouched low on all fours, the mouser's tail made wide, slow sweeps as it prepared to pounce on a gray rat that had remained topside a few minutes too long. Unaware of its stalker, the rodent moved in stops and starts in its search for something to eat.

Anne had taken to sleeping on deck as part of a self-imposed distancing from Mary Read. The closeness of quarters and familiarity were beginning to undermine her resolve, allowing Mary familiarity she had never intended. Now she returned to the cabin only when she knew Mary Read wasn't there and only when she needed to bathe or use the head. It was an inconvenience, but she was glad for the distance and the peace of mind.

But the decision had created new problems. Asku often slept topside as well, and the last thing she wanted was to encourage his attentions. His spot for sleeping was near the bow, so she had sought out a place toward the stern to bed down. Their hours spent together sword training were structured – their relationship defined as master and student. It was this arrangement Anne liked most, and the distance she maintained during the rest of the time ensured that it was their only interaction.

Between constantly second-guessing her decisions and the unrelenting dread of interacting with Mary Read, Anne had begun to see herself as the "woman of distance." There was the physical distance she tried to keep between her and Mary, the emotional distance she maintained from Asku, and the distance she was trying to close between herself and Tye.

Oblivious to Anne's scrutiny, the cat erupted from its perch and trapped the small beast under its paws with nimble precision. Refusing to accept its fate, the rat squeaked and screamed as it thrashed about trying to escape. Then, to Anne's amazement, the rat broke free and tore across the planks in a mad dash to slip under a nearby crate. The mystery was solved the next moment when a kitten dashed from the shadows and leaped upon the rat, pinning it to the deck with needle-like claws. Not finished with the lesson, the mother cat pawed its kitten aside, allowing the tormented rat to escape once more. Again, the kitten pounced, this time snapping the rodent's neck in its jaws.

It was, Anne realized with bitter clarity, the lesson she had neglected to teach her son. Tye had been so young, so independent, and Bath so sheltered from outside threats, she had never taught him how to survive life's darker side. It was her fault that he was now the prey to the predator that was Rader, being used in a game she understood too well.

"My men called him Erik," Gant said.

Startled, Anne jolted upright then rose from her bedding, making sure her back was to the gunwale. That he had come to be so close without having noticed annoyed her.

"What?" she asked out of reflex rather than a desire to know.

"The mouser," Gant said, using the half-loaf of bread he held in his hand to point toward the cat. "They called him Erik the Dread, you know, after the Norseman."

"Then your men must have been a bit daft."

"How so?" he asked, tearing off a chunk of the bread and offering it to her.

Anne accepted the bread and pushed it into her mouth.

"Because," she said as she chewed, "Erik isn't an Erik...she's an Erika."

Gant looked back toward the cat now teaching her kitten how to tear the flesh from its kill. His eyes moved from one to the other a couple of times and then, conceding the obvious, surrendered a slight smile.

"You're right, my men were a bit muddled."

"They had to be to have trusted you."

The comment stung Gant. She could see it in his face and by the way his back stiffened.

*Good,* she thought, *the bastard had hitched his cart to Mary Read and a lot of men had died because of it.* Up to this point, she had seen no good reason why Mary put so much stock in the rogue marine. He had held his own during their scrap with Rader and during Scarlette's initiation, but his intentions were self-serving and – as far as she was concerned – unworthy of trust. In addition to all that, she just didn't like the man.

"They weren't supposed to die," the major said. "Being attacked by *Rackham's Revenge* was never a part of the plan."

"And yet, they died anyway. A fine pair you two make...you and Mary Read. The *Revenge* was barely half a day on the open water and the first ship she runs up against is the very one you were on. Don't you find that a bit curious?"

During the past few days, their pursuit had slowed to a snail's pace, and the drag had stripped away her veneer of civility. What little wind there was carried directly over the bow, forcing them to sail on a beat to make headway. Knowing that Rader might have encountered the same headwind provided Anne no comfort. As a schooner, *Rackham's Revenge* was both faster and easier to maneuver. She was also new to the water, meaning her hull was not yet fouled by barnacles to slow her down.

But Rader's biggest advantage was that he knew his destination. And although Mary Read knew where he was going as well, it was possible that he could stop anywhere along the coast to take on water, plunder a random merchant ship, or wait somewhere for Wennell to catch up. Or, rather than follow the coast, he could turn for the open sea for several hours or days, then tack back toward the coast and his final destination. By now, Rader was three, maybe four days ahead of them and getting farther away with each passing minute. Anne's fuse had burned shorter as the distance between them had grown, and Gant was the random spark that would set her off.

"I hope it was worth it, betraying men who trusted you with their lives," she said, a rush of sadistic pleasure surging through her veins. "Yes, I was a piratress and killed those who needed killing...but I never betrayed my mates. It takes a special kind of evil to be a traitor. And for what purpose? How much swag can a man get in exchange for his honor these days?"

Gant's face drew taut and his eyes turned dark. Free to strike back for a change, Anne felt the same pleasure one feels when giving in to an itch caused by poison ivy. The words that followed were like fingernails tearing into tender flesh savaged by the rash.

"Frankly major, perfidy sticks to you the way stink follows the arse end of a polecat. I didn't trust you from the first moment I saw you on the beach. Everything about you...your manner, your words, your actions...reek of deception. Your vocation is deceit and you pay your debts with other men's lives. When the fighting starts and you don't see me...turn around...I'll be behind you where I can keep my eyes on you. I only allow people I trust to stand at my back."

Anne held his gaze just long enough to make sure her words had found their mark, then took a step toward her quarters.

"Wait!" Gant ordered, grabbing her arm.

Anne spun around, breaking his hold with a twist of her arm. She felt the familiar heat of rage surge through her body as her hand went to the knife sheathed on her belt. Vague thoughts of suppressing the frenzy flitted across her consciousness then vanished as quickly as they had come. Control be damned, it was release she craved.

"Careful, dear," Mary Read said, her coarse voice chastising Anne as though she were talking to a child about to break her favorite toy. "We're going to need Major Gant's martial skills soon. We wouldn't want to give the advantage to your friend Rader by offing him now, would we?"

Anne gripped the knife's hilt harder but willed herself to leave it sheathed. Once again, Mary had inserted herself into her business, but this time the trespass carried a harsher sting. Anne's unreleased frustration began to fester in a pool of bitterness.

It would be so easy. A flick of my wrist and my knife would find her throat before she bats her eye.

"You still don't know where Rader is going," Mary Read said as if reading her mind.

The cording wrapped around the knife's hilt bit into Anne's palm. She relaxed her grip. The need to find Tye was the one thing that could stay the rage smoldering in her core. And though the crisis had passed, the frustration of falling farther behind Rader assaulted her with renewed vigor. If they did not make better headway today, she would go insane.

Movement toward the bow caught her attention. Stealing a quick glance, she saw Asku beginning to stir and cursed the timing. If he looked their way and thought that she was in trouble, he would try to intervene. As much as she liked Asku, his presence made almost everything she did harder.

Once again, she started to the cabin but stepped on her bedding. Kneeling on the deck, she began rolling up the mat and blanket, acting as if nothing had happened.

Seeing that the danger had passed, Gant released a sigh of tension, gave a nod to Mary Read and headed toward the galley.

"He's not all that bad, you know," Mary Read said when he was gone. "He has reasons for the things he's done."

"We all have reasons for the things we've done," Anne said as she tied off her bedroll with a length of rawhide. "That doesn't make it right."

"Tell me," Mary said, "exactly when did you become a paragon of virtue? I seem to remember you being a bit too casual with other people's lives and living by scruples that would make a reiver appear as a saint."

"About the same time I found myself with a child to care for and no means to provide for it. It brings clarity of purpose and a sense of right and wrong you couldn't begin to understand."

Instead of backing down, Mary Read drew as tight as an anchor line.

"Poor, pitiful Ophelia, 'incapable of her own distress,'" she quoted, sarcasm dripping from her words. "Do next we find that you have fallen from a willow tree to drown in a brook? You make me want to hurl my chowder. I thought there was hope for you. I thought a little salt air in your lungs and the feel of coarse hemp in your hands might bring you back from the dead. But there can be no hope for Anne Bonny because Anne Bonny no longer exists. Not the Anne Bonny I knew."

Anne clenched her jaw and steeled herself for another wave of rage – but the blinding red fury never came. Bewildered, she looked at Mary Read a moment, and then she understood. In her heart, she knew that Mary spoke the truth. She wasn't that Anne Bonny anymore, and it was impossible for her to muster a rage over words that were true. The question she could not answer with certainty was whether that was a good thing. Instead of lighting a fire, Mary Read's words were a bucket of cold water thrown upon dying embers.

"Think what you like," she said. "Once I get Tye back you'll never see me again. I didn't kill you right off because I need you to find Tye. When this is done, I'll let you live because of who you...we...used to be, even though you've earned no mercy from me. But make no mistake, after that, if you ever see me again, it will be the last thing you ever see."

Tucking the bedroll under her arm, she brushed passed Mary Read and started toward their quarters. As she reached for the latch, the door swung open to reveal Will Scarlette on his way out, having retrieved several charts he would need for the day's sail.

"Top o' the morn," Scarlette said with unusual civility. It was the first time in several days he had spoken to her. "Looks like it's going to be a good day. Maybe we be lucky an' catch a fair wind, 'eh?"

Anne made a motion to pass to his left, but Scarlette stood his ground, waiting for Anne to return his greeting. She moved to pass to his right, and again he did not budge.

"What's the matter with you? Wake up on the wrong side of the cot?"

"Piss off!" Anne shot back. She hadn't been awake ten minutes and her whole day had already gone to hell.

In disbelief, she watched as the hint of a grin appeared at the corner of Scarlette's mouth. Not only did Anne find this disturbing – she couldn't believe the man had a grain of humor in his body – the idea that he was having a laugh at her expense was about to set her off yet again.

Spinning on her heels, she headed toward the bow with purpose, leaving Scarlette to think what he damned well pleased. All she wanted was a place to be alone, an impossible task on a ship that seemed to be growing smaller with each passing hour. As she stormed away, Scarlette released a belly laugh that rolled across the deck like a bowling ball, knocking her wits about like a row of maple pins.

Too late, she realized her folly. Her escape from Scarlette had brought her straight to the bow and the spot where Asku slept. Only, now he wasn't sleeping. He was wide-awake and sitting up with his back against the bowsprit. Looking down, she saw that he held a narrow length of wood, working its contours over with a pumice stone.

He remained focused on his work, pretending that he had not seen her stupid little dance with Scarlette nor heard the laugh that had chased behind her. The realization that he had, twisted another knot in Anne's nerves. The ship shrank smaller still.

"He's yankin' your line," Asku said without looking up. "You know that, right?"

Anne leaned back against the gunwale in surrender – the fight in her doused by the conspiracy of cockeyed happenstance. *If this is going to be my day from hell, I might as well stop trying to fight it.*

"What's that you're working on?"

"A bow," Asku said, holding the wood up so she could have a closer look. "I found a long plank of red oak in stores, just the right length. Once I get the curve shaved in I'll wrap her with sinew and she should be as good as the one Rader took from me."

"What about arrows?"

"I've been working on those in between the shaping an' the fire-hardening of the bow. Plenty of scrap wood to work with, though I wish I could get my hands on some good dogwood. The seagulls provide the fletching and the smith gives me all the metal scraps for arrowheads I need."

The frantic, shrill shrieks of a seagull from the day before flashed through Anne's memory and she understood how Asku had come by the feathers. It wasn't hard to imagine why the bird's cries had come to an abrupt end. Despite all of the morning's distractions and frustrations, Anne could still appreciate the man's resourcefulness.

"I've been meaning to ask you about something that's been bothering me," she said. It seemed to be as good a time as any to ask.

"What's that?" Asku replied, turning his attention back to the bow.

"Back at Cedar Island, when I first came around...your mother...Ona...called John White a coward and a fool. Remember?"

"I guess. I heard her say that so many times over the years, I don't doubt she said it then, as well."

"But, wouldn't John White be her great-grandfather?"

"Add a couple more 'greats' and...yeah. I couldn't read it, but I was told that our Bible shows-" Asku stopped, realizing that their Bishops' Bible would have been lost in the same fire that had killed his mother. "Our Bible showed that Virginia was born to Elenora...John White's daughter...an' Ananias Dare on August eighteenth, fifteen hundred an' eighty-seven. An' it showed those who came after all the way down to me."

"And yet, she still thought him to be a coward, even though she was a direct descendant?

Asku smiled but kept focused on his bow work.

"That was my mum. She blamed John White for abandoning Ananias, Elenora, and Virginia. I think it was the mother in her that made her feel that way. And maybe it was the way the women of my family handed that story down through the years. I don't know. What I do know is that if I had lost my daughter and beautiful granddaughter to the wild, and thought there was any chance that they were still alive...I would search the ends of the earth until I found them...or knew for certain that they were dead."

The idea that Tye could be dead was a possibility that Anne had refused to consider. She remained quiet as she tried to force the cold truth back down the hole where she kept it hidden.

"I'm... I'm sorry," Asku said, pausing from his work. "I didn't mean to say that Tye might be...you know."

"Don't worry yourself with it," she said, exhausted by the rapid-fire succession of emotions. "I know what you meant. And now you begin to understand how I feel. I won't give up, either. And if anything happens to Tye, I'll spend the rest of my days hunting down Blyth Rader."

Relieved that he had caused no harm, Asku went back to sanding his bow. Anne remained silent and closed her eyes, allowing the soft grinding of the pumice stone as it carried across the wood in a rhythmic beat to sooth her taut nerves. The morning sun warmed her face while at the same time the day's first breeze provided cool relief. Behind and below her she could hear water beginning to lap against the ship's hull. A corner of one of the sails found the growing breeze and snapped with the anticipation of catching the coming wind. The scent of red oak, salt, rosin, and pitch filled the air with a fragrance that appealed to Anne more than any of Mary Read's toilet waters or perfumes.

With eyes still closed, she felt the breeze beginning to grow stronger, though it still came over the bow. Without warning, a strong gust tore through the rigging, coaxing a sonatina of small howls and whistles as the wind plucked at the strings that were the instrument called *Hazard*. The gust subsided for a moment then returned even stronger. With it came a voice, carried over miles and miles, harmonizing with the melody formed in the ship's rigging.

Opening her eyes, Anne gestured for Asku to stop sanding the bow and held her breath. Looking about in search of where the voice may have come from, her gaze fell on Mary Read still standing abaft. A chill cascaded over the length of her spine like ice melt flowing over the rocks of a mountain stream. Mary was looking out past the stern, her arms hanging at her sides with her palms turned out as if ready to catch something. And while everything around her remained still, Mary Read's hair whipped about her head as though she were standing in the center of a tempest.

The air's current shifted, swirled, then found a different set of cords. Its music grew louder and with it came the voice, stronger than before. This time, Anne understood what it was trying to tell her. If they were going to catch Rader, they would have to go to the one place on earth she never wanted to see again.

"Scarlette!" Anne shouted over the growing wind. "Run out as much canvas you dare and set heading for south-by-southwest. I know where Rader is."

The graybeard looked at her for a moment trying to decide if she were serious or crazy.

"NOW, Scarlette, or I swear...!"

Bemused but leery, Scarlette raised an eyebrow and asked the obvious question.

"An' exactly how is it you expect us to be sailing south-by-southwest when the wind is still coming-"

The rest of his words were drowned out by a howling gust as it tore through the ship's rigging and spars. Scarlette grabbed his hat, saving it from flying off his head and over the side. The wind pushed his large frame forward a step and then back again as it buffeted about the deck. Upon regaining his balance, Scarlette looked back at Anne who was staring at Mary Read. Though the wind whorled all around, Mary stood as if in the eye of a storm, calm and unaffected. When the assault began to subside, Scarlette realized that the wind had shifted 180 degrees and was now coming across the stern at the perfect angle for making top speed.

"As I was saying, captain, south-by-southwest. We're going to Charles Town."

"Charles Town? Rader would be crazy to go to Charles Town. It's a walled fortress with dozens of heavy cannon primed and ready for pirates. Even Blackbeard wasn't crazy enough to try an' take Charles Town head on."

"Crazy or not, that's where he'll be. Trust me, as far as I'm concerned, Charles Town might as well be hell. I wouldn't take us there if I wasn't certain."

"Charles Town it be then," he agreed, though his voice betrayed lingering doubts. He yelled out a couple of orders and men began scrambling all over the ship.

Despite the commotion on deck and overhead, Anne saw that Mary Read was now looking at her, sizing her up with her one good eye. The look on Mary's face told her that she was right about Charles Town. It also told her that Mary had willingly given away her trump card. Other than the realization that a fight between them would be one bloody affair, there was now nothing to keep Anne from seeking revenge, if she so chose.

"What is it about Charles Town that makes it a hell for you?" Asku asked.

"Because," Anne said as she continued staring at Mary Read, "Charles Town is my home."

# PART THREE

## CHAPTER TWENTY-NINE

AFTER THE LAST PATRON DEPARTED and the heavy, double doors to the Buford House were closed for the night, Sweets Nightingale ventured out onto the second-story balcony for a moment of solitude. Though the narrow balcony was primarily used by the whores to promote themselves to potential clients on the street below, the only people out at this early morning hour were the watchmen charged with enforcing Charles Town's strict curfew requiring all sailors, slaves, and free men of color to be off the streets. Respectable white women would not venture out alone at this hour in any event, and their satiated husbands - having been shooed away from the Buford and other brothels - were now all back in their homes with their devoted and willfully ignorant wives.

Most of the prurient businesses in this vibrant port town were small, well-managed operations providing a service while at the same time adhering to the local proclivity for discretion. Charles Town's women pretended not to know that such places existed - or at least what went on inside them - and Charles

Town's men were happy to let them. One did not complain about that which did not exist.

Strategically located on Bay Street close to the Court of Guard on the Half Moon Battery and the wharf's main gate, the Buford was the best bordello in Charles Town, and Sweets Nightingale was the most sought after bawd in the southern colonies, at least this year. At nineteen, she knew her special appeal would soon start to fade, but she was a smart girl and had big plans. For the time being, she would continue to demand a high fee, save her coin and play the local gentry for the gullible fools they were.

One of her more subtle skills was pretending to be the fascinated admirer while making sure her clients' cups were never empty. The more they drank, the more they liked to talk and brag. For every dollar she made on her back, she made four more investing in schemes and business deals she learned about through her patrons' boasts. Conducting business as a woman, and worse, as a prostitute, was not an easy undertaking, but certain favors bestowed upon the right man had bought her a proxy who invested her earnings where she directed. As it turned out, her proxy had substantially increased his wealth by advancing his own money toward the same schemes Sweets chose and had profited so greatly he no longer had to be manipulated to do her bidding.

Juggling her two lives was time-consuming and tiring, and these few moments of respite each night were her one self-indulgence. She never tired of looking at the diamond-like stars that spilled from the sky onto the black velvet waters of Charles Town Bay. On moonlit nights, she enjoyed picking out the silhouettes of the merchant ships scattered about the bay port and trying to imagine the exotic places from which they hailed and the far-away ports where they would soon return.

The only thing between the Buford and the six-foot high fortress rampart were the ever-shifting cobblestones loosely planted in the street of sand that ran all the way from the Ashley River to the Huguenot Church in the French Quarter. On the other side of the brick and mortar wall was the broad wharf and its several piers jutting out into the harbor. During the day, the wharf side of the wall was filled with continuous waves of activity – a place where ships docked to unload old cargo and take on new. Lighter boats would dash back and forth to fetch and deliver their loads to the ships with hulls too deep to allow access to the piers. Sailors, merchants, slavers, fishermen, speculators, coopers, smiths, and people of all types crowded the wharf, making deals, selling merchandise and slaves, and declaring goods to the exchange authorities.

At night, all the activity passed through the wall's several gates to the west side where ordinaries and taverns sold room and sustenance for the empty souls and empty bellies, while brothels like the Buford House provided sustenance of the carnal kind. And though the thick, oak wood gates were still operational, in the four years she had been working at the Buford, Sweets had never seen them closed. Threats from the sea – pirates and Spanish invaders – had dwindled over time. The people of Charles Town, however, had long memories and they were not yet ready to declare the need for fortress walls unnecessary. So, the waterfront wall – along with the defensive earthworks and moats surrounding the rest of the city – remained, even if some of its sections were in disrepair.

Looking over the wall and out toward the water, Sweets was treated to a rare sight. Tonight, instead of the black pool of nothingness that was the bay in darkness, a rare cool air from the northwest had traveled down the coast to sweep across the anchorage's warm brackish waters. The contrasting temperatures created a blanket of fog that spread across the entire bay, engulfing the hulls of the merchant ships so that they looked like toys that had been gently placed upon a field of gray cotton.

Movement far out on the harbor where there should be none caught Sweets' attention. It was just inside the inlet and was so slight that she had almost missed it. Whatever it was had given itself away only because it blocked out the stars that hung just above the horizon as it crept toward the wharf.

When the thing reached the outer perimeter of ships anchored near the wharf, she was able to make out what it was – and it still made no sense. Beyond all reason, a ship had managed to find the inlet, pass through it, sail across the bay, and wind its way through the anchored merchant ships in the dark of night. Why its crew had done such a thing defied reason. Crossing the bar and sailing at night was beyond dangerous, it just wasn't done.

With a start, Sweets realized that the dark vessel was gliding toward the central pier. If they managed to dock, it would be a short stroll down the walkway to the main gate and the streets of Charles Town. Her inner voice kept nagging her to call out, to let the someone know that a ship with a crew of fools was navigating the bay in the dark and about to claim prime docking space. Instead, she remained silent as the ship floated in on the fog, catching enough breeze with its topsail to keep moving with a silent, sinister grace. As it turned to present its broadside to the end of the pier, a new thought flashed into her mind, and she shivered.

Could this be a ship of ghosts?

In answer to her question, a series of hushed commands floated across the water and she was able to make out crewmen striking sail while others leaped upon the dock with mooring lines. A few moments later the ship was secured. Instead of ghosts, flesh and blood men began spilling out onto the pier in quiet chaos. As they came closer to the wharf with the low-lying fog swirling around their legs, Sweets saw that the men were heavily armed with muskets, pistols, and cutlasses.

Thus far she had not been seen, and making a move to go inside now might draw their attention. Again, the voice inside her called for her to yell for a watchman or scream for help. Instead, she gripped the wrought iron rail of the balcony with detached fascination, unable to tear her eyes away from the unfolding scene.

The invaders began splitting into small groups, one stealing into the guardhouse while others fanned out across the city. Muffled noises from the Court of Guard and the lack of an alarm told her that the town's security had been compromised. Movement at the end of the pier brought her attention back to the ghost ship. Like dead beings ascending from the depths of hell, several men strode through the main gate onto Bay Street, wisps of fog swirling around their feet and ankles. Stepping into the faint light of a street lantern, Sweets saw what had to be the leader of the group and knew that her life was about to become a lot more interesting.

Dressed in finely tailored clothes and a wide-brimmed hat adorned with an incredible assortment of feathers and tatting, the fellow who had come to a stop below her balcony was unlike any man she had ever seen. The air about him spoke of sophistication, worldliness, and unimaginable horizons. Even in the dim light, she could see that his eyes reflected great intelligence and he wore confidence as if it were an exquisite coat of silk and silver. Except for his strange looking nose, he was a striking figure of a man.

Sweets felt a warm wave of desire flood her body and marveled at the sensation. Though she had dutifully attended to the wanton needs of her clients, it had been several years since she had felt any such desires of her own.

"Good evening," she said, the words springing out before realizing she was going to speak.

Startled, Rader's men readied their swords and pistols and looked about trying to locate the potential threat. Unlike the others, Rader simply looked up at the woman and responded with equal casualness.

"Good morning," he corrected.

Despite the odd circumstances of their meeting, something about the man made Sweets want to impress him. With practiced subtlety, she shifted her posture so as to accent her best features while diminishing the cues that might betray her for the tart she was. Blessed with a sharply-lined chin, rounded cheeks, and soulful eyes that reached into men's hearts, she understood the power of her allure. And with her long straight hair colored so light that it was almost white, she also knew why men coveted the exception and not the rule. A growing charge filled the gulf between them like converging storms.

"Excuse me, cap'n," Curlee Leathers said, interrupting the moment. He had just come from the Court of Guard. "We've secured the guardhouse. Some of the raidin' parties should be comin' back with hostages soon. Do you want them taken to the ship or the guardhouse cellar?"

"Secure the hostages on the *Revenge*, below deck," Rader ordered, not taking his eyes off Sweets. "I want them as far from any possible rescuers as possible. If the militia comes, be prepared to follow through on our plan to convince them to leave. They should get the message very quickly."

"What about you, cap'n?"

"Take these men back to the ship with you and have them escort our two blacksmiths to the guardhouse cellar. Keep the boy, the idiot and...my guest...in my cabin. I'll be here if you need me. There's someone I want to introduce myself to."

Looking up for the first time to see what Rader was staring at, the first mate saw the young beauty on the balcony and understood. Motioning for the men to follow, Leathers headed back toward the ship, leaving Rader on his own.

# CHAPTER THIRTY

FROM THEIR POSITION ON THE *REVENGE*, Tye, Dyonis, and Clairette weren't able to see who the woman on the balcony was talking to because of the fortress wall blocking their view of the street. Yet, Tye somehow knew it was Rader. He also feared that Clairette believed it as well. That she was on the deck at all had been at his insistence, having persuaded Rader that one more helper was crucial if he was going to make his calculations quickly enough to navigate the inlet. Using Clairette, he had argued, would prevent tying up any of the crewmen Rader needed for sailing the ship.

Tye's true intent was to have her on deck in case they had a chance to escape. There had been several opportunities, and had Kofi and Briebras not been locked up in Tye's room, they could have slipped away long ago. But being no fool, Rader had made sure all five of them were not together in the same place at the same time.

Tye was watching Curlee Leathers and his men make their way back to the ship when he heard Clairette gasp. Any doubts whether the woman with the white hair had been talking to Rader were swept away when the captain stepped onto the balcony and greeted her with a grand bow.

The air around them turned icy and heavy with dread. If Clairette was going to survive, they needed to escape, now. With a new woman in the picture, Rader would have no use for Blackbeard's daughter.

"You three, come with me!" Leathers ordered as he stepped across the gangway.

"Where are we go–"

"Shut up boy an' do as I say!"

Not waiting for them to comply, Leathers' men forced the three inside Rader's cabin and locked the door. Except for the dim moonlight shining through the transom windows, the cabin was completely dark. Though fortunate that no harm had come to them, any hope of escape was gone.

"I wonder what time it is?" he asked without thinking.

"Greenwich Time or our time?" Dyonis asked.

"Our time," Tye said, kicking himself. It had not occurred to him that he would forever have to distinguish between the two times, even when asked as a casual question.

"It's five twenty-three A M."

"Very good, Dyonis. You were magnificent tonight."

"I am Timekeeper."

They had all done well given the circumstances. As planned, Rader had sailed due east from the island at Edisto River until they were far out into the ocean and over the horizon. Even if ships following the coastline had been searching for *Rackham's Revenge*, they would not have been spotted. As soon as the sun had set, they made slow sail toward Charles Town. After each new sighting with his octant, Dyonis would announce the time in Greenwich while Clairette held the lantern close so that Tye could do the calculations.

Passing through the channel at night using nothing but navigation plots had been like trying to walk across an open field blindfolded and passing through an open doorway without running into the wall around it. At one point, Tye thought he had made a terrible miscalculation when the ship had come to a sudden stop, pitching men and anything not tied down across the deck. Many of the crew had cried out in panic and there had been much shouting and cursing. Rader had stared at him with a look so vile Tye was sure that he was about to be thrown overboard.

"The keel!" Tye had said. "You forgot to retract the centerboard."

Several of the crew had then swarmed the capstan and raised the keel, freeing the *Revenge* from the sandbar with a sudden lurch.

Next came the inlet, a featureless black hole of water defined by two points of land that were only a little less dark. When they began to pass across the churning confluence of the incoming tide and the outgoing river waters they truly understood the insane folly of what they were attempting to do. Everyone aboard had held their breath as the schooner passed between the spits of land on either side of the ship that, in the darkness, seemed only feet away.

"HURRAY THE BOY!" several of the men had shouted when they had finally slipped into the fog-blanketed bay without incident.

"Silence!" Rader had yelled back, as loud as he dared. They may have made it through the inlet, but there were other dangers awaiting them.

At this point, the crew no doubt believed that fate was smiling upon them. All they had to do was wind their way through the anchored merchant ships and dock at the wharf sitting at the foot of the giant oyster named Charles Town. Done with their part, Tye, Dyonis and Clairette tried to be as inconspicuous as possible as Curlee Leathers took over piloting the ship by sight.

"Why are half the crew looking off port side and the other half looking toward Charles Town?" Clairette had asked.

"You can't see it, but Fort Johnson is there to the south," Tye had said. "It's a palisade with a dozen or more cannon. The men looking over the bow are worried about the battery on the bastions and redans jutting out from the town's wall."

"Will they shoot us with big guns?" Dyonis asked, remembering how Rader had used the cannon to destroy his mother's home.

"Probably not," Tye said. "I don't see any light where the fort should be, so I doubt that the militia is there. It's been a long time since anybody invaded the harbor and it's likely not manned until a call to arms is issued. And unless somebody sounds an alarm in Charles Town, the cannons there won't be manned either."

"I don't understand," Clairette said. "If the city has a wall and is armed with cannon, why is there a second fort?"

"Fort Johnson is why the French, the Spanish, and even pirates have all failed to take the city. The Charles Town cannons and the Fort Johnson cannons create a crossfire that invaders have never been able to breach. Any ships attacking the city have to come through the inlet, and to make it through the inlet they have to cross during the day...that is...until we did it tonight. The channel pilots and lookouts have always been able to see approaching ships, meaning there was no chance that invaders could mount a surprise attack. Every force that has ever tried to take Charles Town from the ocean has been easily defeated, thanks to the crossfire they can bring to bear. It's like shooting fish in a barrel."

As the city's wall had begun to emerge from the darkness and take on detail, Tye saw the cannon peering at them from the brickworks and shuddered. There was no way to tell if the cannon were unmanned silent sentinels or if a hundred cannoneers stood behind them, ready to unleash iron hell that would send them to the bottom of the bay.

When it was clear that the cannon were not going to fire, several of the crew scrambled over the side and onto the dock to secure the ship. Behind them came the raiding parties that were sent out to find the homes Rader had targeted. Now, as they sat locked inside the cabin waiting for something to happen, Tye began to wonder about the details of Rader's plan and what he intended to do with the people they kidnapped.

"It will be dawn shortly and the townspeople will be screaming mad. I don't know how Rader will use the hostages. Unless he takes them out to the ocean, I don't think the townspeople will sit still for long. I expect they will quickly lose patience and storm the ship if it's not moved."

"What's a hostage?" Dyonis asked.

"It's what you become after you are kidnapped. Pirates hold people they've kidnapped as hostages until their families pay a ransom...that is...give the pirates something of value to get them back."

"You mean like gold or...parrot feathers!"

"Yes, things like that. Once you give them the ransom they let the hostage go back to their families."

"Who do you think they are kidnapping?" Clairette asked.

"Well, it's got to be people who are important. Maybe the governor or the provost marshal, somebody like that. Somebody they will threaten to kill if they don't get what they want."

"But...Rader told me he wants the whole town. He wants to turn it into a haven for pirates. Does he really think that the townspeople will let him take over without a fight, even if he does have hostages?"

"I don't know," Tye replied. "It seems like a weak plan when you say it that way. Maybe he–"

The sounds of shuffling feet and people dragging chains across the deck forced Tye to stop. Straining to see what was going on through a crack in the door, Tye felt his heart sink as he watched several of the pirates escort Kofi and Briebras through the gangway and down the pier toward the guardhouse. After they disappeared inside the two-story building and the door was closed, he knew that any hope of them escaping together was gone.

Someone on deck shouted out a challenge and a few moments later the clatter of boots trampling across the gangplank and onto the deck announced that the first raiding party had returned. The men gathered in a tight circle a few feet away, looking at their captor.

"Well done," the deep voice belonging to Curlee Leathers said. "Take him below an' put him in the storage room. They'll be more joinin' him in a minute or two."

The wall of bodies kept Tye from being able to see whom they were forcing down the steps, but it had to be one of the hostages Rader had targeted. He began to wonder why, if people were being dragged out of their homes, nobody had sounded an alarm or fired shots. Placing his ear to the crack, he listened for noises of the town being awakened and people coming together – but heard nothing.

"What is it?" Clairette asked.

"They just took the first hostage below. I don't understand why nobody is coming after them yet."

"Maybe they snuck in like Indians and took them without making any noise," Dyonis said.

"Wait! I hear something," Tye said.

He peered through the crack again in time to see two of the raiding parties come in at the same time, each with a hostage in tow. Leathers greeted the men then looked at their captives.

"Awww... ain't he pretty in his little nightgown. An' he's got curly blond hair just like a little girl."

Tye heard the pitiful sound of a small child whimpering.

"Now you done, it Curlee," one of the men said. "You went and made the other one start crying. An' she was doing fine till you went rapping on her little mate that way."

"Why are you crying, girlie?" Leathers asked, bending over to put his face an inch or two from hers. "We ain't gonna hurt ya. No. We're just gonna keep you here for awhile until we get everything from your mum and dad that we want...and then we're gonna put you in a big ol' pot of boiling water and cook you for supper!"

The men laughed and the children began to cry in earnest.

"Take them below and put them with the other one," Leathers ordered. "When you're done with that, make sure your powder is still dry an' come back here. I want our cannon what's aligned with the pier to be loaded with grapeshot and aimed right at that gate. If the militia tries to take us, they'll be in for a jig of a surprise."

One of the men on deck shouted and Tye spied another group of raiders crossing the gangplank carrying another child. As the full intent of Rader's plan became clear, the fatigue and stress Tye had battled all day sapped the strength from his legs and he slumped to the floor, his back pressing against the door.

"Tye!" Clairette cried, coming to his side. "What is it? What did you see?"

"They're children," he said, gripping Clairette's arm. "They've kidnapped little children."

"They will be all right," Dyonis said. "Once their parents pay their ransom, they'll be let go, remember?"

"Has Rader let me go?" Tye snapped, immediately regretting his harshness. "Look, Dyonis, they are in great danger. Rader knows that the townspeople won't do anything that would cause their children to be hurt. But Rader might hurt them if the townspeople don't give up the city."

"And he will," Clairette said. "He will kill them if it suits his purpose. You know he will."

They all fell silent for a moment, thinking about what evils Rader might commit against the children to get what he wanted. He was capable of anything. Tye, teetering on the edge of physical exhaustion, wondered what he could do to help the children being imprisoned below deck – forgetting that he wasn't any older than they were.

The sounds of several more raiding parties coming aboard filtered through the door. This time it was Dyonis who looked through the crack in the door. With great detail, he described what the pirates were doing, what the children looked like, and how they were reacting. In all, they had kidnapped six children and locked them in Tye's room. They were very young, thrown together in a small room with no light and with no idea why they were there or what was going to happen to them.

"Those poor little children," Clairette said. "They have to be terrified. Some of them are so young they could have been torn from their mother's breast! I hope Blyth Rader gets what he deserves this night, the bastard!"

Tye saw her rubbing one of the wounds on her face and feared that she was about to go into one of her torpors. He had to do something to stop her from thinking about Rader.

"The window," Tye said. "They won't be watching the transom. They're all watching the port side, keeping an eye on the gate. We can slip out the window and climb up on the poop deck."

"And jump in the water and get away?" Dyonis asked.

"Maybe. But first we need to see if there is a way we can free those children. We may be the only chance they have of escaping."

"Yes," Clairette echoed. "We have to try to save the children. We cannot allow that beast to have the children."

Tye opened one of the transom windows and let Dyonis climb outside first. Once topside, he leaned back over the side and pulled Clairette and Tye up to join him. Huddled in the stern's starboard corner, they could see that most of the crew was positioned along the port-side gunwale, looking toward the city's main gate.

Tye was about to start to where the children were but stopped short. The sound of a hundred angry voices drifted down Charles Town's main causeway and through the gate. Dozens of torches and lanterns grew brighter as they came closer to the open area created by the intersection of streets and the court surrounding the guardhouse.

"What is it?" Clairette asked.

The answer came as a throng of men and women spilled into the intersection, some wearing clothes hastily pulled on while others wore only nightshirts or robes. Those at the head of the mob paused in the middle of the intersection and looked about trying to determine which way the kidnappers had gone. Sprinkled among them were a number of slaves holding torches and lanterns, leaving their masters' hands free to wield the guns they carried. Someone in the crowd saw movement on the dark ship at the end of the pier and yelled to the others.

"There they are! Look through the gate...the ship at the end of the pier. Get them!"

From the corner of the stern, Tye, Clairette and Dyonis were able to see the mass of people starting toward the gate. Tye knew that Curlee Leathers would wait until a dozen or more had stepped out onto the wharf before firing the cannon. At that range, the grapeshot would pass through two or three rows of people, damming the pier with the bodies of the dead and wounded. If those who followed did not turn around, they would not be able to make it past the pirates' musket fire before the cannon was reloaded and fired again. The slaughter would be obscene. Blood would flow like a river and the sharks would converge by the dozens to finish off the unfortunate souls who fell into the water. Unable to close his eyes, Tye reached over to grip the arms of Clairette and Dyonis hunkered down on either side of him.

"STOP!"

Rader's voice boomed down the street and over the wall. The crowd stopped in its tracks and turned as one to locate the person who had issued the order.

"ONE MORE STEP AND YOUR CHILDREN DIE!" Rader yelled from above them on the Buford House balcony.

People in the crowd looked at each other and then all about the intersection, but saw no signs of their children.

"You're bluffing," a man said, though his voice wavered.

"NO!" Rader shouted so that all could hear. Then in a measured voice, "I have taken your children hostage and they are on that ship...my ship...at the end of the pier."

Placing thumb and forefinger to his lips, he blew out a shrill whistle. The pirates standing at *Revenge's* gunwale shifted about to reveal six children they had retrieved from down below. A crewman stood behind each of the four taller children with a pistol pointed at the child's head. The two smallest children were lifted up and made to stand on the gunwale so the crowd could see them as well.

Spotting her mother among the courtyard throng, one of the girls on the *Revenge* screamed and called out to her. The woman dropped the lantern she carried and bolted toward the gate. A man leaped after her, grabbing her just before she reached the wharf. The woman screamed out for her daughter as she struggled to free herself.

"'LISABETH! MY GOD, THEY HAVE MY 'LISABETH! LET ME GO!"

Others in the crowd spotted their children on the *Revenge* and began calling out to them. Their shouts of concern and reassurance changed to cries of rage. Turning their attention away from the man on the balcony, the crowd began stampeding toward the gate.

The blast of a pistol resounded off the surrounding walls, stilling the crowd. Stunned, the woman who had started the uproar stopped struggling and retreated into her husband's arms.

"If one of you passes through the gate, I will give the order to shoot the oldest child. If you continue toward the ship, I will have the next oldest child shot."

He paused, allowing the full weight of his threat to sink in and ripple out to the farthest edges of the crowd. When their mutterings began to wane, Rader stuck the pistol in his waistband and spread out his arms as if to embrace them.

"Come now people, your children are fine. No harm will come to them...as long as you do as I say."

"Who are you and why have you taken our children?" asked the man who had spoken earlier.

Tye was able to see the man through the gateway. He was a tall, willowy gentleman in his mid-forties with black hair that had grayed at the temples. He wore a white blouse thrown on in haste and not yet tucked into dark, gray pants that had narrow black stripes running down the legs.

"I am the pirate Blyth Rader, captain of the dread ship *Rackham's Revenge*... and you will do well to fear me. I want nothing of your children. I only want your cooperation and, of course, your city. Once you have completed all the tasks I have for you, your children will be returned to you and you will be free to go."

"To go? To go where?"

"Anywhere you want. I don't care. You can even stay here if you swear an oath of allegiance. But somehow I doubt that any of you will be willing to become pirates."

"But...but this is our home. You don't really expect us to just walk away?"

"Walk, run, ride a horse...whatever you please. I don't really care. But you will leave. If you leave on your own, I will let your children cross the drawbridge at the western wall to join you. If you do not cooperate, I will force you to leave at gunpoint and then throw your children over the wall. Perhaps some will even live."

People in the crowd began looking at each other. Others began whispering among themselves and glancing toward the balcony as if trying to make a decision. Finally, a man emerged from the middle of the group and whispered into the willowy man's ear. As they talked, several of the men on the outer edges of the mob started to slowly work their way over to the Buford House.

"I think I found a flaw in your plan," the crowd's apparent leader said.

"Indeed! Please, enlighten me."

"Your men have our children, but in a couple of minutes we'll have you. I think that would be called a stalemate. Or did you give your men orders to let you die should we capture you?"

As he spoke, several men on the periphery bolted toward the Buford House and began pounding on its door, trying to force their way in.

Showing little concern, Rader reached back into the darkness of the room and grabbed for something. With a hard yank, he pulled a boy about twelve-years-old onto the balcony and shoved him to the front for all to see. The crowd's leader yelled to the men at the door to stop.

"People, people," Rader said, pulling a second pistol from his waistband. "Did you think that I had the wits to get this far, but was so simple that I would leave myself open to be taken this easy? Anybody? No? Tell me then, who does this boy belong to?"

Everyone in the crowd looked at the man who had been speaking on their behalf.

"That's my son," the man said. "His name is Jonathan, and if you harm him, I will make you pay with your life. You have my word."

"No doubt," Rader said, waving the pistol about as though it were a riding crop. "But tell me, who are you and what are you to these people."

"My name is John Chastain...Colonel John Rene Chastain of the Saint Phillips Parrish Militia. You will do well to remember it."

The militiaman spoke with slow, drawn-out, precision – his words infused with the smoky, Barbadian enunciation that distinguished the southern Carolinians from other colonists.

Rader placed a hand on the boy's shoulder and drew him closer. The boy cringed.

**300**

"Listen to me closely, Colonel John Rene Chastain. We have a lot to do and very little time in which to do it. Your first job is to spread the word to Charles Town's good people that I want every male slave in the city to be assembled here, at the Half Moon Battery, in one hour. Tell them to have their slaves bring picks and shovels and be prepared to put their backs into repairing the city's fortifications. Charles Town belongs to me now, and I need it made ready to withstand attacks from both land and sea."

"When you are done with that, you will have every white man and woman in the city congregate at the drawbridge where they will be afforded one chance to pass to the outside. Tell them that anyone found inside the walls after that will be shot on sight."

A wave of angry chatter passed through the crowd and Tye feared their outrage would outweigh the need to protect their offspring.

Perhaps having the same concern, Rader took his pistol and drew it across the boy's forehead, brushing back his hair with its barrel. When the end of the gun barrel reached the boy's temple, Rader pulled the child's head closer and cocked the hammer.

"Time is growing short, Colonel Chastain," he said. "I suggest you make up your mind quickly."

# CHAPTER THIRTY-ONE

STANDING BEHIND RADER, hidden in the darkness of the room, Sweets watched the crowd shifting about on restless feet while futilely struggling to fathom the force confronting them. The man who had captured her favor minutes earlier now stood but a few inches away – a raw, primal man, empowered to do great things. She did not understand what force drew her to him, but she was sure that the man called Captain Blyth Rader had been created just for her.

Moving closer to the doorway, she looked over the mob below the balcony, spotting several men who were familiar with her bed – and standing next to them, their wives. First one man and then another spied her standing behind Rader. A series of elbow nudges and whispers passed among the angry assembly until everyone in the intersection understood that one of Charles Town's whores was betraying them and their city.

Sweets gritted her teeth as a long-suppressed resentment began to rise to the surface. This stranger, Rader, had given her more respect in ten minutes than any of the people of Charles Town ever had. She had played by their rules and had lived among them as a non-person – rendering services to the men at night and always acquiescing to their damnable wives. And now they dared act as if she owed them her loyalty? The same people who, in the light of day, gave more consideration to their dogs and their slaves?

She found herself walking out onto the balcony to stand next to the magnificent, bold blackguard who was single-handedly facing down the entire town. Her heart pounded with excitement to see the people beneath her glaring at her with disgust and loathing. Those who had scorned her were now the ones being looked down upon – literally. The sense of power was intoxicating.

"LISTEN TO ME!" the colonel yelled so that all in the crowd behind him could hear. "We must do as he says. Spread the word. Have your slaves here by dawn. Then gather your families, collect everything you can carry and leave by the drawbridge."

No one in the crowd moved.

"You call that leadership, colonel?" said Rader, shaking his head with mock disgust. "You have not convinced anyone to do anything. Here, let me show you how it is done."

"Mister Leathers!"

"Aye, captain!" Leathers' voice came back to them from the ship.

"The girl named Elisabeth. Make an example of her!"

Curlee Leathers placed his pistol to the girl's head and cocked the hammer. A shrill, earsplitting scream pierced the night and everyone turned to see Elisabeth's mother faint.

"ALL RIGHT!" Colonel Chastain yelled. "Everybody. Stand down! Go home or the death of these children will be on your hands! NOW!"

Reluctantly, most of the crowd began moving back up Broad Street toward their homes. But a few of his more defiant neighbors lingered on.

"Jason," the colonel said. "Daniel. All the rest of you. I know it's not your nature to run from a fight, nor is it mine. But now is not the time to stand your ground. For the sake of the children, go home. Make ready to leave. We can't help them now. We must leave so that they will live. Collect what things you can and prepare for the morrow."

Conceding defeat at last, those who remained began following their neighbors into the darkness of Broad Street.

"Jonathan," he said, turning back to the balcony. "Be brave, son. Do as you are commanded and no harm will occur. I promise. Do you understand?"

Trying his best to look brave, the scared boy took a deep breath and gave his father a nod.

"If any harm comes to our children there will be nowhere on earth you can hide," the colonel said. "I will see you again, Blyth Rader. Soon."

Not waiting for Rader to have the last word, he turned and disappeared into the night.

Rader gave a wave toward the ship where Leathers and the other men began taking the children back to Tye's room. Leaving the balcony, he brushed by Sweets as he guided the boy inside and then shoved him toward the two men who had kidnapped him.

"Find a room with a lock and keep him there," Rader said. "Put him in with some of the whores if you have to. Just make sure he stays here in this house. The other children protect the ship. This boy protects us."

Stepping back onto the balcony, Sweets Nightingale threw herself at him as if he were a conquering hero. Rader staggered backward then caught his balance.

"That was...incredible!" she said before planting a lusty kiss full on his mouth. "You were astounding! The way you faced down the whole lot of them. It gave me chills. It gives me chills now! It was as though you were shrouded in St. Elmo's fire, and they were a bunch of chawbacons pissing their pants."

"That?" Rader scoffed. "That was nothing worthy of boast. It's easy to be the calm dictator when you have the upper hand. It's being smart enough to gain the upper hand that matters. My dear girl, you have seen nothing yet."

"Really? You have defeated the militia and taken the town that could not be won. Everything within these walls is yours to do with as you please. What more could there possibly be?"

"Much more, my dear girl. Much, much, more. I intend–"

Shouting arose from the end of the dock forcing Rader to turn his attention toward the *Revenge*. Several of his men had come together at the stern's far corner and appeared to be struggling with someone. Finally, the cluster of crewmen separated enough for Rader to see that it was not one person they had subdued, but three. And then he understood.

"Mason," he called to one of his men outside the door. "Take a message to Leathers. Tell him I want the boy and the idiot taken to the Court of Guard and locked in the cellar with the darkie and the little Frenchman. Tell him to lock the other one up in my cabin until I get back. I think it's time to put my ship back in proper order."

A few minutes later Rader watched from the balcony as the pirates went about securing the *Revenge*, transferring Tye and Dyonis to the Court of Guard, and preparing for the arrival of the town's slaves. Cloaked by the darkness, no one saw the skiff at the far end of the wharf drift out from between the many cargo lighters to be carried into the bay by the current of the Cooper River.

# CHAPTER THIRTY-TWO

"WHAT IS IT THIS TIME?" Mary Read asked as she joined Scarlette and Anne at the wheel.

A shout of "SAIL HO!" from the upper rigging had announced the approach of another vessel, but the crew was showing little interest. They had seen dozens of merchantmen, fishing boats and a couple of packets on their journey to Charles Town. There was no reason to believe that this one would be a concern.

Rather than alter the *Hazard* in an attempt to make it look like a merchantman, Scarlette had chosen to hide in plain sight by flying the red squadron ensign and pretending that the ship was still Royal Navy. Crews on the ships they passed either waved a cordial greeting or ignored them altogether. With most of the king's navy still preoccupied with the Spanish, the graybeard knew they were not likely to cross paths with another royal ship. The merchantmen and fisher boats they did pass saw them as either a friendly force protecting the shipping lanes or – if engaged in less legal endeavors – something to be avoided.

"Looks like a skiff," Scarlette said as he peered out over the bow through a long glass. "Just a couple of darkies looking to net a fish, it would appear."

"Slaves?" Anne asked, extending her hand. "Out on the open water? Let me see."

She took the glass and took a quick survey of the little sailboat.

"They have no nets and they sail too far from shore to be up to any good. They're either runaways or..."

"Or what?" Mary Read asked.

"That's just it. There is nothing else. Not unless they have writs of passage. But still... A writ of passage to venture this far out? To do what? There's no sense to it."

"Helmsman," Scarlette said to the man at the wheel. "Make toward the skiff."

"Why are we wasting time with them?" Mary Read challenged. "What do we care whether they are running to freedom or hunting for whales?"

"He's right," Anne said, closing the glass and handing it back to Scarlette. "They can tell us how far we are from Charles Town. Better to talk to slaves than to anyone else. The darkies won't ask us questions."

But when the *Hazard* was close enough for them to see the ensign, the two slaves struck sail and began waving and yelling to make sure the brig could see them. Though their actions suggested they were anything but runaways, Scarlette was taking no chances. As the vessels came together, he had several of his men line up along bulwark with their muskets at the ready.

"BE SILENT!" Scarlette shouted at the men who were clamoring so loudly neither could be understood. Their dark skin had turned almost black as pitch from countless days of working in the sun, and both men's hands were calloused by years of hauling in nets and pulling on oars. "Now tell me, what is it that's got you so rattled?"

"Thank the Lord you is here!" the older of the two men said, believing he was talking to the captain of a British warship. "Charles Town has been taken over by pirates an' we was just trying to get home to the Salt Plantation."

"Pirates?" Scarlette questioned, unable to believe that Rader had taken over the fortress city. "Are you sure?"

"It could be true," Mary Read said. "That was the plan. But how Rader did it so quickly and with only one ship, I have no idea."

"If pirates took Charles Town, how did you get away?" Scarlette asked.

"We was sleepin' in the boat at the wharf," the second, younger man said. "One minute we was sleepin' an' the next thing we know they was pirates running all up an' down the streets stealing little children from their beds an' standin' them up like they were goin' to shoot every one of them. But then, the town folks came down to the wharf to rescue their children, an' they were loaded for bear. That pirate with the big nose pointed his gun at the colonel's son's head an' told the townsfolk to go home. An' Colonel Chastain...I ain't lying...he was fit to be tied. Yes sir! He wanted to kill them pirates, 'specially that one with the mashed nose. He would've, too, if it weren't for those kidnapped children."

"The man with the queer nose...did he have a thin, looping mustache an' wear a big, foppish hat?"

"Yes sir! That's him, all right. Comes walkin' out on the whore-house balcony like he was the King of Siam. Had that trollop Sweets Nightingale hangin' all over him, an' she was sparkin' on him in front of everybody. Was one of the most disgustin' things I ever did see. An' the whole town was watchin'. Yes sir. Downright disgustin', that's what it was."

"What about the children?" Mary Read asked. Fear of what might have happened dampened the rasp of her voice to a weak clatter.

"The children are all right as far as we could tell. Took all of them down inside the ship after the militia left, but for a few minutes we thought for sure they was goin' to shoot them right there in front of their parents. But that's when the militia and the rest of the towns folk went back to their homes."

"Rader, the pirate with the funny nose, he just let them go home?" Anne asked.

"No," Mary said. "Not just go home. The plan was to use the threat of the children's lives to force their parents and the others to leave town. They would have gone to their homes to get just a few essential things and then leave."

"That's right!" the older darkie said, surprised that the woman already knew what had happened.

"What?" Anne asked in disbelief. "That was your plan? It was your idea to kidnap children?"

"It worked, didn't it?"

"Seriously? Children? Your plan included possibly killing children?" Her words came out as a muddle of venom and disbelief.

"Worry over it later," Scarlette said, looking to avoid the squall he saw coming. Then to the two men in the boat, "How did you get away if you was there when all this was goin' on?"

"It was a miracle, that's what it was!" the man continued. "Like I said before, we were sleepin' in this here boat waiting for the break of dawn to take supplies back to the plantation. We woke up because of all the racket they was makin', an' when we saw that the pirates had takin' over, we decided we better get out whilst the gettin' was good! So I slipped the rope off the mooring an' let the boat find the current. As soon as we were out of sight, we raise sail an' begged the Lord to send us a breeze."

"So, I take it the two of you know the waters here well," Scarlette said, weighing his options. "You can pilot us back through the channel and get us to the wharf, true?

"No sir!" the older man said. "We can't goes back, not to that place. No sir. Those pirates would blow us out of the water before we get anywhere near the wharf."

"But, there's less than a hundred of them," Scarlette said. "They can't defend the town an' their ship an' guard the harbor all at the same time. They're spread too thin."

"It's not just Rader's men we'll have to face," Mary Read said, reaching up to grab one of the standing rig lines. "By now, he's offered freedom to every slave in Charles Town. In exchange, they will work to reinforce the walls and take up arms to fight as free men. The crewmen from the merchant ships...most of them...will have sworn pirate loyalty to Rader's cause. Those who haven't will have been escorted across the bridge and driven into the wilderness to fend for themselves. Convinced that they are about to acquire unimaginable riches, Rader's converts will have taken control of the ships they served on and have anchored them at the mouth of the inlet. Unsuspecting merchant ships entering the harbor will be let in, but none will be allowed to leave. If we sail into the harbor now, we'll be trapped between the town's cannons and those on Rader's new ships."

Anne watched Scarlette as he pulled on his beard, struggling to think up a new plan. His eyes grew darker and the lines on his face drew deeper with each idea that had to be rejected. The man had spent more than a decade biding his time and had traveled more than three hundred miles to get to this point.

"I know a way into the city," Anne said, guessing the cause of his frustration.

Scarlette arched his eyebrows and looked at the fiery-haired piratress with renewed hope.

"We can sail this floating bum fodder to the Stono River. I'm not sure how far up river we can go, but if we can make it to the big bend, we'll be about two miles west of Charles Town. They won't be looking for us or anybody else to come at them from across the Ashley River. Trust me."

"All right, then," Scarlette said, making his decision. "Let those two go. They're of no more use to us."

When the sails were trimmed to catch the wind again, they resumed the south by southwest course that would take them past Charles Town's harbor. A half hour later, almost every man on board was standing at the starboard rail when they sailed past the inlet, trying to catch a glimpse of the ships Mary Read had assured them would be just inside the mouth of the harbor. It was not until they were to the south side of the inlet that they spotted two ships. Rather than being anchored directly in front of the inlet in the path of incoming merchantmen, they had taken up a position off to the side. Rader had strategically placed them in a position where they would not be noticed until entering trade vessels were well into the harbor.

They all held their breath, waiting to see if a third ship might be sent out to pursue them, but they sailed on by the inlet without threat. There were so many merchantmen sailing into the harbor and having the "door" closed behind them, that it made no sense for Rader's pirates to give chase. And each ship that sailed into the harbor added to their riches and their fleet – never even having to fire a shot.

It was midafternoon when they reached the Stono Inlet. Anne took up a position at the bow, leaning forward as far as she could to look ahead for sandbars. Being a minor inlet of no importance to shipping, merchant ships never came this way. With no local pilots to guide them through the channel, they had to move slowly or risk running aground. By extending her arms left or right to guide the helmsman, Anne was able to keep the ship centered on the deep water of the channel as they moved from the ocean into the river.

Any hopes they had of proceeding up the Stono River unobserved were immediately dashed when the ship glided into the calm, inland haven where the brackish confluence of the river converged with marsh water. Nestled on a protrusion from the mainland ahead of them was an assembly of grass huts and crude fishing boats beached on the sandy riverbank. The smoke from several outdoor fires spiraled into the air, the aroma hinting at unimaginable foods. No longer needed at the bow, Anne returned to the wheel where Asku and Gant had joined the others.

"It's a Gullah fishing village," she said, answering the question written upon their faces.

"Gullah?" Scarlette grunted.

"Africans," Asku said. "Slaves who are almost free, but still slaves."

"The Gullah are slaves that work the rice fields part of the year and fish during the rest," Anne said. "The women smoke or salt the fish and weave baskets. Some of the fish are sold on the market and some go to the plantations for food."

The unusual arrival of the ship had not gone unnoticed, as twenty-five or thirty members of the village had come to the water's edge to gawk at them. The river was deep enough for ships as big as the *Hazard*, but there was little reason for them to sail up the Stono. And though the Africans were familiar with merchant ships, they had never been this close to a warship.

"Where is their overseer?" Gant asked.

"The overseer or plantation owner will visit once a week or so. These slaves are pretty much left on their own, as long as they are producing."

"Why don't they just run away?"

"The slave patrols are well regulated and would come across them before they got past the county line. The Gullah know the boundaries and they know that if they stray too far, what freedom they have will be taken from them...forever. These slaves live just about the same way they did in Africa, so there is little incentive to attempt an ocean crossing to a place they don't know how to find and to a future that could be worse than their lot here."

"What's to keep one of them from runnin' to his master an' lettin' him know that there's a big, fat English warship comin' up the river?" Scarlette asked. "We could hold our own here for a time if need be, but I don't like sittin' in the open with my arse 'hanging out for any damned local yeoman with a musket to take pot shots."

"A threat," Anne said. "Or maybe a bribe. We won't know until we talk to them. But there's no reason for them to alert their owner unless we do something that appears threatening. Otherwise, we're just a curiosity."

"You an' your friend with the bow know more about them than anybody else, so how about you an' him take the longboat over there an' figure out how to handle this. Take fancy buttons with you for good measure."

"I'm going too," Mary Read said. "I've been too many days on this boat and I need to feel the earth under my feet."

"No," Scarlette said. "If somethin' goes bad, the *Hazard* can turn tail an' run back out to sea. If that happens, I want you here with me. You owe me a treasure map, an' I'll not run the risk of losin' you just so you can have a nice walk on the beach."

Mary Read bristled at the idea that Scarlette could dictate her comings and goings. She began rubbing her middle finger along the bottom length of her scar, trying to think of a way around their agreement. A habit that had become more frequent the past few days, the constant rubbing had turned her left cheek rosy-red, making her black eyepatch all the more pronounced.

"Allow me four men to row us over to their village and I'll take care of it," Anne said, reclaiming Scarlette's attention.

"Then it's done," Scarlette agreed. "Just be sure to be back afore dark. I'll not be puttin' the *Hazard* in jeopardy by dropping anchor here if we don't know what these people are about."

A few minutes later, as the longboat drew closer to the crowd on the beach, Anne began to wonder if she had promised more than she could deliver. It had been many years since she had left the South Carolina low country, and she had no idea if the things she had told Scarlette still held true. A lot could have changed since she had left her home at the age of sixteen.

The thought brought back memories of Charles Town's early days when the colony was still young and struggling to find its place in the New World. For her, it had been a tumultuous time, filled with uncertainties about her parentage and the ambiguity of her place in society. It had also been a time when her passions had burned red hot and her father's expectations had been beaten into her on a weekly basis. Some of her remembrances were flittering and vague – a series of ill-formed images hinting at wrongdoings and willful acts of malevolence.

Despite her efforts to hold them at bay, recollections of things she would have preferred to leave unremembered began to resurface. Like the time she had nearly killed a servant girl with a knife for being too slow to fetch her jacket. She also had once humiliated her fencing instructor by denuding him in public at the point of her sword for making an uncomplimentary suggestion about her femininity. Even more shameful was the night she attempted to burn down the plantation's manor in a drunken stupor because her father refused to recognize her elopement to James Bonny.

The sound of wood scraping across wet sand and the sudden slowing of the longboat as it plowed onto the embankment ended her musings. The women and children of the village gathered around them in a semicircle. Their men were nowhere to be seen.

Anne stepped from the longboat followed by Asku, Gant, and the four crewmen.

"My name is Anne Cormac," she said, surveying the dark faces surrounding them. "My father was William Cormac. Is there anyone here who remembers me or my family name?"

The children giggled, realizing for the first time that Anne was a woman dressed in a man's clothing. The women looked at each other with furtive glances. Anne could not tell whether they were afraid to answer, did not understand the question, or were being silent because no one remembered her.

"Damn, woman," Gant said with clenched jaw, "how many names do you have?"

"Brennan was my mother's maiden name," she said as she continued surveying the women's faces. "She was a maidservant in my father's home in Ireland. Need I explain the rest?"

"How did you come to be here, then?"

"My father's wife at the time was not happy to learn that my mother was polishing more than her husband's brass. When I was born, she gave him an ultimatum...both my mother and me had to leave, or he had to leave. Fortunately for me and my mother, he headed off to the colonies and took us with him. Once he got here he bought a few hundred acres of land and built a plantation in Saint Andrews Parrish named Nua Cork Downs."

At the mention of the plantation's name, Anne noticed a look of recognition flicker across the face of a woman standing near the center of the half circle. The woman looked toward Anne and their eyes met – lingered – and then she remembered.

"Ñuli?"

"An-nie!" the black woman said, her singsong confluence of English and West African tongue declaring itself in a single word.

The two women came together in a violent rush, hugging each other as though long-lost sisters who had finally found each other. The people around them – both black and white – watched the reunion with curiosity, wondering what the bond between the two women might be. When satisfied that the person she embraced was real, Anne stepped back but continued holding the woman at arm's length.

As was the style of her people, she wore a large white wrap around her head, creating a contrast that enhanced her facial features. Her skin was unblemished and evenly colored throughout the nooks and mounds of her face. Her bright, brown eyes spoke of confidence, wisdom and – perhaps – a longing that had never been filled.

"Oh Ñuli, sweet, sweet Ñuli. They told me that you had run away and that I could never again speak your name. But here you are, as alive as me."

"Praise Gawd, you live, An-nie! Buckruh say you de water tief, hung on de isle f'um de tik twine. Me h'aa't hebby fuh libbin' uh taut uh wuh gwi' die. But uh knows you de fox sted de crow. Uh knows et!"

"What the hell was that?" Gant asked. "Was it supposed to be English?"

"Geechee," Asku said. "Gullah creole. A mix of English an' African with a handful of words from the islands thrown in."

"What did she say?"

"Don't know, exactly. Seems they were friends once, and both thought the other was gone forever. We'll have to wait for Anne to fill in the rest."

At last, Anne broke away to rejoin the men and the woman named Ñuli began urging her people back to their encampment.

"They need our help," Anne said. "Their men had gone to Charles Town on a trade run when Rader took over the city. They were pressed into service and are being forced to repair the walls that surround the city. Ñuli says that landowners across the colony are gathering somewhere to the north, trying to decide what to do. If they attack before we get inside the city walls, it will be impossible to sneak in."

"But how, damn it?" Gant asked. "I know a good bit about Charles Town's defenses, and I don't know of any way to get by them."

"By water, at night. But it doesn't really matter, does it? You know as well as I do that we're probably all going to die. So if you've got leaving on your mind, now would be the time. It's not like I'd be trusting you to cover my back anyway."

Anne watched his eyes closely, half expecting him to read for his pistol.

"Have it your way, then," he said, pushing his red coat back at the waist to place his hands on his hips. "One day you'll find out how wrong you are about me. I promise you."

"Maybe, but I doubt it. And right now I don't give a damn. The way I see it, I've got one day...maybe two at the most...to get inside that city and find Tye.

If you're still around after that, we can settle up any way you want. Until then, I suggest you stay out of my way."

"With great pleasure," the major said. "Just let me know when you're ready to share your brilliant battle plan and I'll let you know if I'll go along with it. In the meantime, I'll be talking to some of these...Gullah ladies...to see if there might be a decent meal to be had."

"What is the plan?" Asku asked as Gant walked away.

"We stay here till dusk, then head up river. They have a periauger we can use, and Ñuli will guide us. It seems she's sweet on one of the men Rader pressed into labor."

"Really?" Asku asked a little too quickly.

The bitterness in his voice tore at Anne's core. His quip had been a veiled accusation. She had known that this moment would come but she still wasn't prepared for it. Removing her hat, she stared at the ground for a moment to collect her thoughts.

"I've done you a terrible wrong, Asku. I think you should know, I tried to be like other women, several times, but–"

"Stop," Asku said. "You don't have to explain yourself. You've done nothing wrong, and I know how you are. I've known almost from the beginning. You're a damn good woman, Anne Bonny. If there's any fault here, it's my own. Let's just leave it at that?"

The woodsman's unexpected grace revealed a side of him Anne hadn't seen before. Having met his mother, it really shouldn't have been a surprise. The realization made her both relieved and ashamed.

The thought brought back the memory of their departure from Cedar Island and the promise she had made to Ona when saying goodbye.

"Asku," she said as she shuffled the hat in her hands, turning it in a constant circle. "I made a promise to your mother when we left Cedar Island. What I said to Gant was true. When we go to Charles Town tomorrow...there's a good chance that we'll all be killed. I wouldn't hold it against you if you left now, while there's still time. You don't owe me anything."

Asku's eyes turned gray and his face strained at the sting.

"I wouldn't leave even if I had the want. Rader has my brother, and I won't quit till I've gotten him back."

Anne started to speak but Asku cut her off again.

"You see, Annie, I'm your friend. What with all we been through, I thought you would understand that, above all else. What I do for you, I do for its own sake and with no qualifications. Given that you have Gant ready to kill you at any minute; Mary Read lookin' to kill you when this is done; and Scarlette ready to sell you to the highest bidder; I thought you would have placed a higher value on such a thing. So, I guess you're right thinking that I've had you figured wrong – just not for the reasons you thought."

"I'm going to have the men row me back to the ship now to get what I need for tonight. I suggest you do the same. Scarlette will be fit to be tied by now, wondering what's going on."

Anne watched numbly as Asku walked back toward the longboat. For a moment, she agonized about her penchant for disappointing the people she cared most about – but then shoved the thought back into the hole where she kept her doubts. There would be time enough for self-pity and apologies after she got Tye back – if they lived.

As she started toward the boat a new thought bubbled up through the churning flotsam of her dark musings.

*Did he really just call me 'Annie'?*

# CHAPTER THIRTY-THREE

RADER WAS DEEP IN THOUGHT when Sweets Nightingale came out on the balcony to stand next to him. Steeling her resolve, she grasped his arm with both hands and rested her head against his shoulder in a calculated attempt to hide her growing doubts. The confidence the man with the mutilated nose had exuded when he strolled down Bay Street seemed to diminish a little each day. With each hour that passed, and with each decision he was pressed to make, the bold usurper cracked a little more. The bravado he had served up during his dramatic arrival to Charles Town had devolved into a bubbling stew of impatience, suspicion and sometimes rage. The man she held onto now felt small and hollow, like an oak tree, rotting from the inside.

"We've accomplished a lot in a short time," he said, surveying the flurry of preparations    taking place on both sides of the thick brick and mortar wall running along the waterfront. "But there's much more that needs to be done before this city will be ready for an assault."

The work needed to restore the dirt ramparts and the moat surrounding the other three sides of Charles Town had been extensive. But the slaves who had joined the pirates in exchange for freedom – and the ones forced into labor because they remained loyal to their owners – had been working night and day and the repairs were almost finished. If there were to be an attack, the assault would most likely come from inland. The militia was assembling about twenty miles away and the only way they would be able to re-enter the city would be to take the drawbridge.

Rader had also ordered the best, most experienced crewmen from the merchant ships be assigned to the cannons positioned on the wall's bastions and redans. Although there were now enough cannoneers to operate the city's entire complement of guns, they needed more training. And if any of these men were killed or wounded, they had no reserves to replace them.

"Is his liege pleased with the progress on his new kingdom's fortifications?" Sweets cooed with well-rehearsed affectation. "It is hard to imagine that anyone would attack us now. And as long as we have their children, we will be protected."

"Spoken like a true simpleton," Rader said. "The children won't stop the militia from attacking forever. If they are smart, they will keep the children's parents well away from here so they can't interfere. They may try an overwhelming assault or some trickery to save the children but they will understand what the parents did not...that negotiating for the lives of children is a fool's game. If we give them up, we no longer have them for protection. The militia will know that we will not and can not give them up. So they will have to attack at some point."

"Then why keep them?"

"The children won't stop the militia from attacking, but if they make it into the city, the children can still give us cover to make an escape...but only in a face-to-face standoff, and only for a few minutes."

Sweets struggled to grasp the full implications of Rader's dark words. Thoughts of surviving in a city under siege did not match the Camelot she had imagined Charles Town would become. Nor was fleeing the city a few steps ahead of a vengeful mob in keeping with her fantasy of becoming the Queen of

South Carolina. The thrill fashioned by the events of the past few days was beginning to wane, as was the luster that had once shimmered around the hollow brigand named Blythe Rader.

Blessed with an almost unerring intuition, Sweets Nightingale had a knack for making the right choices. But something about Blyth Rader had blunted her instincts and dulled her powers of observation. She wished she could blame it on having too much drink that night, but she knew that alcohol had not been her failing. It was power she had been drunk on, or the illusion of it. Now that she knew him better, she realized that Rader was a man with little real talent but a cargo hold full of ambition – and luck. Sweets had ambition too, but she did not believe in luck. She believed in taking advantage of opportunity, and she saw this one fading away like a ship dipping below a hazy horizon.

The current crisis of confidence with which Rader was grappling confirmed these notions and more. No longer able to deny the truth, Sweets knew it was time to start planning a way out. Having made her decision, she released the arm she had been clutching and stepped back inside.

"Did you believe that this would be easy?" Rader asked, charging into the room after her. "Does the unsavory industry of war test your genteel sensibilities? I had forgotten that whores were so...delicate. I guess the world takes on a different, harsher perspective when one witnesses it standing upright."

Sweets stopped in mid-stride and spun around. She was about to unleash a tirade, but Rader's face was so dark and contorted it looked as though he had either lost his mind or was possessed. Refusing to be intimidated, she pulled herself together and stared back at him with a poise that belied her fear. She knew that if she did not stand up for herself now, he would beat her down and break her spirit for however long they remained together.

"Captain Rader, I may be a whore, but I am not a simpleton. In fact, I am smart enough to understand that you are standing in water way over your head, which is probably the only reason nobody sees it when you pee your pants. I am also smart enough to have financially secured my future so that I will not be a whore forever, while you, on the other hand, will never have the sand of a real

BLACK HEARTS WHITE BONES

man and will spend the rest of your life with a nose that looks like a squashed toad stool."

Rader's fist smashed into Sweet's face before she saw it coming. A searing, white pain exploded behind her eyes and she brought her hands to her face. Warm, thick blood began running between her fingers, down her forearms, and onto the floor.

Bracing herself, she gasped for breath, then forced her eyes open. This time she saw Rader's balled-up hand an instant before it crashed into the side of her head. Sparks exploded behind her eyes again as her knees hit the floor. A vague notion that she should try to cover her head tried to assert itself into conscious action, but failed. As if from a distance, she heard the flat, meaty sound of Rader's open hand striking the other side of her head. Mercifully, Sweets Nightingale collapsed unconscious onto the floor, her white hair, speckled red with her own blood.

The quiet that filled the void flooded through the Buford House's doorways as if seeking escape from an unimaginable evil. The captive prostitutes inside shivered despite the summer heat, and Rader's guards unconsciously gripped the handles of their weapons. A group of men on the wall paused from their work, feeling the evil as it spilled from the Buford House and into the street. The sense of purpose that motivated them was replaced with a dark foreboding.

At the end of the dock, standing on the deck of the *Revenge*, Clairette had watched the intimate exchange between Rader and his new lover with detached resolution. She had not seen him since he had left the ship the night of their arrival. Seeing them together again confirmed all the fears she had imagined during her long days and nights alone with only the crying of the children below deck to keep her company. Any lingering doubts about the truth of her fate had been scaled away. A few weeks ago she had been full of hope and life, embarking on a great adventure the likes of which rivaled those of her infamous father. Now she was floating on a vast sea of nothingness like a discarded jug of rumbullion. The fall had been far and nothing in her life had prepared her for the impact. She was broken beyond repair and knew what must come next. In some strange way, the dire revelation brought a peace she had never known.

Looking toward the second story of the guardhouse, Clairette wondered if Tye was still being held there. The boy and his three odd friends had treated her with a kindness she had not deserved, and they had done so despite her being largely responsible for their plight. Though resigned to her own fate, she retained enough clarity to regret that Rader would not pay for their suffering. The sense of guilt added to her depression and she found herself wishing she could have been more like her father. Whatever else he may have been, he was not a quitter.

The last thought sparked another and the hint of a smile appeared on Clairette's bruised and battered face.

"I don't know if it will help you," she whispered, still looking toward the guardhouse, "but I promise to try."

# CHAPTER THIRTY-FOUR

AT THE SAME MOMENT, standing on a crate to help him see out the barred window of their prison, Tye felt chilled air drift by and down into the damp darkness behind him. Suppressing a shudder, he turned to see Briebras, Dyonis, and Kofi wearing puzzled looks, wondering what unseen thing had roused them.

"Palsambleu!" Briebras said, pulling his coat tighter. "The ghosts of Stede Bonnet and his thirty crewmen are down here, I tell you. I can feel them all about us. If I do not escape from here soon I shall go mad!"

"Twenty-nine," Kofi said, rising from the floor, his sharp voice pinging off the dungeon's brick walls. For about the hundredth time since being locked up, he began poking around the various sacks and crates from cargo ships that had been stored in their crypt-like prison hoping to find something that would help them escape.

"Twenty-nine what?" Briebras asked.

"Twenty-nine crewmen. Bonnet was hanged with twenty-nine of his crew."

"No, no! Thirty men were hanged, I tell you."

"Right," Kofi agreed.

"Then why did you correct me?"

"Because twenty-nine crewmen and Bonnet make thirty men."

"Mon Dieu, what a fool you are!" Briebras said, realizing how Kofi had twisted the words around. "Now it is a total of thirty-one, counting Stede Bonnet."

"Thirty," Kofi countered, accompanied by the loud screeching of nails being pried from wood as he pulled the lid off a crate.

Briebras stomped around the cell, reeling off a fiery string of French obscenities that no one else could understand. Disturbed by the Frenchman's ranting, Dyonis came to stand next to Tye.

"Don't let them bother you," Tye said as he continued studying the window's iron bars. "They argue about everything. Briebras will stop in a minute. He just has to pump the excess water out of his bilge."

"Bilge?" Dyonis repeated, confused. "Where is his ship?"

"I didn't mean it literally," Tye said. Realizing that Dyonis probably didn't understand what that meant either, he turned away from the window and reached down to place a reassuring hand on Dyonis's shoulder. "It's just a funny way to say something. It's another way of saying that he needs to vanquish his inner demons."

"He has demons?!"

"No! It's a metaphor. I mean...never mind."

"Look," Tye continued, hoping to change the subject. "Do you think you can bend one of these? If we can make the gap between the bars just a little wider I think I might be able to slip through."

Dyonis pulled a crate over to the window and stepped up for a closer look. The curved-topped opening was small, about three feet across and a couple of feet tall at its highest point. With only a short distance between the top and bottom of the frame, the iron bars entrapping them had little give. The bottom of the window was just high enough above the cobblestone courtyard surrounding the guardhouse to keep rainwater from pouring in while still allowing light during the day. A few feet away to the left was the section of the wall that formed the Half Moon Battery. To the right was the open intersection where Broad Street ran into Bay Street and the buildings standing along both of them.

"Well? Go ahead, give it a try," Tye said.

Instead of immediately applying brute strength, Dyonis tested each bar to see if there was any give in their setting. Noticing the quiet collaboration between Tye and Dyonis, Briebras abandoned his pointless rant and climbed onto the box to stand next to the boy.

"No," Dyonis said. "I am Timekeeper. I keep time. I'm not strong enough to bend metal bars, but Kofi the blacksmith might be able to."

As one, they turned to look at Kofi who was still standing next to the crate he had opened. Pooled around his feet lay several yards of cloth, its length leading back to the folds of silk he held close to his face.

"Soft...smooth..." Kofi said, oblivious to the others. He pressed his nose into the cloth to inhale the dyes, then pulled a section of the silk across his cheek. Unwinding another arm's length of material from the bolt, he wrapped it around his shoulders and overlapped the sections across his chest as if it were a shawl.

Tye cast a glance at Briebras, though he was certain he already knew the answer to the implied question. The short Frenchman gave a slight shrug as if to say, "C'est la vie."

"Kofi," Tye called, though the word caught in his throat and sounded more like a cat trying to hack out a fur ball.

"So pretty," Kofi said again, stroking the silk running across his chest.

"Kofi," Briebras said. "Mon ami. We need your help."

The giant blacksmith stiffened and stopped his hand in mid-stroke. Without looking back at the others, he began collecting the scattered silk and stuffing it back into the crate.

"Help. With what?"

"The window, s'il te plait. We need to see if you can bend the bars. Our little friend Tye believes we can escape if you can make the gap wider."

Kofi came to join the others at the window, being careful to avoid looking anyone in the eyes. As he approached, they jumped down from the crates, allowing him room to step up and grab the bars unobstructed. Wrapping his huge hands around the two center bars, he took a deep breath, clenched his jaw and began pulling them in opposite directions. As his muscles bulged from the exertion, Tye and Briebras once again exchanged glances. Despite his incredible efforts, the bars refused to give.

Undaunted, Kofi grabbed one of the bars with both hands, swung his feet up and planted them on the inside of the opening's brick encasement. Tye, Briebras, and Dyonis stood in awed silence. Not only was the huge man suspending himself horizontally, he was pushing against the encasement with his legs and pulling on the bar at the same time.

On and on he pulled, until at last, the iron bar made a slight metallic groan of protest as it surrendered to the Herculean effort. Exhausted, he dropped from his awkward perch and sat on the floor. Looking up, he saw that he had barely moved the bar two inches.

"I am sorry," he said, placing his face in his hands. "I did my best."

"Sorry?" Tye asked. "But why?"

"I couldn't do it," he said, pointing to the window. "We cannot get out through that little gap. I have failed you, my friend."

"Kofi. What are talking about? We don't have to get through. Just me. I can get through and then open the door to let the rest of you out. Kofi, we can all get out now...thanks to you."

The big black man raised his head to look at the bars and then looked back at Tye.

"Are you sure?" he asked, a look of vindication spreading across his face.

"Yes, Kofi. Yes. You did it. We're free!"

"Free...to do what?" Briebras asked.

"I'm not sure," Tye said, realizing that he had not thought through the next steps. "But the first thing we have to do is help the children on the *Revenge*...and Clairette."

"Where will we take them?" Dyonis asked.

"I don't know," Tye said. Once again, he felt the weight of making decisions weighing on his shoulders.

"I know!" Briebras said. "The Huguenots, they are strong here. Once we get the children off the ship, we can take them to the church and hide there. And if someone is there, they will help us. I swear it as a Frenchman and a Huguenot."

"Yes," Tye said. "If we can get them off the ship without anyone knowing, it's not likely they will look for us in a church. They will think that we have somehow escaped the city."

"Oui, Oui. It is perfect!"

"Except for one thing," Tye said.

"What?" Briebras asked.

"Considering how long it's been since you've been to church, and the things you have done, I'm not sure that I want to be standing next to you when God realizes who it is that has come to his house."

Briebras tried to give Tye a hard stare, but the smile spreading across his face betrayed his true heart. A moment later, Kofi, Tye, and Briebras were all laughing at the joke. Dyonis joined in too, though he did not understand what was so funny. The other three laughed harder than they should have, releasing the apprehension that came with realizing that they were about to risk their lives yet again.

# CHAPTER THIRTY-FIVE

THE SUN WAS STILL WELL ABOVE the Palmettos when Anne began transferring her weapons and gear from the longboat that had brought them back to Ñuli's village. The Gullah's thirty-foot, cypress periauger with its flat bottom was designed for the shallows, and could be propelled by either sails, oars, or push poles. Taking the periauger would free up the brig to embark on a separate mission, to lay in wait just outside the inlet to Charles Town Bay, either to provide support by cannon or to recover the raiding party once they had secured the map.

"Where's your friend, Gant?" Asku asked? The only things he carried were his bow and a quiver full of the arrows he had made. "I've looked all over the village and he's nowhere to be found. The Gullah women haven't seen him for at least an hour."

Anne cursed but continued stowing her gear.

"I knew it! I knew the bastard would cut and run. He has no flag in this fight and no reason to risk life or limb for me or Tye. And now we see the worth of his allegiance to Mary Read and his oath to Scarlette. Once the dangers began to outweigh the potential for treasure, he ran like the mercenary he is. Damn his eyes!"

"We should get another person to help with rowing," Asku said.

"No. We'll make do with three. We'll take turns on the oars to save our strength when the time for rowing comes, but I won't have anyone I don't know going with us."

"In that case, I hope this breeze holds, or else we'll be dead tired from rowing before we even set foot in Charles Town."

Something in his voice gave Anne pause.

"You think you'd have a better chance of rescuing Tye and Dyonis if you went alone, don't you?"

"It would be easier for one person to work his way through Charles Town's back streets undetected than it would be for three, especially if that one person had the skills of an Indian."

"And why didn't you say anything until now?"

"Because I knew that you would never agree to stay behind, and I couldn't bring myself to knock you out and leave on my own."

Anne felt the familiar heat of her temper begin to flare, then saw the smile on his face.

"You think you're a real jokester, don't you, Asku Dare? Think you know how to get my goat? Will you be making japes the whole way to Charles Town or will I have to bind and gag you before we leave?"

She really wasn't in a mood to make light, but she saw that he was trying to make amends for their clash earlier.

Instead of replying, Asku nodded toward the huts. Anne's childhood friend was about to join them.

"Are you still sure you want to go?" Anne asked. Ñuli waded to the bow while two other Gullah women, standing knee-deep in the water, held on to the boat. The clothes she wore were plain and dark. Her blouse buttoned up all the way to her chin, her simple skirt reached her ankles. A dark, red scarf replaced the colorful wrap she had worn earlier. Tied around her waist, about the size of a book, was a small, leather pouch with a flap.

"De water tief hab me h'aa't een Chaa's Tun, en' buckruh done yent. If me en' Gawd dun gwi' sabe me bo, den nun gwi' to."

Asku looked at Anne.

"She said 'yes'," Anne said as she moved past him to climb into the boat. "You handle the sail and I'll take the tiller. Ñuli will ride the bow and point the way."

"Can't be any other way," Asku said, climbing in to join her. "I wouldn't be able to tell if she was saying 'left' or 'right.'"

Asku lifted Ñuli up into the boat and Anne made her way to the transom. As she took her seat at the tiller, she stepped on a pile of empty sacks heaped in the bottom of the hull.

"Watch it!" a voice from underneath warned.

"Mary?" Anne asked.

"Of course it's me. Now hurry up and get this thing moving before that long-toothed bastard Scarlette finds out I'm gone. It stinks under here."

Having heard the exchange, Asku raised one of the periauger's sails. As it billowed out with the breeze, the little boat pulled away from the bank, slowly advancing up the Stono River and away from the *Hazard*. Except for a few direction changes called out by Ñuli, they all remained silent, ignoring Mary Read's presence. After a few minutes had passed, their stowaway could no longer restrain herself.

"Tell me when I can come out from under this pile of stinking fish bags," she said, her voice muffled by the sacks.

"Of course," Anne said, "but I think it's safe to talk now."

Asku gave her a sharp glance and shook his head at Anne's deception. A bend in the river had taken them out of sight of the *Hazard* five minutes earlier.

"How did you manage to slip away from Scarlette?"

"The old jack and the rest of the crew were watching you and Asku as you headed back to the village in the longboat. I took the opportunity to throw a line off the stern and slip into the water. I let the current carry me past the fishing village and out of *Hazard*'s line of sight before I came ashore. It didn't take long to circle behind the village and come back to where I could see the boats. When I spotted the periauger, I jumped in and hid under these sacks."

"What about the plan? We all agreed that you and Scarlette would wait to enter the harbor until we gave you some kind of signal."

"That doesn't change just because I won't be there. He'll figure out that I went with you and sail to the inlet just like we planned. He doesn't have a choice...if he still wants that treasure map."

"Are you sure they can still see us?" she asked, pushing enough of the sacks aside to expose her head.

Anne glanced over her shoulder pretending to look back at the ship.

"I'm sure," she said, pushing Mary's head back down. She grabbed a sack tried to throw it over her head. "I'm pretty sure Scarlette is watching us with his long glass right now."

Mary Read started to cover herself with the sack but stopped when she saw that Asku was smiling. And even though Ñuli was at the other end of the boat, the twinkle in her eye was undeniable. Flinging away the sacks, she stuck her head above the gunwale and scanned the water behind them.

"YOU WAGTAIL QUEAN! You kept me in that stench knowing we were clear!"

"Are we?" Anne said, taking a glance over her shoulder. "Well, how about that? My mistake. It's all right to come up now. My, what is that smell?"

Mary Read stared at Anne with thoughts of murder spreading across her face. She rose from the bottom of the periauger and steadied herself. Gauging the distance between them, she took a step toward her antagonist. Anne gave the tiller a hard push making the boat lunge to port. Mary fell backward, landing hard on the bottom of the boat right behind Asku.

Ñuli laughed and Asku cracked another smile. Anne pulled the tiller to bring the boat back on course while keeping a wary eye on Mary Read. Mary took a moment to consider what had just happened, trying to decide whether to give it another go or risk giving Anne another opportunity to dump her on her arse.

"Consider that payback for foisting your worthless friend Gant on us," Anne said. "At least he deserted us now, when it doesn't matter, instead of in the middle of a fight."

Not having realized that the marine was absent, she scanned the forward section of the boat as if to confirm whether Anne was telling the truth.

"Yes, it's true," Anne said. "It seems that your partner had second thoughts about risking his life for a fake treasure map."

"It's not fake. It's real. Why can't you understand that?"

"Oh, of course it's real. I have no doubt that it's real paper and real ink. It's the treasure that's a sham...as phony as your friend Gant."

The truth of the marine's absence wicked away Mary's anger. Without his skills and experience, their chances of making it to *Rackham's Revenge* alive were practically naught. Pushing herself onto the opposite end of Asku's seat, she fell quiet as she considered the futility of their quest.

Anne recognized the vacant look on Mary Read's face and saw opportunity.

"You know, we could stop long enough to let you ashore and you could walk back to the village. Maybe even catch Scarlette before he sets sail."

"No," Asku said, seeing what Anne was trying to do. "It's almost dark and there are likely to be gators resting on the banks. She probably wouldn't make it through the night."

"Then I guess you're stuck with us...at least until we get to the city. Once we're done with the boat you can–"

"Shut up!" Mary Read said. "I have no intention of turning back. Nothing will stop me from claiming what is rightfully mine. Not you. Not Blyth Rader. Not all the cannons in Charles Town."

The force of her reaction surprised Anne. The Mary Read she knew was plenty greedy, but she was also a methodical, practical woman. The young Mary Read would have been in a fever to reclaim the map and find the treasure, but she would have dropped the idea without a second thought once it looked to be a losing proposition. The woman she saw now was obsessed. She didn't understand why, but this Mary Read was not about to turn back for any reason – not even for the sake of her own life.

With the matter settled, they sailed on in silence until darkness began settling in. When she could no longer make out landmarks, Ñuli lit a lantern and hung it on a bow pole to light the way. A few minutes later, she spotted the creek that connected to the Ashley River and signaled for Anne to turn east.

Once they had passed through its narrow mouth and the creek began to widen, the breeze gave its last gasp of the evening. Asku lowered the sail and mounted two oars. For the next hour they took turns, two people rowing, one on the rudder and a spotter at the bow. When it came time for Ñuli to take another turn at the bow, she snuffed out the lantern that had been lighting the way.

"Soon be ta Chaa's Tun," she said as she sat down, though no explanation had been needed.

The stars above the openness of the creek, contrasted by the darkness of the trees on either side, made it easy to stay away from the banks. When the ribbon of stars began to expand into a much broader openness, they knew they were entering the Ashley River. As they left the influence of the creek, the river current carried them along at twice the speed they had made while rowing. Now that they were in territory familiar to Anne, she moved to the bow and Ñuli took the tiller.

"We have to reach the far bank before we pass Vanderhorst's Creek, or else we'll have to row back up river against the current," Anne whispered.

After a few minutes of hard, steady rowing, they reached the far bank and rested as the boat drifted on toward the bay. Rounding a small point, the sudden appearance of lantern and torchlight from the city told them that they were on the verge of missing their mark.

"Here!" Anne said as loud as she dared.

Ñuli leaned into the tiller and Asku dug his oar into the water, using it as a brake to force the boat into a hard turn. When the bow swung toward the mouth of the creek, he fell back into rowing until they broke free of the river's current. Moments later they came to a stop in the creek's still waters.

The next few minutes would be the most dangerous they would face. Anne knew that the creek paralleled the southern wall, and that a few hundred feet ahead was a small stream that flowed out from the city. The creek and the stream ran through a tidal marsh that made approaching this span of the wall on foot almost impossible. The stream passed under a wood footbridge connecting a gap in the earthen wall that allowed boats to come and go. On either side of the gap, a redan and a bastion jutted out from the wall where shooters could easily pick off intruders attempting to enter the city by boat. A short hail of musket balls and cannonade shot would annihilate anyone bold enough or stupid enough to try sneaking in.

But there was one weakness. The guards on the wall had to see them coming to stop them. There was no moon, and the only light this night came from the stars and a few lanterns scattered about the wall.

Anne motioned for the oars to be stowed and then Asku broke out one of the long poles to begin pushing the boat forward. With no specific task to perform, Mary Read gripped the hilt of her sword for reassurance and wished that she had a few pistols.

As they turned up the stream leading into the city, they began to understand the true audacity of their simple plan. Less than a hundred yards in front of them was the footbridge connecting the two sections of wall between which the stream passed. At the midpoint of the bridge, sitting atop a six-foot post, a ship's lantern illuminated everything within a fifty-foot circle. Leaning against the post, a man with a musket peered out into the darkness, a lone sentry who had only to fire one shot to alert the city.

Everyone on the periauger held their breath, fearing that the sentry would spot them any moment. Pressing his weight down on the push pole to anchor it in the muddy bottom, Asku kept the boat from drifting. Unaware that he was being watched, the lookout rested his musket against the post and fished something out of his coat pocket. Raising one of the lantern's glass windows, he lit a splinter of wood in its bright yellow flame. Lowering the glass, he placed a pipe in his mouth and attempted to light the tobacco in its bowl.

Releasing his grip on the pole, Asku reached for his bow with one hand and removed an arrow from the quiver with the other. The flame from the splinter would rob the man of his night vision, but only for a few seconds. Deftly nocking the arrow, he drew back the string, aimed – then let it fly.

The man suddenly stiffened as though listening for something. For several long, agonizing moments, Anne feared that Asku had missed his target and had only succeeded in giving them away. Then the pipe fell from the sentry's mouth, clattering on the bridge as though the thing itself was trying to alert the other guards. Turning toward the redan, he staggered for a step, and then another. One hand came to his chest and one to his back, grasping at the shaft they could now see had passed halfway through his torso. His mouth opened and closed several times as he attempted to call for help, but the only sound that reached the boat was the low, ghastly sucking of air failing to fill collapsed lungs. Staggering forward one more time, he crashed to his knees then pitched over the side of the bridge into the soft marsh. Having landed face first, no one would hear him groaning even if he were still alive.

"Hell of a shot," Anne said.

"I was aiming for his throat. We're lucky he didn't scream and wake the whole town."

Propping the bow and quiver against the gunwale, Asku retrieved the pole and began pushing them toward the bridge. No one looked at the corpse in the marsh grass as they passed through the gap in the wall. Everyone's attention was focused on the tips of the masts and the footbridge overhead. Although the crosswalk had been built to allow for the passage of such boats, they made it under with only inches to spare. Had it not been for the blessing of a low tide, they might not have made it through.

Within minutes of clearing the bridge, Ñuli began waving them toward the eastern side of the stream. As they came closer to the bank, a pair of white bollards appeared out of the darkness and Asku pushed the boat toward the closest one. In one swift motion, Ñuli jumped from the bow onto the landing of rock and oyster shells and wrapped a line around the bollard. When the other three were out of the boat, she started up the path leading toward a darkened house, but then stopped without warning. A low, menacing growl came from the darkness ahead. Asku knew that the only way to take out the dog without rousing the whole city was with an arrow – but as he was at the back of their column he could not see the beast at all. If the dog started barking, they would be caught out in the open.

But Ñuli had come prepared. Hunting dogs could be found in half of the town's households. And though most of the families would have taken their dogs when leaving the city, there had to have been some left behind. Lifting the flap of her leather pouch, she slowly slipped her hand inside.

"Hush...puppy," she said as she tossed a small, round object toward the dog. The animal wolfed the thing down then looked back at Ñuli wanting more.

The Gullah woman pulled another ball of cornbread from the pouch and threw it to the side of the path. With nose to the ground, the dog took off into the higher grass in search of the treat. The trespassers continued up the path unchallenged.

Staying in the shadows when possible, they advanced into the town's dark interior. Having no idea where Tye and the others might be, they had agreed that the best place to start looking was on the wharf. It was likely that they were still on the *Revenge*. If not, they would have to find one of Rader's crew and convince him to reveal their location.

After dashing through an intersection, they paused for a moment to decide their next move. As she looked around, Anne was able to make out enough of the surrounding landmarks to get her bearings. The dark, narrow path ahead was Bedon's Alley. Elliott Street crossed its far end, and another block beyond that – she was almost sure – was Broad Street.

"I know where we are," Anne said, moving past the others. "I'll take the lead now."

But when she tried to pass by Ñuli, Anne's friend grabbed her by the upper arm and pulled her close.

"Uh gone fuh me bo ni," she whispered. "Bad buckruh hol' de Gullah mens deh wes' whal at de fallin' bige."

"What's going on?" Mary Read hissed, annoyed by the black woman's mangled English.

"She says that the men from her village are being held near the drawbridge and she is going to try to free them," Anne said, now as peeved with Mary Read as Mary was with Ñuli.

This was no place to argue, and Anne couldn't fault Ñuli for wanting to help her swain. They were both attempting rescues that were not likely to succeed, but they both had to try to save their loved ones.

Conceding the inevitable, Anne pulled her into a hug and said, "Best of luck, my friend. Thank you for your help. Maybe...maybe we will meet again when this is over."

Anne regretted the words even as she said them. Even if they both managed to survive, it was unlikely they would ever see each other again. But Ñuli was as gracious in her goodbye as she had been with everything else they had ever done.

"No forget, An-nie. No forget."

Anne watched until she disappeared into the darkness. Though they had spent less than a day together, she was grateful for the knowledge that her friend had fared far better than she had been led to believe. And as long as they lived, there was hope.

"Now what?" Mary Read asked.

"We keep moving toward the wharf," Anne said. "If we're lucky, we'll come across someone before we get there and see if we can find out where Tye and the others are."

"They may have put him with the other children they kidnapped," Asku said, "wherever that might be."

Anne had not thought of that. She had, in fact, completely forgotten about the other children. Since leaving the Gullah fishing camp she had thought of only one thing – saving Tye. It was the same single-mindedness that had controlled her when she was younger, and it was going to get them killed if she allowed it to continue.

"This is a port town full of taverns, damn it. There's bound to be a drunken sailor laid out in a side street or back alley somewhere."

"Look," Mary Read said, pointing toward the other side of the street. "See it? Halfway down the block."

Anne looked up and down the street a couple of times before she saw it. Cloaked in darkness and partially hidden by the abundance of ornamental shrubs was an alley running between the buildings. Less than an alley, it was more like a footpath that could only be accessed by people, too narrow for carriages.

"We cross one at a time," she said pulling a pistol from her waistband. "If I make it, then you go next. Asku goes last. We're getting close to the wharf, so keep a sharp eye. We're bound to cross paths with someone soon."

Anne exited the alley, moving cautiously at first, keeping in the shadows on their side of Elliott Street for as long as possible. When she was directly across from the half-hidden alleyway, she took a deep breath then bolted across to the open street. When safely concealed by the shrubs, she listened for signs that someone had spotted her. Hearing nothing, she leaned out of the shadows and waved for Mary Read.

Mary repeated Anne's movements, sticking to the dark for as long as possible, then dashing to the other side of the street. Again, Anne waited for a few moments, listening, then gave Asku the 'all clear' signal.

Asku surveyed the street in both directions, making sure no one was approaching from places that Anne could not see from her position. Seeing nothing, he started to step out of the shadows but pulled up short. Across the street, a flicker of light inside a house next to where the women were hiding caught his eye. It was brief and had been muted by the crown glass of the home's window, but Asku recognized the tell-tale shimmer of light reflecting off of human flesh. Someone was inside the building.

Asku started to wave his arms above his head to warn them but realized his foolishness. It was impossible for them to see him in the dark alley. He would have to step out of shadows and into the street, even though he would be exposing himself.

"NOW!" yelled a man who came charging out of the house next to where Anne and Mary were hiding. "THEY'RE IN THE ALLEY! GRAB THEM QUICK!"

Four other men followed, rushing down the entryway steps and into the street. The door to the house on the other side of the women's hiding place flew open and more men rushed out to join the others. Farther away, Asku heard a third group begin shouting and cursing, closing off any hope of escape. A shot rang out and a man with a lantern appeared from nowhere.

Asku pressed back into the shadows as far as he could and still be able to watch. The flood of men had been too swift and too many for him to help Anne and Mary.

"I thought I saw her waving at someone over there, in the alley," Asku heard one of the men say.

"I'd be careful if I were you," Mary Read said. "There should be about fifty of our group gathered there by now. Probably trying to figure out which of you to kill first. I'm thinking it's you with the light. You're the easiest to see."

The man raised the lantern, allowing its yellow glow to fall on his face.

"Well I'll be damned," Mary said. "Of all the men from my crew of mutinous bastards to run into. It's Curlee Leathers, the ugliest bastard of the lot. Had enough of that sorry sack of bumfodder, Rader, yet? Why don't you take that lantern and stick it up your arse."

"You know, I never did like takin' orders from a woman," he said. "Looks like I'm in charge, now...an' I've got a few orders I can't wait to give you. Care to guess where I'll start?"

"Shut up, you idiot," Mary Read said. "We both know that your orders are to take us to Rader if we're captured. Let's just get on with it."

Anne was sure that the man was going to hit Mary, but he turned to the man standing closest to him instead.

"Here, take this light an' three men. I thought I saw someone else across the street just before we took these two. Go see if anyone is hiding over there...an' be quick about it. I want to get these fish to Cap'n Rader afore they spoil."

Moments later the four men stepped into the alley, filling the narrow backstreet with light. They poked around the shrubs and checked everywhere within a hundred feet of Elliott Street that a man might hide, but found no sign of anyone. Satisfied, they rejoined Curlee Leathers who took the lantern and led his men down the pathway between the houses toward the next street.

When they were gone, Asku swung down from his rooftop-hiding place and dashed across the street in pursuit of the pirates. The light from their lantern made tracking them easy work until it took a sudden turn and disappeared. Quickening his pace, he moved as fast as the uneven path and darkness would allow.

When he got to the point where the light had turned, he stopped and looked around. Given that the street was still another hundred feet or more distant, they had to have entered one of the buildings to his right – but which one? Charles Town's practice of orienting the end of their homes toward the bay to catch prevailing breezes put several entryways in close proximity. And if the presence of candlelight was any indication, people were inside all three of the closest buildings.

Asku studied the three structures for a few moments, looking for anything to implicate one over the others. He had to get it right the first time, there would be no second chances. Then he spotted it. A window on the second story of the middle building was open, and yet no light shown from within. It might not be the right building, but at least he could get inside, and he had to start somewhere.

Calling on the same strength and agility that had helped him escape earlier, the woodsman shimmied up a tree next to the window until reaching a branch that was as high as the sill. Using other limbs above his head for support, he moved as close to the house as possible. Bouncing on the thick branch a couple of time to test its strength, he took careful aim – and jumped.

He crashed into the wall with a hard thud but somehow managed to grasp the windowsill. For the next few moments he clung there, not daring to take a breath as he listened. When he was sure that no one was coming to investigate, he threw his leg over the sill and slid into the room, being careful not to bang his bow against the window frame.

Nothing.

Despite his clumsiness, he had managed to enter the house without being discovered. Across the room, narrow slivers of dim light framed a closed door leading into the building's interior, perhaps a hallway. As his eyes adjusted to the stingy lighting, the room began to reveal itself. To his right was a washstand with a mirror, basin, and water pitcher. Towels hung from bars on either side and more were stacked on a shelf underneath the basin. To his left was a large bed with a canopy and thin curtains of mosquito netting.

Though he neither saw or heard anything to cause suspicion, there was something about the bed that made him hesitate. It was an instinct honed by years of tracking and hunting, and he knew to trust it. With swift, silent motion he unsheathed his knife and moved to the bed. Yanking back the netting, he thrust the knife forward to greet whatever threat might be lying in wait.

What he saw in the dim light was so different from want he had expected, it took him a moment to understand what he was seeing. Cowering at the head of the bed, with their backs wedged into the corner and their knees drawn up tight, were a woman and a boy. The boy – too big to be Tye – held the woman's head tight against his chest as if protecting her. In turn, the woman was using her body to shield the boy. Together, they formed a tightly woven ball of desperate fear, each attempting to draw strength from the other.

Despite swelling that reduced the woman's eyes to slits, Asku saw an ember of defiance still smoldering inside. Whoever the woman was, she had been through hell, and might even be a bit addled. Asku returned the knife to its sheath to show that he meant them no harm. As he did, the woman lunged forward and jabbed a penknife toward his face, stopping a half-inch from his eye. They stared at each other, trying to divine the other's mind. Then the boy reached up, placing his hand on the woman's outstretched arm.

"I... I don't think he is one of them."

The woman relaxed but continued holding the penknife in Asku's face. Still leery of the intruder's intentions, she forced down a swallow with a throat too long without water. Her bruised, cracked lips quivered as she struggled to form words.

"Did Rader send you to kill us?"

# CHAPTER THIRTY-SIX

FROM THE DARKNESS OF THE ENTRYWAY leading down to the undercroft they had escaped moments before, Kofi, Briebras, Dyonis, and Tye assessed the movements of a sentinel posted at the gangway to the *Revenge*. After squeezing through the barred window the boy had circled around the building until he found the door to their dungeon and removed its crossbar to free the others. They had expected to find a number of sentries along the wall, but except for the lone guard, the wharf was deserted.

By the light of a lantern at the sentry's feet, Tye recognized the man as the horribly disfigured Oliver Cullen. It was no surprise that Rader assigned only those he knew and trusted to guard the innocents, for they might end up being the only thing standing between his neck and a noose. But had it not been for those same children, Tye and his three friends would have already commandeered a boat and be escaping Charles Town.

"The children," Briebras whispered to the others. "We must free them now, while there is a chance."

"I will go," Kofi said, his squeaky voice turned shrill by the attempt to speak softly. "One man. No problem."

"No," Tye said. "He will see you coming and cry out to the guards in the watch house. One man will become twenty."

"How, then?" Briebras countered.

"I don't know. Give me a minute to think."

"Think fast, mon ami. We cannot remain here much longer."

Tye closed his eyes and began imagining ways that might get them past the guard, but each idea was discarded in quick succession. The harder he tried to devise a solution, the more impossible it seemed to be. The children may well be lost and it would be his fault. For all his cleverness up till now, he was about to fail those who least deserved to die.

Still, he refused to give up. He refused to believe that there were problems that could not be solved. Though he didn't know it, it wasn't his genius that made him so different from most people, it was his inability to admit defeat.

Instead of trying to come up with a solution through sheer will, Tye shut out the distractions and let go of his inner turmoil. Tapping into a long-denied gift he shared with his mother, he allowed his mind to focus on the one circumstance that would allow him to board the ship safely.

"Palsambleu..." Briebras whispered a few moments later. "Look."

Rader had chosen his guard well. The man was at least as big as Kofi, and few were the men who would want to challenge him. His hideous face made him appear more ogre than man. Even those few who did not fear his size instinctively recoiled from his ghoulish face.

But every man has a weakness, and Rader's chosen guard had been too long without sleep. The hour was well past midnight and the bales of animal pelts on the dock waiting for loading onto to a ship had become too inviting to resist. As they watched the man called Skullen settle his large frame into the pile of furs, Tye knew his chance to steal upon the *Revenge* was nigh.

"Dyonis..."

"I am Timekeeper."

"I'm going to sneak aboard the *Revenge*. I need you to track the time. Can you tell Kofi and Briebras when fifteen minutes have passed?"

"Here or in Greenwich?"

"It doesn't matter. Here. Can you tell them when fifteen minutes have passed?"

"Of course. I am Timekeeper."

"If I'm not back in fifteen minutes, then come get me if you have to."

"What about Skullen?" Dyonis asked. "Won't he call for help?"

"If I'm not back in fifteen minutes, I don't think it will matter. Our best hope will be to cut the *Revenge* free and float away from the wharf...and hope that Rader wants the ship too much to fire on it."

"Wait," Briebras said, grabbing the boy's arm. "I will go. You have done too much already."

"No. I am smaller...lighter...less likely to disturb the guard. And I am quicker."

"Oui, but I am also petit. And you are only–"

Tye wrenched his arm free before Briebras could finish and dashed across the court. Huddling in a pool of darkness created by the sharp angles of the wall's main gate, he checked the guard to make sure he was still sleeping. Stepping out of his shoes, he stole across the wharf and started toward the end of the pier where the *Revenge* waited like a leviathan, ready to devour anyone foolish enough to rouse it from its slumber.

When he neared the circle of light created by the lantern, Tye tread as close to the edge of the pier as he dared. Skullen was making wet, sucking sounds as air passed through his exposed teeth, reminding Tye of the night he had stolen back Dyonis's watch. The boy shuddered at the memory of Cull the Skull bolting upright in his sleep with his eyes wide open, but pushed on. Reaching the gangplank at last, he took a deep breath and darted aboard *Rackham's Revenge*.

The moment his foot touched the deck he sensed that something was wrong. The ship he had come to know better than anyone felt different. It was as though he had stepped into a pool of air so frigid he could feel it in his bones. Almost in a panic, he peered into the darkness around him trying to discern the source of the unnatural onslaught, but the light was feeble and he was barely able to see anything at all. There could be a hundred men on deck hiding in the blackness around him and he wouldn't know it.

Shaking off the sense of dread, he hurried over to the captain's quarters and opened the door. Although his self-appointed task was to free the children, he had to try saving Clairette as well. It would only take a few extra minutes, and he would never forgive himself if he didn't at least try.

Stepping into the darkness as far as he dared, he called out to her in a harsh whisper.

"Clairette! Wake up! It's me, Tye! You must come with me, now!"

He listened for a minute, hoping to hear the young woman stirring from her sleep, but no such sounds reached his ears. Cursing his luck, he moved closer to the bed, arms stretched out before him for fear of bumping into a table or chair. When his hands finally found the bed, he shook it as hard as he dared and began feeling around for her.

Nothing. He had been certain that she was still aboard, but the bed had not even been slept in. If she wasn't in the cabin, where was she?

Feeling his time slipping away, Tye cursed his bad luck and began working his way back to the door. This time he followed the cabin wall, passing behind the chart table and pausing long enough to feel about its nooks. A few moments later, he slipped out the door, hurried across the deck and descended the stairs to the inner hull. When he opened the door to his quarters, the interior was so dark and quiet he could not tell if anyone was inside.

*Had both Clairette and the children somehow been spirited away without anyone knowing?*

"Hello?" a girl's fearful voice whispered from the far end of the room. "Who's there?"

Relief passed over Tye in a wave, but he did not have time to revel over his change of luck. His internal clock told him that his time was almost up.

"Listen to me. I've come to rescue you. Is everyone awake?"

The voice that had called out to him began whispering to the others, urging them to wake up. One of the smaller children began whimpering and another lashed out in anger, demanding to be left alone. When the girl warned them that there was another person in the room, he heard them crowding closer together in the corner.

"My name is Tye and you if want to escape you have to trust me. Do you want to get away?"

"Yes!" the girl said. Several of the children began to ask questions, but she quieted them down.

"All right, then," Tye said, trying to sound authoritative. "There's not much time. We have to leave right now and we have to be very quiet. I want everyone to hold hands and follow me. When we leave the boat, we'll have to go past a guard asleep on the dock. If we make any noise and wake him, we'll all end up back here again...or worse. Do you understand?"

In whispers, the girl and two or three of the older children promised to follow instructions. The younger ones remained silent, allowing themselves to be swept along with the others.

"Come, take my hand. We leave now."

The girl who had first spoken helped the others form a line, deciding who would hold whose hand and directing them to remain quiet no matter what. When they were ready, she led them to the doorway, her hand extended in front of her, feeling for their rescuer.

"You...you're just a boy," she whispered when her hand found his shoulder.

"Honestly, it's not my fault," Tye said. It was a stupid answer, but it was the first thing that had popped into his mind. "Do you want to escape now, or wait for someone older to come along?"

"No! I'm sorry. Please, get us out of here. It's been...horrible."

Tye grasped her hand and led them up to the open deck. It was not until they stepped outside that Tye saw the girl was carrying one of the smaller children on her hip. It was impossible to tell, but Tye guessed that she was only eleven or twelve years old herself.

"What is your name?" he asked.

"Elisabeth...Beth."

"Beth...see the light over there, on the dock? That's where the guard is sleeping. We're all going to cross the gangplank together, but when we get to the other side I want you to wait with the others while I make sure he's still asleep. Once I'm sure it's safe, I'll wave to you. Do you understand?"

"Yes," she whispered, her voice more steady than it had a right to be.

"Good. Now remember, keep your eyes on me. When I give the signal, take the others by him as quickly and quietly as you can."

"I promise I will."

As Tye began skulking his way across the open deck, he felt the same forbidding pool of coldness that had enveloped him earlier. The sense of some sort of presence was overpowering, slowing him down as though he were carrying a weight that grew heavier with each step.

After crossing the gangplank and stepping onto the pier, he paused only long enough to regain his composure. Once again freed from the unbearable pall, he began edging his way toward the pile of animal skins and into the circle of sputtering lantern light. When he reached the halfway point, he glanced over to check on Beth and the other children. Though little more than silhouettes, he could see that they were holding in place as he'd instructed. Turning back around, the shock of seeing Skullen's eyes, wide-open and staring hit Tye like a fist in the chest. His mind screamed at him to run, but his legs refused to obey. He was trapped between the need to save himself and the need to save the children.

"Well, well, well...what do we have here?" Skullen said through his wet, sucking teeth. As he rose to his feet, he picked up the lantern and adjusted its wick. Light spread across the dock. "Ahh... It's Master Tye himself, it is. You wouldn't be tryin' to sneak aboard ship to free the little ones, would you?"

Tye tried to tear his eyes away from the ghastly hole in the side of Skullen's face, but the feeling that he was being confronted by a talking skull addled his brain.

With speed belying his bulk, the big man took a long stride toward Tye, grabbed him by the front of his coat, and stepped back into his nest of pelts. With the boy dangling from his fist like a rag doll, the pirate drew him in close to his face.

"What's the matter, boy? You don't like my looks? Turns your stomach a bit, does it?"

Tye continued to stare, unable to speak.

"It's the same with the women. Ain't a one of them that'll let me storm her castle, not for all the coal in Newcastle. But the way I sees it, a boy can be as pretty as a woman...and a boy don't have no say in the matter. Especially a boy what's been lurking about places he don't belong."

The pirate paused, his mouth twisting into a macabre smile, exposing the white of his cheekbone. From somewhere in a swirling chaos of desperation, Tye wondered if Kofi could see him and if he was even now coming to help. The thought gave him a spark of hope. Taking a deep breath, he started to yell out, but the talking skull slammed him down on the pier, forcing him to his knees.

Dazed, Tye looked up into Skullen's eyes searching for a spark of compassion.

"Now, if you do everything I tell you to do and don't make no noise, I'll let you live," he said, starting to untie the knot on the rope holding up his breeches. "If you don't..."

Vile acid flooded Tye's throat and he struggled to force it back down. With his face just inches from the man's feet, Tye saw that – like most of the pirates who climbed the rigging – he wore no shoes.

"Aye! I'll be having none of that? If you spew your chowder on my feet, I'll bash your teeth in. Understand, whelp?"

"It's... I'm all right," Tye said. Placing his hands on his knees, he braced himself and looked up at the man again. But the skull-faced Cullen – his fingers trembling with eagerness – was fixated on unraveling the reluctant knot. Drool seeped between his teeth and through the gap in his cheek, dripping onto the planks between his feet.

"I have something for you," Tye said, his voice growing stronger. He sat up straight and moved his hands to his hips.

"And what might that be?" Skullen asked, so jacked up with anticipation that the boy's brashness barely registered.

"THIS!" Tye screamed. In one swift motion, he pulled the marlinspike hidden in the outseam of his breeches, raised it above his head with both hands, and drove it down through Skullen's foot and deep into the plank beneath it.

# CHAPTER THIRTY-SEVEN

BLYTH RADER WAS SITTING at a round table in the middle of Sweets' lavishly decorated room when Curlee Leathers delivered his catch. With his back to the door, the usurper ignored the new arrivals as he continued working an oil rag over the wood and metal of a finely crafted dueling pistol. Occasionally he paused to peer across the room and through a set of French doors leading out to the balcony.

Following his gaze, Anne saw that she could see over the city wall and that the object of his scrutiny was a ship moored at the end of a pier jutting out from the wharf. The light of a single lantern near the ship sporadically illuminated sections of the dark vessel as its flame danced about inside its glass cage. With a jolt, she realized that the ship was the *Revenge*. Composing herself, she stole a quick glance about the room to see if anyone had noticed her surprise.

Rader turned the pistol to look down its barrel in search of a rogue speck of dust. Satisfied with his work, he turned to look at the two women. Light from a three-branched candle tree on the table illuminated half of his face, revealing a gaunt countenance more befitting a cadaver than a would-be pirate king.

"Caught them trying to sneak into the city, just like you said they would," Leathers said. "Not sure, but I think the one named Asku was with them. Probably half way back to Ocracoke by now, I'd wager."

Rader stiffened but his eyes continued darting about frantically as if in search of something.

"The tar heel...he got away?" he asked.

"Aye. That's what I mean...if he was there at all. We never saw him for certain. It was too dark, an' these two aren't talkin'."

As he weighed his next step, Rader's eyes once again rambled about the room, focusing on nothing.

"What am I thinking?" he said, as if realizing two old friends had just entered the room. Putting the pistol down, he stood and waved an arm in invitation toward two chairs on the opposite side of the table. "Please! Ladies! Take a seat. You must join me in a glass of scuppernong. It's a delightfully sweet wine, made from a grape indigenous to the Carolinas. I'm thinking of exporting it to England."

Rader held up a half-filled goblet so that they could admire the golden-white beverage, then downed the entire glass.

"It's damn hard to sit when you've got your hands tied behind your back," Mary Read said, her coarse voice knocking the edges off the room's quiet like a wood rasp.

"Free them," Rader said as he refilled his goblet. "They can do no harm now."

As Curlee Leathers cut Mary Read's bindings, he leaned in so close she could feel his breath on the back of her neck. When her wrists sprang free, she took a vicious swing at him with the back of her hand. Catching her arm, Leathers twisted it behind her and forced her into the chair.

Though he repeated the trespass on Anne as he cut her bindings, she ignored his lechery. Her attention was fixed on events unfolding on the pier. Being careful not to let her gaze linger too long in that direction, she watched a slight figure sneak by a sentry guarding access to the *Revenge* and disappear into its main cabin. Given the skulker's size, she could not help but think of Tye, but there were no circumstances she could imagine where her son would be free to roam the docks, so she dismissed the idea as desperate fantasy.

"You did search them for weapons?" Rader asked, beginning to have second thoughts.

"Of course," Leathers said as he shoved Anne into the chair next to Mary. "Especially around their nethers. No weapons there, I promise you that."

"I hope you enjoyed it," Mary Read said as he moved around the table to stand behind Rader. "Men who touch me that way don't tend to fare well."

Taking care to pull his scabbard back so that it would not bang against the table, Rader took his seat again. Reassured that the women posed no threat, he turned his attention back to the pistol.

"Tell me where he is," Rader said, acting nonchalant. "I know he came with you. I bet he follows you around like a puppy in search of its mother's teat."

"Shut up!" Anne said. "There's only one dog in Charles Town that walks on two legs, and he's soon to be gelded."

Rader's face went dark as the embarrassment suffered by Anne's hand at the tar kiln burned white hot in his memory. His scowl turned into a mirthless smile and he began to speak again.

"What they said about you back in Bath," he said, unaware that he had begun to rub his nose. "It's true, you know. You're off the hooks. Mad as May butter."

Anne fought back the rage. Now, more than any other time in her life, she had to keep her wits about her. Tye had to be close by. Losing control might get her Rader's life, but it might also mean the end of her son.

"Mad? You dunderhead. Of course I'm mad. Mad like an adder. You have my son and I'll have him back. Tell me where he is...NOW...and I might let you live."

Rader braced himself, half expecting the woman to dive across the table, and then started laughing.

"Tell me something. It was your friend there sitting beside you that came up with the idea of kidnapping your son, why is it that she still lives? Or didn't you know that?"

**352**

He picked up a powder horn and poured a measure of gunpowder down the pistol's barrel while Anne spoke.

"Her time is coming, but that's none of your concern. Right now, you have Tye, and it is my intent to have him far away when the militia comes to reclaim their city. After that, you and Mary Read can rot in hell."

"Ahhh...the militia," Rader said. He picked up a cotton patch and placed it over the pistol's muzzle, its barrel pointed toward the ceiling. "I wouldn't count on them if I were you. I know that they are going to attack soon, that's why I've moved almost all of my men to the west wall. And at first light, the ships I have guarding the inlet have orders to reposition. The *Discordia* will sail up the Ashley River and the *Abundant* up the Cooper. When the militia comes, they will be caught in a three-sided box of canon fire. Boom...boom...and...boom! They all fall down. No more militia. Pretty clever, don't you think?"

Not waiting for an answer, Rader turned to Mary Read.

"What about you? All I heard from you for two years was how much you looked forward to making Anne Bonny suffer. How much you hated her for leaving you to die in Spanish Town. As I recall, you were going to stuff her dead body into a gibbet like good ol' Calico Jack, hang it from the bowsprit, and then sail from Bath to Jamaica for all to see."

As he continued talking, he took a lead ball from a pouch and placed it on the cotton patch still draped across the muzzle. He then picked up the pistol's ramrod and shoved the ball into the barrel, tapping it a few extra times to make sure it was well packed.

"You do understand, if you had just killed her as planned, you might not be in this fix. The crew would have seen that you meant business. They would have known that the Mary Read of old...the Bloody Mary they feared...was back. My attempts to talk them into mutiny would have never left port. But you went soft."

Picking up the horn again, he tapped a thimbleful of black powder into the flash pan.

"Not true, as you're soon to find out," Mary Read said, the Wapping burr in her voice reasserting itself. "But as far as my vow is concerned, let's just say I had a change of heart."

"Mary Read has a heart?" Rader laughed again. Placing the pistol on the table, he picked up the goblet and took another swallow. "Now that's a handsome thought. More likely you reacquainted yourself with Anne Bonny's beard and found it too savory to live without."

"Whatever you say," Rader continued, snorting at his joke. "The fact is, you two have quite the dilemma. Both of you have declared your intent to kill me, but there is only one of me. So which of you will it be...the one-eyed whore or the shrew so full of anger she doesn't realize she's already dead? And how on earth will you decide?"

From the corner of her eye, Anne saw Mary Read was about to rip off one of her biting retorts when something stilled her tongue. Following Mary's gaze to the darkest corner of the room, she thought she could see – something. Like a faint reflection in a pool of water disturbed by a breeze, she knew the rippling in the darkness had to be the Hollow. What she couldn't know was that, for Mary, the apparition was as undefined and ill-formed as it had been from the beginning, but this time she could see the thing's eyes. They peered at her from the darkness without color or the light of life, providing no clues as to who it had once been. But the longer she looked into its eyes, the more they spoke to her.

"Anne... We have to go. Now."

"What?"

"Tye...and Clairette. Something is wrong. Something has happened."

Rader tilted his head, trying to decide whether Mary Read was attempting a trick or had lost her mind. He glanced over his shoulder at Curlee Leathers and the other men standing behind him to make sure they were at the ready.

Anne had no idea how Mary Ready could know such things, but the urgency in her voice could not be denied. Her mind raced to figure a way out, but the possibility that Tye was in need of help made her frantic, scattering her thoughts. Then her eyes fell upon the candle tree.

"Do you remember the game Blackbeard liked to play?" Anne asked with the casualness of a person asking about the weather.

Mary Read thought for a moment and then smiled

"You mean the one that maimed Israel Hands?"

**354**

"That would be the one."

"Enough of this," Rader said as if chastising talkative schoolchildren. His eyes went from one to the other, studying their faces for a clue as to their skullduggery. "I'll be the one to-"

In a blur, Anne reached across the table and struck the candle tree, sending it flying toward Rader. The last thing she saw as the candles went dark was Rader diving for the floor, the candle tree passing harmlessly over his head. Hot wax splattered into the face of one of the men behind Rader, his scream of agony piercing the darkness.

When Anne lunged for the candle tree, Mary Read placed her hands on the edge of the table and pushed down with all her weight. The opposite side began to rise as the room went black, but she could hear the pistol begin sliding toward her. Coming to a stop when it hit her fingers, Mary seized the weapon and had it cocked before the table crashed back to the floor. Pointing the pistol in the direction Rader had been sitting, she pulled the trigger.

In the flash that came with the flintlock's discharge, she saw her mistake. Rader was on the floor, leaving the man with the hot wax in his eyes to take the shot. Already dead, the man crumpled into a heap.

In the same flash of light, Anne saw that Rader had ended up on all fours directly across from her. Diving toward him through the darkness, she thrust her hand toward his hip. Her fingers slammed into the sword's hilt, sending a numbing jolt up her arm. Ignoring the pain, she seized the grip and yanked it from its scabbard.

Even in the midst of the chaos, she recognized the familiar grain of its cord-wrapped tang and the perfect balance of its triangular blade. This was her prized smallsword - the épée de cour Rader's men had taken from her the night she had been captured on the *Revenge*. Given that it was a superior weapon, there was little wonder that Rader had claimed it for himself. Now, Anne was going to return it to him - tip first. As she drew her arm back to deliver a vicious jab, someone grabbed her by the waist of her breeches and pulled her to her feet.

"This way!" Mary Read yelled, not realizing she had just stopped Anne from delivering a fatal blow. "The balcony!"

One of the men fired his handgun and the ball whizzed between them as they sprinted onto the balcony. Mary Read stuffed the emptied pistol in her waistband and swung over the balustrade. She hung from the rail only long enough to prevent free-falling, then dropped to the street. Anne started to toss her sword to Mary as another shot rang out behind her. The ball hit her in the shoulder, knocking the weapon from her hand. She heard the smallsword clatter on the cobblestones below as she rolled over the balustrade. A moment later, she crashed onto the street, landing face-down next to her errant weapon.

Mary Read could see that Anne was wounded, but her own situation had gone sour and could offer no help. A sentry posted outside the Buford had heard the shots and had been halfway inside the door when the clattering sword had turned him around. As he stepped back onto the street, Mary Read pulled the pistol from her waistband and thrust the muzzle in his face. Struggling, Anne clutched the sword, picked herself up from the cobblestones and limped over to Mary Read's side.

"Hand over your weapons or I'll blow your butt ugly head off!" Mary Read said. "Now!"

Any thoughts of refusing vanished when he heard the menacing click of the pistol's cock locking into place. With his hand beginning to shake, the guard held out his pistol.

Keeping her weapon trained on the guard's head, Mary Read snatched the gun and held it behind her for Anne to take. Unable to use her strong side because of her wound, Anne took the heavy pistol with her left hand. As she did, they heard several of Rader's men on the second floor come outside and lean over the rail.

Cocking the pistol as she stepped backward into the street, Anne pointed it toward the balcony. The sounds of cursing and feet scrambling to get back inside told Mary Read that Anne had bought them a few seconds.

"I'll be taking this one, too," Mary said, snatching a second handgun from the guard's waistband. Tossing the dueling pistol into a shrub, she cocked the new weapon and stuck its muzzle in his face.

"And this too," she said, drawing a cutlass from his scabbard. "Now, go back inside and lock the door. When Rader comes down, he'll want to go back outside, quick. Just remember, the first one through the door gets a lead ball in the ballocks. Understand?"

She pointed the pistol at his crotch for emphasis.

The guard slunk back inside the Buford, but not until they heard the door latch click into place did the women start toward the gate. Fearing that Rader and his men might come back out on the balcony to shoot at them, they kept away from the wall-side of the street with its torches and stayed close to the buildings. When they reached the end of the block, they stopped long enough to peer around the corner of the building, making sure there was no one on Broad Street. In the distance – toward the west wall and the drawbridge – a shot rang out.

"The militia?" Anne wondered aloud. "They may be testing the defenses."

"Or just a nervous guard shooting at shadows in the dark," Mary Read said. "Either way, we are running out of time."

She took a step to cross the open area to the main gate, but Anne yanked her back into the shadows.

"Over there...at the Court of Guard."

Mary looked in time to see three figures spring from the darkness surrounding the guardhouse and dash through the gate to the wharf. At the same moment, an ear-splitting scream of agony pierced the night. They had no idea what waited for them on the other side of the wall, but it sounded as though somebody on the wharf had just placed a foot into the fires of hell.

"There they are!" came a shout behind them.

Turning to look down Bay Street, they saw Rader and his men emerge from the Buford and start toward them.

"The wharf!" Anne yelled, already running toward the gate. "It's our only chance!"

Roused by the scream, one of the men in the guardhouse had come outside to see what the row was about. But instead of spotting the two women, there was something out on the wharf that caught his attention. In an instant, he was back inside yelling for the other guards to grab their weapons and rally to the wharf.

As Anne and Mary sprinted toward the pier, the men from the guardhouse and Rader's crew came together behind them, closing off the gate. Ahead loomed a dark ship at the end of the pier where a crowd of another sort had come together.

With a mighty *WHOOSH*, a section of the pier near the ship burst into flames. A raging bonfire illuminated everything within fifty yards. Anne had caught up to the three men, the light revealing them to be Dyonis, Kofi, and the short one, Briebras. In the middle of the fire, futilely pounding his burning clothes with his bare hands was a huge man with a hideous face screaming in agony. Though it seemed he need only take a few steps to fall into the water and save himself, the burning man inexplicably remained in the middle of the bonfire. On the other side of the fire at the end of the pier, she saw Tye with his arms stretched out wide, herding a group of children away from the flames and back onto – *Rackham's Revenge*!

Still anchored to the spot of his immolation, the burning man's legs buckled and he collapsed backward. Mercifully, the charred lump of flesh that had once been a man stopped screaming as the flames broiled away his life. The only sounds now were the pops and snaps of the fire.

Mary Read looked from Anne and the men she had joined to Tye and the children he was trying to protect. Though they were all looking back in Mary's direction, their eyes were focused on something behind her. She turned to look back at the wall and the city it protected.

To no surprise, Blyth Rader stood inside the gateway brandishing a rapier he had commandeered before leaving the Buford. Standing to his left and right, forming a semicircle around the head of the pier, his men cut off the only access to the wharf.

A smile spread across Mary Read's face as she took stock of the situation. There were only a dozen or so men – and with only enough room on the pier for two or three to advance at a time. With Anne at her side, they would easily be able to defend the pier and those behind them.

"Annie! Come join me. We can hold these bumtags until the *Revenge* casts off."

But movement along the rampart caught Anne's attention and she knew that Mary had spoken too soon. First one man was hoisted atop the wall, followed by another, and then another. As each man stood to look down on the wharf, he unslung his musket and aimed it at Mary Read. In all, six musketeers had been posted, greatly changing the odds against them.

"Hold your fire!" Rader ordered. "I wouldn't want a stray shot to take out one of our little guests on the boat. We still need them. We'll take the pier with sword and cutlass. But if by some miracle anyone gets past us, cut them–"

Rader ate the last word as another, larger bale of hides erupted, its flames fed by the oils used in tanning. Brilliant light again flooded the harbor, forcing the men looking toward the ship to cover their eyes – all except for Blyth Rader.

With her back to the blaze, Anne watched Rader closely, fearing that he might use the distraction to charge. But Rader's eyes were locked on something beyond Anne and those she stood with. His guise of confidence crumbled away like weevil-infested sea biscuits. His eyes grew wide and his face turned white. Then Anne saw that it wasn't only Rader. All of the men beside him and on the wall were transfixed, looking past her as if she wasn't even there.

Though reluctant to turn her back to her adversaries, Anne pivoted around to look back at the *Revenge*. Briebras, Kofi, and Dyonis were also staring at the ship, bound by the same spell as Rader and his men. From their refuge on the ship's deck, Tye huddled the children as they looked up into the ship's rigging. And then – finally – she saw it too.

"NOoooooooooo!" Mary Read screamed, the single word erupting from her lungs in unfathomable agony and undeniable guilt.

Dangling from the rigging that ran between the mainmast and the foremast hung Edward Teach's daughter, the girl Mary had known only as Clairette. The rope around her broken neck had twisted her head down in an unnatural angle, allowing the dead girl to look upon those below with a wicked, frozen smile of morbid satisfaction.

Rader's men shifted about, not sure what to do. The superstitions among seamen were deep-rooted and enduring. Ships were the domain of men. With the exception of viragoes like Anne Bonny and Mary Read, women who came aboard were tolerated for a short time and expected to leave before their presence attracted bad fortune. By hanging herself in the ship's rigging, Clairette had consigned her soul to walk the decks of *Rackham's Revenge* for eternity. As far as Rader's men were concerned, this ship was damned, and anyone foolish enough to sail on her would be as well.

Looking at the men about him, Rader saw that he was losing them. If he could not rouse them long enough to take back the children, his trump card would be lost.

"Kill her!" Rader yelled as he pushed the man closest to him on his left toward Mary Read. The pirate stumbled forward, then stopped in his tracks.

"Kill them all!" Rader shouted to the rest of the men. But they stood their ground, refusing to move toward the pier.

Rader pulled a pistol from his waistband and placed the muzzle at the temple of the closest man's head. The next sound was the distinct click of flint striking metal followed by the roar of black powder exploding. The man dropped to the wharf, still alive but clawing at his head as if trying to dig the pistol ball out of his brain.

Spellbound, the rest of the pirates watched as the dying man beat his legs against the wood planks like mallets on a drum skin. When the gruesome spectacle finally ended, the men looked up to see that Rader had placed the tip of his sword at the back of the crewman he had shoved toward the pier.

"Fools! You don't have to go aboard ship. Just kill them and I'll get the nippers. Kill the women and the men with them...or I swear I will kill you!"

Rader prodded the man toward the pier with his sword at the same moment another shot was fired. The luckless pirate dropped to his knees and then fell flat on his face. Looking down the pier, Rader saw Mary Read with a smoking pistol aimed at his head. Her mouth was twisted into a hate-filled sneer and her eye was black as pine tar.

"Damn it!" she said. "That ball was meant for you."

# CHAPTER THIRTY-EIGHT

"MY NAME IS ASKU DARE and I swear I won't hurt you," Asku said between clenched teeth as he held fast to the woman's wrist. The loud crack of a pistol shot echoing through the house had startled her, allowing the woodsman to snatch the penknife from her grasp. "I'm in search of two women who may have been brought here a few minutes ago, but right now I need to know who's down the hall."

The woman looked at the boy huddled next to her. The sounds of men shouting and furniture being knocked about filled the hallway outside the bedroom. The boy nodded consent and she turned back to Asku.

"Rader. The bastard's name is Blyth Rader. He fancies himself to be a pirate and the King of Charles Town. I don't care who you are. All I ask is that you give me my knife back so I can kill him the next time I see him."

"Who's with him?"

Another shot rattled through the house and then another. There was more shouting. A door at the end of the hall flung open with a bang followed by the sound of heavy boots running down the hall.

"I'm not sure," she whispered, her words coming more quickly. "I thought I heard the thatch-gallows named Curlee Leathers say they had captured two women. One of them spoke, but I couldn't tell if it was a man or a woman."

Again they heard the sound of boots rumbling by the bedroom door. As the men began descending the stairs at the end of the hall, Asku heard Blyth Rader's voice.

"They can't get far. I want them both alive. You hear!"

When the voices and the sound of tramping boots began to fade, Asku went to the door and cracked it open. For some reason, the men had gathered in front of the main door on the first floor but had not yet ventured outside.

"I said open it, you damn fool!" It was Rader's voice again.

"But she's out there, I tell you! Waiting. With a pistol."

"She wouldn't have a pistol if you hadn't let her take yours, so you can go first!"

Asku heard a door being opened followed by sounds of a struggle.

"No! Don't!"

The man Rader had yelled at screamed as he was pushed outside. The next few moments passed in strained silence, as though everyone at the door believed that holding their breath would keep them safe.

"There they are!" someone shouted at last, followed by the sounds of Rader and his men scrambling from the building.

"Now!" the woman said, pulling on Asku's shirt. She and the boy had left the bed and were standing behind him. "Please help us. Take us from here while they are gone! While we have a chance."

"I have to go after them," Asku said, opening the bedroom door. He poked his head into the hallway and looked both ways to make sure it was clear. "They need me. They must be headed toward the wharf and they need my help."

"We need you," she said, pulling on his arm. "He will kill us. He will kill you."

Light from the hallway shown on her face to reveal cuts, bruises, and battered lips. Her silvery-white hair – woven into a long braid that fell over her shoulder – shimmered with the light as though it were a living thing.

"What is your name?"

"Sweets...Nightingale. The boy's name is Jonathan."

"Come with me, Sweets Nightingale. I can't promise you safety, but I can promise you a chance to live."

The determination in his eyes told her it would do no good to argue.

"To the wharf, then," she said.

Asku handed the penknife back to her and then hurried down the hall toward the steps without looking back. Sweets followed with the boy in tow. When they reached the front door, Asku paused long enough to make sure none of Rader's men were lingering behind, then stepped out into the street.

"Stay close to the buildings," he said as he unslung his bow and nocked an arrow. "Stay on this side of the street and follow me from the shadows."

After crossing Bay Street, he used the wall to guide him toward the wharf's main gate. Sweets and the boy followed from the other side of the street, darting from one pool of darkness created by the buildings to the next. As he closed in on the gateway, a burst of flames from the docks lit up the sky. Above him, spaced out along the top of the wall, he saw six men with their muskets pointed in the direction of the fire. Signaling for Sweets and the boy to stop, Asku crouched as low as he could. The closest musketeer was no farther away than the length of his bow.

"Hold your fire!"

Though the shout had come from the other side of the wall, the hollow pitch of Rader's voice was unmistakable.

"NOooooooooooo!"

The scream pierced the night like the shattering of a hundred windows. There was only one person whose voice was capable of making such a sound – Mary Read!

Asku backed away from the wall and into the middle of the street. Taking quick aim, he shot an arrow into the back of the nearest man atop the wall. He then started toward the gate at a slow, steady pace, rhythmically pulling arrows from his quill and shooting the musketeers one by one. Completely enraptured by whatever was occurring on the wharf, the men along the wall were oblivious to the killing of their comrades a few feet away. Just before he reached the entryway to the wharf, the distinct report of another pistol shot rang out from the other side of the wall.

Nocking another arrow, Asku took a deep breath and stepped through the gateway.

Though the fire toward the end of the dock was beginning to wane, he could see every detail of the standoff as though it were the middle of the day. In front of him were a dozen pirates with a dark-skinned brute of a man standing just to their rear. At the head of the pier leading to a docked ship was Blyth Rader – standing between two bodies. A few yards in front of him, Mary Read held a smoking pistol, her face as hard and death-ready as a person can be. In one smooth motion, she tossed the empty weapon aside and deftly passed a cutlass from her left hand to her right.

As the pistol splashed into the water, Anne came to stand beside her with sword in hand. Between them and the fire stood Briebras, Kofi, and – Dyonis! Relief swept over Asku but disappeared as quickly as it had come when he saw Tye and the other children on the schooner, their heads poking over the gunwale, watching the scene unfold on the wharf.

Then he saw the girl named Clairette hanging from the ship's rigging and he understood the vengeance on Mary Read's face. The raven-haired piratress had become death, and Blyth Rader was marked. Transfixed by the incredible scene, Asku did not see the burly pirate closest to him turning around until it was too late.

"To the rear!" Curlee Leathers yelled when he saw Asku. Leathers pointed his pistol at the same time the woodsman aimed his arrow at the pirate.

The two men stared at each other from behind their weapons. Leathers – only having one shot – hesitated. If he missed, he would surely be killed. Asku held his arrow but kept it at full draw. The threat of killing the man would keep the others from shooting.

# CHAPTER THIRTY-NINE

"WAIT!" MARY READ CALLED FROM THE PIER. "Everyone stand down! As a brethren of the sea and crew to *Rackham's Revenge*, I'm declaring my right to challenge Blyth Rader as captain! I never had the chance the night Rader betrayed me, so I'm doing it right here and right now!"

One of the men behind Leathers laughed, but the rest of them looked each at other, not sure whether the challenge was real or a ruse. All of the men who had joined the *Revenge* had signed or made their mark accepting the ship's Articles of Agreement – a long-held practice among pirates. Mary Read knew everything that was in the contract because she had written it. Never having been captain to a crew of pirates, Rader had been happy to leave the job of writing the articles to her. Now, as he watched the original crewmen struggling to decide whether to allow Mary Read's challenge, his mistake became clear.

"For the love of Mike!" Rader said as he looked at each man around him. "You can not seriously be considering her challenge? She wasn't even one of the crew. Being the owner of the ship is not the same as being a member of her crew."

"Not true! Not only do I own the *Revenge*, I also serve as her quartermaster...or did you think the ship's books took care of themselves? If you don't believe me, it's written into the articles me and everybody else signed and is stored in the captain's quarters."

"Leathers! You're the first mate. If she kills me, you'll have to take orders from her...a woman. Is that what you want?"

Though he kept his pistol pointed toward Asku, Leathers turned to look at the rest of the crew. Their faces told him what he already knew – that the only law that mattered to pirates were the Articles of Agreement they signed. Anyone who betrayed those articles was a traitor to the brethren and would be a marked man. The agreement they signed was the only thing that prevented total anarchy.

But there was another piece on the chessboard that nobody but Leathers could see. Mary Read's skill with the sword was known to all. Blyth Rader was believed to be her equal, or close to it. If they somehow managed to kill each other, the ship, the city, and all that went with it would be his.

"The law is the law," he said, lowering his pistol. "You're the ship's captain. The articles are your rules to live by as well as ours."

"Or to die by," Mary Read said.

Rader kept his gaze locked on Leathers just long enough to leave no doubt that the matter would be taken up again later. Then he turned his attention back to the woman standing between him and his dream of creating an empire.

"Now we know the answer to the question," Rader said, forcing a smile.

"What question?" Mary Read asked.

"Which of you will be the one to try killing me."

"I guess it's just my lucky day," she said, giving her cutlass a twirl.

As much as it chafed Anne that she would not face Rader, she had to give Mary Read credit for working the Articles to her advantage. On the other hand, having seen both of them fight, she knew that Mary's victory was not a given. Almost everything Mary Read knew about sword fighting she had learned in the army during her years pretending to be a man. She had tempered her skills in the furnace of military training and honed them to a fine edge in battle. Her techniques were designed to deflect an opponent's blade and kill, or to strike first and kill. Long, drawn out duels were good for show but meant death on the battlefield. Her methods were so exact that – to the commanders watching her fight from afar – it looked as though she were moving through the enemy like a farmer walking through a wheat field, mowing down soldiers with a scythe as she advanced.

Anne's heart raced as Mary Read moved toward Rader. Without realizing it, she was squeezing and releasing her grip on her sword, itching to enter the fray. The lust for fighting she had rediscovered after so many years burned through her veins as liquid fire. Her forehead turned wet with perspiration as she fought to keep her rage in check.

Mary Read's first movement was a feint that Rader bit on hard, leaving his neck exposed. But as her blade came within a breath of finding the fat artery leading to his brain, Rader's incredible quickness saved his life. With a reflexive motion that did not seem possible, he deflected the cutlass away at the last possible instant.

He stumbled back a few steps, his eyes bulging wide by the realization that Mary Read was as good as legend claimed, and that death – his death – was a real possibility.

Attempting to catch him before he recovered, Mary lunged at him again, but this time he was ready. Deflecting the blow with a seconde-style parry, Rader's riposte was instantaneous and well-aimed. The sickening sound of cloth ripping apart filled the night air. The tip of Rader's rapier had cut through Mary's blouse.

Given how much she had come to hate her former friend, she felt as though the strike had wounded her as much as it had Mary. With dread, she watched as Mary felt about her waist and then, raising her hand, looked at her own blood in disbelief. Though the wound was superficial, Anne could see that her confidence was shaken. Never in her life had anyone come so close to delivering a mortal blow to Mary Read. Even worse, Mary was now forced to engage in an extended duel rather than a brief clash. Now she was playing to Rader's strength.

Anne's hopes began to fade as she watched the two go back and forth – attacking, deflecting, counter attacking. Rader was getting the better of Mary Read, and each new wound drew shouts from the pirates. Designed for close-quarters hacking, the cutlass she wielded was ill-suited for dueling in the open. Not only did Rader have quickness, his sword had a longer reach. The fop who had once been Mary's proxy as captain held the advantage

They battled on for several minutes. While the wounds he inflicted upon Mary were many, there were only nicks and scratches. Still, her blouse had turned red and was slashed in so many places it and looked as though it might fall from her body. With no hope of out-dueling Rader with a cutlass, her only option was to keep trying to deliver a powerful blow that would bring him down all at once. But his quickness prevented her from landing a single strike, and the powerful swings she took that never landed were wearing her down.

Anne could see that Mary was at the end of her rope. Though Rader's tactic was simple – he kept performing the same moves over and over – it was working too well. First he would feint to his left, only to change direction and attack her from his strong side. The Mary Read of old would have figured out the pattern and used it to her advantage, but now she seemed incapable of seeing–

*How stupid could I be! He's making her turn her head and then attacking her blind side. The cutlass is too short – it allows him to get in close so she doesn't have enough time to respond to his lunges. The bastard! Without a proper sword, she never had a chance, and he knows it.*

At that moment Rader lunged again, tearing yet another gash into Mary Read's arm. Exhausted and frustrated, she staggered back a few steps, trying to compose herself. To continue what she was been doing thus far meant that she would die. The longer the fight went on, the weaker she would become. If she rushed him, she might get inside the reach of his rapier and gig him like a frog. Though it was the desperate act of someone who was about to die – it was her only chance.

Taking a deep breath, she shook the tiredness from her limbs and straightened her body. Standing tall and defiant with her head held high, she twirled the cutlass in a final act of irreverence and started toward Rader. As she took her first step, she felt a powerful pull on her shoulder as if from nowhere. Reeling sideways, she stumbled over the body of the man she had shot earlier and fell face-first onto the wharf.

"Out of the way, you one-eyed cow," Anne said. "I believe that may be the most embarrassing display of swordsmanship I've ever witnessed. You move with the speed of a manatee and swing your cutlass as though you are chopping wood. Watch me, and I'll show you how it's done."

Pushing herself up off the wharf high enough to turn her head, Mary read looked in time to see Anne closing in on Rader.

"Stand your ground!" Curlee Leathers said, leveling his pistol at Anne's head. By allowing Mary's challenge he had placed himself on precarious ground with Rader. His only hope of staving off his captain's wrath was to enforce the rules all the way to the end, and Anne had no right of challenge. "You were never a member of this crew. You have no stake. Now back off so they can finish."

"No," Rader said, holding up his hand. "Let her be. It was her I wanted anyway."

He paused for a moment to rub his nose, remembering the mutilation and humiliation Anne had inflicted upon him.

"When I'm done with Mrs. Brennan here I'll finish off her friend. And then I'll find the runt and impale him on the bowsprit – alive – and laugh while he jigs in the air."

White-hot bitterness surged through Anne's veins. The roar of blood rushing in her ears drowned out all other sounds. Everything within her narrowing field of vision was tinted red. The resolve she had managed to maintain was slipping – but still she held on.

Rather than square off in a proper dueling stance, Anne willed herself to relax, leaving the smallsword to dangle, its tip pointing straight down. After weeks spent searching for Tye – almost dying from snake bites, suffering swarms of mosquitoes, nearly getting shot escaping the *Revenge*, enduring the hallucinations of Scarlette's skull tonic – their fate would be decided by her sword.

The corner of her mouth turned up to form a smirk. Every minute she had spent in the Spanish Town jail waiting to be hanged, she had cursed herself for surrendering to Barnet and the *Snow-Tyger*. Being imprisoned had taught her that there are some things worse than death, and each night she had prayed and wished for one more chance to die with a sword in her hand, instead of being the star attraction in a freak show. Strange it was indeed – how her wish had come true.

The grin seemed to throw Rader off kilter. But then he saw how she favored her right shoulder and fresh blood matting her blouse.

"I see that your escape did not leave you unscathed," Rader said, his confidence regained. "And now you wish to commit suicide in some desperate, misguided attempt to save your...friend. 'Tis a pity, for you. I, on the other hand, will become known as the man who killed both Anne Bonny and Mary Read. I will become legend."

A wry smile spread across Anne's face.

"And I'm told that the smaller the cock the louder the crow," she said, "and you crow like a rooster with a smashed beak and no bollocks."

Rader started to bring his hand to his nose again, stopped, then thrust the maverick limb behind his back as if it had moved on its own. This time, he would not take her skill for granted – and she was using her weak arm.

Pouncing forward with uncanny quickness, he thrust his rapier toward Anne's heart almost before she realized the attack. But Anne had seen him fight and knew his techniques. Instead of retreating, she stepped into his lunge, deflecting the rapier with the base of her blade. Following the momentum, she smashed the hand guard of her sword into his face, knocking him several steps back.

Stunned, he brought his free hand to his face, blood flowing from his nose. When he had felt the sting of her blade before, he had convinced himself that it was because he had not taken her seriously and because she had been lucky. He had not made that mistake this time, and yet even with an injured wing the bird had gotten the better of him.

With a snap of his wrist, he flung off the blood and turned his shoulder toward Anne.

"Enough of this! I was going to take my time with you, just for the sport. But I've let this drag out too long. It's time to be done with both of you."

Again he advanced, but with more caution. His cockiness had allowed her to draw first blood – he would not let her have a second taste. But instead of coming at him as before, Anne slapped at his blade as she stepped back. Rader lunged again, harder. Again Anne deflected the rapier while stepping backward.

Sensing the advantage, Rader started to lunge a third time, but Anne planted her back foot and thrust her blade toward his heart. The counterattack was simple and poorly done – exactly what might be expected of someone using their weak arm. Catching the tip of her smallsword before it neared his chest, he redirected the momentum of her attack in a circular motion designed to carry the blade outside the width of his body.

The trap was sprung! Anne's series of retreats were feigned weakness – the bait. His response to her feeble attack had tripped the spring.

Never having trained against a left-handed swordsman, Rader could not have known that his defensive move would do the opposite of what was intended. Instead of turning her blade to the outside, he had guided it toward his torso.

When she felt Rader's blade meet hers, Anne threw the full weight of her body into the momentum of her thrust. For the first time in nearly nine years, she felt the strangely satisfying sensation of sharp, pointed metal punching through the soft tissue of a man's flesh and then the tougher gristle of the inner organs.

Reflexively, Blyth Rader grabbed the smallsword protruding from his solar plexus with his free hand and stared at it, unwilling to believe his eyes. As his mind struggled to catch up to the reality of his death, he looked up at Anne as if hoping she would reveal the secret to the trick she had used to so easily kill him.

Anne stared back into Rader's soulless eyes, matching blackness for blackness. Loathing percolated from every cell of her body. She hated him for disrupting the peaceful home she had created. She hated him for stealing Tye and putting his life in jeopardy. Most of all, she hated him for forcing her to remember how good the bad things in her life had been.

Like a stone thrown through a looking glass, the thought shattered the resolve that had been restraining her fury. Stepping in closer, she drove the remainder of the blade into Rader with the full weight of her body. The hand guard hit his stomach hard, knocking the last bit of breath from his lungs. Leaning in so close that her face nearly touched his, she looked still deeper into his eyes, searching for a last flicker of life.

"Tell me, Rader...do you know how to keep a dead fish from smelling?" Spittle flew from between teeth clenched so tight her words rattled out as a string of mutilated syllables.

The rapier fell from Rader's hand, clanging dully on the wharf planks as he tried to focus on Anne's face. A small stream of blood oozed from the corner of his mouth to trail down his chin onto the front his shirt.

"You cut off its nose."

Rader's eyes widened for a moment, fluttered a few times, then stopped. The next instant his legs buckled and his lifeless body slid down the front of her torso until his knees thunked against the wharf. Placing a foot on his chest, Anne pulled her sword from his stomach, allowing the corpse to fall sideways onto the planks.

Turning toward the remaining pirates, she looked each one in the eyes, her jaw muscles rippling with forced restraint. Light from the gateway torches shimmered off the bloodied blade of her smallsword like crimson fire as Rader's lifeblood dripped from its tip. The fury in her black eyes made it clear that she was teetering on the edge of a crazed, killing frenzy like those that had made her infamous.

Still a dozen strong, the men looked back at her in fear and at each other with uncertainty. The speed and ease with which Anne had killed their leader had knocked them off their pins. While they were no strangers to killing and brutality, none of them had ever seen anyone so transformed. And though their reasoning minds told them that they were far too many to be defeated, their eyes told them that the red-haired banshee was not daring them to attack. They saw her demeanor for what it was – an invitation to die.

"Now then, gentlemen! Time to pack it in. I suggest you clear the gate quick, else I might have to stick your mate here and bleed him out...an' we wouldn't want that, now would we Mister Leathers? That is your name, right?"

The pirates spun around to see that Asku had grabbed Leathers from behind and was holding the lethal point of an arrow against his neck. The pistol Leathers was holding fell from his hand.

"Do what he says," Leathers ordered, his hoarse voice reduced to a choked whisper. As the outcome of the duel between Rader and Mary Read had become a certainty, the more his attention had waned from Asku. When Anne stepped in, the clash had been so swift and compelling he had forgotten about the threat just feet away. Not until Asku's arm snaked around his neck and began squeezing off his air did he realize his stupidity.

"Now!" Asku yelled.

As the pirates began shuffling through the gate, the sound of musket fire carried down Broad Street. Realizing that the militia was once again testing the drawbridge's defenses, their uncertainty was beginning to turn into panic.

"Let me go," Leathers said. "I can do you no harm. They need me to lead them, now. I'm the only chance they have."

Though Asku knew he was right, he had no intention of setting a snake free at his feet just to be bitten.

"Our only chance is to stop the militia at the gate," Leathers said, trying a different tack. "The longer the battle goes on, the more time you will have to escape."

"He's right," Anne said. "Let him go. It will give us more time. If you can still see him by the time I count to ten, put an arrow in his back."

Asku released Leathers from his grasp and stepped back, nocking the arrow as he moved.

"One," she said.

Keeping an eye on Asku, Leathers reached down to pick up his pistol.

"Leave it!" Anne said.

Leathers shifted his gaze toward her and smiled.

"Two."

The first mate took a few tentative steps toward the gateway, saw that they were not going to kill him, then led the other pirates up Broad Street until swallowed by the darkness.

"What kind of stupid jest was that?" Mary Read asked. She was sitting up now, her color beginning to return. Her expression showed no shame at having lost to Rader, nor gratitude for having been rescued. "Cut off its nose? I thought he was a man, not a mackerel."

"I told you I was better than you," Anne said, still watching Leathers and his men.

"I must concede that it would appear so...now. It would be a different story if I still had my left eye."

"Are you all right?" Anne asked, offering her hand.

"No," she said as Anne pulled her to her feet. "I have to spend the rest of my life living with the fact that you bested Rader after I didn't. That's not right. Not right at all. I may well have to kill myself."

"You still have one thing," Anne said, their faces nearly touching.

"Yeah, what's that?"

"You can still drink me under the table."

Mary Read studied her for a moment but said nothing.

Anne took the pause to mean that Mary had accepted the concession as a temporary truce. Turning her attention toward the *Revenge*, she peered through the dim light past Briebras and Dyonis in search of Tye.

Her killing of Rader had been brutal and personal. Tye had witnessed the savagery with his own eyes, leaving no doubt that all the things he had heard about Anne Bonny the notorious piratress were true. Fearing the worst, she braced herself. If he looked at her with eyes of hate, she could deal with that. Hatred could be repaired. Fear was another matter. She could not exist as a monster in her son's eyes.

Silhouetted by the reddish-orange hues of the rising sun's first light, she saw Tye shepherding the kidnapped children through the gangway, coaxing them to hurry as they crossed the plank and past the embers of the dying fire. The girl named Elisabeth led the way but stopped at the burned-out section of the pier to help the children cross to safety. As they approached the wharf, Dyonis dropped to one knee, stretching out his arms to gather them in as if they were ducklings.

Stepping onto the pier, Tye turned and looked up at Clairette. Though the early rays did not yet reach the wharf, the sun shone brightly on the ship's upper rigging where the mortal remains of Blackbeard's daughter still dangled. Golden light radiated through her blonde hair, giving her the halo of an angel.

The sight of the wretched girl – appearing greater in death than she had been in life – purged the last remnants of strength from Tye's spirit. Moving by instinct rather than conscious effort, he turned away and started to cross the small bridge of planks that had survived the fire. When he was halfway, he saw the charred remains of Skullen's lower leg jutting up from the smoldering edge of the burned-out section of pier.

Skullen had fallen backward into the middle of the blazing pile of cured animal hides, but even in his horrific death throes, he had not been able to free his impaled foot. When the planking beneath the hides burned away and plunged into the water, his immolated remains had fallen with it. The burnt, brittle tissue of his blackened leg had separated at the knee the way a cooked chicken leg is easily pulled from its thigh.

Anne watched as he eased down onto the unburned section of pier to sit in front of the disarticulated limb, his supple legs flayed out to either side of his bum, creating the shape of a W beneath him. He stared at the thing without moving, his face tired and haggard. Anne knew he needed more time to try and come to terms with what he had done, but circumstances wouldn't allow it.

"I didn't mean to kill him," he said, though he didn't look up. "He...he knocked the lantern over when I stabbed his foot, trying to get away. The tanning oils...they burn...so...easy."

"It's not your fault," Anne said, her heart pounding. She wanted to pull him to his feet, hug him, and tell him it was over. But it wasn't over. For her son – who was teetering between the harsh grays of reality and the total blackness of a traumatized mind – it might never be over.

"What you have done is beyond comprehension. You have endured evils that would have bested grown men and you have saved the lives of many. Tye...son...you have nothing to be ashamed of. Nothing."

She stopped, hoping that he would speak, or at least turn his eyes away from the crusty black monument to piratical perversion that had once been a leg. The sound of musket fire floated down the pier, the shots coming much faster now. Mixed in with the shooting was the dim roar of men shouting and the exertions of hand to hand combat.

"Tye. Do you hear that? It won't be long before–"

"I'm not the son you think I am," he said, grasping the marlinspike. He began twisting the metal tool from side to side and back and forth, working it free from the wood beneath the orphaned foot.

"What?" Anne asked, barely able to choke the word from her throat. She had been braced to be cursed, rejected, and even damned, but she had not expected this.

The planking let go of the spike and the charred leg pivoted off the pier into the water. Tye wiped the tool on his trousers to remove the blood and greasy soot, then guided it back into the outseam of his pant leg. As he began to stand, a cannon from the western side of the city thundered awake. Then another.

Anne looked toward the darkness at the end of Broad Street and back at the brightening sky in the east. If Rader had been telling the truth, the *Discordia* and the *Abundant* had already weighed anchor, unfurled topsails to catch a morning breeze, and were sailing up the Ashley and Cooper rivers. If they managed to establish firing positions before the militia breached the western wall, Charles Town's citizen soldiers would be caught in a crossfire and the city would remain in control of the pirates.

"The *Revenge*!" Mary Read yelled. "There's enough of us to sail her out of here. We can do it!"

"No!" Anne said. "The ships Rader ordered upriver will be coming this way now. We would be caught between them. They'd hit us from both sides and we'd have no way to fire back." She paused, letting the truth of her words sink in. "We have to go back to the periauger and try to get back to Scarlette the way we came."

The cannons to the west roared again, though much louder this time. One – two – three cannons boomed in succession. An unnerving silence followed.

Then a fourth blast came that was louder than the others. The still-dark sky at the end of Broad Street glowed orange-red for a moment then went dark again. The quiet that followed was quickly chased away by the sound of hundreds of feet pounding on the cobblestones and the panicked screams of predators who had suddenly become the prey.

Anne pushed Tye toward the open area of the gateway where they joined the others. Seeing the children huddled around Dyonis, she grimaced.

"What do we do with them?" she said. "We can't just leave them here."

"The church of the Huguenots, it is not far from here," Briebras said. "We can take them there to hide."

"No," Asku said. "There's not enough time. Look."

At the far end of Broad Street where the fireball had erupted, a mass of humanity roiled about like a thousand rats dumped from a burlap sack into a crate. All the men who had joined with Rader were now fleeing the city's western wall, running headlong toward the wharf. Accomplishing the impossible, the militia had managed to breach the city's defenses, turning the usurpers into a panicked horde. The ships moored safely in their slips were their only hope of escape – and the only thing standing in their way was Anne Bonny and the handful who stood with her.

"I'll do it," a voice from the main gate said. Jonathan Chastain stepped out from the shadows followed by Sweets Nightingale – both still dressed in their bedclothes. "The church is only two blocks from here. I'll hide them inside until my father and his men come."

Anne looked from the boy to the battered woman behind him, not sure what to make of them.

"Let him do it," Asku said. "He knows these streets. They'll be all right."

Anne glanced down Broad Street and saw that the churning mob was less than three blocks away and closing in fast.

"Go! Now!" she said, resisting the urge to make a stand to protect them. She could see that the children's best chance would be to distance themselves from the wharf – disappear into the narrow alleys and private courtyards, and then hunker down in the sanctuary of the church.

Feeling the mass of desperate men bearing down upon them, the boy needed no further coaxing.

"'Lisabeth!" he called to the girl who had brought the children away from the *Revenge*. "You lead the way. I'll follow and make sure we don't lose anyone." Then to the children gathered around Dyonis, "Hold hands and stay close to 'Lisabeth. I'm right behind you. Hurry!"

Anne watched the children run through the main gate and scurry north up Bay Street until they had passed the Court of Guard. Satisfied that she had made the right decision, it was time to leave the wharf to the pirates.

"Take me with you," said the young woman who now stood alone. Anne had forgotten about Asku's battered friend. "Please, I...I can't stay here. The townsmen will hang me if they catch me."

Anne cut an anxious glance toward Asku who nodded affirmation. She had no idea what the woman's story was, and right now she didn't care. The pirates at the front of the wave were less than a hundred yards away. At the same time, a deluge of pirates came pouring out of several side streets onto the south end of Bay Street. They were like swollen streams flowing toward the river of men on Broad Street – flash floods that were steps away from converging at the main gate.

"It's too late," Anne said. "We waited too long."

The sickening truth settled into Anne's bones with the finality of a sinking ship slipping below the surface of the water. Behind her – somehow sifting through the rising din of the approaching pirates – the sharp noise of large iron rings clanking against each other in succession reached her ears.

"Kofi will give you time," he said. His massive hands clutched the end of an anchor chain.

"No!" Briebras said. "I beg you, Kofi. S'il te plait, do not do this. You have nothing to prove."

"Go," he said. "This is my time."

Briebras choked down the growing lump in his throat but was forced to accept his friend's decision.

"Kofi," he said as a sad smile spread across his face. "Do you remember the ship at the dock in Bath? The one that brought us Mary Read?"

"Yes?"

"You were right. It was an Indiaman."

"I know," Kofi said, picking up the argument from where they had left off weeks before. Then, realizing that for the first time since becoming friends Briebras was admitting he was wrong, he smiled.

"Briebras," he said, still looking toward the onrushing pirates. "Free Emmie. For me. Swear it!"

"Oui, mon amie. My friend. I swear."

Kofi nodded, took a deep breath, then stepped through the gate into the intersecting streets, dragging the heavy chain behind him. As the first wave of human rats spilled into the open juncture, they ran headlong into the swooshing twelve-foot length of iron rings. The serpentine metal rope powered by the blacksmith's potent arms crushed skulls and broke bones with the efficiency of a butcher's mallet. A cacophony of screams and panicked shrieks filled the square, but the unseeing throng behind the leading wave pressed on in their desperate attempt to make it to the ships and their salvation.

"This way!" Anne shouted, pointing toward the southern bastion. They sprinted along the wharf, keeping the wall between them and the city. The sound of Kofi's iron whip ripping meat from bones – seasoned with an audible marinade of blood-laced moans and gurgling wails of despair – following them as they ran. When they passed by the first of the minor gateways to Bay Street, they saw more pirates, renegade slaves, and traitors approaching the wharf from the side streets. Moments later they came to the final gate that would allow them to access Bay Street and the path back to the periauger.

Spilling into the cobblestone lane, they almost crashed into several guards that had abandoned the southern wall and were running toward the ships. The last to understand that the city had been lost, they were frantic to make the wharf and did not recognize the threat the odd mix of men, women, and children before them posed. Brandishing her smallsword as though it were a parasol, Anne strode through the muddled dullards with a rhythmic motion that denied their eyes the opportunity to fix on the instrument of their deaths. Resuming the single-minded immersion of purpose she had rediscovered in defeating Rader, she followed the flow of her blade and her will until the wicked-beautiful carnage she wreaked came to an end.

As the last man fell, a torrent of musket fire rolled down the street, prompting them to look back toward the main gate. As if in a dream, they saw Kofi attempt to swing his chain one last time, falter, stagger backward, and then collapse to the cobblestones. The immense semicircle of desperate jackals that had put him down rushed through the gateway to the piers.

"Come," Anne said, grasping Briebras by the arm. The little Frenchman continued staring at the dark heap of mutilated flesh in the middle of the square that had been his friend. "We have to keep moving. To die now would be to waste his life."

Briebras continued gaping but yielded to her pull.

The woman who was once and once again Anne Bonny guided them as much by instinct as memory. The only obstacles they encountered now were the mounds of horse dung that littered the streets and the stricken dogs too confounded by the cannon fire to challenge them. Reaching the finger of Vanderhorst's Creek that cut into the city, they followed it to the periauger, still secured to the bollard where they had left it.

Assuming her place at the tiller, Anne had Tye take the bow. Asku handed push-poles to the others and they began propelling the flat-bottom boat back the way they had come. As they approached the footbridge, several musket shots from the west alerted them to a new threat. A strange-looking collection of militiamen with flintlocks and black men with machetes, pitchforks and sticks were running toward them, both atop the earthen wall and on the ground at its base. In a flash of insight, Anne realized that Ñuli had somehow set off the ordinance in the town's powder magazine while the pirates were being bombarded by the cannon fire. During the distraction of its explosion, she freed the loyal slaves who then managed to lower the drawbridge. Seizing the moment, the militia had stormed through the gate, sending the pirates fleeing toward the wharf.

"Look!" Mary Read yelled, pointing to the nearby bastion. "They're not shooting at us...they're shooting at him!"

Rounding the corner where the bastion became the southern wall, they saw Dyonis running as hard as he could, his long, lanky legs covering the distance at a deceptive rate, his wiry arms flailing about like the hands of a clock spinning around on a busted spring. He was racing toward the bridge the boat would pass under.

Asku cursed his carelessness and stupidity. He had been so focused on escaping that he hadn't thought to keep an eye on Dyonis. Remembering how he had embraced the children, he should have known that his brother would follow them until they were safe. It was his nature.

"Keep pushing!" Asku said. "We have to make the river!"

They lost sight of Dyonis as the boat began passing under the bridge, expecting to see him again when they emerged on the other side.

"Look out!" Anne yelled.

Her warning was followed by the sickening sound of wood tearing at wood as the tip of the periauger's front mast lodged itself into the bottom of the footbridge above their heads. The boat came to a sudden stop.

"The water's too high!" Anne said, seeing the confusion on their faces. "The tide! Now we're stuck!"

Asku raised his push pole overhead to see if he could reach the footbridge and push on it to force the boat down, but the pole was too short.

"What the bloody hell do we do now?" Mary Read asked.

A sudden, hard bounce at the front of the boat jolted everyone's attention toward the bow. Somehow, Asku's extraordinary brother had swung down from the crossover and dropped into the boat between Tye and Sweets Nightingale. The added weight made the periauger ride a little lower in the water, freeing the mast from the bridge.

"Hello," he said to the startled Sweets, taking a shallow bow. "My name is Timekeeper. I keep time."

"Well..." Sweets wavered, searching for a retort. Dyonis's dramatic arrival and peculiar clock-like appearance had blunted her quick wit. "It would seem that you made it...just in time."

Liking the joke, Dyonis smiled. He grasped Sweets' braided rope of white hair, delighting in its softness.

"Very pretty," he said. "Pretty like the swan. Do you like swans?"

Too late they heard the crack of a musket and the air-splitting whir of its lead ball passing over Anne's head. The splatting sound the bullet made as it passed through the leg of his breeches punctuated the question. Dyonis looked down to see a red stain spreading across his thigh, then collapsed. His face contorted with a mix of confusion, fear, and pain.

"I...I don't like bees. I hate bees. Asku? Where are you? Make the bees go away. Please. Askuwheteau?"

"Get down!" Anne shouted as Asku scrambled over the cross-seats and fishnets to get to his brother's side. "Everyone, get down!"

Disregarding her own order, Anne rose from her seat at the tiller to stand tall and straight. With willful deliberation, she aimed the pistol Mary Read had commandeered from the Buford House guard and fired it at a militiaman on the crosswalk. The ball passed by the man who held a still-smoking musket without harm, but the musketeers lining up beside him to take shots of their own stepped back and crouched down, fearing that another bullet would follow.

"Push! Anne hissed. "Now! Push with all you have!"

Briebras, Mary Read, Tye, and Sweets stood and leaned on their poles with all the strength they could muster. Again. And again...the muscles in their arms burned with the fire of desperation. Then came the inevitable succession of musket fire, following the periauger as it caught the flow of the river. The musketeers now began firing at will – shooting their weapons as quickly as they could reload. Once again the fugitives dropped to the bottom of the boat to avoid the bullets buzzing around them.

"Damn it!" Anne said. "We're going the wrong way! If we keep drifting toward the bay, we'll run into Rader's gunship. We have to go back the way we came. Asku, can you raise the sail?"

The woodsman finished tying off a makeshift tourniquet on Dyonis's leg and reached for the mainsheet's haul line. A new wave of musket balls hissed overhead like striking copperheads, one splintering the boat's foremast just above his fingertips. Asku looked at Anne and shook his head. The whims of tide and current would determine their fates now.

Popping her head up for a quick look now and again, Anne guided their boat away from the city and into the open bay as best she could. Their drift was swift, riding a current that soon had them out of range of the militiamen's long guns. But Anne knew they were trading the Charles Town frying pan for the fire that was Rader's gunships. The two ships he had ordered up the river to help defend the town's west wall would have weighed anchor at dawn. Still, the morning wind had not arrived as yet, and the same tide that was sweeping them into the bay would be working against the ship headed for the Ashley River. They might still have a chance, now that it was safe to stand and raise sail. A periauger could squeeze momentum out of a slight breeze that would do a ship little good.

"There!" Tye said. "Straight ahead!"

As one, they looked out past the bow to where the boy was pointing. The ship heading toward them was much closer than Anne had imagined it would be. Its bulk seemed enlarged, taking up half the horizon before them.

"It's the *Discordia*," Mary Read said. "That's the one Rader said would take the Ashley."

Though the ship was only running her tops'l – searching for wind that did not yet sweep across the water – Anne could see the crew scampering up the rigging to release more canvas. But something about the way the ship moved wasn't right. Anne could feel the contradiction, but she couldn't make sense of it.

"She's drifting backward on the current," Mary Read said, seeing what Anne could not. "She's turning on her heel."

Indeed, the rudder was biting hard on the water, braking the stern. As the bow turned about to catch up, the ship's broadside presented itself to them – huge, black barrels protruding from a dozen gun ports, any one of which could blow them out of the water.

"Is this how we die?" Anne wondered aloud. "With no defense and no rebut?"

"It wouldn't be such a bad way to go if you think about it," Mary Read said. "But it's not going to happen. Not today. Look, off to the port."

"Palsambleu!" It was the first word Briebras had uttered since seeing Kofi die. "It can not be."

"But it is," Mary Read said. Having recovered from the exhaustion of her duel with Rader, her voice had returned to its full, stone-crunching resonance.

With its taller mainmast reaching a few feet higher than the *Discordia*'s, the *Revenge* was catching just enough breeze to make forward progress. Before them lay the open water of Charles Town Bay. Beyond that was the inlet to the Atlantic Ocean.

"Who?" Sweets asked, refusing to believe. "How did–"

"Curlee Leathers," Mary Read said.

"I should have killed him when I had the chance," Asku said. Though he remained by his brother's side, he had risen to his knee to see what the others were looking at.

"But the girl? I thought–"

Sweets' question hung in the air where Mary Read had chopped it off with a hard, one-eyed stare. Sweets felt the periauger shrinking around her, wishing there was somewhere to hide.

"Fear for your life trumps fear of the unknown," Anne answered for them all. "With the militia closing in, they had nowhere else to go. Leathers would have had little trouble convincing enough of them to board the *Revenge*, even with Clairette's body swinging over their heads."

"He signaled the gunship and ordered them to join him," Mary Read added. "And unless I miss my guess... Yes! Look there...coming down the Cooper."

Curlee Leathers' makeshift flotilla was now complete. The two ships that had been guarding access to the bay – the same ships that Rader had ordered up the two rivers to defend his city fortress against the militia – had joined Leathers in a desperate but slow run for the inlet.

"Charles Town's cannon are the only things that can stop them now," Anne said. "But I doubt they will rally the gun crews in time to dispense colonial justice. Even in this calm, Leathers and the other two ships will soon be out of range."

Leaning against the tiller, the stress of the past day had robbed her of the strength to continue. She felt weak, puny, and ashamed. Rescuing Tye should have been enough, but as she watched the three ships inch their way toward the inlet she knew it wasn't. That she wanted revenge was true enough and easily admitted. But what she wanted most was absolution for allowing her son to have been kidnapped in the first place, and for not having told him the truth. Her entire life since Jamaica had been a lie, and it had almost led to the death of an entire city. But even that painful truth meant nothing compared to the damage she had done to her bond with Tye.

Sensing that the moment was not hers alone, Anne looked up to see Mary Read studying her. Though she was trying to keep her face blank, Anne saw a smirk tug at the corner of Mary's mouth. It was the kind of smile people smile when they know something that others don't. Anne sat up straight, her back stiff with resentment. The fire in her belly roared back to life.

"What's that?" Sweets asked, unaware of the soundless confrontation behind her. "It's...it looks like...sails. It's another ship!"

Anne held her gaze on Mary Read for a few long moments, then looked toward the inlet. A ship under feeble sail had found its way through the unguarded channel and was tacking its way toward the *Revenge* and its two escorts.

"I'll be damned," Mary Read said. "The crusty old bastard found his teeth and wants to hunt with the young dogs."

"Must have seen or heard the explosion and took it as the signal," Asku said, remembering the vague plan Scarlette had agreed to before leaving the Gullah camp. "It will be three against one an' nowhere to run, now that he's in the bay. The question is, will he fight or will he try to join with them?"

"Damn!" Mary Read sighed, peeved at having missed something so obvious. "I didn't think of that."

As if in answer, the captured brig – still flying its British naval jack – slowly began a turn that would bring its starboard guns to bear on the three ships heading toward it. But Curlee Leathers was a survivor and had no intention of waiting for the inevitable. A moment later, the *Abundant* and the *Discordia* slowly peeled off in different directions, preparing to deliver broadsides of their own. At the same time, the crew of the *Revenge* began loading the twin bow guns that would propel the deadly spinning chain shot toward the *Hazard* – the same shot that had so devastated it during the first encounter.

"At least Scarlette is a man of his word," Anne said as they watched the ships creeping along to establish their battle positions. "I'll give him that."

"He's also an idiot," Mary Read said. "If he somehow sinks the *Revenge*, the Pellicane map goes with it. He'd be smarter, richer, and less dead if he tried to make a deal."

Though absorbed in the sluggish nautical maneuvering unfolding before them, Tye shifted in his seat at the bow as though discovering he had been sitting on a splinter. Anne watched as he adjusted his coat and vainly tried to regain a comfortable position. The current had taken them well out into the bay, far from the city and the sounds of fighting. A quiet had fallen over the boat, the only sounds were those of small ripples slapping against the hull and the distant screech of soaring seagulls, oblivious to the battle about to take place beneath them.

"You know," he said, coming to a decision. "We have oars. We could start row–"

They felt the blast before they heard it, the concussion slamming into them like a moving wall of air somehow turned solid. An instant later, the tremendous roar of a cannon assaulted their ears, forcing everyone aboard the periauger to duck below the gunwale. The distinctive, rolling whoosh of a forty-two-pound cannonball cut through the air over their heads, finally splashing into the water fifty yards in front of the slow-moving *Revenge*.

Leather's crew, that moments before had been focused on the on-coming *Hazard*, now turned to look directly toward the periauger. But it wasn't the little boat they began pointing at, but rather a billowing puff of smoke rising from one of the cannons at Fort Johnson. Unwittingly, Anne had piloted them to a point halfway between the fort's defensive cannon and Curlee Leathers' fleeing ships.

"Holy hell," Mary Read said. "This isn't good. This isn't good at all. I think now would be a really good time to break out those oars."

"Look!" Briebras said before anyone had a chance to move. "Standing on the wall – do you see what I see?"

Though the distance from their boat to the battery of guns was too great to distinguish detail, they could clearly see a man perched atop the fort's palisade. The man, who appeared to be shouting orders to the gun crews below was easy to spot because of the brilliant red coat he wore.

"No..." Anne said. "You don't think...?"

"You know it is," Mary Read laughed, a sound akin to a basket of oyster shells being thrown on a pile of more oyster shells. "I told you he was a man of reliable consequence."

"But can he aim cannon with accuracy?" Briebras asked, eyeing the distance between the fort and *Rackham's Revenge*. It wasn't an idle question. Gant's ability to direct cannon fire could determine whether they lived or died.

The answer came a few moments later when a half dozen or more of the fort's guns fired almost in unison. Like a swarm of giant hornets, the cannonballs passed over their heads and crashed into the *Revenge*'s bow. Flying sections of splintered wood slammed gun crews into the ocean and across the deck. Other cannonballs struck the bow at the waterline, opening a gaping hole. Because the cavity was so far forward, the ship took on water as if it were a huge scoop, halting what little forward momentum it had been able to muster.

The ship was floundering, but it could still defend itself. Gun port lids on the starboard side began flipping up randomly as Curlee Leathers' untrained gun crews raced to return fire against the new threat. The odds were not as favorable as they had been, but with three ships at his command, he still had a chance.

Anne thought she could hear the burly pirate's commands drifting across the water when a second torrent of cannon fire erupted from the island. Again, the cannonballs screamed over the periauger, coming together to strike a narrow section amidships, right at the waterline. Water rushed through the enormous hole so rapidly that the ship began to pitch over on its side. When the cannon were finally ready to fire, the ship was listing so badly they could not be elevated high enough to do any good. What would have been a defiant roar became the ship's silent death knell.

The schooner sank so quickly that most of the crew had no time to jump overboard. Many became entangled in the rigging and sails and were dragged under the water never to surface again. They were the lucky ones. The pirates that survived would soon be dancing to a piper on a Charles Town gallows.

"Mon Dieu..." Briebras said as the ship slid into the dark bay waters. "Did you see? Gant, he makes a hell of a gun capitaine. And look, the other ships have reefed their sails and now fly the white flag. It is over."

"Fools," Anne said. "If they had both made a run for the inlet, at least one would make it. The half-wits have consigned themselves to the gibbet."

Though they stood shoulder to shoulder, Mary Read did not offer a response. With a quick glance, Anne saw that the raven-haired piratress from Wapping stood as if in a trance, fixated on the spot where the *Revenge* had gone under. The display of sadness and regret splayed across her friend's face touched Anne in a way she had not thought possible.

"I'm sorry," she said. "Your beautiful ship..."

"My beautiful map," Mary Read said.

Anne reeled. The schooner Mary Read had built was an asset that could have provided her a comfortable income as a merchantman for the rest of her life. The map was little more than a clever work of fiction, designed to foster greed and – ultimately – disappointment. Mystified, she ran a hand through her tangled red hair and wondered at the absurdity.

"We're soon to have company," Tye called out. "Look, a longboat comes this way from the fort."

"Oui," Briebras said, "and Scarlette brings the *Hazard* this way. It appears that we will be the point of rendezvous."

The brig made it to the periauger first, retrieving the raiding party and those they had reclaimed from the city. By the time Gant's boat joined them, Scarlette's men were hauling the wounded Dyonis up the side of the ship on a broad plank. Asku hung from the harness, making sure the litter did not bang against the hull lest it jar his brother. When safely aboard, Asku and several of the crew used the broad plank as a litter to carry him to the surgeon's cockpit below the waterline.

"Wait for me," Gant ordered the oarsmen as he climbed up a rope ladder. As he came over the gunwale, Scarlette stepped back to give him more room. Sweets Nightingale, who had been standing next to the large man and unable to see, found herself face-to-face with Gant. Their eyes met and held for a moment.

"This way," he said, leading Scarlette and the group of survivors to the far side of the deck so that the men in the longboat below could not hear.

"I told you that you were wrong about me," Gant said to Anne as they congregated next to the gunnel, the words popping off his tongue with proper English crispness. His eyes smiled even as the corner of his mouth presented her with a twisted sneer.

"So it would appear," Anne said with a nod, though the tinge of sarcasm in her voice gave away her true feelings. "How did you know that we weren't on the *Revenge?* We would all be dead now if you had made the wrong call."

Gant locked his arms behind his back, military style, as he reconsidered Anne.

"Because the crew was preparing the bow cannon to fire on Scarlette...which would have been a stupid thing to do if you had been aboard and in charge. Unless, of course, you were in the act of betraying the oath we all took back at Ocracoke...and were intending to sink the *Hazard* along with our alliance. Either way, I estimated that sinking the was the right thing to do. Would you disagree?"

"No," Anne conceded once again. Gant had painted her into a corner, and as much as she hated losing, the man's reasoning was spot on. "But, why didn't you tell us what you were up to...and how in the hell did you manage to take command of the fort?"

"I didn't tell you I was leaving because I knew you wouldn't believe that my intentions were honorable. You've left little doubt as to what you think about me, but I knew there was a good chance that the guns at Fort Johnson would make the difference, one way or the other. Either they could be used to our advantage...which is what happened...or they could be used against us. I was ready to make sure that would not happen if events had turned the wrong way."

"Getting the militia to do my bidding, that was easy enough. When militiamen see a red coat, they tend to fall in line, pell-mell. They believe I was sent here on assignment...that there had been rumors of a pirate resurgence and I was dispatched to reassure the colony that ships and troops were on the way, only I got here too late. After that, they did everything I told them to do."

"They don't suspect you...yet," Mary Read said, cutting to the chase. "But they will, once the militia in Charles Town pokes some of Rader's men for information. And what about right now? How do you explain me and Anne and our long-in-the-tooth friend here, Bloody Bill?"

"You too?" Gant asked. "That she would doubt me, I can understand. But you? Truly, I am hurt."

"I doubt anything that might lead to a noose around my neck," she said, not in a mood for banter. "Best you tell us your scheme while there's still distance between us and those in Charles Town aching to wrap good hemp around the necks of anyone they believe was party to Rader's scheme."

A loud snap from overhead cut off Gant's reply.

"The wind is on the rise," Scarlette said, nodding at the topsail, "an' the tide will make the inlet an easy go. We need to make sail, now."

"Perfect," Gant said, reclaiming their attention. "My plan is simple. You see that ship, the *Discordia*? In a few minutes I'm going to convince the captain, whoever he is, that if he wants to live he will follow the *Hazard* through the inlet and haul the wind for all it's worth, regardless of direction."

"An' what's goin' to stop the battery at Fort Johnson from sinking both ships?" Scarlette scowled, wary of cannon that were now under the control of the militia. "Pellicane's map was lost with the *Revenge,* and the longer we remain in the open the more likely it is we'll sail into trouble. We need to leave, now."

"The fort's captain would gift me his adolescent daughter after the dressing down I gave him. The man is a total incompetent. The fort is in disrepair. There was barely enough dry powder to fire the second barrage, and the forty-two pounder was rendered useless after the first shot, leaving me with only the use of the smaller cannon. You don't have to be a quartermaster to see that the fool has been lining his pockets with funds intended to maintain the garrison. Even if they could scrape together enough powder to try and sink us, he would much rather I be gone than take the chance I'll expose his incompetence."

"And what about Charles Town's cannons?" Anne asked, still skeptical. "You think the militia will just let us leave without firing a shot?"

"The *Hazard* is flying the king's colors," Gant said, glancing toward the jack. At just that moment a gust of wind made the flag snap as if to make a point. "As far as they know, this is a proper British ship of the line that came to the rescue. As long as I keep the *Discordia* close on her heel, they won't dare fire at her. By the time they fully understand what has transpired, we'll be far and away."

"Um... Excuse me," Sweets broke in, trying to sound as if she was asking an innocent question. "Where, exactly, do you plan to go?"

Anne and Mary Read exchanged a glance. The young doxy had not even been introduced to Gant yet and she was already trying to manipulate him. Even a blind man could see where this was heading.

Gant looked at the girl and then to Anne and Mary as if asking, "Who is she and what's her story?"

"I don't know what her name is," Anne said, "but she apparently has an uncanny knack for picking the worst of men. Other than that, all I know is that she can't go back to Charles Town. We'll have to wait for Asku to tell us the rest."

"My name is Sweets Nightingale," she said, ignoring Anne's slight. "I'm a woman of means...or I will be once I convince a few of Charles Town's gentry that they had better send me what's mine or have their secrets revealed."

"Sweets Nightingale?" Mary whispered in Anne's ear. "What kind of made-up name is that?"

Gant looked back at Sweets expecting her to say more. Instead, she let the outer wrap of her nightclothes slip down below her shoulders and eyed Gant, waiting for his answer.

"I don't know, to be true," Gant said. "As far away from here as possible. The fort's captain is a scoundrel, but the man spouts rumors as though he were the town crier. According to him, England is close to signing a treaty with Spain...information he claims the merchant ship captains brought with them before Rader shut down the port. If there is a treaty, the admiralty will be free to send ships back to protect the trade routes. And once they hear about Rader's attempt make Charles Town a pirate stronghold, they will descend upon the southern colonies like sharks. If I show up as the sole survivor of the *Hazard*'s crew, they'll ask a lot of questions I won't be able to answer very well. If they find me living out of uniform, I'll be hanged as a deserter."

"There won't be a safe harbor anywhere in the colonies for any of us," Mary Read said, beginning to realize the consequence of her failed plans.

"Same for the Caribbean," Anne said. "Once they discover that Anne Bonny and Mary Read still live, they will post a bounty. Every ship in the Atlantic outfitted with a swivel gun will be looking for us. We'll have to go to the frontier...or leave America and go...somewhere."

Anne shook her head in disgust. After all they had been through, the thought of returning to a hand-to-mouth existence made her sick with loathing. It would not work for her, and it would not work for Tye. Never again would they be content scratching in the dirt to grow food, collecting loose parrot feathers to make penny crafts, and grinding winter grist for the meal dust left between the stones. But what else could they do? Where else could they go?

"Excusez-moi," Briebras said. "Mesdemoiselles. Major. May I offer a suggestion? There is a petit but growing settlement in La Louisisane...named La Nouvelle-Orléans. I am told that it is a place where a man can become someone other than himself. A place that welcomes all, no matter from where they hail. It would be an easy voyage in the *Discordia*...if you can make it past the Spanish strongholds in La Florida."

Gant palmed the stubble on his face as he considered the idea. The location of the settlement and westward expansion all but guaranteed that it would become a thriving port city.

"Yes," he said. "It makes sense. If we make it there safely, I can either keep the *Discordia* and become a sea merchant, or I can sell it and buy land to establish a business or a plantation. Briebras, my friend, you are a smart man, indeed. New Orleans makes for an excellent choice."

"I've heard that New Orleans is a wonderful place," Sweets said, employing her Charles Town drawl to maximum effect.

Well played, Anne thought. Perhaps the marine might even think his next thought concerning her would actually be his own.

"What about you?" Gant asked, looking to Anne and Mary Read.

"I'm staying here on the *Hazard*, with Asku and his brother," Anne said, offering no further explanation.

"And I go where she goes," Mary Read said. "We have...a few things yet to resolve."

Whether Mary was talking about their ongoing feud or something else, Anne no longer cared. She had Tye back, and that was all that mattered. But by staying, Mary Read had absolved the major of any obligations associated with their unsuccessful partnership. They were free to go their separate ways.

A few minutes later, as she watched Gant and Sweets board the *Discordia*, Anne began to wonder whether she had made the right decision. Though she knew nothing about New Orleans or Louisiana, she understood that it would have afforded her and Tye a new start. But she could not just sail away and abandon Asku to take care of Dyonis alone. She owed them and their mother far too much.

After Scarlette piloted the *Hazard* through the inlet and the *Discordia* veered off to take a southerly heading, Anne pondered the wispy hues of crimson blazoned across the morning sky. She recognized it for the omen it was – the omen that sailors had heeded for as long as there had been ships built worthy enough to sail the open seas.

*Red sky at night, sailors delight. Red sky at morning...*

# CHAPTER FORTY

SAILMAKER PEPPERS - THE AGING CREWMAN who had once been Scarlette's spy aboard *Rackham's Revenge* and had tailored Tye's calico suit - also acted as the ship's surgeon in times such services were needed. It was a natural transition for a man with skills using needles, thread, and the sharp blades of scissors. But even though his fingers were still nimble and steady when poking a needle through sailcloth, his frayed constitution balked at the idea of sawing through flesh and bone.

Removing maimed limbs was an unenviable task. Sawing off the leg of a man who fancied himself to be some sort of clock - a man who screamed in horrific agony and begged for his mother as the instrument's teeth cut through vital bone - was a deeply disturbing and gruesome job that he would gladly have shirked off on another. Only, there were no others.

"It's a patch of cloth what's infecting his wound," he had explained. "When the ball passed through his breeches it punched out a bit of cloth on the way in. It's too late to take it out. The only chance he has now is to take off his leg."

Dyonis was a bleeder. It had taken the sailmaker more than half a day to stanch the wound. It was because of the profusion of blood that he had missed the cloth while extracting the musket ball. Infection had set in soon after, turning the wound into a purple, engorged mound of pus. Amputation had been the only option.

Several times during the procedure the sailmaker's hand slipped from the saw, its grip made slippery by the torrent of blood that followed each cut. When he was finally done, the sight of the butchery he had committed made him sick. Instead of a clean, precise cleave, Dyonis's stump looked more like it had been hacked off with an ax. Hours later, after he had somehow managed to reduce the bleeding, the old man left his patient in the hands of his brother and retreated to the refuge of his hammock. Retrieving a jug of rumbullion he had been hoarding from its hiding place, Sailmaker Peppers had commenced drinking his way to the bottom.

It was deep into the next morning when he awoke. Despite the pounding in his head, he could tell that the weather had changed and they were no longer under sail. Struggling from his hammock, he staggered up the steps to the main deck. Though the wind had subsided, the sky was still heavy with black clouds and the rain showed no sign of relenting. As his eyes became accustomed to the gray light, he saw Asku at the port rail with a handful of crewmen lowering the unconscious Dyonis into the periauger. The small boat's sails that had been tented over the hull to the deflect the rain were reattached to the masts. What they planned to do with it now mystified him, but the answer came a moment later when Scarlette, the two women, the Frenchman, and the boy exited the captain's quarters to join Asku.

"As I told you afore, Brunswick Town is ten miles or so up river on the west bank," Scarlette said to the others. The wide brim of his hat sheltered his face from the rain, funneling the water down his back. "It ain't much of a town, but it's all there is to be had around here. With a little luck, you might find a real doctor."

Peppers winced at the unintended insult, though he had done more than should have rightly been expected of him. He was not a doctor and had never laid claim to being one. He had performed the surgery out of necessity. He could live with that. What he couldn't live with were the haunting echoes of Dyonis's pitiful, child-like screams bouncing around inside his head. Those, he feared, would last forever. One thing he did know for sure – he would never do another surgery. There wasn't enough rum in the world to convince him otherwise. Let them find some other fool to amputate their mangled arms and legs. He was done.

"What about you?" Anne asked. "Nobody knows that you were a part of this...except us...and as brethren, we will keep our oath of silence. Scuttle this brig and no one will be the wiser."

"Ocracoke is a small island," the graybeard said. "Too damn small for this seaman. The only reason we stayed as long as we did was because of the treasure. Now that the map is gone, there's nothing to hold us there. Those that want to stay, can. The rest of us will collect our families and find a new place to live."

"Just like that?" Mary Read asked. "And where will you go? What will you do?"

"From where I'm standing, your man Gant made a sound choice. The Caribbean won't be safe for us when the king's navy returns in force. Not if we stay with the *Hazard*. We'll have to have a vote, but most of the men are like me. We'd rather take our chances on the open sea than wait to be tracked down on land like dogs. We'll head to the Gulf and figure out what to do once we get there. But we won't be staying here, that's for certain."

It was as much of a goodbye as Scarlette was apt to give them. The allegiance they had sworn had bound their fates together. The battle they had fought in Charles Town Bay had earned them the old pirate's trust. They were free to go their own way, both sides satisfied that the other would take their secrets to the grave.

As the periauger pulled away from the *Hazard*, Anne turned to take a last look at Bloody Bill Scarlette and the ship that had brought them so far. But it wasn't the graybeard she saw standing amidships, lingering at the gunwale. It was the sailmaker – the man who had butchered Dyonis's leg. The rain and the distance between them made the dark, hunched-back figure appear more like a vulture than an old man. Waiting... Waiting... Waiting... A harbinger of a death not yet realized.

A gust of wind sent a rush of water down the open front of Anne's coat and she began to shiver. The wound to her shoulder was beginning to heal, but it was too tender to work the tiller so she steered the boat with her left arm. Adjusting the sling to where she could grasp her lapels together, she piloted the boat through the channel into the Cape Fear River.

With the wind picking up again, she had Asku and Mary Read stow the oars and release the sail. They had miles to go and little chance of finding help, but they had to try. She had to try for Dyonis's sake as well as Tye's. As long as Asku's brother had breath, she would not give up. Vultures and old sailmakers be damned.

The farther up the river they sailed, the harder the rain fell. When it was clear that Briebras couldn't keep up with the water collecting in the boat, Asku picked up a hollowed-out gourd and settled into a fast-paced rhythm that would outpace the rain. Tye continued to hover over Dyonis, occasionally offering him a sip of water or wiping his brow.

With nothing else to do, Mary Read assumed the job of lookout – a curious task for the only person on the boat who didn't have two eyes. Every time she wiped the rainwater from her face, Anne could see her wince. An ointment Peppers had given her was working but the collection of cuts and punctures about her body were still painful.

*Good thing for Mary that the sailmaker made a far better apothecary than he did a surgeon,* Anne thought.

"There!" Mary Read said, pointing to several buildings on the riverbank emerging from the gloom. "That must be it. Brunswick Town."

Anne pulled on the tiller and peered through the rain, trying to get a better sense of what they were sailing into. Calling the small collection of rough structures a town was generous. A single pier extending from the riverbank was the little port's most noticeable feature. Behind it stood a large brick building that doubtless served as the community's commerce center. A handful of single-story log cabins and stone hovels extended out to either side, creating a haphazard main street along the waterfront.

Behind those, barely visible through the rain, were the few buildings that made up the rest of the town, including a two-story clapboard that had all the signs of being an ordinary. As much as she had grown to dislike Bath, Anne grudgingly conceded that her adopted home was a lustrous pearl compared to the raw, greenwood settlement spread out along the riverbank. Brunswick Town might one day grow to be a Bath or even a Charles Town, but to Anne, it looked like an arbitrary collection of structures destined to collapse because of its lack of ambition.

After securing the periauger they wasted no time carrying Dyonis to the ordinary. Asku and Mary Read took the two front corners of the makeshift litter while Anne and Briebras held up the corners at the rear – Briebras bearing his share of the load on his shoulder. Tye led the way, making sure the path was clear. When they reached the ordinary, he pushed the door open and stepped aside. Rough-looking seamen, fur traders, and dockworkers packed the room, driven to find shelter from the relentless rain.

Halfway inside, Asku and Mary Read stopped in their tracks to avoid crashing into the back of a huge trapper. Far past the point of drunk, the man dressed in buckskins did not realize he was blocking their entry until a sudden blast of damp air and the sound of splattering rain told him the door was open. As he shuffled around to look, the man's red-bearded face turned into a sneer, exposing a jagged collection of yellow teeth.

"What the hell!" he said. The foul odor of rotting gums and festering sores almost made Asku heave. "Shut the damn door or I'll skin you alive and tan your hide!"

The constant assault of rain, lack of sleep, and days of living on edge had chafed Asku's tolerance to a thread. In a move that seemed impossible for a man supporting a litter, Asku jerked his knee straight up and then thrust his heel into the trapper's sternum with all his might. The sickening crackle of shattering bone filled the stillness that had enveloped the room. The red beard stumbled backward, crashed into a table and then fell onto the floor with a dull thud. Clutching his chest as he rolled from side to side, he called out for help between groans of agony.

Responding to his calls, another trapper emerged from the crowd and started toward Asku. In a flash of steel, the tip of Mary Read's sword appeared just below the man's Adam's apple, forcing him to stop.

"We need a room for our friend," she called out, her stare remaining locked on the man at the end of her blade. She continued holding her corner of the litter despite a growing sensation that her shoulder was about to be pulled from its socket.

Though no one said anything, almost everyone in the ordinary turned to look at a plain looking man across the room. Standing behind a rough-hewn bar, the man who had to be the owner looked back at them like a rabbit caught in the open, frozen between the impulse to run and the desperate hope that not moving would somehow save him.

"There are no rooms," he said at last. "We're full up."

Mary Read tilted her head to peer at the man through thick ropes of sopping wet hair that fell across her face and her shoulders.

"I... I mean...you can have my room," he said.

"Where?" Asku asked.

"Top of the stairs," the man said, nodding the direction. "First door on your left."

"Do you have a doctor hereabouts?" Anne asked as they started toward the stairway.

"Not unless a ship with a doctor has ported. I'll have to ask about."

"You do that," Mary Read said as they started up the stairs, "and be quick about it."

After they had moved Dyonis from the makeshift litter to the innkeeper's bed, Mary bolted the door then went to the room's only window.

"Well, that was a hell of an entrance," she said. The confrontation had resurrected her trill to its full glory. "No doubt they're tryin' to figure out who we are and what might have happened to Asku's brother."

As she spoke, she pulled back a ragged square of sailcloth covering the window, trying to get her bearings. The room overlooked an ally that opened into the street passing in front of the inn. At the other end of the alleyway, barely visible in the gloom, was a horse barn.

"I don't like it," Anne said. She was sitting on the edge of the room's only chair, watching Asku mop his brother's fevered brow with a damp cloth. "News travels fast, and Charles Town isn't that far away. The people here may not know that the militia has re-taken the city, but they surely know about Rader and the siege. We won't be able to stay here long. We have to leave, as soon as possible."

"Oui," Briebras said. "But to where? You cannot go back to Bath. It is pas un option. I forbid it!"

"Forbid it? What do you mean...you forbid it?" Anne asked.

"Anne. Mon 'amie. You do not understand. Do you not remember when Kofi said–" His voice cracked and a tear came to his eye. "Do you not remember when we first boarded the *Revenge* and you challenged Kofi's loyalty? Do you remember my words then...about practicing the art of subterfuge...and that I would reveal all later?"

Anne did recall the moment. Briebras had promised to explain himself, but there had been no time, and she had long since forgotten to ask about it.

"Oui. You do remember. I see it in your eyes. That is what I am trying to tell you. Isaac Ottiwell, the customs collector in Bath, recruited Kofi to sign on as crew to the *Revenge* to spy on Mary Read and Blyth Rader."

Hearing her name, Mary let the curtain slip from her grasp and turned to look at the little Frenchman.

"Monsieur Ottiwell was certain that his assistant, Kilby Bloodhoff, was conspiring with the pirates, giving them information as to what goods the departing ships carried. He also told them which ships were expected to arrive and what goods they were expected to bring. And, most important, he was giving them information about the king's warships."

Anne looked at Mary Read. Mary Read stared back, her face expressionless.

"Kofi agreed because he wanted to save enough money to buy the freedom of his sister...Emmie...so when Monsieur Ottiwell offered him a large sum to spy on the pirates, he accepted without hesitation. The money he would earn as a spy would have been more than enough to buy Emmie's freedom."

"Was there nothing you didn't have your claws into?" Anne said to Mary Read. "You had Gant on the *Hazard*, Rader tipping cups with Bath's assemblymen, and the colony's assistant customs collector tucked in your pocket. Just how big did you weave your web? What else do we need to know?"

"I don't know," Mary Read said, tracing the scar above her eye as though having just discovered it. "I'm a complicated woman. My byzantine nature manifests itself in many ways."

"The point is," Briebras rushed to continue, "you cannot go back to Bath because Monsieur Ottiwell already knows about Mary Read, and by now he knows who you really are as well. I must return to Bath. The information I have to deliver is now moot, but it will fulfill the contract. After that, I will go to the Virginia colony and keep my promise to Kofi."

"Asku!" Dyonis called out, his voice weak and pleading. "Askuwheteau! Where are you? I need you. Asku...."

"I'm here, Dyonis," Asku said, grasping his hand. "I'm right here beside you."

"I'm cold, Asku. So cold. Could you close the window...before you get in trouble."

"Yes," Asku said. It was clear to all that Dyonis was reliving a childhood memory. "I'll close it in a minute. Here, maybe this will help."

Though his voice remained strong, Anne saw that Asku's hands were shaking as he covered Dyonis with a quilt.

"Well, that's just fine for you, isn't it?" Mary Read said to Briebras, filling the silence. "You have a vow to keep that takes you back to Bath, but we can't go...because of you and Kofi."

"That's strange," Tye said, speaking for the first time since entering the room. "I thought you would want to go back to Portsmouth Island."

"Portsmouth Island?" Mary Read said. "There's nothing for me there. If the *Revenge* hadn't been sunk and I still had the..." Her voice trailed off, realizing that Tye's question was really a comment.

"...the map," Tye finished for her. Now that he had their attention, Tye pulled back the left side his calico jacket to reveal a leather spyglass case, its strap passing over his shoulder.

"You mean, the treasure map hidden inside the long glass inside this case?"

"The map!" Mary Read said in disbelief. "How? Where did you..."

Anne suppressed a surge of anger. Once again circumstances were conspiring to push the divide between her and her son ever farther apart. Voicing ridicule of the damned map would ring hollow and petty, given its importance to Tye. Responding as though its recovery was a good thing would sound contrived. Caught in the middle of lose and lose, she said nothing.

"When I snuck aboard the *Revenge*, I went to the captain's cabin to look for Clairette. Of course, she wasn't there, but I grabbed the long glass on my way out."

"But how did you even know that the map was in the long glass?"

"I stumbled upon it while looking for the riddle...the one hidden behind the mirror. I knew the map was important to you, so I put the glass in this case and put it on under my coat before going below deck to free the children."

"Why didn't you say something before? Why tell me now?"

"Because," Anne said, "he knows how I feel about your stupid map."

No one spoke for a moment, thrown off by the raw honesty of her statement.

"There just really hasn't been a good time to bring it up, until now," Tye continued. "You see, I know that the map shows the treasure is somewhere on Portsmouth Island, not far from the village. So now you have a destination and a reason to go there. We can find Blackbeard's treasure...I'm sure of it."

"Then, you will have to find it quickly," Briebras said. "I will travel back to Bath by road. That will give you six or seven days before I make my report to the customs collector. Perhaps ten, if I experience difficulties on the way. But no more. I will have to explain my whereabouts to Monsieur Ottiwell and my story must ring true. He must not suspect that Kofi was working with the two of you, or else he might refuse to pay."

"Askuwheteau..." Dyonis's call cut through their conversation in a hushed rattle. "Look at my feathers! My beautiful feathers! Asku, I can fly! I can really fly! And it is...wonderful."

Asku pulled his brother's hand to his lips, kissed it, then pressed it against his cheek. He attempted to speak, but a shudder stifled the words. Anne rose from the chair and motioned to the others. When they were all in the hallway, she closed the door, leaving Asku the privacy to grieve for his brother in ways he might not want them to see.

"Let's go downstairs and ask what there is here to eat," she said, leading the way.

The darkness of evening had overcome what little light the storm had allowed. And though there were only a handful of candles illuminating the ordinary's main room, it was enough for the patrons who remained to see who was joining them. All eyes turned to look at the newcomers and the dull hum of their many conversations grew quiet.

"Looks like we made quite an impression on locals," Mary Read said as they took seats at an empty table. "I bet they'd all pee their breeches if I said 'boo' real loud."

Anne scanned the faces around the room and saw that it was true. It struck her as strange, given that these were not the type of men who scared easily. They were trappers, hunters, frontiersmen, dockworkers, and merchant sailors who had faced dangers almost every day. It was odd that men of such ilk were so easily cowed by two women, a half-sized Frenchman, and a boy.

A woman came to serve their table and the muted drone of conversations around the room resumed. The fare was limited – venison stew with cornbread – but the rumbullion would continue to flow for as long as they had coin with which to pay. When she had finished her stew, Mary Read dropped her spoon into the empty bowl and wiped her mouth with the back of her coat sleeve.

"There's something wrong here," she said as softly as her bristly voice would allow. "Every jack and lubber in this place has been cutting us eyes since we sat down."

"I know," Anne said. "I've been watching them too. Usually by this time, at least one drunken sot would be at the table wanting one or both of us to be his companion for the night. It's as if they-"

"-know who we are," Mary Read said, finishing the sentence for her.

"Mes amies," Briebras whispered. "Do not look, but five...six men just came in through the front door. Three of them are making their way toward the back of the room. the other three remain at the door."

"The group moving to the back have stopped at a table," Tye said, taking over for Briebras as the men moved into his line of sight. "They are talking to...a man. It's dark, but... Oh, it's the man you held at sword point."

"We need a plan," Mary Read said, grasping the hilt of her sword for reassurance.

"I suggest we move back to the-"

A loud, piercing wail of grief emanating from the second floor cut off the rest of Anne's words. Part war cry and part torment, the soulful lamentation rolled down the stairway and into the open room to still the tongues of everyone in the ordinary.

"Quick," Anne said, seizing the moment. "Start walking to Asku's room and act as though you haven't noticed anything going on down here. I have an idea."

"We're going to check on our friend," Anne called out to their server as the others started toward the stairs. "Fix me a bowl of stew I can take to him. I'll be back in a minute to get it."

The woman nodded, not sorry to have the odd group leave.

Anne felt all eyes in the room burning into her back as she followed the others upstairs. Making sure the promise to return had been spoken loud enough to be overheard, she was gambling that the brigands gathering to attack them would rather wait until Asku and Mary Read - the main targets of their revenge - were delivered into their waiting hands.

Though relieved to have gained a little time, the pall of grief saturating the room when Anne re-entered was crushing. Asku stood at the head of the bed holding Dyonis's pallid face in his hands. The others watched silently as he stared into his brother's eyes as if searching for a flicker of life.

"It is the custom of his people," Briebras said. "They believe that by staring into the eyes of a loved one when he dies, all the ancestors that came before can be seen. I think it is their way to give death...purpose."

"All right, Mrs. Rackham," Mary said to Anne. "Now what? Tell us what your plan is?"

"My plan? My plan was to get us out of the main room where we were outnumbered and trapped. Beyond that, I-"

A breezed ruffled the curtain behind Mary Read, catching her attention.

"The window! We'll go out the window and steal our way to the boat. If we leave now, we'll be gone before the chawbacons downstairs realize it."

"I won't leave Dyonis," Asku said. "Go if you have to, but I'll not leave him here with no family to bury him proper. I promised my mother that I would watch over him, no matter what. I may have broken all my other promises, but I'll not be breaking this one...even if it kills me."

Anne shook her head, unwilling to accept Asku's ultimatum. If they rushed the men in the tavern, one or two of them might make it through. But which ones? And what of Tye? The risk was too great. If they went out the window and left Asku, it wouldn't be long before the men would come looking for them. Asku could hold them off for awhile, but in the end, he would surely die. It was a conundrum she had experienced only one other time in her life – the day that Barnet and the *Snow-Tyger* had attacked them – and the whole crew of the *William* had been below deck, dead drunk.

"Mister Dare," Tye said, placing his hand on the woodsman's arm. "Asku. Your brother once told me that you made another promise to your mother. He told me that you gave her your word that you would bring him home. You don't have to break that promise. There's still a way."

Asku looked at the boy.

"He's right," Anne said, grasping the straw for all it was worth. "We can carry Dyonis to the boat and take him back to Cedar Island."

Asku considered the idea for a moment, but doubt still clouded his face.

"Oui!" Briebras said, attempting to lend an air of certainty to the scheme. "It is true. We can tie the sheet around him so that you and I can lower him down to the others. the boat is not that far away."

"But we have to go now," Anne said, sensing that their time was running out. Asku looked Anne in the eyes.

"Either we all leave or we all stay," Anne said. "It's your call."

Put that way, she knew he had no real choice. If they all stayed, they would all die, and she knew he would not want to be the cause of their deaths. A run for the boat would at least give them a chance.

"Then we leave," Asku said.

As the others hurried to prepare the body for the escape, Mary Read climbed through the window and dropped to the alley. Anne went next, with Asku helping her because of her shoulder, and then Tye. Asku and Briebras maneuvered Dyonis's body through the opening with as much dignity as the situation would allow, then gently lowered him to the others.

"I've got him from here," Asku said when he and Briebras were on the ground. "Briebras, you and Tye lead the way."

"No," Briebras said as Asku lifted his brother across his shoulders. "I am sorry, but I must leave you now."

"But, you can't stay here by yourself," Anne said. "They will kill you."

Above them, the sound of someone banging on the door of their room rolled out of the window they had just exited.

"S'il te plait! You must hurry! I will hide in the woods till daylight and then find the trail that leads to Bath. They will believe that we all left by boat and will not be looking for any of us to be traveling on foot. I will be all right."

Not waiting for anyone to object, he grasped Asku's hand and shook it.

"Your frère was a good man. I was proud to have known him."

The heavy thud of shoulders pounding into the door of their room signaled that their time was almost up.

"Remember," Briebras said as he disappeared into the darkness of the ally, "you only have about ten days. Que Dieu soit avec vous, mes amis."

"And with you," Anne said under her breath, though she doubted that God would heed any prayer that came from her lips.

Although the rain had stopped, the clouds made the night as dark as a cavern. Only by following the occasional splash of light spilling out of a window or doorway cracks were they able to navigate the muddy lanes leading to the wharf. Asku followed Anne's barely visible silhouette, while Tye led the way, his young eyes able to discern obstacles that the others could not. Mary Read brought up the rear, her sword drawn and ready to dispatch anyone who pursued.

As they approached the dock, the splintering crash of solid wood yielding to unrelenting shoulders heralded the end of their stealth. A wave of curses and shouts rolled through the lanes like a horn announcing that a fox had been flushed. The dogs were in pursuit. Racing as fast as he dared, Tye led them to the periauger and scrambled aboard. While Anne and Asku struggled to get Dyonis's body into the boat, Mary Read stood squarely in the middle of the dock, looking toward the village. Only a few moments had passed when the light of several lanterns spilled out into the lane followed by an angry band of thugs bent on taking revenge.

"Mary!" Anne called. "You must come, now! Hurry!"

Freed of its moorings, the river's current pulled the periauger away from the dock. For a few moments, Anne wondered if Mary Read might stand her ground and try to dispatch the sorry collection of riffraff that dared to chase them. It would be a wicked justice – the best kind.

"I still have the map," Tye called out, tugging at the string he knew would get her attention.

Despite the dire circumstances, the gambit did not go by Anne unnoticed. During the few weeks they had been separated, her son seemed to have developed an uncanny ability to say the right thing at the right time, and in far more measure than his years would suggest possible – especially with things that involved the raven-haired woman who had kidnapped him in the first place.

Mary Read took a final look at the approaching band of village idiots and shook her head in regret. With a running start, she leaped from the end of the dock toward what she hoped was the center of the boat. Though she overshot her mark, Asku caught her before her momentum carried her over the side. A moment later, the rabble spilled onto the dock with lanterns held high so as to light as much of the darkness around them as possible – but to no avail. The strangers they chased had disappeared into the pitch-black night as anonymous as they had arrived.

Anne sat at the tiller, letting the current guide the boat. As the light from the lanterns on the dock diminished, the probability of their escape grew more certain. Even if the men chasing them took to boat it would take awhile for them to catch up. And though there was still a hundred and fifty miles between them and Cedar Island, they had a good chance of making it if they could get back to the ocean.

"Well, that worked out pretty good, I'd say," Mary Read said, interrupting Anne's thoughts. "What's your plan now?"

It was a reasonable question, but the burden of making decisions for their little troupe was taking its toll. Sapped by living every moment of every day for weeks with the fear that she would not reach Tye in time, her resolve was in tatters and her nerves teetered on a razor's edge. Sucking in a long breath of air between clenched teeth, she dug down deep to tap into the last ounce of grit she could muster.

"If the weather clears, we should be able to travel the open water during the morning calm," she said, making up a plan as it came to her. "If we can round the cape before the wind rises in earnest, we can cut behind the islands...stay in the lee where it will be safer."

"Safer from the ocean wind and waves," Mary Read said, "but not from alligators, Indians, and river bandits looking to snatch a trader's goods."

"If you have a better idea, then by all means, throw it on the skillet and let's see if it'll dance. Otherwise, I'll thank you to shut up and help us get back to the inlet. I don't know if the wharf rats we left back there will take to boat to find us, but I don't intend to be on this river come sunrise to find out."

For a moment, the world around the periauger seemed to stand still. The chirping of crickets along the river's banks filled the silence with a steady tempo while the bubbling river added a somber melody. Then Mary Read let go a sound that was more like the cracking of brittle bones than the laugh it was meant to be.

"Now THAT'S the Annie I know and love. Welcome back, Mrs. Rackham. You've been too long gone."

Though it hadn't been loud, the harsh rasp of Mary Read's chuckle had been enough to silence the crickets. The unexpected response had knocked

Anne off-kilter. Having no place to target her rage, the fatigue she had experienced moments before returned to fill the void.

"You know something," Anne said, resting her weight on the arm of the tiller. "Sometimes, you're as worthless as a lobcock."

Grabbing a phrase from her nearly forgotten repertoire of Molly-house speak, Mary Read fired back a retort without missing a beat.

"And you, my sweet, short-fused friend, can sometimes be a cupid stunt."

Neither Asku nor Tye understood why, but Anne began laughing so hard it echoed off the trees on the riverbank.

"For pity's sake," Mary Read pleaded between escalating chortles of her own, "put a cork in it! You'll give us away as sure as cannon fire."

But neither woman could stop. The more they tried, the harder they laughed. Tye joined in, though he still didn't understand the joke. As antidote to weeks of stress and danger, the laughter would not be denied. Even Asku couldn't help but smile at the absurdity of it all.

A loud splash along the far bank brought the raucous laughter to a sudden halt. There were any number of animals that could have caused the noise, but there was only one that could threaten them in the middle of the river – and in the dark, no one wanted to wait around to find out for certain if it was, indeed, an alligator.

"All right," Anne said, taking up the tiller again. "Let's find the mouth of this river. We need to be ready and waiting to pass through the inlet as soon as day breaks. If we can make it over the bar before anyone spots us, they'll never find us."

The dawn brought clear skies, calm waters, and just enough breeze to help them navigate the inlet. They never saw any sign of the men from Brunswick Town but they took no chances. Anne held the boat as close to the shore as possible so as not to silhouette themselves against the horizon. Taking advantage of the first day of easy sailing since having left Charles Town, they followed the coast until they reached the southern end of Topsail Isle when the afternoon winds made the seas too rough for the periauger. Soon after entering the island's lee, they stopped to make camp on an islet between Topsail Isle and the mainland. Within minutes of securing the periauger and starting a fire, the exhausted travelers slept wherever there was enough open beach on which to lie down – except for Asku.

Anne awakened the next morning with a start, at first unable to remember where she was or how she had gotten there. Grabbing the hilt of her sword, she took a frantic look about the clearing, cursing herself for allowing them to be exposed and unguarded the entire night. Movement by the periauger caught her eye and she jumped to her feet. Her sword was halfway drawn when she stopped, realizing that it was Asku. The woodsman was kneeling in the sand, hunched over an object hidden by the boat. He was working at something, making slow, deliberate motions she could not fathom.

Securing her weapon, she moved to the boat's bow to get a better look. Stretched out on a section of sailcloth lay Dyonis, the clothes removed from his pasty, white skin. A thin sheen of wax covered his exposed body from head to toe. With a pang of shame, Anne realized that they had left Dyonis's body in the boat with only a sheet to cover him.

"Asku,' she said, barely able to speak. She looked away from Dyonis's nakedness out of respect. "I'm sorry. I... We... It wasn't right."

"It doesn't matter," he said as he began piling small green leaves on his brother. "His soul is what matters, not his body. I just need to get him home before...well...you know."

He paused for a moment.

"I gathered all the myrtle berries I could find, then boiled the wax out of them. The myrtle leaves will help a little, too. He'll be all right for awhile, but we need to move on."

"Of course," Anne said, unable to say more. An onslaught of guilt paralyzed her tongue and numbed her brain. After everything Asku had done for her, she had not even shown the decency to care for his dead brother. And had it not been for Dyonis, Tye would have never made it into or out of Charles Town alive. They had given her almost everything there was to give – and she had given back nothing.

She watched in silence as Asku completed the primitive embalmment. When he finished coating Dyonis's body with the waxy leaves, he carefully rolled it up inside the sailcloth and then bound it tight with a strand of hemp. As he stooped to lift the bundle into the boat, Anne stepped over to help.

"No!" Asku said. "I will do this. He's my brother."

"NO yourself!" Anne shot back with a fire that equaled Asku's. "The thing of it is, I made a promise to your mother, too. I may have failed her, but I won't fail you and I won't fail Dyonis."

Asku stared back at her and for a moment Anne feared that he was going to strike her – a possibility that both scared and surprised her. It was then she realized that the once boyish-looking woodsman she had come to know in Bath had changed. His face – tempered by an unrelenting succession of narrow escapes, great victories, and even greater loss – was that of a man. It was a revelation that greatly saddened her.

Coming to a decision, Asku shifted around to place his hands under his brother's shrouded shoulders and then looked at Anne. Needing no further explanation, she grasped the opposite end of the heavy bundle with her good hand and together they gently lifted it into the boat. When she was sure that Asku no longer needed her help, she wakened Tye and Mary Read.

"Gather your things as quick as possible and get to the boat," she said. "And no whining about food – we'll find something to fill your bellies later."

"What's the rush?" Mary Read asked, not sure whether to be angry or concerned.

"Asku spent the night covering Dyonis with wax so as to preserve his body, but it won't last long. We need to make sail right off and get them both home as quick as we can. It's the right thing to do."

"The right thing to do?" Mary Read repeated. "That's a laugh. Since when did you start caring about doing what's right?"

"Since about ten minutes ago," Anne said as she started back toward the boat. "Now, gather your things and let's go. Or stay here. It's your call."

"I'll be damned if I can figure her out," Mary Read muttered. "One minute she's the dread piratress Anne Bonny, and the next she's St. Clare of Assisi. I'd give up Israel Hand's map if I could just have my old Annie back."

"You don't have the map – I do, "Tye said giving her a start. She had completely forgotten about the boy.

"Which brings up an interesting question," Mary said. "When are you going to give it back? It belongs to me, you know."

"Not anymore, it doesn't. It belongs to me, now. But I'll give it back when I'm ready."

"And when will that be?"

Tye finished stuffing the few things he had into a sack fashioned from spare duck cloth and tied off the ends.

"When I'm sure that you and her have...worked things out."

"I could take it from you, you know?"

"You could. But you won't."

"And how do you know that?"

"Because...I just know."

Throwing the sack over his shoulder, he left the befuddled Mary to help Asku and Anne push the periauger back into the water.

"Last chance!" Anne called out. "You coming or not?"

Startled, Mary Read saw that the boat was already free of land and drifting with the current. In a wild rush, she snatched up her hat and coat and ran to the periauger.

# CHAPTER FORTY-ONE

IT TOOK TWO DAYS to reach Cedar Island from the islet. On the morning of the third day, Asku buried Dyonis next to their mother with most of the villagers on hand to pay their respects. Anne watched Asku throughout the service, wondering if he would cry or breakdown in some way. But the morose, withdrawn expression on his face never varied. Even when Gerald Gurkin read the Twenty-Third Psalm, he showed no grief or bitterness. The darkness enveloping him was thick and impenetrable.

Anne did not look at Mary Read during the service for fear of what she would see. The edges between them had smoothed somewhat during the trip, but a new tension was beginning to fill the void. Anne believed that while her thrashing defeat of Rader had curbed Mary's appetite for confrontation, the blistering stare-down administered to her raven-haired friend while escaping Brunswick Town had ignited a fire of a different sort.

Mary Read's change had forced Anne to reconsider her vow of retribution – a contingency she had not anticipated and now loathed. Desire for a reckoning had kept her going almost as much as her fear for Tye's life. It had provided warmth and clarity. The notion of forgiveness was cold and ambiguous. So what if Mary Read had helped save them? Were four lives saved fair compensation for the three lost and the hell she had put them through?

Without the defiant swagger, there was no malice. Without malice, there was no threat. If there was no threat, she would have no rage – and she could never kill Mary Read in cold blood. If there was no longer any reason for them to be at each other's throats – the only thing Anne feared was what she would feel if their eyes met and lingered for too long.

Nor could Anne dare to look at Tye for fear of what she would not see. There was a wall between them she could not understand. He wasn't disrespectful or spiteful. He was just distant – brushing off her attempts to connect at any level and otherwise ignoring her. It was obvious that Dyonis's death pained him deeply, but it was equally clear that the gulf between them had nothing to do with the loss of his friend. With everyone else, he was as he had always been – open, amenable, curious. And even more so with Mary Read. Only with his mother was there a discordance.

Having run out of ideas on how to bridge the impasse, Anne quit trying. As hard as it was for her to do nothing – and as much as it maddened her to see Tye becoming ever closer to Mary Read – forcing the issue would only drive him further away. Her only option was to bide her time and hope that he would eventually forgive her for lying.

When the dedication was over, Asku extended his hand and dropped a single emerald-hued feather onto Dyonis's coffin. All the other villagers attending the service did the same, leaving the cedar wood box covered in a layer of green, yellow and orange parakeet plumage like those of the cloak Dyonis had worn.

"Eternity has no need for a Timekeeper," Asku said, "but an angel must have feathers for his wings."

After the service, Anne, Mary, and Tye stopped at the village only long enough to gather their few belongings and say goodbye to Asku. But to Anne's surprise, the woodsman fell in with them as they approached and continued on to the periauger.

"Why?" she asked. "You've done everything you promised. You owe me nothing...and you know that there is little chance I can give you what you want."

"There is nothing for me here. I have no family left and there are too many ghosts here for me. Besides, I think Dyonis would want me to do this. To see if we can find the treasure, for Tye's sake."

"There's a better chance that we'll all hang than there is of finding treasure."

"All the more reason I should come along. Somebody has to save you and Mary Read from yourselves."

Anne shot him a wicked glance, not sure if he was insulting her.

"Don't give me the witch's eye," he said. "You know what I'm talking about. If there was no one around, you two would throw down right here in the middle of the path and have it."

Anne pulled up short. There could be no doubts about his meaning this time. Her face flared red and fire burned in her eyes.

"Hell's bells!" he said, cutting her off before she started. "It's as obvious as the nose on Blyth Rader's face. You're as twisted as wormed glass...trying to figure out this and that and the other. But it's all about nothing that really matters, and you won't find peace until you do something about the thing that burns inside you. Everyone sees it but you – and it follows you like a squall."

He paused for a moment, letting his words sink in.

"Do yourself and the rest of us a kindness, Anne Bonny. Make amends with this woman and get on with it...before it kills you."

The truth of truth set Anne back on her heels. By the time she recovered, Asku had caught up to Mary and Tye.

She kept to herself during their short sail to Portsmouth, trying but failing to dismiss Asku's words as raffish, backwoods conjecture. When they came into sight of Portsmouth Village, Mary and Asku began discussing whether they should stay there or at Ocracoke. Anne remained muted, offering only grunts or nods in answer to their questions.

"There's a pilot who lives in Portsmouth that's missing his boat," Mary reminded them. "The one you stole to board the *Revenge* that night. He may not have connected you to that bit of larceny, but the crew Rader left with the *Hazard* had one night ashore to tell tales before we took her. Better to stay at

Ocracoke than risk a chance meeting with an irate pilot and his extended family seeking reparation for his missing craft."

Finding a place to stay was easier than they had expected. Scarlette, his crew, and their families had already departed. Their exodus had left a good many shacks and lodges around the village abandoned, including Scarlette's large house on the sound side of the island. Its distance from the village shielded them from prying eyes and its access to the water made it an easy choice.

Wasting no time, they ventured into Ocracoke's village on the first night of their arrival in search of food, drink, and information about a fellow named Jack. According to the map, if they were going to find the treasure, they first had to find Jack's home on Portsmouth Island. But to find Jack's home they first had to figure out who Jack was. It seemed a simple task, but it took only a few minutes at the first ordinary to discover the folly of their quest. The problem wasn't that there weren't any "Jacks" to be found in the area. The problem was that a man couldn't swing a dead cat by the tail in either village without hitting several men named Jack. Without a last name, it would take several days to identify each man named Jack and locate his home.

Worn down from the days of travel, Asku took Tye back to Scarlette's house to get some much-needed sleep. Disheartened by the enormity of the task before them, Anne and Mary remained at the ordinary to plan their next steps and to find a bit of solace in a bottle of rumbullion.

"I know a Jack," a man sitting at a corner table who had overheard their conversation said.

The two women braced themselves in anticipation of the unwanted advance that was sure to follow. But the face illuminated by a candle on the table was that of a the leathery-skinned fisherman rather than a lecherous drunkard.

"What's his last name?" Mary asked.

"'Jack' is his last name," the fisherman said, taking a draw on a white clay pipe. The tobacco in its bowl glowed red as he sucked air through its long stem. A moment later he released a cloud of smoke from the corner of his mouth.

"Really," Anne said, her interest piqued. It had not occurred to her that "Jack" might be a surname. "Tell us then, what's his given name?"

"His first name would be Hatteras...as in Hatteras Jack."

"Hatteras is the name of the cape north of here," Anne shot back, growing impatient. "It's not the name of a man."

"Didn't claim him to be a man," the fisherman said.

"Not a man?" She was beginning to tire of his cryptic manner. "'Jack' is a hell of a stupid name for a woman."

"Didn't say he was a woman, neither," the fisherman said, oblivious to Anne's growing irritation. "Hatteras Jack is a fish – a white porpoise."

The fisherman's face was so cracked from years of sun and wind, it was hard to judge his true age. He could have been 45 or he could have been 60, it was impossible to say. But as he spoke, Anne saw truth in his light blue eyes.

He took another puff off his pipe and then continued.

"Hatteras Jack 'as been guiding boats through the inlet for twenty year or more. Some folks say he's spawned from the union of a lovesick sailor an' a mermaid, but I don't hold with that. Truth is, he just likes to be with people. Likes to help them out and maybe show off a little. Anyway, that's the way I see it."

The two women exchanged a glance. They were sure they had found the Jack referenced on the Pellicane map. Now all they had to do was find where he lived. To show their appreciation and keep the information coming, Anne poured the weather-beaten old man a cup of rum.

Relieved that they had finally found proof of the map's authenticity, Mary Read let Anne continue with the questions. The steady drone of Anne's voice and the rum in her full belly brought on a restfulness she had not felt in a long time. As her senses dulled, the subtleties of her surroundings blended together like the disconnected wisps of a bad dream, nudging her toward the realization that all was not as it was supposed to be.

Being careful not to let on that anything was wrong, Mary searched the room for the malevolence making the hair on the back of her neck stand on end. Other than a few patrons absorbed in their conversations, there was nothing close by to see. But farther away, in the dark recesses and corners of the room, there was a scattering of men who could possibly pose a threat.

Unsettled, Mary peered into the dark crannies harder, half-hoping to see the wavering gray form of the Hollow – and immediately dismissed the notion. Whatever it was that had crawled under her skin was far different and darker than the Hollow.

"Tell me," Anne asked the fisherman as he took a sip of his spirits, "where exactly does this Jack go when he's done for the day? We are of the understanding that there is a cove or the like on the sound side of Portsmouth Island where he takes shelter. Any idea where that might be?

"No. But I can't say I've ever thought about it much. Once he guides a ship through the inlet, he goes his own way. Sailors and fishermen got no reason to follow him."

Though she would have liked more details, Anne wasn't discouraged. They had at least found the "Jack" they were looking for. From here it would be a simple matter of following the beast to its home, finding the building shown on the map, and go from there.

Six days later they were no closer to finding the treasure than they had been since the first night. Once again, as they had done the previous five days, the four of them navigated the periauger through Ocracoke Inlet out onto the ocean, then waited for the albino dolphin to appear. About an hour before sunset, just as he had done the previous five days, Hatteras Jack appeared beside their boat and let loose a series of high-pitched chirrups in invitation to follow. Yet again, they raised one of the sails and tagged along behind until they reached the point on the sound side where the channels converged.

"Twisty rickets!" Mary Read yelled from her perch at the bow. "He's doing it again! He's turning to starboard instead of port. What the hell is wrong with this stupid fish?"

"He's not a fish!" Tye yelled back, though he was kneeling on the cross seat next to her. "I keep telling you, Jack is a dolphin...a mammal...not a fish."

"Call him whatever you want," she said. "I'll soon be calling him supper if he doesn't show us the way."

Frustrated, she flipped up her patch and rubbed her scarred eye socket with the back of her hand. The days of repeatedly sailing out of the inlet and then following the dolphin back through were taking their toll.

Anne felt it too, but frustration wasn't the only thing making her head hurt. Even taking his time, Briebras would have made his way to Bath by now. It would not be long before Customs Collector Ottiwell had a bounty on their heads. Once the world found out that Anne Bonny and Mary Read still lived, there would be no place under the English flag that would be safe for them to hide.

To make matters worse, the captains of the merchant ships passing through the inlet on the way to Bath were bringing more bad news. Peace talks in Seville were going so well that the British Admiralty had released more ships to patrol the colonies. Having learned of the battle between the *Hazard* and a pirate ship believed to be named *Rackham's Revenge*, the Royal Navy was now searching for both ships. Every merchantman they happened upon was stopped and questioned in hope of discovering who the pirates were and what might have become of their brig. It would only be a matter of days before their sails would dot the coast along the Outer Banks.

"Take us back to the village," Anne called out to Asku, sitting at the rudder. "There's no point in going around the back side of Ocracoke again. The stupid map says Jack is supposed to go behind Portsmouth Island – not Ocracoke. Either the map is wrong or the dolphin's habits have changed since Pellicane made it. Either way, we'll never find the treasure if we can't find the exact spot to look. And at this point, all we are doing is putting ourselves at risk for nothing."

Asku guided the periauger into a slow jibe, deftly completing the turn without snapping the boom. Anne set the trim then sat facing the bow.

"Time has run out," she said to Mary. "We've got to leave. You know that, right?"

Still sitting at the bow beside Tye, Mary Read turned so Anne could see her face.

"One more day," she said. "We give it one more day. You know it's here...somewhere. It has to be."

"It's the map," Tye said, more to himself than the others. He was staring into the distance off the port bow, watching the dolphin as it occasionally broke the surface on its way behind Ocracoke. "We're missing something. We've got to be."

Anne mulled the situation for a moment more, trying to resolve the probability of their imminent capture with what might possibly be the last chance to regain her son's respect. She had come too close to feeling the prickly strands of the hangman's rope around her neck the first time she had been captured. But his indifference toward her was taking its toll, and she was not sure how much more she could take before she slipped and did something that would close the door between them forever.

"One more day," she said. "Come morning, day after tomorrow, we leave this place forever. No matter what. Agreed?"

A twitch at the corner of Mary Read's mouth hinted at a smile as if to say, "I knew you would see it my way."

By the time they reached the small, makeshift pier at Scarlette's house, Anne had stewed in her misery to the point she could no longer think straight. Not only was she trapped by circumstance, Mary Read was pulling her strings like a marionette. Although Anne's perception that she was the one in control was not a total illusion, she realized that its scope was narrow.

Desperate to distance herself from the others, she leaped from the boat before it had come to a stop, tromping off the pier and up the path toward the village without saying a word.

"You should go after her," Asku said as he tied the boat down.

"Me?" Mary Read asked. "Why not you?"

"Because, I'm not the one causing her to do a slow burn."

"I suppose you're right," she said as Anne disappeared in the live oaks and junipers. "There's still some things that need to be made right. Might as well be now."

She caught up to Anne at Teach's Bloody Head, the ordinary closest to Scarlette's house. It's most distinctive feature was a passable likeness of Blackbeard's head, dangling at the end of a chain suspended from a mock bowsprit over the entrance. Carved out of cypress, the painted knot of wood wore a wig and beard made of twisted hemp dyed jet black, its stark white eyes peering down at all who entered.

Inside, the tavern was nearly filled to capacity with men from around the village, consuming their liquid recompense for a day's hard labor. Somehow – sitting in the center of the room like a boulder around which a river of human motion flowed by – Anne had managed to stake out a table for herself. That no one had dared to sit at the table with her was no surprise. The entire village could now recognize Anne Bonny on sight. And knowing who she was, no one but a fool would have violated the solitude of the black-hearted killer whose dark face and brooding manner left no doubt that she wanted to be left alone.

"You ready to toe the line with me again?" Mary Read asked as she took the seat to Anne's right.

Instead of looking up, Anne studied the rum in her cup, swirling the amber-colored liquid around until it almost ran over the lip.

The one-eyed piratress grabbed a used cup from the tray of a passing server and poured herself a generous portion from the jug sitting in front of Anne. She then plopped her heels up on the edge of the table and rocked her chair back until it was balanced on two legs.

"No? I guess I don't blame you. You can't out-drink me...and besides that, you make a really sloppy drunk."

Anne's eyes cut across the top of her cup, slicing Mary Read into little pieces. Mary had forgotten that their last drinking bout had been prelude to Tye's abduction. Gritting her teeth, she considered her next move. She was tired of holding back and having nothing good come of it. She needed to know whether Mary was true about leaving – or if she was so blinded by treasure she would force them to linger around until it was too late.

"Tell me," Anne said from behind the cup. "Tell me what it was you–"

She stopped in mid-sentence, realizing that Mary was no longer listening. Her one eye was darting back and forth, looking about the room as if in search of someone or something. One at a time, Mary removed her feet from the table, let the chair come to rest on all four legs, and stood so as to see beyond the men standing around them.

"Is it the Hollow?" Anne asked, half-hoping that it was. Better the apparition than a bounty hunter or a search party from a newly arrived ship of the line.

"No..." Mary breathed. "I mean...yes. I think it's here. But it's not the Hollow I'm feeling. There's someone...something...a vile, depraved thing...watching us."

Instead of looking about the room, Anne stared at Mary for a few moments, trying to decide whether to put her faith in the woman's darker talent. Mary's revelation about the Hollow had rung true enough. Whether the thing truly existed really didn't matter – it was real enough to her. But the thing that held Mary in its grip now was different. Much different. Sensing that its effect on Mary would only get worse, Anne grasped her arm and pulled.

"Come on," she said. "We need to get out of here. Now."

Mary took a half-step, then balked. Fishing a coin out of her pouch, she tossed it on the table and grabbed the bottle of rum.

"Now I'm ready," she said.

Anne kept looking over her shoulder as they wound their way through the live oaks. Even though no one appeared to be following, she felt no sense of relief. Everyone in the village knew where they were staying. If anyone wished to find them, they need only follow the same path and it would lead right to their door.

Neither Tye nor Asku were in the house when they returned, which suited Anne just fine. She was in no mood for idle talk or explanations about what had happened in the village. Nor was she concerned for her son. As long as he was with the woodsman, she needn't worry for his safety.

With dusk coming on and the wind long since stilled, the steamy-hot summer air made sitting inside a dismal option. Hoping that a breeze off the water would afford a little relief, she led the way upstairs to the main bedroom and its small balcony overlooking the sound. Having recovered her wits by the time they passed through the bedroom, Mary grabbed two small pewter cups kept under the room's washbasin. When she stepped out onto the balcony, Anne was already sitting in one of two rush chairs situated on either side of a cask serving as a table.

"Come on, Annie," Mary Read said as she placed the jug of rumbullion and cups on top of the cask. "Have a drink with me. No dancing with the devil this time. Just a friendly tip. What do you say?"

Anne had no desire to drink to their past, but she needed more liquid fortification than she had been afforded at Teach's Bloody Head. In answer, she picked up one of the cups and held it out.

Mary filled their cups and took the empty chair on the other side of the cask.

"To Calico Jack Rackham," Anne said with a wry smile. "If not for him, we would have never known one another."

She left it to Mary to decide whether she meant it as a toast to good fortune or bad.

"And to the women he left behind," Mary added with equal vagueness, "wherever they may find themselves."

Anne's smile grew to a smirk, conceding a small measure of appreciation for the quick-witted riposte.

After tapping their cups together and downing the rum, they watched in silence as the sun began to kiss the glassy surface of the Pamlico Sound. The slight hint of a breeze teased them with the promise of cooler air. The only sounds were the occasional splash of fish out by the landing and the chirping of a pair of cardinals coming to nest for the evening.

"What was that?" Anne asked, holding out her cup to be refilled. "Back there at the tavern?"

"What do you mean?"

"Don't play the village idiot with me, Mary Read. You know damn well what I'm talking about. That thing you see...the Hollow. I understand that. Lots of people claim to see ghosts. But this was different."

Mary refilled their cups and then settled back in her chair. Her gaze lingered on the horizon for a few moments as if in search of an answer – or a good lie. Finally, she sighed, swallowed half the rum in her cup, and took a deep breath.

"As far as I can remember, this...extra thing that I have...has been with me since birth. The older I got, the more obvious it became to others, and the more my mother tried to hide it from them. I could see people who weren't really there and they would talk to me. I hated the damned things...and it's why I still do. At other times, I would walk into a room and a bowl or a candlestick or an apple would fly about or fall on the floor for no reason. It started happening so much that my mother became concerned for our lives. People started to say that I was possessed by the devil, or that I was a witch."

She downed the rest of the rum and filled the cup again.

"It got worse when my brother Mark died. I think he had rubeola. I don't know for sure, but it doesn't matter. People said it was somehow my fault. That I had cast a spell on him. Me! And only four years old. I remember my mother waking me in the middle of the night and rushing off to London with nothing but the clothes we wore. Years later, she told me that a cousin had come to our house, pounding on the door. He was frantic with news that some of the villagers and farmers had gotten together in a tavern to discuss the 'little witch' down the road and what they should do about her. By the time he left to come warn her, the men were heavy into their cups and talking about burning me and my mother at the stake. We got away just in time."

"But, I thought you had always lived in London," Anne said, realizing they had never really discussed much of Mary's childhood. Given their youth and the wildness of their situation at the time, it wasn't the kind of thing they would have talked about.

"No. My mother left London when she started to become heavy with me. My father had been missing at sea for nearly six months when I appeared in her belly. She left for the country to be with relations in Devon County...I believe it was a farm near a village along the River Taw...to hide my birth from my father's people."

"If your father was dead, what did it matter?"

"No one knew for sure if he was dead or not. There were reports that his ship had gone down off the coast of Africa, but it was never confirmed. My mum feared that he would show up one day, and I would be a bit hard to explain, given that the union that created me would have occurred after he'd left port."

She paused for a moment to sip from her cup again.

"It was after we got back to London that my mother started dressing me like a boy. She convinced my grandmother that I was Mark, and as a male heir, it was only fitting that she be afforded a crown a week to help support me. Somehow, it worked. But the part I remember most is that as soon as I started wearing my brother's clothes, I stopped seeing people no one else could, and things no longer flew off the tables and shelves when I walked into a room. All of it...gone. And gladly so, as far as I was concerned. The farmers and villagers were a superstitious lot, to be sure, but their fear was real. Londoners were just mean and brutal, especially in Wapping. Being different in the way I was different was to be shunned and ridiculed. When you're four or five years old...you may not be able to understand why people fear you and hate you and look at you different...but you know that they do. It was a hard thing for a child to bear...even me. Or it was until I became my brother."

The muted rays of the setting sun played across Mary's face, accenting every age line she had earned as well as the jagged edges of her scar. To Anne's amazement, a small tear had begun to pool at the bottom of Mary's good eye.

"Mary...," Anne said, but paused, trying to make sense of the thoughts swirling through her head.

"Well look at you," Mary said. "Your cup is empty again. We can't be having that."

Picking up the jug, she pulled the cork and refilled the small cup.

"You do realize," she continued, "that there's a reason I was always able to drink you under the table, right?"

"And how's that?" Anne asked, well aware that Mary was shifting the conversation – and happy to let her.

"I cheated. Every time we had a drink I'd pour half of mine into my boot, a crack in the floor, or just throw it over my shoulder when you weren't looking. And you, always fighting fair, drinking every single drop as if there was a tallyman keeping track."

"What?" Anne asked, placing her cup on the cask top. "Why the hell would you do that? Were you so driven to be better than me that you had to foul the fellowship of our drinking?

"No, Annie." She placed her hand on Anne's. "I did it because, unless you were at least two sheets in the wind's eye, you would never own up to who you are. To what you are. What we are. Oh, you put on a good face about it when you were sober, but without a drink or three, you were as stiff and tight-legged as a vicar's daughter. Your heart was willing enough, but your puritanical upbringing stifled your passions such that I might as well have been doing the bed sheet dance with a broomstick. But put a pint of rum in your belly, well, you were a woman on fire...leading me to places I had never been and haven't seen since. That's why I cheated. I wanted the passionate Annie. The real Annie. The Annie that I would have died for. It was a selfish act, I know, but I knew what I wanted and I took it. If that makes me wrong in your eyes, then so be it. But at least I was true to myself. So I ask you...can you really hate me for that?"

The familiar touch of Mary's hand released a torrent of memories and desires. Anne struggled to make out her words over the rush in her ears. She gripped the cup harder to still her trembling fingers, but could do nothing to hide the flush on her face. Eight years had passed since being rescued from prison. In saving her, her father had killed what little meaning her life had held. In the span of a minute, and with only a few dozen words, Mary Read had ripped away the veil she had been hiding behind since first having spied the magnificent, raven-haired blade on the deck of Jack's captured merchantman.

Anne pulled her hand away from Mary's without letting go of the cup. She started to take a sip, then changed her mind.

"I have only one question," she managed to whisper. "Why? Why didn't you kill me when you had the chance? Why did you take from me the one thing I cherished beyond all else? Did you hate me that much?"

"Several reasons," Mary said, leaning across the chair's arm to come closer. "I was going to kill you that first night, in the ordinary. Oh...I had such hate for you...leaving me in Jamaica to die. Killing you was all I thought about, day and night. It fed me and kept me alive. When I heard rumors that you might be living in Bath, I altered my plans so that I could commission my ship in there and look for you. I collected every penny I was due and sold every asset I had to send Rader to Bath. He oversaw progress of the *Revenge* while I put the

**426**

final pieces together...enlisting Gant to help spy on the navy and bribing Kilby Bloodhoff to keep track of the fat merchant ships and the goods they carried. Everything was perfect."

"And then you walked into the Poisoned Oak as brash and bold as ever. Your hair flowing about your shoulders like crimson wheat, shimmering in the wind. The cut of your clothes unable to hide the form of your body, turned hard as iron by years of work. And when I looked into your eyes, all the hatred I harbored disappeared as though a mirage. I knew at that moment that I couldn't kill you. But neither could I allow you to go unpunished. So I took the boy. Even then, I knew that I would bring him back to you...at some point. I'm almost sure of it."

Resisting the urge to laugh at Mary's clumsy explanation, she placed her cup on the cask and leaned across the arm of her chair the same way Mary had done.

"I told you before...I did try to come back for you. As God is my witness, I did. I tried everything I could. Even when my father forbade me from speaking of it, I refused to give up. I waited until he was drunk one night and stuffed all the silverware and settings I could carry into a pillowcase. I was going to go to Williamsburg, sell it to a silversmith, and use the money to come buy your way out. But I tripped as I was coming down the stairs in the dark and lost my grip on the pillowcase. The racket it made would have wakened the dead...and my father was far from that. The light of his lamp exposed my pilfering and, realizing what I was up to, he came at me in a drunken rage. I remember him yelling about how I was betraying him for a tribade and that my existence was an affront to God. And then he struck me with the back of his hand."

"I was addled. Me, Anne Bonny, the bloody piratress known to have murdered a hundred men, or so they say. And my father thought he was going to box me around like I was a fifteen-year-old twit. Before I could recover, he struck me again. When he tried to hit me a third time, I stopped his blow and pushed him backward. He tripped and fell, spilling the lamp onto the floor. By the time he was able to sit up, the curtains had caught fire...and in a matter of moments the whole house was ablaze. I grabbed Tye and made it to my boat with only the clothes on my back and one silver tray."

"I sailed for as long as I could, but Tye's needs eventually forced me to find port. I came across a merchantman on the Pamlico Sound heading east and followed it, knowing that it had to be going to Bath. My father died about two months later, though I didn't find out about it for several years. The plantation survived the fire, but nothing was left to me. It didn't matter anyway. It was too late to save you, or so I believed. Everyone said you were dead. And the truth is, a part of me had died with you. Had it not been for Tye, I would have died a pauper or as gin-sodden drab long ago."

She paused at this point, irritated for having revealed so much, and refusing to admit why she had.

"And what about you, Annie?" Mary asked, taking advantage of the lull. "Why didn't you kill me? You had your chances. You could kill me right now if you wanted. You have every right, given what I did. But yet, here I am...sitting next to you....drinking rum as if we had never stopped."

Anne started to avert her eyes, but Mary Read had no intention of letting her escape. With a subtle swiftness, she slid from her chair and came to kneel in front of Anne.

"There's a reason for that, Annie," she said, grasping her forearms. "Don't you understand? Can't you admit that...even now?"

Mary's words sliced through years of denial and excuses – exposing the simple truth she had struggled so hard to deny. And having been laid bare, she could no longer pretend that the truth did not matter. But still she averted her eyes.

A thousand thoughts flitted about inside her head, like dust caught in a shaft of sunlight. She had a vague sense that, if she could only manage to focus her thinking for a moment, she would have the perfect response. But the warm touch of Mary's hands on her arms made the scattered specks of thought swirl about even faster. Like her fits of rage, once inflamed, her passion became all consuming.

Misinterpreting Anne's silence, Mary relaxed her grip and dropped her head, believing that she had missed her chance. For the first time in her life, her instincts had failed her. There would be no reconciliation. And now she felt the grand fool for having revealed herself. Not wanting to rub salt into her self-inflicted wound, she was about to stand and go to the bedroom when she felt Anne rise from her seat. She looked up to see Anne offering a hand to help her stand.

"Here I am, Mary Read. It's truly me...Anne Bonny. I'm as sober as the day and in full control of my faculties. You have been patient beyond measure, and I'd only be lying to myself if I didn't admit the truth. I'm ready. I want to know you...Mary...heart, body, and soul. And if you have the will and the grit...and desire...to come with me, there's a few more places I've yet to take you."

Mary took the outstretched hand in her own and rose to her feet.

Taking Mary into her arms, the last hushed rays of the day's light fell upon her face. As if seeing her for the first time, Anne consumed the peaks and valleys and lines that somehow came together to create perfect beauty. When her gaze fell upon the eyepatch, she reached behind Mary's head, untied the knot, and let it drop onto the cask. With trembling lips, she softly kissed the jagged scar – first above her eyebrow, then on her cheek, and finally on her eyelid.

Mary gasped and leaned into Anne, raising her chin to expose her neck. It was a familiar maneuver, and Anne smiled to herself as she accepted the invitation. Starting near the hollow at the bottom of her neck, she softly kissed her way up until she reached Mary's ear. With long-forgotten practice, she caught Mary's earlobe between her lips, pulled on it gently, then nibbled at the sweet spot underneath.

An errant wisp of Anne's hot breath found its way into Mary's ear and she shuddered. Pushing back a little, she stared into Anne's eyes to see whether it was all real. Still feeling the sting from seemingly having her affection rejected just moments before, she had to be sure.

Caught in a swirl of different needs, Anne dismissed the last of her doubts and damned the consequences. Having tasted the familiar salts of Mary's flesh, she had to have more. Pulling her back into her embrace, their mouths came together in a bruising kiss. With desperate urgency, she felt for Mary's breasts through her blouse, then started to pull the offending garment over her head.

Mary grasped Anne's wrists, making her stop. She knew Anne better than anyone, and she knew that Anne was incapable of saying such things if she did not mean them. The bond that had seemed lost beyond hope only moments before, had somehow been rescued from the abyss.

"Come," she said, releasing Anne's wrists to take her hand. Mounting anticipation softened the rasp of her voice, turning the hard edges of her words into a purr. "Let's go...inside."

# CHAPTER FORTY-TWO

BELOW THE BALCONY, where he had been standing for several
minutes, Tye watched the two women disappear inside the room, hand in
hand. Though still very much a boy, he understood what men and women did
in the darkness of their bedrooms. He also understood that what the two
women were doing was considered an offense to the mores of most people –
though he did not understand the seeming contradiction. Without the
advantage of experience, one seemed little different than the other. So it was
that he had observed their touching and fondling – not with a lewd eye – but
with the same curiosity and analytical reasoning he applied to almost every new
thing he encountered.

"Best you come back to the barn, now," Asku said, giving the boy a start.
His approach had been so silent, Tye had not realized he was no longer alone.

"I wasn't spying," Tye said without sounding defensive. He held up two
striped bass taken off the trot line as proof that his presence was accidental.

"I know," Asku said, placing his hand on the boy's shoulder. "It's all right."

When they got to the barn, Tye filleted the stripers while Asku started a fire in a smithing forge. With the dog days of summer setting in, it was too hot to cook inside, so Asku had converted the forge into a grill and had been cooking on it since their return. When the fire had died down, he retrieved a couple of cedar planks that had been soaking in a bucket of water, placed the fillets on them, and then laid the planks across the coals.

While Asku kept an eye on the planks to make sure they didn't catch fire, Tye lit a candle and began going over the map as he did every night, trying to see what they might have missed. It was such a simple diagram, he could not imagine they were doing anything wrong. The crudely drawn outlines did not even attempt to show the two islands in their entirety – only the southwestern end of Ocracoke and the northeastern end of Portsmouth and the inlet passing between them. Nor did the handful of little squares on each island seem to hold any significance beyond depicting the two villages.

Then there was the drawing of Blackbeard's ensign, with its horned skeleton holding a spear in one hand and an hourglass in the other. Meant to instill fear, Tye had come to despise the lineament that looked back him each time he unrolled the map – taunting him for having failed to unravel its mysteries.

In the bottom-right corner of the parchment was the map's four-point compass rose. Again, in its simplicity, the directional letters for north, east, south, and west had not been filled in. But anyone who knew they were looking at a map of Ocracoke Inlet would know how the rose aligned. The rose was confirmation that the map was exactly what it appeared to be.

Frustrated, Tye put the map down to give his mind a rest. He was tired of considering the same possibilities over and over, only to come to the same conclusions. He needed a new perspective. He needed a distraction. Taking out a blank sheet of parchment he had found in the house, he began drawing with a shard of charcoal he'd retrieved from the forge earlier.

Asku got up to tend to the fish and saw that Tye was no longer studying the map.

"What are you drawing?" he asked, pushing the planks around. A blast of steam rose from the forge as he poured a ladle of water on the coals.

"I'm not sure what to call it," Tye said without looking up. "I lost my father's octant when the *Revenge* went down. I thought I would try to make a new one, but I think I've come up with a better idea. You do know what an octant is, don't you?"

"Of course. It's an instrument used for navigating. What makes your idea better?

"An octant measures things in the heavens relative to the instrument itself. If I can make it work, this instrument would measure objects relative to the horizon. I also think I can make it smaller and that would make it easier to use."

"Perhaps so," Asku agreed, pushing the planks back over the cooler coals.

"Mister Dare," Tye said, changing the subject. "Can you tell me why it is that a man can be with a woman, but a woman cannot be with another woman? I mean, in the biblical way."

Given what had transpired on the balcony, the question could not have come as a surprise to Asku. But instead of responding right away, he stared into the glowing coals. Tye realized too late that it wasn't fair to have posed such a question to the woodsman. Even he could see that the man was in love.

As the moments passed without hearing a reply, Tye began to fear that he may have offended Asku or hurt him in some way. Turning his attention away from the drawing to check, Tye caught the reflection of the forge's red hot coals in the quenching bucket. From his perspective, the image on the water's surface appeared upside down – just as it should. But the casual observation triggered a memory of the day he had found the riddle hidden behind the mirror on the *Revenge*. He remembered being entertained by how the mirror reversed left and right, but not top and bottom. The image in the water was upside down only because of the position from which he viewed it, not as a property of reflections. It was the same as if someone had taken a picture and turned it upside down.

With a jolt, he grabbed the map and held it up in front of the candle. A quick glance at the compass rose confirmed his theory. The letters N, E, S, and W had been scratched into the parchment's reverse side and were all but invisible until revealed by shining light through it. And as he had expected, the letters were oddly written and out of place. The N for north appeared below the compass point where the S should have been. Not only was the S where the N should have been, the letter looked as if it had been written backward. And while the W and the E were in the right places, the W looked like an M.

Smiling with satisfaction, Tye turned the map over – not in a circle like a ship's wheel, but from top to bottom. The compass rose now appeared in the top-right corner of the map and the letters appeared as they should. The ends of the two islands were so similar, and their outlines on the map so crudely drawn, there was no distinction between one or the other.

"I've got it!" Tye said.

"Got what?" Asku asked, startled from his musings.

"The reason why we haven't been about to find the treasure. Jack's home isn't on the lee of Portsmouth...it's behind Ocracoke we're supposed to go. He's been trying to take us to the right place all along!"

# CHAPTER FORTY-THREE

"STAY WITH HIM!" Mary Read yelled from her usual seat at the bow. "It can't be too much farther! We're getting close...I can feel it."

But instead of leaving them behind, the dolphin was making the most of having people follow him beyond the inlet for a change. Sometimes he would slow down to let the periauger come up beside him, then rush ahead to show them the channel running behind the island. After so many years, it appeared that the map drawn by Anders Pellicane, commandeered by Israel Hands, and accepted as an article of faith by Mary Read was about to reveal its secrets.

"There!" she shouted, pointing off to the starboard. Her raspy voice quaked with excitement, showing that even her stolid nature had its limits. "Keep following him toward... Wait! He's gone! Where did he go?"

They spent several frantic minutes scanning the water hoping to catch their guide breaking the surface again. Had the dolphin tired of his game, deciding to leave them just when they were so close?

"Asku," Anne said at last. "Give us just enough sail to beat the current. I'm steering us toward the bank in the direction he was last headed."

Anne deftly guided the boat up to the marshy bank until they were almost close enough to jump ashore.

"Look," Mary said as the periauger glided past a break along the bank. "It's a small channel hidden by overlapping spits. You have to be right on top of it to see it. Jack must have gone through there."

Asku worked the sail as Anne brought the boat about and steered it through the cut. Only a hundred feet long, the channel opened into a cove that would have been considered a small lake if it had been completely closed off. Like a small eruption, the dolphin burst out of the water, using its powerful tail to move backward along the length of the boat. Apparently satisfied that he had given his new friends a proper welcome, the dolphin took off across the cove, leaving them alone to consider their next move.

"The map just shows a square with the words 'Jack's home,'" Tye said. "I think this cove is his home and we need to find a cabin or a shack nearby."

"Where do we start?" Anne asked.

"The map shows it as being straight across from where we entered, but I don't see it. You would think we'd be able to see something as big as a shack even this far away."

"We'll start here an' follow the bank 'round the cove," Asku said. "It won't take long to get to the other side."

A few minutes later they had come full circle, finding themselves back where they had started.

"We must have missed it," Mary Read said, crossing her arms. "Go back around, now."

"It's all right," Anne said. "It's been ten years since Pellicane drew that map. Anything could have happened. The place could have been knocked down in a big blow or swept away during a 'cane. Let's go back around but in the opposite direction. If we don't see anything, we'll stop at the mid-way point and take a look around on foot."

The tension between the two women was gone. Every aspect of their interactions had changed – the way they looked at each other, the words they chose, the familiar touching. The bad blood between them had been let and drained during their night together. The women who had once been Peg Brennan and the nameless señora from Saint-Domingue were gone. Anne Bonny and Mary Read had returned in their place, almost as if they had never been separated.

"I think I see something," Mary said as they neared the midpoint. "Yes! See it? Just past the marsh grass at the edge of the brush. Something black...charred looking."

As the boat came closer to the bank, they began to see the remnants of what had once been a make-shift dock just beneath the water's surface. Not waiting for the boat bottom out on the bank, Mary vaulted over the side, dashed through the knee-deep water and up the incline toward the blackened object.

"This is it!" she said.

After throwing the anchor onto the bank, the others joined Mary with shovels in hand.

"We found it!" Mary said. "It's burned down...but this has to be it. I knew we would find it. Where does the map say we go now?"

Tye removed the map from the long glass case and held it up to the sun.

"West is still west and east is still east...but north and south are reversed," he said to himself as he oriented their position to the inverted image. Glancing from the map to the ground, he positioned himself at the burned-out shack's northeast corner. Flipping the map back over to study the instructions, he said, "From this point we head directly across the island toward the ocean, about a hundred yards or so."

"But...how?" Anne asked, waving a hand toward the forest of red cedars and thick underbrush a few yards away. "Shovels won't help us get through that."

Asku walked to the edge of the trees and knelt to one knee.

"Here," he said, pointing to the ground and then to the woods. "It's a game path. And it looks like the banker ponies use it as well."

"It's not an exact match to the map," Tye said, "but–"

"Pellicane would have been in a hurry," Mary interrupted. "He would have followed the trail, not make a new one."

Mary Read took the path into the woods, not waiting to see if the others fell in behind. The cedars soon surrendered to the overpowering live oaks, their long strands of Spanish moss hanging from massive boughs. The canopy of limbs and thick clusters of gray tree-hair blocked much of the sun's rays, turning the thick woods into an arboreal cavern almost devoid of underbrush.

Coming to a point where a second game trail crossed the one they followed, Mary stopped to look around.

"We must be close," she said, hoping to spot something that looked out of place or might hint at where they should dig.

"I counted off my paces," Tye said as he unrolled the map again. "We've come at least two hundred and ninety-five feet by my count."

"What does the map say?" Anne asked.

"It says, 'X marks the spot.'"

"What?" Anne shot back. Though she had grudgingly accepted that the map might be real, she had never felt compelled to look at it. She had left that to the true believers – Tye and Mary. But with this, the scale in her gut that had teetered between believing and not believing had just bottomed out on the side of utter horse shite. "X marks the spot! I can't believe it. Is it a poor joke that Pellicane was making? What else does it say? Is there a tree or a rock or anything we're supposed to look for?"

"No," Tye said. "It just says to go a hundred yards from the shack and then there's an X that shows where we are supposed to dig."

"Let me see that," Mary Read said.

While the others looked at the map, Asku went to the closest oak, pulled himself up on a low-hanging limb, then rose to his feet to look down at the others.

"I found it," he said.

"Found what?" Anne asked.

"The X. You're standing on it."

Anne, Mary, and Tye looked down at the same time, then backing away to get a better perspective, realized that the crossing paths did indeed create an X.

"You're right," Mary said, the raspy edges returning to her voice. "This has to be it. This is where we dig."

By the time Asku had swung down from the limb, Anne and Mary were shoveling away the soft, sandy soil where the two paths crossed. Less than a minute later Mary's shovel struck something solid. Anne dropped to one knee to brush away the dirt, revealing a human rib bone. Looking up, she saw that Mary had backed away from the hole, her face drained of color.

"What is it?" Anne asked. "An old bone wouldn't make you swoon like a school girl. Is it the Hollow? Something else?"

"I'm not sure. It's... I can't make sense of it."

"Give me the shovel," Asku said, taking the tool from her hands. "Go with Tye an' sit down against the tree."

"It looks like we've stumbled onto a grave instead of the treasure," Asku said as Tye led Mary away. "What do we do now?"

"Keep digging," Mary said over her shoulder. "This is just another one of Pellicane's tricks, I'm sure of it. He killed the men who helped dig the hole, then buried the treasure with the poor buggers on top to scare away anybody who happened to dig in the right place."

Too stirred up and leery to sit, Mary leaned against the oak and tried to catch her breath. Tye remained beside her, unable to take his eyes off of the pile of bones beside the hole growing ever larger.

"I've got something!" Anne said. "Something made of wood!"

"And metal," Asku said as he wiped the top layer of dirt off with his hands. "It looks to be a wine cask covered with tar."

"No," Anne said, pointing to a brass handle attached to the end she had uncovered. "It's a rum barricoe. An eight-gallon one, by the looks of it."

"You're right," Asku said, grasping the handle with both hands.

Taking a deep breath, he gave the cask-like drum a mighty heave, but the barricoe didn't budge.

"Blood and hounds!" he said. "The thing weighs more than an anchor. Give me a hand."

Anne gripped the handle on the opposite end and together they managed to drag the barricoe out of the hole and onto the path.

"Look at the size of the bung," Asku said, prying the oak stopper out of the opening with his hunting knife.

"The opening is big enough to put your hand inside," Anne said, her voice cracking with the anticipation of what that implied.

Asku reached into the hole, his fingers barely passing through the opening before hitting something hard inside. He felt around for a moment, then removed his hand.

"Well I'll be damned," Anne said, staring at the bounty of gold coins Asku clutched in his fist. "The map was real. Blackbeard's treasure is real!"

"Mary!" she called out as she stared at the shimmering coins. "You were right all along. Pellicane... Israel Hands... It was all—"

Anne's last word stuck in her throat, choked off by the sight she spied over Asku's shoulder. With a desperate leap, she sprang from the hole and drew a pistol from her waist sash. Asku dropped the coins and drew his own pistol, whirling around to face the unknown threat.

Frigid tentacles of fear that can only be caused by threats from an unnatural being gripped every cell of Anne's body. Her limbs turned to water. Her mind screamed *LIE!* But her eyes could not be denied. One of the oak trees had come to life. The bark-covered creature had Tye pinned against its trunk with a limb covered in flowing gray moss. Its other, moss-covered limb held a knife to the boy's throat. A few feet away, Mary Read stood before them with pistol drawn, her face a knotted mix of fear, anger, and indecision.

"Welcome back to Ocracoke," the man-sized mass of wood and moss said. "I thought you clagnuts would never find this place."

The voice was strained and shrill. Anne was sure she had heard it before – *but from where?* Her mind reeled, trying to make sense of the absurd.

"I knew Pellicane buried the gold somewhere around here, he told me that much. But I could have dug holes for a hundred years and never found it. The day I saw you two bawds come sailing back into Ocracoke I knew you had returned for the treasure. And I knew you would show up here, eventually. All I had to do was wait."

"I don't know who you are," Mary Read said through clenched teeth, "and I don't care. You can have the gold. Take it. Just let the boy go or I'll shoot you where you stand."

Anne bit the inside of her cheek, quelling words that might reveal too much. As obsessed as Mary had been with finding Teach's treasure, the woman had just offered to give it all away without a second thought. And though their night together held the promise of better things to come, even in their best days together Mary Read would never have made such a sacrifice – not even for her.

"Well...aren't you the generous cow," the moss-thing said. Pressing the knife's blade closer to Tye's throat, he removed his hat with his free hand. Long gray strands of Spanish moss stitched into the cap's fabric came off with it, falling into a pile beside his feet. "But I want something more precious than gold. I'm here to collect my pound of flesh."

"Harry Wennell!" Anne said.

The would-be pirate captain that Mary Read had unmanned on the deck of the *Hazard* was almost unrecognizable. Pudgy and soft-looking, he had added at least thirty pounds of fat. His eyes were swollen and red from too many nights without sleep. A stringy, gray beard fell from his face to blend with the tree hair draped around his body, making it hard to tell where the man ended and the flora began.

"NO!" he said. With a shrug of his shoulders, a cape of Spanish moss fell to the ground, revealing a leather baldric with three pistols strung across his chest. "You killed Harry Wennell the man! Now I'm nothing but a pathetic eunuch who lives each waking moment cursing the day I was born."

His speech became more shrill with each word. Every pause was accented with the sound of wet air passing through his teeth as he took another breath. Hunching his shoulder, he turned his head to wipe away a string of drool from the corner of his mouth.

"Do you have any idea what it's like to have desires...to want a woman...but not be able to act on those desires? To know that not even the whores will have anything to do with you...at any price? But the need keeps gnawing at you, day after day, night after night. Then one morn you wake up...and you're insane. You know you're insane because you find yourself humping a beast of burden like a hatter in a drunken stupor. But even then, in the depths of my darkest depravities, I never considered taking my own life. You know why?"

Mary saw the trap and refused to take the bait.

"This pound of flesh you spoke of? I remember very clearly what it was you lost that day, and I have to say, I think a pound is an unfair bill by far."

Wennell's bloodshot eyes bulged from their sockets and the veins in his neck looked as though they would burst. He came just to the verge of dropping the boy and charging the woman who had haunted his nightmares...but stopped.

"You'd like that, wouldn't you?' he said, sucking air through his teeth ever harder. "Have me forget about the boy and rush you? But I'm not stupid. I see what you're doing. Harry Wennell was stupid...but Harry the Eunuch is much, much smarter. I hate you and I intend to kill you."

"Then kill her, and kill me too," Anne said. "But let the boy go. He's done nothing to you. He's an innocent."

Wennell shifted his gaze to Anne, his eyes running up and down the length of her body as though an undertaker sizing her up for a casket.

"First things first," he said. "All of you throw your pistols as hard as you can toward that far tree and I'll consider your proposition."

Anne hesitated. Once they were disarmed, they would be at the mercy of the madman holding a blade to Tye's throat.

"Do it!" Mary Read said. Not waiting for the others, she threw her pistol toward the tree. "Do it or Tye is already dead. I see it in his eyes. It's the only chance Tye has."

Anne hesitated as a dozen different ways to kill Wennell flashed through her mind. But as she looked from Mary to Tye and back to Harry Wennell, she knew Mary spoke the truth. She had no choice but to give the man what he wanted. She pitched her weapon toward the tree and Asku followed suit.

"VERY good," Harry Wennell said, combing the boy's hair with his greasy fingers. "Such a noble crew we have. Now...let me tell you what's in store for little Tye here. First, I'm going to castrate the little bugger like you did me."

"NO!" Anne yelled, stepping toward them.

"Stop!" Wennell ordered, pulling the boy's head back to expose his throat.

Anne froze. Wennell's sick, rotting mind had concocted a sadistic conundrum. Doing nothing would leave her son mutilated for life and almost certainly condemn him to the same madness Wennell suffered. And though reason told her that, by comparison, making a desperate move that caused Tye's death would be an act of kindness – her heart would have none of it. Not while there was still a sliver of hope.

Seeing defeat in Anne's eyes, a smug smile spread across Wennell's bloated face.

"Lost your bluster, have you? And I haven't even gotten to the good part yet. Oh yes, yes, there's more. You see these pistols? One. Two. Three. One for each of you. Now, why would I have brought a pistol for each of you?"

He paused, savoring the tortured looks on their faces.

"They're not for you. No. Not the pistols. Just the pistol balls. Once I've turned the boy into a gelding, I'm going to shoot each of you in turn. First the white Indian. Then the boy's mother. And then...you...the raven-haired, one-eyed pirate bitch from hell. And you will die knowing that you condemned the boy to the same life of pent up lust and madness as you did me."

Wennell's smile turned into a tight-lipped sneer, moist air continuing to sluice back and forth through his teeth. After weeks of spending every waking hour imagining how he would make the women who had robbed him of his captaincy and his manhood suffer, he was in no hurry.

As Wennell continued to talk, Tye felt for the marlinspike hidden in the outseam of his breeches. He had just started to work the splicing tool out of the threaded furrow when Wennell made a wild gesture, jerking his hand away. For a few moments, the insane seaman held him at such an awkward angle he was unable to move his hand. Wennell made another exaggerated move and Tye found that his fingertips could just reach the spike. Being careful to hide his efforts, he dug his fingernails in the seam and inched the tool farther out of its nest.

From where she stood, Anne could see what the boy was trying to do. If he managed to coax the marlinspike out of the seam there he would doubtless use it. But what then? It wasn't likely that stabbing Wennell would do little more than enrage him. Instead of saving himself, it was more likely that Tye would be hastening his death. The only hope was that if he did manage to stab Wennell, it would distract him for at least a moment. But the only person close enough to reach them in time was Mary – and it was impossible for her to see what the boy was trying to do from where she was standing.

When the sharp-pointed spike at last came free of its hiding place, Anne watched Tye work the tool around in his fingers with slow, deliberate moves until he was able to grasp it firmly in his hand. As he brought his arm up to jab the tool into Wennell's leg, he glanced up at Anne. In the brief moment their eyes met, her heart stopped. One way or other, it would all be over in a moment. There wouldn't be a second chance.

"HAH!" Wennell said, grabbing the boy's wrist. "Thought you would save yourself by sticking me with your little marlinespike, did you? I saw what you was doing the whole time."

The ruse that Tye had used to save himself from Skullen had failed this time. Defiant until the end, he looked up at the man about to slit his throat and spit in his face.

Henry Wennell screamed with the agony of the damned. Dropping the blade he held to Tye's throat, he reached up to pull Asku's hunting knife from his shoulder. As he did, Tye dropped to the ground and rolled away.

Mary Read had begun her rush when she saw Asku's hand go for his knife and throw it at Wennell. Realizing his mistake, the eunuch forgot about the knife and drew a pistol from his baldric. A heartbeat later Mary crashed into him at full tilt. As the two fell to the ground, the gun went off.

For several long moments the others held their breath, waiting to see if either of the two had been injured by the shot. Not until Mary began to push herself off of Wennell's still body did they breathe again. But their relief was short-lived. A black stain spreading across Mary's midsection and the twisted expression of pain on her face revealed the bitter truth.

No longer trapped, a dazed Henry Wennell began to stir. Propping himself up on one elbow, he looked at Mary Read, trying to understand why she was on the ground next to him. When his gaze fell on Anne it all came rushing back. He reached for a second pistol but the weapon never cleared the baldric.

Without a sound, Asku sprung across the distance between them to land on Wennell's stomach, knees first. Pulling his hunting knife from the man's shoulder, he grasped the bone and leather handle with both hands and drove the blade into Wennell's chest again and again and again. By the time Anne was able to grasp Asku's shoulder, Henry Wennell's upper torso looked as though it had been torn apart by wolves.

With the entire front of his body soaked in blood, Asku sat back on his heels and watched the mutilated eunuch take his last breath. It wasn't until that moment that Asku began to understand the brutality of his act. With the pirate's warm blood still dripping from his face, he looked up at Anne.

"It's all right," she said. "I would have done worse had I gotten to him first. Come now. We must see to Mary."

Together, they lifted the raven-haired piratress and carried her to the nearby oak. Placing her between two large roots with her back against the trunk, they gathered around to comfort her as best they could.

"Take my hat off," she said. "I want to die as a woman...not as a man. I never wanted to be a man...I wanted to be better than a man."

"You are," Anne said as she removed the hat, allowing the thick strands of sable hair to cascade over Mary's shoulders. "You are better than any man I've ever known...and you're not going to die. You're too damn stubborn to die."

"No, my sweet Annie. The bastard shot me in the gut. It's a slow painful death he's given me. We've seen it too many times to pretend otherwise."

Anne struggled to swallow and cursed the wetness collecting in her eyes. Mary Read would mock her for being weak, and she would not allow that. Not now.

"Why did you do it? It should have been me. It would have been me had you not gotten to him first."

"I had to save the boy. I had to save...Tye."

Had it been almost anyone else, Anne would have believed her without question. But this was Mary Read, a woman who had never made a sacrifice for anyone but herself.

"I know you and Tye became close after you... I mean...during your time together. But...I..."

Mary cut her off with a laugh.

"But you can't believe I would sacrifice my life for that of another?" Her laughing ended in a series of coughs. When the spasms passed, she continued.

"Oh Annie. My sweet, sweet Annie. For such a smart woman, sometimes you're as dumb as a stump. Even now you don't see the truth of it, do you?"

Anne looked at her, not sure she even understood the question.

"Annie, my love. It's not your child I was saving...it was mine."

Anne's confusion changed to complete bewilderment. No matter how hard she tried to resolve Mary's words, they made no sense.

"The fever gripped you first, remember? You were weathering the worst of it when you gave birth to your child...a girl it was. But you can't remember any of that because you were mad with pain and sickness. You were so delirious I had to tie you down with bunk webbing to stop you from thrashing about. When the baby came, the cord was wrapped around her neck. I tried to rouse her. Truly I did. But I don't know anything about bringing life...just taking it. The baby died before she had a chance to draw her first breath."

As Mary let the words sink in she glimpsed movement behind the others. A form as gray and wispy as the Spanish moss was coming toward them, slowly making its way through the oaks. For a moment she feared Wennell may have had an accomplice who wore a similar cloak of moss, but then she understood. The Hollow was coming to her, its form becoming clearer with each step.

"But...if my baby died, where did Tye..." Her voice trailed off as she began to understand.

"Aye. I birthed Tye early the next morning and put him to your breast. Your father had come to Spanish Town by then, and we both knew he would buy your way out. I knew the boy would have a better chance at life with you than me. And the truth be known...I thought it a kindness that you would never know that your girl had died."

Anne looked at Tye as if seeing him for the first time. She recalled their falling out and that it had started after he had seen Mary at the shipyard. She thought of the friction between them these past weeks and the easy way he and Mary had formed a bond.

"You knew," she said. "You knew all along, but you never said a word."

Tye looked back at her with a mix of sadness and relief, grateful that the truth had finally been revealed.

"Of course he knew," Mary said. "After all, he shares his mother's gift, even if just a little."

She coughed again and dark red fluid began to trickle from the corner of her mouth. She wiped the blood away with the back of her hand and focused on the Hollow, now standing next to Anne. At long last, she could see the wraith's features in detail. Her face was kind and wise, despite her youth. Her eyes hinted at knowledge of the beyond, like light chasing back the darkness feared by all those who come to stand at death's door.

And now that she could recognize the apparition for who she was, Mary understood why the child had followed her all these years, across land and sea – past trials and travails and every danger that could be imagined.

"Your baby...you never told me what you were going to name her if it was a girl. I had to bury her in our cell with no name – just 'Baby Bonny.'"

Anne shook her head, realizing the irony of the long-forgotten decision she had made.

"I never told you because it was going to be a surprise. My last gift to you before we were hanged. I was going to name her...Mary."

"Well..." she smiled weakly. "Don't that just make the ship's bell ring. And all I gave you was misery. Not much of a trade, was it?"

"That's not true," Anne said, grasping Mary's hand. "You gave me purpose...and it saved my life, for I surely would have found a way to die had I not been driven to care for Tye."

"Fair enough," Mary said. "But, I wish we could talk about it while we killed the devil one more time."

"Only if you promise not to cheat."

They both smiled, but the mirth in Anne's eyes turned to darkness, knowing that they would never drink rumbullion together again.

Mary squeezed her hand then looked at the Hollow.

"I see your daughter. I see her as she would have been...the same age as Tye, just as tall and just as favored. Her skin is fair, like yours, and her hair is the color of polished copper. Her eyes are gray and kind and..."

She stopped in mid-sentence and closed her eye for a moment. A breeze drifted through the trees making the Spanish moss flutter like topsails catching an orphaned wind. For a moment, Anne feared that her once and once again love had passed, but then Mary came back to her one last time.

"The Hollow...little Mary...is gone," she said, gripping Anne's hand. "And it's time for me to go as well."

"No!" Anne said. "Not now, damn you! Not after all this time. Not when I've finally found you again. I forbid it!"

"I lived much longer than I should have...but I made the most of it. You'll have to live the rest of your life for the both of us."

Placing her hand on Anne's cheek, she drew her in to kiss her softly on the lips.

"Annie," she whispered. "I... I have to tell you..."

"I know," Anne said, not sure that she could handle hearing the words. "You don't have to say it."

"But...I do," Mary insisted, struggling to breathe. "Annie...the map...I told you it was real."

Anne looked at her in disbelief, then saw the wicked smile on her face and in her eye.

"Mary Read, you crazy, magnificent, beautiful woman. I love you, too, my duchess. I-"

But Mary's hand fell from her cheek before Anne could finish - the words that would have followed unable to make it past her throat. Forcing back a sob, Anne ran her finger along the scar that would have driven a lesser woman to hide her face from the world, and wondered at what could have been. The rage that always simmered just below the surface began to burn hot, stoked by the bellows the injustice of it all. She longed for something - someone - to strike out at. The fury almost erupted when she felt Asku's hand on her shoulder, but realizing his intent, held the madness at bay.

"I can't pretend to know your pain," he said. "But I do know this. I would give my arm to have for just one day what you and Mary had. I mean that, true. And if you can't see the truth of what I'm saying, then you betray her and all the good about the two of you that matters."

The insight was as cool water, drowning a fury with no place to go. As she embraced the peace Asku had granted her, a line from a play she had seen as a young girl sprang from the recesses of her memory. They were simple words that she thought she had understood at the time but now took on a much deeper meaning.

"The course of true love," she whispered, "never did run smooth."

# CHAPTER FORTY-FOUR

"SHE'LL BE AS ONE with the sea and the sky, now," Asku said as they watched the flames rise into the morning sky. "Her spirit will be the wind that fills the sails of great ships. Her ashes will become the salt of the sea, from the tears she never shed."

Anne nodded approval, not daring to speak for fear her voice would fail. She shook off a shiver that somehow found its way under her skin despite the warm August morning and the heat of the fire. She had insisted that they not bury Mary's body for the worms and grubs. And she could not bear the idea of taking her back to the village for the gawkers to stare at her and the souvenir hunters to tear the clothes and hair from her body.

Instead, they carried her to the ocean side of the island and began to build a pyre of driftwood and fallen branches from the oak grove. Asku found the dried-out broken hull of a pilot's boat and had rolled it bottom-up atop the growing pile of wood – a platform upon which they placed Mary's body. Once the pyre was completed, they waited until morning to light it for fear that one of the Royal Navy's ships said to have returned to the area might mistake it for a distress signal. When the sun finally began to crest the horizon, Asku took a burning shard from the campfire he had built and placed it at the base of the pyre. The seasoned wood burned quick and hot, consuming enough of Mary Read's mortal remains that her true fate would forever remain a mystery to the world.

"What do we do now?" Asku asked when the flames began to die. "We have to have a plan."

"We take the periauger back to Scarlette's place, if the barricoe doesn't sink it first," Anne said, not yet ready to look away from the fire. Tye stood next to her nestled under her arm, his head resting in the curve of her waist. They understood each other now, and for this he allowed himself to be a little boy, if only for a few minutes. "Then we find a merchantman that will take us on as passengers and sail as far away from Bath and Ocracoke and the bloody Royal Navy as we possibly can."

"What about Briebras? We owe him a share of the coins, for certain."

"We'll give him two...one for Kofi and one for him. He can give the extra share to Kofi's sister or do whatever he wants with it, but I don't want the blacksmith's gold. He paid for it with his blood."

A wave of guilt washed over her, forcing her to turn her gaze away from the fire long enough to look at Asku. He too had given more than gold could buy. He had been faithful until the end, despite losing both his mother and his brother. Anything she said or did to express her gratitude would sound hollow, even asinine.

"What about you? Are you sure you don't want to go back to Cedar Island? Maybe go to the frontier? You have enough riches to last you a lifetime, you know. You can do anything you want?"

But the last descendant of the Dares no longer had family to hold him to the land, and he had never considered a future without such ties.

"No," he said. "I'll figure it out, eventually. But right now I want to make sure you two leave this place in one piece. And the only way I'll know for sure that you do is to go with you."

His mouth and eyes shifted into a sly smile.

"Besides, it's not like I don't enjoy the company. And as you once said, you never know what might happen."

Anne smiled back at him and wondered at what entity or power it might have been that had favored her with such a friend.

"But you haven't said...where is it that you plan on taking us?"

Anne looked back at what was left of the pyre. The lapping waves brought closer by the rising tide were beginning to wash the ashes and bones out to sea.

"Well...I don't know for sure, but I've heard tell that New Orleans is a place where people can go to make new lives for themselves."

# THE END

# AUTHOR'S NOTES

The true history of Anne Bonny and Mary Read is shrouded in mystery, misinformation, legend, and wishful thinking. What the record left blank has been gratuitously filled-in by those who love pirate stories and those who have adopted them as their champions. Having grown up in a part of the world that celebrates its pirate history with great relish, I found it odd that so little has been done to examine their lives and to further their legend. Not only did these women exist in one of the most male-dominated cultures in history, they thrived in it. As a writer and as a student of history, I found these facts too compelling to pass up.

When I began my research I quickly discovered that, although largely unknown to most people, there are two groups who are very familiar with Anne Bonny and Mary Read – pirate aficionados and the gay community. (OK, mostly lesbians.) I remember growing up, that most history books and articles gave only a cursory reference to their existence, if they were mentioned at all. I suspect this may have been because of the fear (in those days) that they might have qualified to belong to the second group mentioned above. Better to rush past that awkward part of history than have to explain to little Johnny and Susie why these two female pirates were really, really close. From where I'm sitting, all of this makes their story that much more compelling.

My own beliefs are reflected in my story.

Although I first read about the claim that Cedar Island is the real location of the Lost Colony in 1993, written accounts about the theory have been around since at least the 1940s and probably by oral history for hundreds of years. Perhaps what gives the theory credence that it otherwise would not have is the fact that many Cedar Island natives believe themselves to be decedents of the colonists and point to shared surnames as proof. And even if it was not the original location of the colony itself, it is possible that some members of Sir Walter Raleigh's group of settlers eventually made their homes on Cedar Island. Anyone who has visited certain areas of the Outer Banks where the natives still speak with a distinct cockney-like brogue finds the theory that Raleigh's colonists were not lost, but abandoned, very plausible.

While the history of "Charles Town" has been far overshadowed by the history of "Charleston" and its role in Southern secession, its colonial history is much broader and, in many ways, more compelling. Given that it was the only British settlement in North America to have been fortified with a wall speaks volumes about its environment and its precarious hold in the New World. Given that it had to be constantly vigilant for attacks by Native Americans, Spanish colonists, and pirates, it is little wonder that the people of South Carolina's Lowcountry developed a warrior culture that manifested itself in 1861.

I will apologize in advance to readers who are sticklers for details when it comes to tall ships and nautical terminology. Despite having conducted hours and hours of research and sought advice from many sources, there are bound to be a few errors. While I tried to keep such mistakes to a minimum – and allowing for creative license – the incredible breadth of all things nautical makes it extremely difficult to get it 100 percent correct. In the same vein, despite extensive research to find the correct names of the real ships referenced in the story, there is a lot of conflicting information in the historical accounts and records. Whenever there were conflicts, I settled on the name that was mentioned most often by the more accepted sources.

Finally, I wish to pay tribute to Charles Harry Whedbee, perhaps North Carolina's best known author of coastal lore. Judge Whedbee's collections of stories about pirates and ghosts have been a staple of Outer Banks vacationers and sports fishermen for many decades. His accounts of Anne Bonny and Mary Read, Hatteras Jack, and Blackbeard's Cup helped inspire several of the scenes in my story. Unfortunately for history buffs, Judge Whedbee liked to keep his readers guessing as to which stories were supposedly true and which ones were fiction. The one exception is his account of Blackbeard's Cup, which was written in first person and sworn by him to be true. In fact, he was so convinced that he had drank from the cup as a young man, he had a standing offer to pay $1,000 to "the person who loans me the cup from which I drank." Judge Whedbee passed away in 1990, never having realized his dream of proving the cup's existence.

## A PERSONAL REQUEST FROM THE AUTHOR

The success of independently published writers such as myself is almost totally dependent on reader reviews. If you enjoyed this novel and would like to see more of my stories make it to print, please post a revew on GoodReads.com, Amazon.com/books, Kindle.com, or other book-related websites. And please be sure to tell your friends. Thank you.

Made in the USA
Middletown, DE
08 December 2019

80273817R00274